JANE AUSTEN was born in 1775 in Hampshire, England, to George Austen, the rector of Steventon, and his wife, Cassandra. Like many girls of her day, she was educated at home, and began her literary career by writing parodies and skits for the amusement of her large family. Although Austen did not marry, she did have several suitors and once accepted a marriage proposal—but only for one evening. Austen never lived apart from her family, but her work nevertheless shows a worldly and wise sensibility. Her novels include *Sense and Sensibility* (1811), *Pride and Prejudice* (1813), *Mansfield Park* (1814), *Emma* (1816), and *Northanger Abbey* and *Persuasion,* published together posthumously in 1818. Austen died in 1817.

MARGARET DRABBLE is the highly acclaimed novelist, biographer, and editor of *The Oxford Companion to English Literature.* Her novels include *The Gates of Ivory, The Radiant Way, Realms of Gold,* and *The Needle's Eye.* She lives in London.

Sense
and
Sensibility

Jane Austen

**With a New Introduction by
Margaret Drabble**

A SIGNET CLASSIC

SIGNET CLASSIC
Published by New American Library, a division of
Penguin Group (USA) Inc., 375 Hudson Street,
New York, New York 10014, U.S.A.
Penguin Books Ltd, 80 Strand,
London WC2R 0RL, England
Penguin Books Australia Ltd, 250 Camberwell Road,
Camberwell, Victoria 3124, Australia
Penguin Books Canada Ltd, 10 Alcorn Avenue,
Toronto, Ontario, Canada M4V 3B2
Penguin Books (N.Z.) Ltd, Cnr Rosedale and Airborne Roads,
Albany, Auckland 1310, New Zealand

Penguin Books Ltd, Registered Offices:
80 Strand, London WC2R 0RL, England

Published by Signet Classic, an imprint of New American Library,
a division of Penguin Group (USA) Inc.

First Signet Classic Printing, May 1961
First Signet Classic Printing (Drabble Introduction), August 1997
10

Introduction copyright © Margaret Drabble, 1989
All rights reserved

 REGISTERED TRADEMARK—MARCA REGISTRADA

Library of Congress Catalog Card Number: 95-74957

Printed in the United States of America

Introduction

Sense and Sensibility is without doubt Jane Austen's most painful and disturbing novel. It is the fashion these days to look for the painful and disturbing side of every comedy and light romance, and Jane Austen in particular has this century discovered many interpreters eager to attack the various myths that surround her reputation—that she is cozy, complacent, middle class, conservative, unemotional, dry. But in the case of *Sense and Sensibility,* a dark interpretation seems unavoidable—her biographer John Halperin[1] has gone so far as to call it "bleak and black and nasty." This overstates the case, but it is an unhappy, almost tragic book, full of raw emotions which her other works carefully control or distance. The novelist George Moore said of it that it "gives us all the agony of passion the human heart can feel ... it is here that we find the burning human heart in English prose narrative for the first, and, alas, for the last time."[2]—a somewhat surprising but not inappropriate accolade. We see here suffering undisguised, and despite the author's harsh judgement of its causes we cannot help knowing it for what it is. Marianne Dashwood, the representative of the "Sensibility" of the title, comes as near the edge of tragedy as her author can allow her, and it is by no means clear that she is rescued at the end. No amount of exegesis of the "Sentimental Novel" and praise of Elinor's fine qualities of "Sense" can conceal what happens here.

Having said that, it is of course necessary for an introduction to attempt to place the novel in a historical context, and to discuss its relationship to the cult of sensibility which plays such a dominant part in the plot. It is at once clear that that relationship is much more oblique than the relationship of *Northanger Abbey* to the Gothic novel which it parodies and exploits. One could begin by looking back at the treatment of "Sentiment" and "Sensibility" in Jane Austen's Ju-

---

[1] John Halperin, *The Life of Jane Austen*, Harvester Press, London, 1984.
[2] *Avowals*, privately printed 1919, Heinemann, London, 1936.

venilia, stories composed when she was still a girl. There, we find evidence of her wide reading, particularly of fiction, and of her talent for burlesque. Some have expressed surprise that she should have been drawn to parody at so young an age, and John Halperin[3] even suggests it indicates a "cold" and "cynical" nature, but it seems natural enough for a young person leading a fairly quiet village life amongst a limited acquaintance to imitate and make fun of fictional models—she knew more heroines from novels than she knew real people, a not uncommon predicament for a girl of her age. And the talent for parody tends to flourish even amongst young people who have plenty of company, as any school or college magazine then or now would show. Indeed, one of Jane's earliest efforts may have included a contribution to *The Loiterer*, the magazine her brothers edited (1789–90) at Oxford, itself an admiring "imitation" of the great periodicals of the eighteenth century, *The Spectator* and *The Idler*.[4] It had been a great age for satire and caricature, and Jane Austen inherited much of the tradition—including, in these early works, a coarseness and broadness that she was later to refine away.

The objects of her wit are, however, illuminating. She takes on many targets—the epistolary form, the Gothic novel, the stage comedy, the objectivity of historians—but one of her most recurrent themes is the "Sentimental Novel" and the dangerous emotions it expressed and encouraged. This form of fiction, although rooted in some of the earlier codes of Fielding and Richardson, flourished mainly in the later years of the century, and may (in broad generalization) be seen both as a precursor of Romanticism and as a reaction against the balanced rationalism of the Augustan age. It drew on Rousseau's immensely influential *Julie, ou la Nouvelle Héloïse* (1761) and Goethe's much-imitated *Sorrows of Young Werther* (1774), and tended to elevate "feeling" above "reason." Its heroes and heroines were virtuous and unselfish, and much given to sudden passions, fits of weeping and fainting, and acts of wild generosity. Better-known writers in the genre include Henry Brooke (*The Fool of Quality*, 1765–70), Henry Mackenzie (*The Man of Feeling*, 1771, and

[3] *South Atlantic Quarterly*, Summer, 1982.
[4] See Park Honan, *Jane Austen: Her Life*, Ch. 5, Weidenfeld & Nicolson, London, 1987.

Julia de Roubigné, 1777), Oliver Goldsmith (*The Vicar of Wakefield*, 1766) and, more indirectly, Sterne, particularly with his *Sentimental Journey*. One of the basic tenets of the form was the natural goodness of unspoiled human nature, which was often portrayed as flourishing in the picturesque poverty of a country cottage. It has been the fate of most of these novels in recent years to have been remembered more for their caricaturists than for their content, and for this Jane Austen herself bears some responsibility.

Her principal assault is found in one of her longer efforts, *Love and Friendship* (1790), an epistolary novel of some 10,000 words, in which we follow the raptures and disasters of the narrator Laura from a rustic cot in the Vale of Usk to a "romantic Village in the Highlands of Scotland." Some of its phrases are justly famous—for instance, the moment when Laura and her friend Sophia faint "Alternately on a Sofa"—but the whole story has considerable verve and at times a manic energy. It parodies such clichés of the novel as "love at first sight" and instant, passionate declarations of friendship; Lady Dorothea is judged inferior in "Delicate feelings, tender Sentiments, and refined Sensibility" because on introduction she manages to stay half an hour without confiding "any of her Secret thoughts," whereas Laura and Sophia at first meeting "flew into each other's arms and after having exchanged vows of mutual Friendship for the rest of our Lives, instantly unfolded to each other the inward Secrets of our Hearts." There are implausible separations, implausible recognitions and reunions; many sudden journeys and geographical improbabilities (one character finds himself in South Wales, "I know not how it happened," on the way from Bedfordshire to Middlesex); and, perhaps most significantly, we are invited to laugh at the extravagant claims of disinterest and impractical, unselfish generosity. Poverty and imprudence, in the sentimental novel, are held up for admiration, but in this caricature, they hide mercenary behavior and indeed theft. The heroines and their lovers may protest their delicacy and sensibility, but they in fact act with a ruthless self-interest that is not above stealing bank notes while despising the insensitivity of those from whom they steal. Jane Austen reveals herself, if not as a cynic, at least as a disabused observer of the human capacity for deceiving itself and others, and of dressing up base behavior with fine sentiments.

In *Sense and Sensibility,* a work separated at the time of its original composition (in 1795?) by only a few years from *Love and Friendship,* we find some striking connections. It too was originally composed in the epistolary form, under the title "Elinor and Marianne"; its romantic younger heroine, like the recipient of Laura's letters, is called Marianne; and it too displays an extraordinary interplay between the conventionally generous assumptions of the heroine and the cold calculations of the mercenary world. (One should not make too much of Jane Austen's use of names, as she employed a limited range and tended perhaps oddly to use and re-use those of her own family circle, but it is worth noting that the name "Marianne/Mariana," like "Julie," had strong emotional and literary resonance, and that elsewhere in her early fragments we find Dashwoods and a jilt named Willoughby. "Mariana" is the dejected and deserted lover abandoned by Angelo in Shakespeare's *All's Well that Ends Well,* who was to reappear so hauntingly, possibly even overlaid with memories of Jane Austen's Marianne, in Tennyson's poem "Mariana": "He will not come, she said/ She said I am a weary, a weary/Oh God, that I were dead.")

But the differences are made even more striking by the similarities. For here, in the later, more mature work (begun in its present form in late 1797, but much reworked before its eventual publication in 1811) we find that the tone and the balance have completely altered. Marianne, unlike Laura and Sophia, is exonerated of all hint of duplicity or self-seeking. Her attitude to life may be wrong, even tragically wrong, as her sister believes it to be, but we are not for a moment given to believe that it is insincere.

The novel is full of insincerities, but they are of a much more calculated kind. It is a novel in which some of the characters are, even by Jane Austen's standards, obsessed by money, and the financial map of the plot is extremely complicated. It must take most readers several attempts to unravel the complex family and legal relationships of the first chapter, but even as we struggle to take them in, we cannot help noticing that the principal issue governing family destiny is money. The word "estate" appears three times in the first paragraph, and is closely accompanied by "inheritor," "succession," "fortune" and "life interest": in no time at all we are led to Fanny Dashwood's brilliantly contrived (and coolly disingenuous) disinheriting of her stepmother and

half-sisters-in-law, in the name of "family-sentiment."
Throughout, there is a brutal and precise calculation of what
each character is worth on the marriage market, and John
and Fanny Dashwood, Lucy Steele and even Willoughby are
seen to be motivated almost entirely by money. One of the
most shocking passages comes at the end of Volume II,
Chapter 11 when John Dashwood, after describing his own
notional poverty, caused in part by the state of the stock
market, and after (mistakenly and a little enviously) congratulating Elinor on the prospect of her marrying Colonel
Brandon's two thousand a year, remarks on Marianne's recent illness: " 'She looks very unwell, has lost her colour,
and is grown quite thin. Is she ill?'

"She is not well; she has had a nervous complaint on her
for several weeks,' " replies Elinor, to which he gallantly responds:

> "I am sorry for that. At her time of life, anything of an ill-
> ness destroys the bloom forever! Hers has been a very short
> one! She was as handsome a girl last September, as any I
> ever saw—and as likely to attract the men ... I remember
> Fanny used to say that she would marry sooner and better
> than you ... She will be mistaken, however. I question
> whether Marianne *now* will marry a man worth more than
> five or six hundred a year, at the utmost."

In other words, Marianne's stocks have gone down, and
her cheapened value is calculated to the nearest hundred
with a niceness that is appallingly tasteless and tactless, but
alas not unconvincing. The passage reminds one forcibly of
W. H. Auden's comments on Jane Austen, in his "Letter to
Lord Byron":

> You could not shock her more than she shocks me;
> Beside her Joyce seems innocent as grass.
> It makes me most uncomfortable to see
> An English spinster of the middle-class
> Describe the amorous effects of 'brass',
> Reveal so frankly and with such sobriety
> The economic basis of society.

The spectacle of rampant but disguised self-interest introduced through Fanny Dashwood in the opening chapters
makes us turn with relief to the different values expressed in

Mrs. Dashwood's instinctive revulsion from her "indelicacy" and "ungracious behaviour"—only to find, in the space of another paragraph, that we cannot rest here. We must find a middle way, between avaricious calculation and spontaneous emotion: picturesque poverty is not to be our model. Our guide to the middle ground is to be the precociously wise Elinor, who at nineteen is everything that Mrs. Dashwood and Marianne are not.

Elinor has (in this order) "strength of understanding," "coolness of judgment," "an excellent heart," an affectionate disposition, and strong feelings which she knows "how to govern." We are told this, in a firm authorial tone that brooks no denial, though we have not yet seen any of these qualities in action. Marianne, in contrast, suffers from an "excess of sensibility" which she indulges rather than attempts to control. We are informed of all this in a schematic, deliberate manner which is compounded by the dismissal, in the last paragraph, of the somewhat superfluous younger sister, Margaret, as one who had "already imbibed a good deal of Marianne's romance, without having much of her sense," and who does not therefore "bid fair to equal her sisters at a more advanced period of life."

This high-handed manner towards the reader's freedom of response may alienate those who do not like to be told too clearly what to think and what to feel, and may even risk arousing a small rebellion, as didacticism is wont to do. And as the novel progresses, the tightness of control appears to continue. Elinor and Marianne are carefully contrasted, in their attitudes to men, poetry, painting and prudence, in their conception of love and their discretions or indiscretions of speech. Their not-dissimilar situations are carefully balanced and contrasted; they are both in love with not wholly satisfactory objects—Elinor with the mysteriously dejected and unforthcoming Edward, Marianne with the high-spirited but mysteriously disappearing Willoughby. We are clearly to admire Elinor's prudence in keeping her feelings to herself, for thus she avoids exposing herself to public ridicule; and we are to see that Marianne's impetuous trust of her own heart and the good intentions of others will lead to disaster.

But the neat abstract, eighteenth-century antithesis of "sense" and "sensibility" does not work out quite as neatly as we at first think it will. We are forewarned against Willoughby by the author's tone and by Elinor's doubts, but nevertheless he continues to astonish us. His first gallant, dashing apparition as the handsome stranger and "preserver" of Marianne clearly refers back to the "love-at-first-sight" convention mocked in *Love and Friendship,* where the stranger-hero arrives unheralded on a December evening at the heroine's cottage, at once falls in love, and is married to her before the night is out. But Willoughby steps beyond the role of parody, and his final encounter with Elinor provides one of the most troubling scenes in the whole of Jane Austen's work. One would have expected the author to have dismissed Willoughby as decisively as she dismisses her other philanderers, the mercenary Wickham and the wealthy Henry Crawford (both of whom are allowed, of course, to have great charm). But Willoughby refuses to be distanced by Elinor's sense and Austen's morality and irony. He insists on being heard. His reappearance, on a cold and stormy night as Marianne lies, as he thinks, desperately ill, is as melodramatic as his original introduction, but far more seriously intended, and his long attempt at self-exoneration is oddly moving, and quite beyond Austen's usual emotional range. And the sensible Elinor, despite herself, is impressed. She tries to "harden her heart" against compassion for him, but she does not quite succeed. She listens to him with feeling, and her reflections on the injuries done to his character by "idleness, dissipation, and luxury," "extravagance and vanity," seem conventional beside the real pain and confusion with which he infects her. We see her visibly struggling, in the face of his passionate plea for forgiveness, for "control." Her "gentle counsel" to him seems inadequate, even presumptuous, and we are relieved to hear that despite all her common sense she begins to think of him as "poor Willoughby," and even for a moment wishes him, for Marianne's sake, a widower. The irredeemable and "diabolical" villain has become, through the urgency of his emotion and the power of his presence, almost acceptable as a brother-in-law.

One of the most curious features of this curious novel is the way in which it manages to suggest the power of the forces it tries to control and subdue. How intentional this may be, it is hard to guess: it is tempting to suppose that Jane Austen, like her spokeswoman Elinor, is a little carried away by her villain-hero, and cannot resist giving him better lines and better feelings than his conduct and his role in the plot warrant. And a similar ambivalence surrounds the treatment of all the manifestations of "nature" and "sensibility," which go far beyond the measures required for light comedy or burlesque. Clearly, we are meant to find Mrs. Dashwood charming as well as imprudent, for much is made of her "attaching" manners, "sweetness of address" and warmth of heart. Marianne herself is a complex character, not a caricature (even that first appraising introduction concedes she has "sense" as well as feeling), and we are given to understand she has real taste and talent: she is no self-important drawing-room prima donna, like poor Mary Bennet in *Pride and Prejudice,* and her feeling for poetry and nature resembles that of the author-approved Fanny Price. If she sins by excess, there is no direct criticism of the aesthetic or (sexual?) emotions in which she indulges: the indulgence alone is condemned. There are moments here where we breathe a freer air than usual in Austen, and feel ourselves on the brink of another kind of experience.

Take the treatment of the picturesque cottage, that requisite of the sentimental novel, in which the not-quite-desperately but sufficiently impoverished Dashwoods find themselves through the generosity of Mrs. Dashwood's relative, Sir John Middleton. At first we think the cottage-concept is to be treated in characteristically satiric vein (as Edward treats the Gilpinesque raptures that prefer dead leaves and ruins to healthy trees and neat farms) but although the cottage itself is dismissed as being structurally sound and aesthetically "defective," its neighborhood is evoked with some feeling. High hills, beautiful walks, open downs, wooded slopes are mentioned with approval, and when Marianne and Margaret set off on the fateful walk that introduces them to Willoughby, we might almost think ourselves in the company of a Dorothy Wordsworth who, at precisely the period of composition (1798), was writing her Alfoxden Diaries and describing the beauties of neighboring Somerset. The Austen world and the Wordsworth world, usually so far apart, meet as we read of the two girls laughing as they make their way against the wind, "rejoicing . . . at every glimpse of blue sky." It is a robust, healthy, refreshing scene, with no hint of sentimental falsity or exaggeration: the turn-of-the-century outdoor spirit of the Wordsworths and the Romantic revolution has prevailed over the eighteenth-century sketchbook raptures, rules and "compositions" of Gray and Gilpin. Marianne herself, we see, despises the "jargon" of aesthetic rapture: we do not doubt that she, like Dorothy Wordsworth, feels the real thing. True, Jane Austen soon pours (literal) cold water upon the outing, proving the pessimistic Elinor to have been annoyingly right about the weather, but the girls have had their walk, they have escaped, if briefly, from the "confinement" of the cottage and of their author's knowingness.

A romantic feeling for nature makes its way through the author's determined anti-romantic emphasis on muddy lanes, and similarly and more dangerously, sexual passion makes its way through the cool dissection of prudence, hypocrisy, self-seeking and financial exigencies. We have seen that Willoughby comes very near to justifying himself through the intensity of his love for Marianne and his own capacity for suffering—just as, in Richardson's *Clarissa,* the warmth and passion of the rake and seducer Lovelace contrast favourably with the cold and cruel calculations of Clarissa's family, and have captivated many (perhaps masochistic?) readers. Indeed, if the novel in some aspects looks forward to the Romantics, in others it looks back to the freer manners and standards of the eighteenth century. We hear that the respectable and eligible Colonel Brandon, for instance, is suspected of having a love-child, and nobody seems to think any the worse of him for it. We learn that he has fought a duel with Willoughby over his ward's seduction, and although Elinor sensibly shakes her head "over the fancied necessity of this," she does not appear unduly surprised to hear it—whereas if Mr. Bennet had in fact engaged Wickham in a duel (as Mrs. Bennet hysterically suggests he might), we would have been very surprised indeed. (Duelling, in fact, was still current in the early nineteenth century but the practice was much frowned upon, and Beau Nash had attempted to ban it at Bath in the 1720s.) The story of Colonel Brandon's early love, Eliza, who runs from a forced and unhappy marriage to a succession of seducers and finally dies of consumption in great financial distress in a spunging house, belongs more to the world of *Clarissa* than to the world of Emma Woodhouse, and in her later novels, Austen was much more wary about treating such extreme subject matter—perhaps wisely, as the Eliza story is much less plausibly handled than, for instance, the low machinations of Lucy Steele.

It is in the portrayal of Marianne's sufferings, however,

that we reach the heart of the novel's power, and find ourselves face to face with the conflict between emotion and control. Novels, since the birth of the genre, have been full of rejected, seduced, and abandoned maidens, whose proper fate is to die, as Eliza and Clarissa obligingly do, and as did a host of heroines in lesser works. Sometimes they die of sorrow, sometimes of disgrace, sometimes in childbirth, sometimes of disgrace-induced sickness or poverty. They may even, following the fashion of Goethe's Werther, take their own lives. Such deaths are exemplary, intended to warn other young women from passion and abandon. One remembers that harsh little eighteenth-century song of Goldsmith's, "When lovely woman stoops to folly," which concludes that the only art that can cover Woman's guilt and "give repentance to her lover/And wring his bosom—is to die." Marianne, of course, is not guilty (i.e., she has not been seduced) but she has allowed—indeed, as we see, encouraged— herself to fall recklessly and visibly in love, and she pays the full price of a very public rejection. She has also, as John Dashwood remarks, lowered her own market value.

She suffers more intensely than any other Austen heroine, most of whom, of course, have to endure trials, misunderstandings and separations—sometimes lengthy, as in the case of Anne Elliot. But none of these other heroines manifest their distress in anything worse than headaches, fits of weeping (in which even Elinor indulges), low spirits and fatigue. Marianne nearly dies. In the course of the novel, she has two severe illnesses, the first induced by her rejection by Willoughby, to whom she had considered herself all but engaged, and the second by a "putrid fever" brought on by lingering romantically on a twilight walk in wet grass (and neglecting to change her shoes and stockings). Both illnesses are thus the product of imprudence and indulgence of sensibility, and we cannot doubt that they are linked: her constitution has been weakened by the first bout, making her far more vulnerable to the second (the gravity of which, we are half-satisfied to note, the sensible Elinor underestimates, thus showing the occasional failure of too much "sense").

The description of the first, psychosomatic "broken heart" illness is peculiarly vivid and realistic. We note her feverish waiting for a letter from Willoughby and her desperate attempts at optimism as she justifies his absence; in company she is already "wholly dispirited, careless of her appearance." When the blow of his public rejection of her falls, she turns "dreadfully white"; on her return home, we learn of her wandering restlessly from room to room, her deathlike paleness, her choking bursts of tears, her faintness and giddiness, her "almost screaming" with agony, her hysterical nervous fever, her violent headaches, her inability to eat. It is clear that we are not here in the Lucy Steele realm of disappointed financial prospects, and that Marianne is suffering the extreme shock of betrayed trust. Compare the calmer behavior of Jane Bennet, who, when Bingley unexpectedly disappears, is indeed much distressed, but will hardly admit it even to her sister Elizabeth, insisting that she had no right to believe that Bingley loved her, therefore she has no right to feel rejected. Marianne clearly (and justifiably) does feel she has this right. Note, also, that it is not the public nature of his rejection that most shocks her—she specifically says that "misery such as mine has no pride," however embarrassed Elinor may be on her behalf. She is beyond the reach of social considerations, both for good and ill, and both the extremity and psychological details of her illness are extremely convincing. While I would not go so far as Tony Tanner,[5] who suggests that "her behaviour is pathological in a way which for the late eighteenth century can have been construed as madness," I entirely endorse his emphasis on the central importance (and verisimilitude) of Jane Austen's treatment of the illness: this is not satire of a conventionally distressed heroine from a sentimental novel, it is an observed and felt portrait. (Observed from whom, one cannot but impertinently speculate: we do not know the answer.)

Elinor, of course, grieves over the "impropriety" and "imprudence" that have led to this suffering, and urges her sister to "exert herself." She is desperate for Marianne to regain control, for she cannot bear the sight of such abandoning of the self to unrestrained grief. But we do not now feel that Marianne is indulging herself: her state is real, not self-induced, and Elinor's exhortations to resistance seem out of place. More apposite, perhaps, to a modern mind, might be the homely advice of Mrs. Jennings, who (while uselessly offering all sorts of titbits and treats as consolation) says that "she had better have her cry out at once and have done with it." The wisdom of this is not recognized by Elinor, although

[5] *Jane Austen*, Macmillan, London, 1986.

she is grateful for her hostess's good heart and good intentions: and we suspect that she and Jane Austen might think it the silliest comment in the world. Elinor veers more to the "pull-yourself-together" school of thinking, known to be peculiarly unhelpful in cases of depression like this—and although we see that her sustained and loving concern for her sister is instrumental in bringing her back from the brink of despair, we also note her stress on "thinking of others" and preserving the social fabric. Powerful, undisguised emotion is selfish: we must learn to control and submit.

Are we intended to read some awareness of the limitations of Elinor's "Sense," in its contrast with Marianne's demonstrably dangerous "Sensibility"? Does the need to "control" sometimes mislead? Most critics have accepted that Elinor is, throughout, Jane Austen's representative and voice, but there is room for a little doubt. As we have seen, Elinor errs in the direction of taking Marianne's second illness too lightly, and is persuaded at least to pity Willoughby. And one might observe that her own behavior is not always wholly what her own high standards would require: she is forced to compromise and to dissimulate. Some of the instances are trivial enough—as when, for example, she finds herself obliged to flatter Lady Middleton because Marianne is too honest to bother with the mere forms of politeness. But when Lucy Steele confides her secrets to her, and binds her not to divulge them, she finds herself in an unpleasant predicament, unable to be open with her sister or her mother: Marianne can quite rightly reproach her (as she does) for reticence. Lucy Steele, with her malicious and manipulative divulgence of unwanted and painful intimacies, is indeed something of a parody of a sentimental heroine, but Elinor's predicament as recipient of these confidences is more complex.

Should we feel that a little of Marianne's spontaneity and warmth would have done Elinor no harm, and would have rescued Edward from a loveless marriage? As it is, she follows the dictates of prudence, and only a *deus ex machina* in the shape of the somewhat unconvincing match between Robert Ferrars and Lucy saves Edward from a life of undoubted misery. It is possible that we are intended to reflect (as we must) that Edward's scrupulous abiding by his engagement is almost as unwise as Willoughby's breaking of faith. It is significant that it is Marianne herself who praises Edward (to Lucy) in these terms:

> "And I really believe he *has* the most delicate conscience in the world, the most scrupulous in performing every engagement however minute, and however it may make against his interest or pleasure. He is the most fearful of giving pain, of wounding expectation, and the most incapable of being self-ish of anybody I ever saw."

While the chief function of Marianne's speech lies in the dramatic irony with which it embarrasses "two thirds of her auditors," it also suggests that Edward himself might with more "sense" or more "sensibility" have found some other way out of the empty form in which he has trapped not only himself but also Elinor.

As it is, the plot resolves happily for Edward and Elinor, and the two hesitant lovers are freed to declare themselves and to enjoy the living at Delaford so conveniently prearranged by Colonel Brandon. The conclusion of Marianne's story is not quite so satisfactory. We note that she greets the news of Elinor's engagement "only by tears"... and that "her joy, though as sincere as her love for her sister, was of a kind to give her neither spirits nor language." As we have seen, she is widely considered by the world to have lost stock in the marriage market, but we have been told not to rely too much on the world's opinion. The author returns to her only in the last seven paragraphs of the book, where she informs us that "Marianne Dashwood was born to an extraordinary fate" and proceeds to describe the complete reversal of her world picture and her marriage, at nineteen, to the flannel-waistcoated thirty-seven-year-old Colonel Brandon—who, the author points out, satisfies symmetry and perhaps also the demands of sentiment by having "suffered no less than herself under the event of a former attachment."

Most readers and some critics have with reason found this resolution somewhat unsatisfactory. It is usually objected that Colonel Brandon is too sketchy a character to be accepted as a fitting husband for the complex and demanding Marianne: Marvin Mudrick calls him a "vacuum."[6] Also, the disparities in age alarm us almost as much as they alarmed

[6] *Irony as defence and discovery*, University of California Press, 1952.

the sixteen-year-old Marianne herself, and we must question the happy ending that portrays her as one who "could never love by halves" and who therefore "became, in time, as much devoted" to her husband as she had been to Willoughby. This scepticism is not based on her own romantic (and then commonly held) view that "second attachments" are always inferior to first, but on the suspicion that in the real, untold, uncontrolled version of this story she has succumbed to a worldly marriage and the pleasures of two thousand a year (she is to be the "patroness of a village") and the even stronger suspicion that her creator approves this decision. Austen does her best to render plausible Brandon's somewhat unlikely passion for Marianne, but there is little to suggest that anything other than a certain failure of hope and spirit would have persuaded her to settle for him. The conclusion Austen chooses falls between two more likely stories—the version of "sense," paradoxically, tells us that Marianne would have been more likely (in her own world's marriage market) to have remained single or to have married the Colonel for status, and it is only a romantic fictitious convenience that can pass off her marriage to the Colonel as one of perfect happiness and growing compatibility. Of all Jane Austen's heroines, she seems temperamentally most resolutely set for an unhappy ending, and the conventional denouement must disturb and disappoint.

In this novel, Austen invokes emotions that cannot so easily be brought under "control" by "exertion," and comes too close for comfort to "the burning heart of passion." As Mudrick argues, "against her moral will and conscious artistic purpose" she has created in Marianne "a creature wholly sympathetic," who he believes to represent "an unacknowledged depth of her author's spirit." Marianne is forcibly distanced at the end, into a formal framework where no detail, no inner motions may be observed. Now, had Jane Austen's art permitted her to pursue Colonel and Mrs. Brandon (eagerly watched from afar by Willoughby) through the middle years of their marriage, we would have had another novel altogether. It would have been the nineteenth-century novel; consider George Eliot's *Middlemarch* and Flaubert's *Madame Bovary*, both of which portray heroines who read too much and love unwisely. *Sense and Sensibility* rests between *Clarissa* and *Middlemarch*, looking both ways. It lacks the near-perfect poise of its companion volumes, but offers insights into emotional depths unique in its author's *œuvre*, and suggests powers that she perhaps deliberately chose not to pursue.

—*Margaret Drabble*
London, 1989

VOLUME I

Chapter 1

THE FAMILY of Dashwood had been long settled in Sussex.
Their estate was large, and their residence was at Norland
Park, in the centre of their property, where, for many gen-
erations, they had lived in so respectable a manner as to
engage the general good opinion of their surrounding acquaintance. The late owner of this estate was a single man
who lived to a very advanced age, and who for many years
of his life had a constant companion and housekeeper in his
sister. But her death, which happened ten years before his
own, produced a great alteration in his home; for to supply
her loss, he invited and received into his house the family of
his nephew Mr. Henry Dashwood, the legal inheritor of the
Norland estate, and the person to whom he intended to be-
queath it. In the society of his nephew and niece, and their
children, the old gentleman's days were comfortably spent.
His attachment to them all increased. The constant attention
of Mr. and Mrs. Henry Dashwood to his wishes, which proceeded not merely from interest, but from goodness of heart,
gave him every degree of solid comfort which his age could
receive; and the cheerfulness of the children added a relish
to his existence.

By a former marriage, Mr. Henry Dashwood had one son:
by his present lady, three daughters. The son, a steady respectable young man, was amply provided for by the fortune
of his mother, which had been large, and half of which de-
volved on him on his coming of age. By his own marriage,
likewise, which happened soon afterwards, he added to his
wealth. To him, therefore, the succession to the Norland estate was not so really important as to his sisters; for their fortune, independent of what might arise to them from their
father's inheriting that property, could be but small. Their

mother had nothing, and their father only seven thousand pounds in his own disposal, for the remaining moiety of his first wife's fortune was also secured to her child, and he had only a life interest in it.

The old gentleman died; his will was read, and like almost every other will gave as much disappointment as pleasure. He was neither so unjust, nor so ungrateful, as to leave his estate from his nephew; but he left it to him on such terms as destroyed half the value of the bequest. Mr. Dashwood had wished for it more for the sake of his wife and daughters than for himself or his son; but to his son and his son's son, a child of four years old, it was secured in such a way as to leave to himself no power of providing for those who were most dear to him, and who most needed a provision, by any charge on the estate, or by any sale of its valuable woods. The whole was tied up for the benefit of this child, who, in occasional visits with his father and mother at Norland, had so far gained on the affections of his uncle, by such attractions as are by no means unusual in children of two or three years old; an imperfect articulation, an earnest desire of having his own way, many cunning tricks, and a great deal of noise, as to outweigh all the value of all the attention which, for years, he had received from his niece and her daughters. He meant not to be unkind however, and as a mark of his affection for the three girls, he left them a thousand pounds apiece.

Mr. Dashwood's disappointment was at first severe; but his temper was cheerful and sanguine, and he might reasonably hope to live many years, and by living economically, lay by a considerable sum from the produce of an estate already large, and capable of almost immediate improvement. But the fortune, which had been so tardy in coming, was his only one twelvemonth. He survived his uncle no longer; and ten thousand pounds, including the late legacies, was all that remained for his widow and daughters.

His son was sent for, as soon as his danger was known, and to him Mr. Dashwood recommended, with all the strength and urgency which illness could command, the interest of his mother-in-law and sisters.

Mr. John Dashwood had not the strong feelings of the rest of the family; but he was affected by a recommendation of such a nature at such a time, and he promised to do everything in his power to make them comfortable. His father was rendered easy by such an assurance, and Mr. John Dashwood had then leisure to consider how much there might prudently be in his power to do for them.

He was not an ill-disposed young man, unless to be rather cold-hearted and rather selfish is to be ill-disposed: but he was, in general, well-respected; for he conducted himself with propriety in the discharge of his ordinary duties. Had he married a more amiable woman, he might have been made still more respectable than he was: he might even have been made amiable himself; for he was very young when he married and very fond of his wife. But Mrs. John Dashwood was a strong caricature of himself: more narrow-minded and selfish.

When he gave his promise to his father, he meditated within himself to increase the fortunes of his sisters by the present of a thousand pounds apiece. He then really thought himself equal to it. The prospect of four thousand a year, in addition to his present income, besides the remaining half of his own mother's fortune, warmed his heart and made him feel capable of generosity. "Yes, he would give them three thousand pounds: it would be liberal and handsome! It would be enough to make them completely easy. Three thousand pounds! He could spare so considerable a sum with little inconvenience." He thought of it all day long and for many days successively, and he did not repent.

No sooner was his father's funeral over than Mrs. John Dashwood, without sending any notice of her intention to her mother-in-law, arrived with her child and their attendants. No one could dispute her right to come; the house was her husband's from the moment of his father's decease; but the indelicacy of her conduct was so much the greater, and to a woman in Mrs. Dashwood's situation, with only common feelings, must have been highly unpleasing; but in *her* mind there was a sense of honour so keen, a generosity so romantic, that any offence of the kind, by whomsoever given or received, was to her a source of immovable disgust. Mrs. John Dashwood had never been a favourite with any of her husband's family; but she had had no opportunity till the present of showing them with how little attention to the comfort of other people she could act when occasion required it.

So acutely did Mrs. Dashwood feel this ungracious behaviour, and so earnestly did she despise her daughter-in-law for it that on the arrival of the latter she would have quitted the house forever, had not the entreaty of her eldest girl induced her first to reflect on the propriety of going, and her own tender love for all her three children determined her afterwards to stay, and for their sakes avoid a breach with their brother.

Elinor, this eldest daughter whose advice was so effectual, possessed a strength of understanding and coolness of judgment which qualified her, though only nineteen, to be the counsellor of her mother, and enabled her frequently to counteract, to the advantage of them all, that eagerness of mind in Mrs. Dashwood which must generally have led to imprudence. She had an excellent heart; her disposition was affectionate, and her feelings were strong; but she knew how to govern them: it was a knowledge which her mother had yet to learn, and which one of her sisters had resolved never to be taught.

Marianne's abilities were in many respects quite equal to Elinor's. She was sensible and clever, but eager in everything; her sorrows, her joys, could have no moderation. She was generous, amiable, interesting: she was everything but prudent. The resemblance between her and her mother was strikingly great.

Elinor saw with concern the excess of her sister's sensibility, but by Mrs. Dashwood it was valued and cherished. They encouraged each other now in the violence of their affliction. The agony of grief which overpowered them at first was voluntarily renewed, was sought for, was created again and again. They gave themselves up wholly to their sorrow, seeking increase of wretchedness in every reflection that could afford it, and resolved against ever admitting consolation in future. Elinor, too, was deeply afflicted; but still she could struggle, she could exert herself. She could consult with her brother, could receive her sister-in-law on her arrival, and treat her with proper attention; and could strive to rouse her mother to similar exertion, and encourage her to similar forbearance.

Margaret, the other sister, was a good-humoured well-disposed girl; but as she had already imbibed a good deal of Marianne's romance, without having much of her sense, she did not at thirteen bid fair to equal her sisters at a more advanced period of life.

Chapter 2

MRS. JOHN DASHWOOD now installed herself mistress of Norland, and her mother and sisters-in-law were degraded to the condition of visitors. As such, however, they were treated by her with quiet civility, and by her husband with as much kindness as he could feel towards anybody beyond himself, his wife, and their child. He really pressed them, with some earnestness, to consider Norland as their home; and as no plan appeared so eligible to Mrs. Dashwood as remaining there till she could accommodate herself with a house in the neighbourhood, his invitation was accepted.

A continuance in a place where everything reminded her of former delight was exactly what suited her mind. In seasons of cheerfulness, no temper could be more cheerful than hers, or possess in a greater degree that sanguine expectation of happiness which is happiness itself. But in sorrow she must be equally carried away by her fancy, and as far beyond consolation as in pleasure she was beyond alloy.

Mrs. John Dashwood did not at all approve of what her husband intended to do for his sisters. To take three thousand pounds from the fortune of their dear little boy would be impoverishing him to the most dreadful degree. She begged him to think again on the subject. How could he answer it to himself to rob his child, and his only child too, of so large a sum? And what possible claim could the Miss Dashwoods, who were related to him only by halfblood, which she considered as no relationship at all, have on his generosity to so large an amount. It was very well known that no affection was ever supposed to exist between the children of any man by different marriages; and why was he to ruin himself and their poor little Harry by giving away all his money to his half sisters?

"It was my father's last request to me," replied her husband, "that I should assist his widow and daughters."

"He did not know what he was talking of, I dare say; ten to one but he was light-headed at the time. Had he been in his right senses, he could not have thought of such a thing as begging you to give away half your fortune from your own child."

"He did not stipulate for any particular sum, my dear Fanny; he only requested me in general terms to assist them and make their situation more comfortable than it was in his power to do. Perhaps it would have been as well if he had left it wholly to myself. He could hardly suppose I should neglect them. But as he required the promise, I could not do less than give it: at least I thought so at the time. The promise, therefore, was given, and must be performed. Something must be done for them whenever they leave Norland and settle in a new home."

"Well, then, *let* something be done for them; but *that* something need not be three thousand pounds. Consider," she added, "that when the money is once parted with, it never can return. Your sisters will marry, and it will be gone forever. If, indeed, it could ever be restored to our poor little boy—"

"Why, to be sure," said her husband very gravely, "that would make a great difference. The time may come when Harry will regret that so large a sum was parted with. If he should have a numerous family, for instance, it would be a very convenient addition."

"To be sure it would."

"Perhaps, then, it would be better for all parties if the sum were diminished one half. Five hundred pounds would be a prodigious increase to their fortunes!"

"Oh! beyond anything great! What brother on earth would do half so much for his sisters, even if *really* his sisters! And as it is—only halfblood!—But you have such a generous spirit!"

"I would not wish to do anything mean," he replied. "One had rather on such occasions do too much than too little. No one, at least, can think I have not done enough for them: even themselves, they can hardly expect more."

"There is no knowing what *they* may expect," said the lady, "but we are not to think of their expectations: the question is, what you can afford to do."

"Certainly—and I think I may afford to give them five hundred pounds apiece. As it is, without any addition of mine, they will each have above three thousand pounds on their mother's death—a very comfortable fortune for any young woman."

"To be sure it is: and, indeed, it strikes me that they can want no addition at all. They will have ten thousand pounds divided amongst them. If they marry, they will be sure of doing well, and if they do not, they may all live very comfortably together on the interest of ten thousand pounds."

"That is very true, and therefore I do not know whether, upon the whole, it would not be more advisable to do something for their mother while she lives rather than for them, something of the annuity kind I mean. My sisters would feel the good effects of it as well as herself. A hundred a year would make them all perfectly comfortable."

His wife hesitated a little, however, in giving her consent to this plan.

"To be sure," said she, "it is better than parting with fifteen hundred pounds at once. But then if Mrs. Dashwood should live fifteen years, we shall be completely taken in."

"Fifteen years! My dear Fanny; her life cannot be worth half that purchase."

"Certainly not; but if you observe, people always live forever when there is any annuity to be paid them; and she is very stout and healthy, and hardly forty. An annuity is a very serious business; it comes over and over every year, and there is no getting rid of it. You are not aware of what you are doing. I have known a great deal of the trouble of annuities; for my mother was clogged with the payment of three to old superannuated servants by my father's will, and it is amazing how disagreeable she found it. Twice every year these annuities were to be paid; and then there was the trouble of getting it to them; and then one of them was said to have died, and afterwards it turned out to be no such thing. My mother was quite sick of it. Her income was not her own, she said, with such perpetual claims on it; and it was the more unkind in my father, because otherwise the money would have been entirely at my mother's disposal without any restriction whatever. It has given me such an abhorrence of annuities that I am sure I would not pin myself down to the payment of one for all the world."

"It is certainly an unpleasant thing," replied Mr. Dashwood, "to have those kind of yearly drains on one's income. One's fortune, as your mother justly says, is *not* one's own. To be tied down to the regular payment of such a sum on every rent day is by no means desirable: it takes away one's independence."

"Undoubtedly; and after all you have no thanks for it. They think themselves secure, you do no more than what is expected, and it raises no gratitude at all. If I were you, whatever I did should be done at my own discretion entirely. I would not bind myself to allow them anything yearly. It may be very inconvenient some years to spare a hundred, or even fifty pounds from our own expenses."

"I believe you are right, my love; it will be better that there should be no annuity in the case; whatever I may give them occasionally will be of far greater assistance than a yearly allowance, because they would only enlarge their style of living if they felt sure of a larger income and would not be sixpence the richer for it at the end of the year. It will certainly be much the best way. A present of fifty pounds, now and then, will prevent their ever being distressed for money, and will, I think, be amply discharging my promise to my father."

"To be sure it will. Indeed, to say the truth, I am convinced within myself that your father had no idea of your giving them any money at all. The assistance he thought of, I dare say, was only such as might be reasonably expected of you; for instance, such as looking out for a comfortable small house for them, helping them to move their things, and sending them presents of fish and game, and so forth, whenever they are in season. I'll lay my life that he meant nothing further; indeed, it would be very strange and unreasonable if he did. Do but consider, my dear Mr. Dashwood, how excessively comfortable your mother-in-law and her daughters may live on the interest of seven thousand pounds, besides the thousand pounds belonging to each of the girls, which brings them in fifty pounds a year apiece, and of course they will pay their mother for their board out of it. Altogether, they will have five hundred a year amongst them, and what on earth can four women want for more than that? They will live so cheap! Their housekeeping will be nothing at all. They will have no carriage, no horses, and hardly any servants; they will keep no company, and can have no expenses of any kind! Only conceive how comfortable they will be! Five hundred a year! I am sure I cannot imagine how they will spend half of it; and as to your giving them more, it is quite absurd to think of it. They will be much more able to give *you* something."

"Upon my word," said Mr. Dashwood, "I believe you are

perfectly right. My father certainly could mean nothing more by his request to me than what you say. I clearly understand it now, and I will strictly fulfil my engagement by such acts of assistance and kindness to them as you have described. When my mother removes into another house my services shall be readily given to accommodate her as far as I can. Some little present of furniture too may be acceptable then."

"Certainly," returned Mrs. John Dashwood. "But, however, *one* thing must be considered. When your father and mother moved to Norland, though the furniture of Stanhill was sold, all the china, plate, and linen was saved, and is now left to your mother. Her house will therefore be almost completely fitted up as soon as she takes it."

"That is a material consideration undoubtedly. A valuable legacy indeed! And yet some of the plate would have been a very pleasant addition to our own stock here."

"Yes, and the set of breakfast china is twice as handsome as what belongs to this house. A great deal too handsome, in my opinion, for any place *they* can ever afford to live in. But, however, so it is. Your father thought only of *them*. And I must say this: that you owe no particular gratitude to him, nor attention to his wishes, for we very well know that if he could, he would have left almost everything in the world to *them*."

This argument was irresistible. It gave to his intentions whatever of decision was wanting before; and he finally resolved that it would be absolutely unnecessary, if not highly indecorous, to do more for the widow and children of his father than such kind of neighbourly acts as his own wife pointed out.

Chapter 3

MRS. DASHWOOD remained at Norland several months; not from any disinclination to move when the sight of every well-known spot ceased to raise the violent emotion which it produced for a while; for when her spirits began to revive, and her mind became capable of some other exertion than that of heightening its affliction by melancholy remembrances, she was impatient to be gone and indefatigable in her inquiries for a suitable dwelling in the neighbourhood of Norland; for to remove far from that beloved spot was impossible. But she could hear of no situation that at once answered her notions of comfort and ease, and suited the prudence of her eldest daughter, whose steadier judgment rejected several houses as too large for their income, which her mother would have approved.

Mrs. Dashwood had been informed by her husband of the solemn promise on the part of his son in their favour, which gave comfort to his last earthly reflections. She doubted the sincerity of this assurance no more than he had doubted it himself, and she thought of it for her daughters' sake with satisfaction, though as for herself she was persuaded that a much smaller provision than 7000£ would support her in affluence. For their brother's sake too, for the sake of his own heart she rejoiced; and she reproached herself for being unjust to his merit before in believing him incapable of generosity. His attentive behaviour to herself and his sisters convinced her that their welfare was dear to him, and for a long time she firmly relied on the liberality of his intentions.

The contempt which she had very early in their acquaintance felt for her daughter-in-law was very much increased by the further knowledge of her character, which half a year's residence in her family afforded; and perhaps in spite of every consideration of politeness or maternal affection on the side of the former, the two ladies might have found it impossible to have lived together so long had not a particular circumstance occurred to give still greater eligibility, according to the opinions of Mrs. Dashwood, to her daughters' continuance at Norland.

This circumstance was a growing attachment between her eldest girl and the brother of Mrs. John Dashwood, a gentlemanlike and pleasing young man who was introduced to their acquaintance soon after his sister's establishment at Norland, and who had since spent the greatest part of his time there.

Some mothers might have encouraged the intimacy from motives of interest, for Edward Ferrars was the eldest son of a man who had died very rich; and some might have repressed it from motives of prudence, for except a trifling sum, the whole of his fortune depended on the will of his mother. But Mrs. Dashwood was alike uninfluenced by either consideration. It was enough for her that he appeared to be amiable, that he loved her daughter, and that Elinor returned the partiality. It was contrary to every doctrine of hers that difference of fortune should keep any couple asunder who were attracted by resemblance of disposition; and that Elinor's merit should not be acknowledged by everyone who knew her, was to her comprehension impossible.

Edward Ferrars was not recommended to their good opinion by any peculiar graces of person or address. He was not handsome, and his manners required intimacy to make them pleasing. He was too diffident to do justice to himself; but when his natural shyness was overcome, his behaviour gave every indication of an open affectionate heart. His understanding was good, and his education had given it solid improvement. But he was neither fitted by abilities nor disposition to answer the wishes of his mother and sister, who longed to see him distinguished—as—they hardly knew what. They wanted him to make a fine figure in the world in some manner or other. His mother wished to interest him in political concerns, to get him into parliament, or to see him connected with some of the great men of the day. Mrs. John Dashwood wished it likewise; but in the meanwhile, till one of these superior blessings could be attained, it would have quieted her ambition to see him driving a barouché. But Edward had no turn for great men or barouchés. All his wishes centered in domestic comfort and the quiet of private life. Fortunately he had a younger brother who was more promising.

Edward had been staying several weeks in the house before he engaged much of Mrs. Dashwood's attention, for she was at that time in such affliction as rendered her careless of surrounding objects. She saw only that he was quiet and unobtrusive, and she liked him for it. He did not disturb the wretchedness of her mind by ill-timed conversation. She was first called to observe and approve him further by a reflection which Elinor chanced one day to make on the difference between him and his sister. It was a contrast which recommended him most forcibly to her mother.

"It is enough," said she; "to say that he is unlike Fanny is enough. It implies everything amiable. I love him already."

"I think you will like him," said Elinor, "when you know more of him."

"Like him!" replied her mother with a smile. "I can feel no sentiment of approbation inferior to love."

"You may esteem him."

"I have never yet known what it was to separate esteem and love."

Mrs. Dashwood now took pains to get acquainted with him. Her manners were attaching and soon banished his reserve. She speedily comprehended all his merits; the persuasion of his regard for Elinor perhaps assisted her penetration, but she really felt assured of his worth: and even that quietness of manner which militated against all her established ideas of what a young man's address ought to be, was no longer uninteresting when she knew his heart to be warm and his temper affectionate.

No sooner did she perceive any symptom of love in his behaviour to Elinor, than she considered their serious attachment as certain and looked forward to their marriage as rapidly approaching.

"In a few months, my dear Marianne," said she, "Elinor will in all probability be settled for life. We shall miss her, but *she* will be happy."

"Oh! Mama, how shall we do without her?"

"My love, it will be scarcely a separation. We shall live within a few miles of each other and shall meet every day of our lives. You will gain a brother, a real, affectionate brother. I have the highest opinion in the world of Edward's heart. But you look grave, Marianne; do you disapprove your sister's choice?"

"Perhaps," said Marianne, "I may consider it with some surprise. Edward is very amiable, and I love him tenderly. But yet—he is not the kind of young man—there is a something wanting—his figure is not striking; it has none of that grace which I should expect in the man who could seriously attach my sister. His eyes want all that spirit, that fire, which at once announce virtue and intelligence. And besides all this, I am afraid, Mama, he has no real taste. Music seems scarcely to attract him, and though he admires Elinor's drawings very much, it is not the admiration of a person who can understand their worth. It is evident, in spite of his frequent attention to her while she draws, that in fact he knows nothing of the matter. He admires as a lover, not as a connoisseur. To satisfy me, those characters must be united. I could not be happy with a man whose taste did not in every point coincide with my own. He must enter into all my feelings; the same books, the same music must charm us both. Oh! Mama, how spiritless, how tame was Edward's manner in reading to us last night! I felt for my sister most severely. Yet she bore it with so much composure; she seemed scarcely to notice it. I could hardly keep my seat. To hear those beautiful lines which have frequently almost driven me wild, pronounced with such impenetrable calmness, such dreadful indifference!"

"He would certainly have done more justice to simple and elegant prose. I thought so at the time; but you *would* give him Cowper."

"Nay, Mama, if he is not to be animated by Cowper!—But we must allow for difference of taste. Elinor has not my feelings, and therefore she may overlook it and be happy with him. But it would have broke *my* heart had I loved him to hear him read with so little sensibility. Mama, the more I know of the world, the more am I convinced that I shall never see a man whom I can really love. I require so much! He must have all Edward's virtues, and his person and manners must ornament his goodness with every possible charm."

"Remember, my love, that you are not seventeen. It is yet too early in life to despair of such an happiness. Why should you be less fortunate than your mother? In one circumstance only, my Marianne, may your destiny be different from hers!"

Chapter 4

"WHAT A pity it is, Elinor," said Marianne, "that Edward should have no taste for drawing."

"No taste for drawing," replied Elinor; "why should you think so? He does not draw himself, indeed, but he has great pleasure in seeing the performances of other people, and I assure you he is by no means deficient in natural taste, though he has not had opportunities of improving it. Had he ever been in the way of learning, I think he would have drawn very well. He distrusts his own judgment in such matters so much that he is always unwilling to give his opinion on any picture; but he has an innate propriety and simplicity of taste, which in general direct him perfectly right."

Marianne was afraid of offending and said no more on the subject; but the kind of approbation which Elinor described as excited in him by the drawings of other people was very far from that rapturous delight which, in her opinion, could alone be called taste. Yet, though smiling within herself at the mistake, she honoured her sister for that blind partiality to Edward which produced it.

"I hope, Marianne," continued Elinor, "you do not consider him as deficient in general taste. Indeed I think I may say that you cannot, for your behaviour to him is perfectly cordial, and if *that* were your opinion, I am sure you could never be civil to him."

Marianne hardly knew what to say. She would not wound the feelings of her sister on any account, and yet to say what she did not believe was impossible. At length she replied:

"Do not be offended, Elinor, if my praise of him is not in everything equal to your sense of his merits. I have not had so many opportunities of estimating the minuter propensities of his mind, his inclinations, and tastes, as you have; but I have the highest opinion in the world of his goodness and sense. I think him everything that is worthy and amiable."

"I am sure," replied Elinor with a smile, "that his dearest friends could not be dissatisfied with such commendation as that. I do not perceive how you could express yourself more warmly."

Marianne was rejoiced to find her sister so easily pleased.

"Of his sense and his goodness," continued Elinor, "no one can, I think, be in doubt, who has seen him often enough to engage him in unreserved conversation. The excellence of his understanding and his principles can be concealed only by that shyness which too often keeps him silent. You know enough of him to do justice to his solid worth. But of his minuter propensities as you call them, you have from peculiar circumstances been kept more ignorant than myself. He and I have been at times thrown a good deal together while you have been wholly engrossed on the most affectionate principle by my mother. I have seen a great deal of him, have studied his sentiments and heard his opinion on subjects of literature and taste; and upon the whole, I venture to pronounce that his mind is well-informed, his enjoyment of books exceedingly great, his imagination lively, his observation just and correct, and his taste delicate and pure. His abilities in every respect improve as much upon acquaintance as his manners and person. At first sight his address is certainly not striking; and his person can hardly be called handsome till the expression of his eyes, which are uncommonly good, and the general sweetness of his countenance, is perceived. At present I know him so well that I think him really handsome; or, at least, almost so. What say you, Marianne?"

"I shall very soon think him handsome, Elinor, if I do not now. When you tell me to love him as a brother, I shall no more see imperfection in his face than I now do in his heart."

Elinor started at this declaration and was sorry for the warmth she had been betrayed into, in speaking of him. She felt that Edward stood very high in her opinion. She believed the regard to be mutual; but she required greater certainty of it to make Marianne's conviction of their attachment agreeable to him. She knew that what Marianne and her mother conjectured one moment, they believed the next: that with them, to wish was to hope, and to hope was to expect. She tried to explain the real state of the case to her sister.

"I do not attempt to deny," said she, "that I think very highly of him—that I greatly esteem, that I like him."

Marianne here burst forth with indignation—

"Esteem him! Like him! Cold-hearted Elinor! Oh! worse than cold-hearted! Ashamed of being otherwise. Use those words again and I will leave the room this moment."

Elinor could not help laughing. "Excuse me," said she, "and be assured that I meant no offence to you by speaking in so quiet a way of my own feelings. Believe them to be stronger than I have declared; believe them, in short, to be such as his merit and the suspicion—the hope of his affection for me may warrant without imprudence or folly. But further than this you must *not* believe. I am by no means assured of his regard for me. There are moments when the extent of it seems doubtful; and till his sentiments are fully known, you cannot wonder at my wishing to avoid any encouragement of my own partiality by believing or calling it more than it is. In my heart I feel little—scarcely any doubt of his preference. But there are other points to be considered besides his inclination. He is very far from being independent. What his mother really is we cannot know; but from Fanny's occasional mention of her conduct and opinions, we have never been disposed to think her amiable; and I am very much mistaken if Edward is not himself aware that there would be many difficulties in his way if he were to wish to marry a woman who had not either a great fortune or high rank."

Marianne was astonished to find how much the imagination of her mother and herself had outstripped the truth.

"And you really are not engaged to him!" said she. "Yet it certainly soon will happen. But two advantages will proceed from this delay. I shall not lose you so soon, and Edward will have greater opportunity of improving that natural taste for your favourite pursuit which must be so indispensably necessary to your future felicity. Oh! if he should be so far stimulated by your genius as to learn to draw himself, how delightful it would be!"

Elinor had given her real opinion to her sister. She could not consider her partiality for Edward in so prosperous a state as Marianne had believed it. There was at times a want of spirits about him which, if it did not denote indifference, spoke a something almost as unpromising. A doubt of her regard, supposing him to feel it, need not give him more than inquietude. It would not be likely to produce that dejection of mind which frequently attended him. A more reasonable cause might be found in the dependent situation which forbad the indulgence of his affection. She knew that his mother neither behaved to him so as to make his home comfortable at present, nor to give him any assurance that he might form a home for himself without strictly attending to her views for his aggrandizement. With such a knowledge as this, it was impossible for Elinor to feel easy on the subject. She was far from depending on that result of his preference of her which her mother and sister still considered as certain. Nay, the longer they were together the more doubtful seemed the nature of his regard; and sometimes, for a few painful minutes, she believed it to be no more than friendship.

But whatever might really be its limits, it was enough when perceived by his sister to make her uneasy; and at the same time, (which was still more common), to make her uncivil. She took the first opportunity of affronting her mother-in-law on the occasion, talking to her so expressively of her brother's great expectations, of Mrs. Ferrars's resolution that both her sons should marry well, and of the danger attending any young woman who attempted to *draw him in*; that Mrs. Dashwood could neither pretend to be unconscious nor endeavour to be calm. She gave her an answer which marked her contempt and instantly left the room, resolving that, whatever might be the inconvenience or expense of so sudden a removal, her beloved Elinor should not be exposed another week to such insinuations.

In this state of her spirits, a letter was delivered to her from the post, which contained a proposal particularly well timed. It was the offer of a small house, on very easy terms, belonging to a relation of her own, a gentleman of consequence and property in Devonshire. The letter was from this gentleman himself, and written in the true spirit of friendly accommodation. He understood that she was in need of a dwelling, and though the house he now offered her was merely a cottage, he assured her that everything should be done to it which she might think necessary, if the situation pleased her. He earnestly pressed her, after giving the particulars of the house and garden, to come with her daughters to Barton Park, the place of his own residence, from whence she might judge, herself, whether Barton Cottage, for the houses were in the same parish, could by any alteration be made comfortable to her. He seemed really anxious to accommodate them, and the whole of his letter was written in so friendly a style as could not fail of giving pleasure to his cousin; more especially at a moment when she was suffering under the cold and unfeeling behaviour of her nearer connections. She needed no time for deliberation or inquiry. Her resolution was formed as she read. The situation of Barton, in a county so far distant from Sussex as Devonshire, which but a few hours before would have been a sufficient objection to outweigh every possible advantage belonging to the place, was now its first recommendation. To quit the neighbourhood of Norland was no longer an evil; it was an object of desire; it was a blessing in comparison of the misery of continuing her daughter-in-law's guest: and to remove forever from that beloved place would be less painful than to inhabit or visit it while such a woman was its mistress. She instantly wrote Sir John Middleton her acknowledgement of his kindness and her acceptance of his proposal; and then hastened to show both letters to her daughters, that she might be secure of their approbation before her answer was sent.

Elinor had always thought it would be more prudent for them to settle at some distance from Norland than immediately amongst their present acquaintance. On *that* head, therefore, it was not for her to oppose her mother's intention of removing into Devonshire. The house, too, as described by Sir John, was on so simple a scale, and the rent so uncommonly moderate, as to leave her no right of objection on either point; and therefore, though it was not a plan which brought any charm to her fancy, though it was a removal from the vicinity of Norland beyond her wishes, she made no attempt to dissuade her mother from sending her letter of acquiescence.

Chapter 5

No SOONER was her answer dispatched, than Mrs. Dashwood indulged herself in the pleasure of announcing to her son-in-law and his wife that she was provided with an house, and should incommode them no longer than till everything were ready for her inhabiting it. They heard her with surprise. Mrs. John Dashwood said nothing, but her husband civilly hoped that she would not be settled far from Norland. She had great satisfaction in replying that she was going into Devonshire. Edward turned hastily towards her on hearing this, and in a voice of surprise and concern which required no explanation to her, repeated, "Devonshire! Are you indeed going there? So far from hence! And to what part of it?" She explained the situation. It was within four miles northward of Exeter.

"It is but a cottage," she continued, "but I hope to see many of my friends in it. A room or two can easily be added; and if my friends find no difficulty in travelling so far to see me, I am sure I will find none in accommodating them."

She concluded with a very kind invitation to Mr. and Mrs. John Dashwood to visit her at Barton, and to Edward she gave one with still greater affection. Though her late conversation with her daughter-in-law had made her resolve on remaining at Norland no longer than was unavoidable, it had not produced the smallest effect on her in that point to which it principally tended. To separate Edward and Elinor was as far from being her object as ever; and she wished to show Mrs. John Dashwood by this pointed invitation to her brother, how totally she disregarded her disapprobation of the match.

Mr. John Dashwood told his mother again and again how exceedingly sorry he was that she had taken an house at such a distance from Norland as to prevent his being of any service to her in removing her furniture. He really felt conscientiously vexed on the occasion; for the very exertion to which he had limited the performance of his promise to his father was by this arrangement rendered impracticable. The furniture was all sent round by water. It chiefly consisted of household linen, plate, china, and books, with an handsome pianoforte of Marianne's. Mrs. John Dashwood saw the packages depart with a sigh: she could not help feeling it hard that as Mrs. Dashwood's income would be so trifling in comparison with their own, she should have any handsome article of furniture.

Mrs. Dashwood took the house for a twelvemonth; it was ready furnished, and she might have immediate possession. No difficulty arose on either side in the agreement; and she waited only for the disposal of her effects at Norland and to determine her future household before she set off for the west; and this, as she was exceedingly rapid in the performance of everything that interested her, was soon done. The horses which were left her by her husband had been sold soon after his death, and an opportunity now offering of disposing of her carriage, she agreed to sell that likewise at the earnest advice of her eldest daughter. For the comfort of her children, had she consulted only her own wishes, she would have kept it; but the discretion of Elinor prevailed. *Her* wisdom too limited the number of their servants to three: two maids and a man, with whom they were speedily provided from amongst those who had formed their establishment at Norland.

The man and one of the maids were sent off immediately into Devonshire to prepare the house for their mistress's arrival; for as Lady Middleton was entirely unknown to Mrs.

Dashwood, she preferred going directly to the cottage to being a visitor at Barton Park; and she relied so undoubtingly on Sir John's description of the house, as to feel no curiosity to examine it herself till she entered it as her own. Her eagerness to be gone from Norland was preserved from diminution by the evident satisfaction of her daughter-in-law in the prospect of her removal, a satisfaction which was but feebly attempted to be concealed under a cold invitation to her to defer her departure. Now was the time when her son-in-law's promise to his father might with particular propriety be fulfilled. Since he had neglected to do it on first coming to the estate, their quitting his house might be looked on as the most suitable period for its accomplishment. But Mrs. Dashwood began shortly to give over every hope of the kind, and to be convinced from the general drift of his discourse that his assistance extended no farther than their maintenance for six months at Norland. He so frequently talked of the increasing expenses of housekeeping, and of the perpetual demands upon his purse, which a man of any consequence in the world was beyond calculation exposed to, that he seemed rather to stand in need of more money himself than to have any design of giving money away.

In a very few weeks from the day which brought Sir John Middleton's first letter to Norland, everything was so far settled in their future abode as to enable Mrs. Dashwood and her daughters to begin their journey.

Many were the tears shed by them in their last adieus to a place so much beloved. "Dear, dear Norland!" said Marianne as she wandered alone before the house on the last evening of their being there; "when shall I cease to regret you! When learn to feel a home elsewhere! Oh! happy house, could you know what I suffer in now viewing you from this spot, from whence perhaps I may view you no more! And you, ye well-known trees! But you will continue the same. No leaf will decay because we are removed, nor any branch become motionless, although we can observe you no longer! No, you will continue the same: unconscious of the pleasure or the regret you occasion and insensible of any change in those who walk under your shade! But who will remain to enjoy you?"

Chapter 6

THE FIRST part of their journey was performed in too melancholy a disposition to be otherwise than tedious and unpleasant. But as they drew towards the end of it, their interest in the appearance of a country which they were to inhabit overcame their dejection, and a view of Barton Valley as they entered it gave them cheerfulness. It was a pleasant fertile spot, well-wooded, and rich in pasture. After winding along it for more than a mile, they reached their own house. A small green court was the whole of its demesne in front, and a neat wicket gate admitted them into it.

As a house, Barton Cottage, though small, was comfortable and compact; but as a cottage it was defective, for the building was regular, the roof was tiled, the window shutters were not painted green, nor were the walls covered with honeysuckles. A narrow passage led directly through the house into the garden behind. On each side of the entrance was a sitting room about sixteen feet square, and beyond them were the offices and the stairs. Four bedrooms and two garrets formed the rest of the house. It had not been built many years and was in good repair. In comparison of Norland, it was poor and small indeed! But the tears which recollection called forth as they entered the house were soon dried away. They were cheered by the joy of the servants on their arrival, and each for the sake of the others resolved to appear happy. It was very early in September; the season was fine, and from first seeing the place under the advantage of good weather, they received an impression in its favour which was of material service in recommending it to their lasting approbation.

The situation of the house was good. High hills rose immediately behind and at no great distance on each side, some of which were open downs, the others cultivated and woody. The village of Barton was chiefly on one of these hills, and formed a pleasant view from the cottage windows. The prospect in front was more extensive; it commanded the whole of the valley and reached into the country beyond. The hills

which surrounded the cottage terminated the valley in that
direction; under another name, and in another course, it
branched out again between two of the steepest of them.

With the size and furniture of the house Mrs. Dashwood
was upon the whole well satisfied; for though her former
style of life rendered many additions to the latter indispensable, yet to add and improve was a delight to her; and she
had at this time ready money enough to supply all that was
wanted of greater elegance to the apartments. "As for the
house itself, to be sure," she said, "it is too small for our
family, but we will make ourselves tolerably comfortable for
the present as it is too late in the year for improvements.
Perhaps in the spring if I have plenty of money, as I dare say
I shall, we may think about building. These parlours are both
too small for such parties of our friends as I hope to see often collected here; and I have some thoughts of throwing the
passage into one of them with perhaps a part of the other,
and so leave the remainder of that other for an entrance; this,
with a new drawing-room which may be easily added, and a
bedchamber and garret above, will make it a very snug little
cottage. I could wish the stairs were handsome. But one
must not expect everything, though I suppose it would be no
difficult matter to widen them. I shall see how much I am
beforehand with the world in the spring, and we will plan
our improvements accordingly."

In the meantime, till all these alterations could be made
from the savings of an income of five hundred a year by a
woman who never saved in her life, they were wise enough
to be contented with the house as it was; and each of them
was busy in arranging their particular concerns, and endeavouring, by placing around them their books and other possessions, to form themselves a home. Marianne's pianoforte
was unpacked and properly disposed of, and Elinor's drawings were affixed to the walls of their sitting room.

In such employments as these they were interrupted soon
after breakfast the next day by the entrance of their landlord,
who called to welcome them to Barton, and to offer them
every accommodation from his own house and garden in
which theirs might at present be deficient. Sir John
Middleton was a good looking man about forty. He had formerly visited at Stanhill, but it was too long ago for his
young cousins to remember him. His countenance was thoroughly good-humoured; and his manners were as friendly as

the style of his letter. Their arrival seemed to afford him real satisfaction, and their comfort to be an object of real solicitude to him. He said much of his earnest desire of their living in the most sociable terms with his family, and pressed them so cordially to dine at Barton Park every-day till they were better settled at home, that, though his entreaties were carried to a point of perseverance beyond civility, they could not give offence. His kindness was not confined to words; for within an hour after he left them, a large basket of garden stuff and fruit arrived from the park, which was followed before the end of the day by a present of game. He insisted moreover on conveying all their letters to and from the post for them, and would not be denied the satisfaction of sending them his newspaper every day.

Lady Middleton had sent a very civil message by him, denoting her intention of waiting on Mrs. Dashwood as soon as she could be assured that her visit would be no inconvenience; and as this message was answered by an invitation equally polite, her ladyship was introduced to them the next day.

They were of course very anxious to see a person on whom so much of their comfort at Barton must depend; and the elegance of her appearance was favourable to their wishes. Lady Middleton was not more than six or seven and twenty; her face was handsome, her figure tall and striking, and her address graceful. Her manners had all the elegance which her husband's wanted. But they would have been improved by some share of his frankness and warmth; and her visit was long enough to detract something from their first admiration, by showing that though perfectly well-bred, she was reserved, cold, and had nothing to say for herself beyond the most commonplace inquiry or remark.

Conversation however was not wanted, for Sir John was very chatty, and Lady Middleton had taken the wise precaution of bringing with her their eldest child, a fine little boy about six years old, by which means there was one subject always to be recurred to by the ladies in case of extremity, for they had to inquire his name and age, admire his beauty, and ask him questions which his mother answered for him while he hung about her and held down his head to the great surprise of her ladyship, who wondered at his being so shy before company as he could make noise enough at home. On every formal visit a child ought to be of the party, by way of provision for discourse. In the present case it took up ten minutes to determine whether the boy were most like his father or mother, and in what particular he resembled either, for of course everybody differed, and everybody was astonished at the opinion of the others.

An opportunity was soon to be given to the Dashwoods of debating on the rest of the children, as Sir John would not leave the house without securing their promise of dining at the park the next day.

Chapter 7

BARTON PARK was about half a mile from the cottage. The ladies had passed near it in their way along the valley, but it was screened from their view at home by the projection of the hill. The house was large and handsome; and the Middletons lived in a style of equal hospitality and elegance. The former was for Sir John's gratification, the latter for that of his lady. They were scarcely ever without some friends staying with them in the house, and they kept more company of every kind than any other family in the neighbourhood. It was necessary to the happiness of both; for however dissimilar in temper and outward behaviour, they strongly resembled each other in that total want of talent and taste which confined their employments, unconnected with such as society produced, within a very narrow compass. Sir John was a sportsman, Lady Middleton a mother. He hunted and shot, and she humoured her children; and these were their only resources. Lady Middleton had the advantage of being able to spoil her children all the year round, while Sir John's independent employments were in existence only half the time. Continual engagements at home and abroad, however, supplied all the deficiencies of nature and education, supported the good spirits of Sir John, and gave exercise to the good breeding of his wife.

Lady Middleton piqued herself upon the elegance of her table and of all her domestic arrangements, and from this kind of vanity was her greatest enjoyment in any of their parties. But Sir John's satisfaction in society was much more real; he delighted in collecting about him more young people than his house would hold, and the noisier they were, the better was he pleased. He was a blessing to all the juvenile part of the neighbourhood, for in summer he was forever forming parties to eat cold ham and chicken out-of-doors, and in winter his private balls were numerous enough for any young lady who was not suffering under the insatiable appetite of fifteen.

The arrival of a new family in the country was always a matter of joy to him, and in every point of view he was charmed with the inhabitants he had now procured for his cottage at Barton. The Miss Dashwoods were young, pretty, and unaffected. It was enough to secure his good opinion, for to be unaffected was all that a pretty girl could want to make her mind as captivating as her person. The friendliness of his disposition made him happy in accommodating those whose situation might be considered in comparison with the past as unfortunate. In showing kindness to his cousins, therefore, he had the real satisfaction of a good heart; and in settling a family of females only in his cottage, he had all the satisfaction of a sportsman; for a sportsman, though he esteems only those of his sex who are sportsmen likewise, is not often desirous of encouraging their taste by admitting them to a residence within his own manor.

Mrs. Dashwood and her daughters were met at the door of the house by Sir John, who welcomed them to Barton Park with unaffected sincerity; and as he attended them to the drawing room repeated to the young ladies the concern which the same subject had drawn from him the day before, at being unable to get any smart young men to meet them. They would see, he said, only one gentleman there besides himself, a particular friend who was staying at the park, but who was neither very young nor very gay. He hoped they would all excuse the smallness of the party and could assure them it should never happen so again. He had been to several families that morning in hopes of procuring some addition to their number, but it was moonlight and everybody was full of engagements. Luckily Lady Middleton's mother had arrived at Barton within the last hour, and as she was a very cheerful agreeable woman, he hoped the young ladies would not find it so very dull as they might imagine. The young ladies, as well as their mother, were perfectly satisfied with having two entire strangers of the party and wished for no more.

Mrs. Jennings, Lady Middleton's mother, was a good-humoured, merry, fat, elderly woman, who talked a great deal, seemed very happy and rather vulgar. She was full of jokes and laughter, and before dinner was over had said many witty things on the subject of lovers and husbands, hoped they had not left their hearts behind them in Sussex, and pretended to see them blush whether they did or not. Marianne was vexed at it for her sister's sake and turned her eyes towards Elinor to see how she bore these attacks, with an earnestness which gave Elinor far more pain than could arise from such commonplace raillery as Mrs. Jennings's.

Colonel Brandon, the friend of Sir John, seemed no more adapted by resemblance of manner to be his friend, than Lady Middleton was to be his wife, or Mrs. Jennings to be Lady Middleton's mother. He was silent and grave. His appearance however was not unpleasing, in spite of his being in the opinion of Marianne and Margaret an absolute old bachelor, for he was on the wrong side of five and thirty; but though his face was not handsome, his countenance was sensible, and his address was particularly gentlemanlike.

There was nothing in any of the party which could recommend them as companions to the Dashwoods; but the cold insipidity of Lady Middleton was so particularly repulsive, that in comparison of it the gravity of Colonel Brandon and even the boisterous mirth of Sir John and his mother-in-law was interesting. Lady Middleton seemed to be roused to enjoyment only by the entrance of her four noisy children after dinner, who pulled her about, tore her clothes, and put an end to every kind of discourse except what related to themselves.

In the evening, as Marianne was discovered to be musical, she was invited to play. The instrument was unlocked; everybody prepared to be charmed, and Marianne, who sang very well, at their request went through the chief of the songs which Lady Middleton had brought into the family on her marriage, and which perhaps had lain ever since in the same position on the pianoforte, for her ladyship had celebrated that event by giving up music, although by her mother's account she had played extremely well, and by her own was very fond of it.

Marianne's performance was highly applauded. Sir John was loud in his admiration at the end of every song and as loud in his conversation with the others while every song lasted. Lady Middleton frequently called him to order, wondered how anyone's attention could be diverted from music for a moment, and asked Marianne to sing a particular song which Marianne had just finished. Colonel Brandon alone, of all the party, heard her without being in raptures. He paid her only the compliment of attention; and she felt a respect for him on the occasion, which the others had reasonably forfeited by their shameless want of taste. His pleasure in music, though it amounted not to that ecstatic delight which alone could sympathize with her own, was estimable when contrasted against the horrible insensibility of the others; and she was reasonable enough to allow that a man of five and thirty might well have outlived all acuteness of feeling and every exquisite power of enjoyment. She was perfectly disposed to make every allowance for the colonel's advanced state of life which humanity required.

Chapter 8

MRS. JENNINGS was a widow with an ample jointure. She had only two daughters, both of whom she had lived to see respectably married, and she had now therefore nothing to do but to marry all the rest of the world. In the promotion of this object she was zealously active as far as her ability reached and missed no opportunity of projecting weddings among all the young people of her acquaintance. She was remarkably quick in the discovery of attachments, and had enjoyed the advantage of raising the blushes and the vanity of many a young lady by insinuations of her power over such a young man; and this kind of discernment enabled her soon after her arrival at Barton decisively to pronounce that Colonel Brandon was very much in love with Marianne Dashwood. She rather suspected it to be so on the very first evening of their being together, from his listening so attentively while she sang to them; and when the visit was returned by the Middletons' dining at the cottage, the fact was ascertained by his listening to her again. It must be so. She was perfectly convinced of it. It would be an excellent match, for *he* was rich and *she* was handsome. Mrs. Jennings had been anxious to see Colonel Brandon well married ever since her connection with Sir John first brought him to her knowledge; and she was always anxious to get a good husband for every pretty girl.

The immediate advantage to herself was by no means inconsiderable, for it supplied her with endless jokes against them both. At the park she laughed at the colonel, and in the cottage at Marianne. To the former her raillery was probably, as far as it regarded only himself, perfectly indifferent; but to the latter it was at first incomprehensible; and when its object was understood, she hardly knew whether most to laugh at its absurdity, or censure its impertinence, for she considered it as an unfeeling reflection on the colonel's advanced years and on his forlorn condition as an old bachelor.

Mrs. Dashwood, who could not think a man five years younger than herself so exceedingly ancient as he appeared to the youthful fancy of her daughter, ventured to clear Mrs. Jennings from the probability of wishing to throw ridicule on his age.

"But at least, mama, you cannot deny the absurdity of the accusation, though you may not think it intentionally ill-natured. Colonel Brandon is certainly younger than Mrs. Jennings, but he is old enough to be *my* father; and if he were ever animated enough to be in love, must have long outlived every sensation of the kind. It is too ridiculous! When is a man to be safe from such wit if age and infirmity will not protect him?"

"Infirmity!" said Elinor. "Do you call Colonel Brandon infirm? I can easily suppose that his age may appear much greater to you than to my mother, but you can hardly deceive yourself as to his having the use of his limbs!"

"Did not you hear him complain of the rheumatism? And is not that the commonest infirmity of declining life?"

"My dearest child," said her mother, laughing, "at this rate you must be in continual terror of *my* decay; and it must seem to you a miracle that my life has been extended to the advanced age of forty."

"Mama, you are not doing me justice. I know very well that Colonel Brandon is not old enough to make his friends yet apprehensive of losing him in the course of nature. He may live twenty years longer. But thirty-five has nothing to do with matrimony."

"Perhaps," said Elinor, "thirty-five and seventeen had better not have anything to do with matrimony together. But if there should by any chance happen to be a woman who is single at seven and twenty, I should not think Colonel Brandon's being thirty-five any objection to his marrying *her*."

"A woman of seven and twenty," said Marianne, after pausing a moment, "can never hope to feel or inspire affection again, and if her home be uncomfortable, or her fortune small, I can suppose that she might bring herself to submit to the offices of a nurse for the sake of the provision and security of a wife. In his marrying such a woman therefore there would be nothing unsuitable. It would be a compact of convenience, and the world would be satisfied. In my eyes it would be no marriage at all, but that would be nothing. To me it would seem only a commercial exchange in which each wished to be benefited at the expense of the other."

"It would be impossible, I know," replied Elinor, "to convince you that a woman of seven and twenty could feel for a man of thirty-five anything near enough to love to make him a desirable companion to her. But I must object to your dooming Colonel Brandon and his wife to the constant confinement of a sick chamber merely because he chanced to complain yesterday (a very cold damp day) of a slight rheumatic feel in one of his shoulders."

"But he talked of flannel waistcoats," said Marianne; "and with me a flannel waistcoat is invariably connected with aches, cramps, rheumatisms, and every species of ailment that can afflict the old and the feeble."

"Had he been only in a violent fever, you would not have despised him half so much. Confess, Marianne, is not there something interesting to you in the flushed cheek, hollow eye, and quick pulse of a fever?"

Soon after this, upon Elinor's leaving the room, "Mama," said Marianne, "I have an alarm on the subject of illness, which I cannot conceal from you. I am sure Edward Ferrars is not well. We have now been here almost a fortnight, and yet he does not come. Nothing but real indisposition could occasion this extraordinary delay. What else can detain him at Norland?"

"Had you any idea of his coming so soon?" said Mrs.

Dashwood. "I had none. On the contrary, if I have felt any anxiety at all on the subject, it has been in recollecting that he sometimes showed a want of pleasure and readiness in accepting my invitation when I talked of his coming to Barton. Does Elinor expect him already?"

"I have never mentioned it to her, but of course she must."

"I rather think you are mistaken, for when I was talking to her yesterday of getting a new grate for the spare bed-chamber, she observed that there was no immediate hurry for it, as it was not likely that the room would be wanted for some time."

"How strange this is! What can be the meaning of it! But the whole of their behaviour to each other has been unaccountable! How cold, how composed were their last adieus! How languid their conversation the last evening of their being together! In Edward's farewell there was no distinction between Elinor and me: it was the good wishes of an affectionate brother to both. Twice did I leave them purposely together in the course of the last morning, and each time did he most unaccountably follow me out of the room. And Elinor, in quitting Norland and Edward, cried not as I did. Even now her self-command is invariable. When is she dejected or melancholy? When does she try to avoid society, or appear restless and dissatisfied in it?"

Chapter 9

THE DASHWOODS were now settled at Barton with tolerable comfort to themselves. The house and the garden, with all the objects surrounding them, were now become familiar, and the ordinary pursuits which had given to Norland half its charms were engaged in again with far greater enjoyment than Norland had been able to afford since the loss of their father. Sir John Middleton, who called on them everyday for the first fortnight, and who was not in the habit of seeing much occupation at home, could not conceal his amazement on finding them always employed.

Their visitors, except those from Barton Park, were not many; for in spite of Sir John's urgent entreaties that they would mix more in the neighbourhood, and repeated assurances of his carriage being always at their service, the independence of Mrs. Dashwood's spirit overcame the wish of society for her children; and she was resolute in declining to visit any family beyond the distance of a walk. There were but few who could be so classed; and it was not all of them that were attainable. About a mile and a half from the cottage, along the narrow winding valley of Allenham, which issued from that of Barton, as formerly described, the girls had in one of their earliest walks discovered an ancient respectable looking mansion, which by reminding them a little of Norland interested their imagination and made them wish to be better acquainted with it. But they learned, on inquiry, that its possessor, an elderly lady of very good character, was unfortunately too infirm to mix with the world and never stirred from home.

The whole country about them abounded in beautiful walks. The high downs, which invited them from almost every window of the cottage to seek the exquisite enjoyment of air on their summits, were a happy alternative when the dirt of the valleys beneath them shut up their superior beauties; and towards one of these hills did Marianne and Margaret one memorable morning direct their steps, attracted by the partial sunshine of a showery sky, and unable longer to bear the confinement which the settled rain of the two preceding days had occasioned. The weather was not tempting enough to draw the two others from their pencil and their book in spite of Marianne's declaration that the day would be lastingly fair, and that every threatening cloud would be drawn off from their hills; and the two girls set off together.

They gaily ascended the downs, rejoicing in their own penetration at every glimpse of blue sky; and when they caught in their faces the animating gales of an high southwesterly wind, they pitied the fears which had prevented their mother and Elinor from sharing such delightful sensations.

"Is there a felicity in the world," said Marianne, "superior to this? Margaret, we will walk here at least two hours."

Margaret agreed, and they pursued their way against the wind, resisting it with laughing delight for about twenty minutes longer, when suddenly the clouds united over their heads, and a driving rain set full in their face. Chagrined and surprised, they were obliged, though unwillingly, to turn

back, for no shelter was nearer than their own house. One
consolation however remained for them, to which the exi-
gence of the moment gave more than usual propriety; it was
that of running with all possible speed down the steep side
of the hill which led immediately to their garden gate.

They set off. Marianne had at first the advantage, but a
false step brought her suddenly to the ground, and Margaret,
unable to stop herself to assist her, was involuntarily hurried
along, and reached the bottom in safety.

A gentleman carrying a gun, with two pointers playing
round him, was passing up the hill and within a few yards
of Marianne when her accident happened. He put down his
gun and ran to her assistance. She had raised herself from
the ground, but her foot had been twisted in the fall, and she
was scarcely able to stand. The gentleman offered his services, and perceiving that her modesty declined what her situation rendered necessary, took her up in his arms without
further delay and carried her down the hill. Then passing
through the garden, the gate of which had been left open by
Margaret, he bore her directly into the house, whither Margaret was just arrived, and quitted not his hold till he had
seated her in a chair in the parlour.

Elinor and her mother rose up in amazement at their entrance, and while the eyes of both were fixed on him with an
evident wonder and a secret admiration which equally
sprung from his appearance, he apologized for his intrusion
by relating its cause in a manner so frank and so graceful,
that his person, which was uncommonly handsome, received
additional charms from his voice and expression. Had he
been even old, ugly, and vulgar, the gratitude and kindness
of Mrs. Dashwood would have been secured by any act of
attention to her child; but the influence of youth, beauty, and
elegance, gave an interest to the action which came home to
her feelings.

She thanked him again and again; and with a sweetness of
address which always attended her invited him to be seated.
But this he declined, as he was dirty and wet. Mrs. Dashwood then begged to know to whom she was obliged. His
name, he replied, was Willoughby, and his present home was
at Allenham, from whence he hoped she would allow him
the honour of calling to-morrow to inquire after Miss
Dashwood. The honour was readily granted, and he then de-

parted, to make himself still more interesting in the midst of an heavy rain.

His manly beauty and more than common gracefulness were instantly the theme of general admiration, and the laugh which his gallantry raised against Marianne, received particular spirit from his exterior attractions. Marianne herself had seen less of his person than the rest, for the confusion which crimsoned over her face, on his lifting her up, had robbed her of the power of regarding him after their entering the house. But she had seen enough of him to join in all the admiration of the others, and with an energy which always adorned her praise. His person and air were equal to what her fancy had ever drawn for the hero of a favourite story; and in his carrying her into the house with so little previous formality, there was a rapidity of thought which particularly recommended the action to her. Every circumstance belonging to him was interesting. His name was good; his residence was in their favourite village; and she soon found out that of all manly dresses a shooting-jacket was the most becoming. Her imagination was busy; her reflections were pleasant; and the pain of a sprained ankle was disregarded.

Sir John called on them as soon as the next interval of fair weather that morning allowed him to get out of doors; and Marianne's accident being related to him, he was eagerly asked whether he knew any gentleman of the name of Willoughby at Allenham.

"Willoughby!" cried Sir John; "what, is *he* in the country? That is good news however; I will ride over to-morrow, and ask him to dinner on Thursday."

"You know him then," said Mrs. Dashwood.

"Know him! To be sure I do. Why, he is down here every year."

"And what sort of a young man is he?"

"As good a kind of fellow as ever lived, I assure you. A very decent shot, and there is not a bolder rider in England."

"And is *that* all you can say for him?" cried Marianne indignantly. "But what are his manners on more intimate acquaintance? What his pursuits, his talents and genius?"

Sir John was rather puzzled.

"Upon my soul," said he, "I do not know much about him as to all *that*. But he is a pleasant, good humoured fellow, and has got the nicest little black bitch of a pointer I ever saw. Was she out with him to-day?"

But Marianne could no more satisfy him as to the colour of Mr. Willoughby's pointer, than he could describe to her the shades of his mind.

"But who is he?" said Elinor. "Where does he come from? Has he a house at Allenham?"

On this point Sir John could give more certain intelligence; and he told them that Mr. Willoughby had no property of his own in the country; that he resided there only while he was visiting the old lady at Allenham Court, to whom he was related, and whose possessions he was to inherit; adding, "Yes, yes, he is very well worth catching, I can tell you, Miss Dashwood; he has a pretty little estate of his own in Somersetshire besides; and if I were you, I would not give him up to my younger sister in spite of all this tumbling down hills. Miss Marianne must not expect to have all the men to herself. Brandon will be jealous if she does not take care."

"I do not believe," said Mrs. Dashwood with a good humoured smile, "that Mr. Willoughby will be incommoded by the attempts of either of *my* daughters towards what you call *catching him.* It is not an employment to which they have been brought up. Men are very safe with us, let them be ever so rich. I am glad to find, however, from what you say, that he is a respectable young man, and one whose acquaintance will not be ineligible."

"He is as good a sort of fellow, I believe, as ever lived," repeated Sir John. "I remember last Christmas, at a little hop at the park, he danced from eight o'clock till four without once sitting down."

"Did he indeed?" cried Marianne, with sparkling eyes, "and with elegance, with spirit?"

"Yes, and he was up again at eight to ride to covert."

"That is what I like; that is what a young man ought to be. Whatever be his pursuits, his eagerness in them should know no moderation and leave him no sense of fatigue."

"Aye, aye, I see how it will be," said Sir John. "I see how it will be. You will be setting your cap at him now and never think of poor Brandon."

"That is an expression, Sir John," said Marianne warmly, "which I particularly dislike. I abhor every commonplace phrase by which wit is intended; and 'setting one's cap at a man,' or 'making a conquest,' are the most odious of all. Their tendency is gross and illiberal; and if their construction could ever be deemed clever, time has long ago destroyed all its ingenuity."

Sir John did not much understand this reproof; but he laughed as heartily as if he did and then replied,

"Aye, you will make conquests enough, I dare say, one way or other. Poor Brandon! He is quite smitten already, and he is very well worth setting your cap at, I can tell you, in spite of all this tumbling about and spraining of ankles."

Chapter 10

MARIANNE'S PRESERVER, as Margaret, with more elegance than precision, styled Willoughby, called at the cottage early the next morning to make his personal inquiries. He was received by Mrs. Dashwood with more than politeness; with a kindness which Sir John's account of him and her own gratitude prompted; and everything that passed during the visit tended to assure him of the sense, elegance, mutual affection, and domestic comfort of the family to whom accident had now introduced him. Of their personal charms he had not required a second interview to be convinced.

Miss Dashwood had a delicate complexion, regular features, and a remarkably pretty figure. Marianne was still handsomer. Her form, though not so correct as her sister's, in having the advantage of height, was more striking; and her face was so lovely, that when in the common cant of praise she was called a beautiful girl, truth was less violently outraged than usually happens. Her skin was very brown, but from its transparency, her complexion was uncommonly brilliant; her features were all good; her smile was sweet and attractive, and in her eyes, which were very dark, there was a life, a spirit, an eagerness which could hardly be seen without delight. From Willoughby their expression was at first held back by the embarrassment which the remembrance of his assistance created. But when this passed away, when her spirits became collected, when she saw that to the perfect good breeding of the gentleman, he united frankness

and vivacity, and above all, when she heard him declare that
of music and dancing he was passionately fond, she gave
him such a look of approbation as secured the largest share
of his discourse to herself for the rest of his stay.

It was only necessary to mention any favourite amusement
to engage her to talk. She could not be silent when such
points were introduced, and she had neither shyness nor reserve in their discussion. They speedily discovered that their
enjoyment of dancing and music was mutual, and that it
arose from a general conformity of judgment in all that related to either. Encouraged by this to a further examination
of his opinions, she proceeded to question him on the subject of books; her favourite authors were brought forward
and dwelt upon with so rapturous a delight that any young
man of five and twenty must have been insensible indeed
not to become an immediate convert to the excellence of
such works, however disregarded before. Their taste was
strikingly alike. The same books, the same passages were
idolized by each; or if any difference appeared, any objection arose, it lasted no longer than till the force of her arguments and the brightness of her eyes could be displayed. He
acquiesced in all her decisions, caught all her enthusiasm;
and long before his visit concluded, they conversed with the
familiarity of a long-established acquaintance.

"Well, Marianne," said Elinor, as soon as he had left them,
"for *one* morning I think you have done pretty well. You
have already ascertained Mr. Willoughby's opinion in almost
every matter of importance. You know what he thinks of
Cowper and Scott; you are certain of his estimating their
beauties as he ought, and you have received every assurance
of his admiring Pope no more than is proper. But how is
your acquaintance to be long supported under such extraordinary dispatch of every subject for discourse? You will
soon have exhausted each favourite topic. Another meeting
will suffice to explain his sentiments on picturesque beauty,
and second marriages, and then you can have nothing further
to ask."

"Elinor," cried Marianne, "is this fair? Is this just? Are
my ideas so scanty? But I see what you mean. I have been
too much at my ease, too happy, too frank. I have erred
against every commonplace notion of decorum; I have been
open and sincere where I ought to have been reserved, spiritless, dull, and deceitful: had I talked only of the weather

and the roads, and had I spoken only once in ten minutes, this reproach would have been spared."

"My love," said her mother, "you must not be offended with Elinor; she was only in jest. I should scold her myself if she were capable of wishing to check the delight of your conversation with our new friend." Marianne was softened in a moment.

Willoughby, on his side, gave every proof of his pleasure in their acquaintance, which an evident wish of improving it could offer. He came to them every day. To inquire after Marianne was at first his excuse; but the encouragement of his reception, to which every day gave greater kindness, made such an excuse unnecessary before it had ceased to be possible by Marianne's perfect recovery. She was confined for some days to the house; but never had any confinement been less irksome. Willoughby was a young man of good abilities, quick imagination, lively spirits, and open, affectionate manners. He was exactly formed to engage Marianne's heart, for with all this, he joined not only a captivating person, but a natural ardour of mind which was now roused and increased by the example of her own, and which recommended him to her affection beyond everything else.

His society became gradually her most exquisite enjoyment. They read, they talked, they sang together; his musical talents were considerable; and he read with all the sensibility and spirit which Edward had unfortunately wanted.

In Mrs. Dashwood's estimation he was as faultless as in Marianne's; and Elinor saw nothing to censure in him but a propensity, in which he strongly resembled and peculiarly delighted her sister, of saying too much what he thought on every occasion without attention to persons or circumstances. In hastily forming and giving his opinion of other people, in sacrificing general politeness to the enjoyment of undivided attention where his heart was engaged, and in slighting too easily the forms of worldly propriety, he displayed a want of caution which Elinor could not approve in spite of all that he and Marianne could say in its support.

Marianne began now to perceive that the desperation which had seized her at sixteen and a half, of ever seeing a man who could satisfy her ideas of perfection, had been rash and unjustifiable. Willoughby was all that her fancy had delineated in that unhappy hour and in every brighter period as

capable of attaching her; and his behaviour declared his
wishes to be in that respect as earnest as his abilities were
strong.

Her mother too, in whose mind not one speculative
thought of their marriage had been raised by his prospect of
riches, was led before the end of a week to hope and expect
it and secretly to congratulate herself on having gained two
such sons-in-law as Edward and Willoughby.

Colonel Brandon's partiality for Marianne, which had so
early been discovered by his friends, now first became perceptible to Elinor when it ceased to be noticed by them.
Their attention and wit were drawn off to his more fortunate
rival; and the raillery which the other had incurred before
any partiality arose was removed when his feelings began
really to call for the ridicule so justly annexed to sensibility.
Elinor was obliged, though unwillingly, to believe that the
sentiments which Mrs. Jennings had assigned him for her
own satisfaction were now actually excited by her sister; and
that however a general resemblance of disposition between
the parties might forward the affection of Mr. Willoughby,
an equally striking opposition of character was no hindrance
to the regard of Colonel Brandon. She saw it with concern;
for what could a silent man of five and thirty hope when opposed by a very lively one of five and twenty? And as she
could not even wish him successful, she heartily wished him
indifferent. She liked him; in spite of his gravity and reserve,
she beheld in him an object of interest. His manners, though
serious, were mild; and his reserve appeared rather the result
of some oppression of spirits than of any natural gloominess
of temper. Sir John had dropped hints of past injuries and
disappointments which justified her belief of his being an
unfortunate man, and she regarded him with respect and
compassion.

Perhaps she pitied and esteemed him the more because he
was slighted by Willoughby and Marianne, who, prejudiced
against him for being neither lively nor young, seemed resolved to undervalue his merits.

"Brandon is just the kind of man," said Willoughby one
day when they were talking of him together, "whom everybody speaks well of, and nobody cares about; whom all are
delighted to see, and nobody remembers to talk to."

"That is exactly what I think of him," cried Marianne.

"Do not boast of it, however," said Elinor, "for it is injustice in both of you. He is highly esteemed by all the family at the park, and I never see him myself without taking pains to converse with him."

"That he is patronized by *you*," replied Willoughby, "is certainly in his favour; but as for the esteem of the others, it is a reproach in itself. Who would submit to the indignity of being approved by such women as Lady Middleton and Mrs. Jennings, that could command the indifference of anybody else?"

"But perhaps the abuse of such people as yourself and Marianne will make amends for the regard of Lady Middleton and her mother. If their praise is censure, your censure may be praise, for they are not more undiscerning than you are prejudiced and unjust."

"In defence of your protegé you can even be saucy."

"My protegé, as you call him, is a sensible man; and sense will always have attractions for me. Yes, Marianne, even in a man between thirty and forty. He has seen a great deal of the world; has been abroad; has read, and has a thinking mind. I have found him capable of giving me much information on various subjects, and he has always answered my inquiries with the readiness of good breeding and good nature."

"That is to say," cried Marianne contemptuously, "he has told you that in the East Indies the climate is hot and the mosquitoes are troublesome."

"He *would* have told me so, I doubt not, had I made any such inquiries, but they happened to be points on which I had been previously informed."

"Perhaps," said Willoughby, "his observations may have extended to the existence of nabobs, gold mohrs, and palanquins."

"I may venture to say that *his* observations have stretched much farther than *your* candour. But why should you dislike him?"

"I do not dislike him. I consider him, on the contrary, as a very respectable man, who has everybody's good word and nobody's notice; who has more money than he can spend, more time than he knows how to employ, and two new coats every year."

"Add to which," cried Marianne, "that he has neither genius, taste, nor spirit. That his understanding has no brilliancy, his feelings no ardour, and his voice no expression."

"You decide on his imperfections so much in the mass," replied Elinor, "and so much on the strength of your own imagination, that the commendation *I* am able to give of him is comparatively cold and insipid. I can only pronounce him to be a sensible man, well-bred, well-informed, of gentle address, and I believe possessing an amiable heart."

"Miss Dashwood," cried Willoughby, "you are now using me unkindly. You are endeavouring to disarm me by reason and to convince me against my will. But it will not do. You shall find me as stubborn as you can be artful. I have three unanswerable reasons for disliking Colonel Brandon: he has threatened me with rain when I wanted it to be fine; he has found fault with the hanging of my curricle, and I cannot persuade him to buy my brown mare. If it will be any satisfaction to you, however, to be told that I believe his character to be in other respects irreproachable, I am ready to confess it. And in return for an acknowledgment which must give me some pain, you cannot deny me the privilege of disliking him as much as ever."

Chapter 11

LITTLE HAD Mrs. Dashwood or her daughters imagined when they first came into Devonshire, that so many engagements would arise to occupy their time as shortly presented themselves, or that they should have such frequent invitations and such constant visitors as to leave them little leisure for serious employment. Yet such was the case. When Marianne was recovered, the schemes of amusement at home and abroad, which Sir John had been previously forming, were put in execution. The private balls at the park then began; and parties on the water were made and accomplished as often as a showery October would allow. In every meeting of the kind Willoughby was included; and the ease and familiarity which naturally attended these parties were exactly calculated to give increasing intimacy to his acquaintance with the Dashwoods, to afford him opportunity of witnessing the excellencies of Marianne, of marking his animated admiration of her, and of receiving in her behaviour to himself the most pointed assurance of her affection.

Elinor could not be surprised at their attachment. She only wished that it were less openly shown; and once or twice did venture to suggest the propriety of some self-command to Marianne. But Marianne abhorred all concealment where no real disgrace could attend unreserve; and to aim at the restraint of sentiments which were not in themselves illaudable appeared to her not merely an unnecessary effort but a disgraceful subjection of reason to commonplace and mistaken notions. Willoughby thought the same; and their behaviour at all times was an illustration of their opinions.

When he was present she had no eyes for anyone else. Everything he did, was right. Everything he said, was clever. If their evenings at the park were concluded with cards, he cheated himself and all the rest of the party to get her a good hand. If dancing formed the amusement of the night, they were partners for half the time; and when obliged to separate for a couple of dances, were careful to stand together and scarcely spoke a word to anybody else. Such conduct made them of course most exceedingly laughed at; but ridicule could not shame and seemed hardly to provoke them.

Mrs. Dashwood entered into all their feelings with a warmth which left her no inclination for checking this excessive display of them. To her it was but the natural consequence of a strong affection in a young and ardent mind.

This was the season of happiness to Marianne. Her heart was devoted to Willoughby, and the fond attachment to Norland which she brought with her from Sussex was more likely to be softened than she had thought it possible before, by the charms which his society bestowed on her present home.

Elinor's happiness was not so great. Her heart was not so much at ease, nor her satisfaction in their amusements so pure. They afforded her no companion that could make amends for what she had left behind, nor that could teach her to think of Norland with less regret than ever. Neither Lady Middleton nor Mrs. Jennings could supply to her the conversation she missed; although the latter was an everlasting talker, and from the first had regarded her with a kindness which ensured her a large share of her discourse. She had already repeated her own history to Elinor three or four times; and had Elinor's memory been equal to her means of improvement, she might have known very early in their acquaintance all the particulars of Mr. Jennings's last illness and what he said to his wife a few minutes before he died. Lady Middleton was more agreeable than her mother, only in being more silent. Elinor needed little observation to perceive that her reserve was a mere calmness of manner with which sense had nothing to do. Towards her husband and mother she was the same as to them; and intimacy was therefore neither to be looked for nor desired. She had nothing to say one day that she had not said the day before. Her insipidity was invariable, for even her spirits were always the same; and though she did not oppose the parties arranged by her husband, provided everything were conducted in style and her two eldest children attended her, she never appeared to receive more enjoyment from them than she might have experienced in sitting at home; and so little did her presence add to the pleasure of the others by any share in their conversation, that they were sometimes only reminded of her being amongst them by her solicitude about her troublesome boys.

In Colonel Brandon alone, of all her new acquaintance, did Elinor find a person who could in any degree claim the respect of abilities, excite the interest of friendship, or give pleasure as a companion. Willoughby was out of the question. Her admiration and regard, even her sisterly regard, was all his own; but he was a lover; his attentions were wholly Marianne's, and a far less agreeable man might have been more generally pleasing. Colonel Brandon, unfortunately for himself, had no such encouragement to think only of Marianne, and in conversing with Elinor he found the greatest consolation for the total indifference of her sister.

Elinor's compassion for him increased, as she had reason to suspect that the misery of disappointed love had already been known by him. This suspicion was given by some words which accidentally dropped from him one evening at the park, when they were sitting down together by mutual consent while the others were dancing. His eyes were fixed on Marianne, and after a silence of some minutes, he said with a faint smile, "Your sister, I understand, does not approve of second attachments."

"No," replied Elinor, "her opinions are all romantic."

"Or rather, as I believe, she considers them impossible to exist."

"I believe she does. But how she contrives it without reflecting on the character of her own father who had himself two wives, I know not. A few years however will settle her opinions on the reasonable basis of common sense and observation; and then they may be more easy to define and to justify than they now are by anybody but herself."

"This will probably be the case," he replied; "and yet there is something so amiable in the prejudices of a young mind, that one is sorry to see them give way to the reception of more general opinions."

"I cannot agree with you there," said Elinor. "There are inconveniences attending such feelings as Marianne's which all the charms of enthusiasm and ignorance of the world cannot atone for. Her systems have all the unfortunate tendency of setting propriety at nought; and a better acquaintance with the world is what I look forward to as her greatest possible advantage."

After a short pause he resumed the conversation by saying—

"Does your sister make no distinction in her objections against a second attachment? Or is it equally criminal in everybody? Are those who have been disappointed in their first choice, whether from the inconstancy of its object or the perverseness of circumstances, to be equally indifferent during the rest of their lives?"

"Upon my word, I am not acquainted with the minutia of her principles. I only know that I never yet heard her admit any instance of a second attachment's being pardonable."

"This," said he, "cannot hold; but a change, a total change of sentiments— No, no, do not desire it—for when the romantic refinements of a young mind are obliged to give way, how frequently are they succeeded by such opinions as are but too common, and too dangerous! I speak from experience. I once knew a lady who in temper and mind greatly resembled your sister, who thought and judged like her, but who from an enforced change—from a series of unfortunate circumstances—" Here he stopped suddenly; appeared to think that he had said too much, and by his countenance gave rise to conjectures which might not otherwise have entered Elinor's head. The lady would probably have passed without suspicion, had he not convinced Miss Dashwood that what concerned her ought not to escape his lips. As it was, it required but a slight effort of fancy to connect his emotion with the tender recollection of past regard. Elinor attempted no more. But Marianne, in her place, would not have done so little. The whole story would have been speedily formed under her active imagination; and everything established in the most melancholy order of disastrous love.

Chapter 12

As ELINOR and Marianne were walking together the next morning the latter communicated a piece of news to her sister, which in spite of all that she knew before of Marianne's imprudence and want of thought, surprised her by its extravagant testimony of both. Marianne told her, with the greatest delight, that Willoughby had given her a horse, one that he had bred himself on his estate in Somersetshire, and which was exactly calculated to carry a woman. Without considering that it was not in her mother's plan to keep any horse, that if she were to alter her resolution in favour of this gift, she must buy another for the servant, and keep a servant to ride it, and after all, build a stable to receive them, she had accepted the present without hesitation, and told her sister of it in raptures.

"He intends to send his groom into Somersetshire immediately for it," she added, "and when it arrives we will ride everyday. You shall share its use with me. Imagine to yourself, my dear Elinor, the delight of a gallop on some of these downs."

Most unwilling was she to awaken from such a dream of felicity, to comprehend all the unhappy truths which attended the affair; and for some time she refused to submit to them. As to an additional servant, the expense would be a trifle; mama she was sure would never object to it; and any horse would do for *him*; he might always get one at the park; as to a stable, the merest shed would be sufficient. Elinor then ventured to doubt the propriety of her receiving such a present from a man so little, or at least so lately known to her. This was too much.

"You are mistaken, Elinor," said she warmly, "in supposing I know very little of Willoughby. I have not known him long indeed, but I am much better acquainted with him than I am with any other creature in the world, except yourself and mama. It is not time or opportunity that is to determine intimacy; it is disposition alone. Seven years would be insufficient to make some people acquainted with each other, and seven days are more than enough for others. I should hold myself guilty of greater impropriety in accepting a horse from my brother than from Willoughby. Of John I know very little, though we have lived together for years; but of Willoughby my judgment has long been formed."

Elinor thought it wisest to touch that point no more. She knew her sister's temper. Opposition on so tender a subject would only attach her the more to her own opinion. But by an appeal to her affection for her mother, by representing the inconveniences which that indulgent mother must draw on herself if (as would probably be the case) she consented to this increase of establishment, Marianne was shortly subdued; and she promised not to tempt her mother to such imprudent kindness by mentioning the offer, and to tell Willoughby when she saw him next that it must be declined.

She was faithful to her word; and when Willoughby called at the cottage, the same day, Elinor heard her express her disappointment to him in a low voice, on being obliged to forego the acceptance of his present. The reasons for this alteration were at the same time related, and they were such as to make further entreaty on his side impossible. His concern however was very apparent; and after expressing it with earnestness, he added in the same low voice, "But, Marianne, the horse is still yours, though you cannot use it now. I shall keep it only till you can claim it. When you leave Barton to form your own establishment in a more lasting home, Queen Mab shall receive you."

This was all overheard by Miss Dashwood; and in the whole of the sentence, in his manner of pronouncing it, and in his addressing her sister by her Christian name alone, she instantly saw an intimacy so decided, a meaning so direct, as marked a perfect agreement between them. From that moment she doubted not of their being engaged to each other; and the belief of it created no other surprise than that she, or any of their friends, should be left by tempers so frank to discover it by accident.

Margaret related something to her the next day which placed this matter in a still clearer light. Willoughby had spent the preceding evening with them, and Margaret, by being left some time in the parlour with only him and Marianne, had had opportunity for observations, which, with a most important face, she communicated to her elder sister when they were next by themselves.

"Oh! Elinor," she cried, "I have such a secret to tell you about Marianne. I am sure she will be married to Mr. Willoughby very soon."

"You have said so," replied Elinor, "almost everyday since they first met on High-church Down; and they had not known each other a week, I believe, before you were certain that Marianne wore his picture round her neck; but it turned out to be only the miniature of our great uncle."

"But indeed this is quite another thing. I am sure they will be married very soon, for he has got a lock of her hair."

"Take care, Margaret. It may be only the hair of some great uncle of *his*."

"But indeed, Elinor, it is Marianne's. I am almost sure it is, for I saw him cut it off. Last night after tea, when you and mamma went out of the room, they were whispering and talking together as fast as could be, and he seemed to be begging something of her, and presently he took up her scissors and cut off a long lock of her hair, for it was all tumbled down her back; and he kissed it, and folded it up in a piece of white paper, and put it into his pocketbook."

From such particulars stated on such authority, Elinor could not withhold her credit: nor was she disposed to it, for the circumstance was in perfect unison with what she had heard and seen herself.

Margaret's sagacity was not always displayed in a way so satisfactory to her sister. When Mrs. Jennings attacked her one evening at the park, to give the name of the young man who was Elinor's particular favourite, which had been long a matter of great curiosity to her, Margaret answered by looking at her sister and saying, "I must not tell, may I, Elinor?"

This of course made everybody laugh; and Elinor tried to laugh too. But the effort was painful. She was convinced that Margaret had fixed on a person whose name she could not bear with composure to become a standing joke with Mrs. Jennings.

Marianne felt for her most sincerely; but she did more

harm than good to the cause by turning very red and saying in an angry manner to Margaret:

"Remember that whatever your conjectures may be, you have no right to repeat them."

"I never had any conjectures about it," replied Margaret; "it was you who told me of it yourself."

This increased the mirth of the company, and Margaret was eagerly pressed to say something more.

"Oh! pray, Miss Margaret, let us know all about it," said Mrs. Jennings. "What is the gentleman's name?"

"I must not tell, ma'am. But I know very well what it is; and I know where he is too."

"Yes, yes, we can guess where he is: at his own house at Norland to be sure. He is the curate of the parish I dare say."

"No, *that* he is not. He is of no profession at all."

"Margaret," said Marianne with great warmth, "you know that all this is an invention of your own and that there is no such person in existence."

"Well then he is lately dead, Marianne, for I am sure there was such a man once, and his name begins with an F."

Most grateful did Elinor feel to Lady Middleton for observing at this moment "that it rained very hard," though she believed the interruption to proceed less from any attention to her than from her ladyship's great dislike of all such inelegant subjects of raillery as delighted her husband and mother. The idea, however, started by her, was immediately pursued by Colonel Brandon, who was on every occasion mindful of the feelings of others; and much was said on the subject of rain by both of them. Willoughby opened the pianoforte, and asked Marianne to sit down to it; and thus amidst the various endeavours of different people to quit the topic, it fell to the ground. But not so easily did Elinor recover from the alarm into which it had thrown her.

A party was formed this evening for going on the following day to see a very fine place about twelve miles from Barton, belonging to a brother-in-law of Colonel Brandon, without whose interest it could not be seen, as the proprietor, who was then abroad, had left strict orders on that head. The grounds were declared to be highly beautiful, and Sir John, who was particularly warm in their praise, might be allowed to be a tolerable judge, for he had formed parties to visit them at least twice every summer for the last ten years. They contained a noble piece of water; a sail on which was to form a great part of the morning's amusement; cold provisions were to be taken, open carriages only to be employed, and everything conducted in the usual style of a complete party of pleasure.

To some few of the company it appeared rather a bold undertaking, considering the time of year and that it had rained every day for the last fortnight; and Mrs. Dashwood, who had already a cold, was persuaded by Elinor to stay at home.

Chapter 13

THEIR INTENDED excursion to Whitwell turned out very differently from what Elinor had expected. She was prepared to be wet through, fatigued, and frightened; but the event was still more unfortunate, for they did not go at all.

By ten o'clock the whole party were assembled at the park, where they were to breakfast. The morning was rather favourable, though it had rained all night, as the clouds were then dispersing across the sky, and the sun frequently appeared. They were all in high spirits and good humour, eager to be happy, and determined to submit to the greatest inconveniences and hardships rather than be otherwise.

While they were at breakfast the letters were brought in. Among the rest there was one for Colonel Brandon. He took it, looked at the direction, changed colour, and immediately left the room.

"What is the matter with Brandon?" said Sir John.

Nobody could tell.

"I hope he has had no bad news," said Lady Middleton. "It must be something extraordinary that could make Colonel Brandon leave my breakfast table so suddenly."

In about five minutes he returned.

"No bad news, Colonel, I hope," said Mrs. Jennings as soon as he entered the room.

"None at all, ma'am, I thank you."

"Was it from Avignon? I hope it is not to say that your sister is worse."

"No, ma'am. It came from town and is merely a letter of business."

"But how came the hand to discompose you so much if it was only a letter of business? Come, come, this won't do, Colonel; so let us hear the truth of it."

"My dear Madam," said Lady Middleton, "recollect what you are saying."

"Perhaps it is to tell you that your cousin Fanny is married?" said Mrs. Jennings, without attending to her daughter's reproof.

"No, indeed, it is not."

"Well, then, I know who it is from, Colonel. And I hope she is well."

"Whom do you mean, ma'am?" said he, colouring a little.

"Oh! you know who I mean."

"I am particularly sorry, ma'am," said he, addressing Lady Middleton, "that I should receive this letter today, for it is on business which requires my immediate attendance in town."

"In town!" cried Mrs. Jennings. "What can you have to do in town at this time of year?"

"My own loss is great," he continued, "in being obliged to leave so agreeable a party; but I am the more concerned, as I fear my presence is necessary to gain your admittance at Whitwell."

What a blow upon them all was this!

"But if you write a note to the housekeeper, Mr. Brandon," said Marianne eagerly, "will it not be sufficient?"

He shook his head.

"We *must* go," said Sir John. "It shall not be put off when we are so near it. You cannot go to town till to-morrow, Brandon, that is all."

"I wish it could be so easily settled. But it is not in my power to delay my journey for one day!"

"If you would but let us know what your business is," said Mrs. Jennings, "we might see whether it could be put off or not."

"You would not be six hours later," said Willoughby, "if you were to defer your journey till our return."

"I cannot afford to lose *one* hour."

Elinor then heard Willoughby say in a low voice to Marianne, "There are some people who cannot bear a party of pleasure. Brandon is one of them. He was afraid of catching cold, I dare say, and invented this trick for getting out of it. I would lay fifty guineas the letter was of his own writing."

"I have no doubt of it," replied Marianne.

"There is no persuading you to change your mind, Brandon, I know of old," said Sir John, "when once you are determined on anything. But, however, I hope you will think better of it. Consider, here are the two Miss Careys come over from Newton, the three Miss Dashwoods walked up from the cottage, and Mr. Willoughby got up two hours before his usual time, on purpose to go to Whitwell."

Colonel Brandon again repeated his sorrow at being the cause of disappointing the party, but at the same time declared it to be unavoidable.

"Well then, when will you come back again?"

"I hope we shall see you at Barton," added her ladyship, "as soon as you can conveniently leave town; and we must put off the party to Whitwell till you return."

"You are very obliging. But it is so uncertain when I may have it in my power to return that I dare not engage for it at all."

"Oh! he must and shall come back," cried Sir John. "If he is not here by the end of the week, I shall go after him."

"Aye, so do, Sir John," cried Mrs. Jennings, "and then perhaps you may find out what his business is."

"I do not want to pry into other men's concerns. I suppose it is something he is ashamed of."

Colonel Brandon's horses were announced.

"You do not go to town on horseback, do you?" added Sir John.

"No. Only to Honiton. I shall then go post."

"Well, as you are resolved to go, I wish you a good journey. But you had better change your mind."

"I assure you it is not in my power."

He then took leave of the whole party.

"Is there no chance of my seeing you and your sisters in town this winter, Miss Dashwood?"

"I am afraid none at all."

"Then I must bid you farewell for a longer time than I should wish to do."

To Marianne he merely bowed and said nothing.

"Come, Colonel," said Mrs. Jennings, "before you go, do let us know what you are going about."

He wished her a good morning, and attended by Sir John, left the room.

The complaints and lamentations which politeness had

hitherto restrained now burst forth universally, and they all agreed again and again how provoking it was to be so disappointed.

"I can guess what his business is, however," said Mrs. Jennings exultingly.

"Can you, ma'am?" said almost everybody.

"Yes, it is about Miss Williams, I am sure."

"And who is Miss Williams?" asked Marianne.

"What! Do not you know who Miss Williams is? I am sure you must have heard of her before. She is a relation of the Colonel's, my dear; a very near relation. We will not say how near, for fear of shocking the young ladies." Then lowering her voice a little, she said to Elinor, "She is his natural daughter."

"Indeed!"

"Oh! yes, and as like him as she can stare. I dare say the Colonel will leave her all his fortune."

When Sir John returned, he joined most heartily in the general regret on so unfortunate an event; concluding however by observing, that as they were all got together, they must do something by way of being happy; and after some consultation it was agreed, that although happiness could only be enjoyed at Whitwell, they might procure a tolerable composure of mind by driving about the country. The carriages were then ordered. Willoughby's was first, and Marianne never looked happier than when she got into it. He drove through the park very fast, and they were soon out of sight; and nothing more of them was seen till their return, which did not happen till after the return of all the rest. They both seemed delighted with their drive, but said only in general terms that they had kept in the lanes while the others went on the downs.

It was settled that there should be a dance in the evening and that everybody should be extremely merry all day long. Some more of the Careys came to dinner, and they had the pleasure of sitting down nearly twenty to table, which Sir John observed with great contentment. Willoughby took his usual place between the two elder Miss Dashwoods. Mrs. Jennings sat on Elinor's right hand; and they had not been long seated, before she leaned behind her and Willoughby, and said to Marianne loud enough for them both to hear, "I have found you out in spite of all your tricks. I know where you spent the morning."

Marianne coloured, and replied very hastily, "Where, pray?"

"Did not you know," said Willoughby, "that we had been out in my curricle?"

"Yes, yes, Mr. Impudence, I know that very well, and I was determined to find out *where* you had been to.—I hope you like your house, Miss Marianne. It is a very large one I know, and when I come to see you, I hope you will have new-furnished it, for it wanted it very much when I was there six years ago."

Marianne turned away in great confusion. Mrs. Jennings laughed heartily; and Elinor found that in her resolution to know where they had been, she had actually made her own woman inquire of Mr. Willoughby's groom, and that she had by that method been informed that they had gone to Allenham and spent a considerable time there in walking about the garden and going all over the house.

Elinor could hardly believe this to be true, as it seemed very unlikely that Willoughby should propose or Marianne consent to enter the house while Mrs. Smith was in it, with whom Marianne had not the smallest acquaintance.

As soon as they left the dining-room, Elinor inquired of her about it; and great was her surprise when she found that every circumstance related by Mrs. Jennings was perfectly true. Marianne was quite angry with her for doubting it.

"Why should you imagine, Elinor, that we did not go there, or that we did not see the house? Is not it what you have often wished to do yourself?"

"Yes, Marianne, but I would not go while Mrs. Smith was there, and with no other companion than Mr. Willoughby."

"Mr. Willoughby however is the only person who can have a right to show that house; and as we went in an open carriage, it was impossible to have any other companion. I never spent a pleasanter morning in my life."

"I am afraid," replied Elinor, "that the pleasantness of an employment does not always evince its propriety."

"On the contrary, nothing can be a stronger proof of it, Elinor; for if there had been any real impropriety in what I did, I should have been sensible of it at the time, for we always know when we are acting wrong, and with such a conviction I could have had no pleasure."

"But, my dear Marianne, as it has already exposed you to

some very impertinent remarks, do you not now begin to doubt the discretion of your own conduct?"

"If the impertinent remarks of Mrs. Jennings are to be the proof of impropriety in conduct, we are all offending every moment of all our lives. I value not her censure any more than I should do her commendation. I am not sensible of having done anything wrong in walking over Mrs. Smith's grounds, or in seeing her house. They will one day be Mr. Willoughby's, and" . . .

"If they were one day to be your own, Marianne, you would not be justified in what you have done."

She blushed at this hint; but it was even visibly gratifying to her; and after a ten minutes' interval of earnest thought, she came to her sister again and said with great good humour, "Perhaps, Elinor, it *was* rather ill-judged in me to go to Allenham; but Mr. Willoughby wanted particularly to show me the place; and it is a charming house I assure you. There is one remarkably pretty sitting-room upstairs of a nice comfortable size for constant use, and with modern furniture it would be delightful. It is a corner room, and has windows on two sides. On one side you look across the bowling-green, behind the house, to a beautiful hanging wood, and on the other you have a view of the church and village, and beyond them, of those fine bold hills that we have so often admired. I did not see it to advantage, for nothing could be more forlorn than the furniture, but if it were newly fitted up—a couple of hundred pounds, Willoughby says, would make it one of the pleasantest summer-rooms in England."

Could Elinor have listened to her without interruption from the others, she would have described every room in the house with equal delight.

Chapter 14

THE SUDDEN termination of Colonel Brandon's visit at the park, with his steadiness in concealing its cause, filled the mind and raised the wonder of Mrs. Jennings for two or three days; she was a great wonderer, as everyone must be

who takes a very lively interest in all the comings and go-
ings of all their acquaintance. She wondered with little intermission what could be the reason of it; was sure there must
be some bad news, and thought over every kind of distress
that could have befallen him, with a fixed determination that
he should not escape them all.

"Something very melancholy must be the matter, I am
sure," said she. "I could see it in his face. Poor man! I
am afraid his circumstances may be bad. The estate at
Delaford was never reckoned more than two thousand a
year, and his brother left everything sadly involved. I do
think he must have been sent for about money matters, for
what else can it be? I wonder whether it is so. I would give
anything to know the truth of it. Perhaps it is about Miss
Williams—and, by the bye, I dare say it is, because he
looked so conscious when I mentioned her. Maybe she is ill
in town; nothing in the world more likely, for I have a notion she is always rather sickly. I would lay any wager it is
about Miss Williams. It is not so very likely he should be
distressed in his circumstances *now,* for he is a very prudent
man, and, to be sure, must have cleared the estate by this
time. I wonder what it can be! Maybe his sister is worse at
Avignon and has sent for him over. His setting off in such a
hurry seems very like it. Well, I wish him out of all his trouble with all my heart, and a good wife into the bargain."

So wondered, so talked Mrs. Jennings, her opinion varying with every fresh conjecture, and all seeming equally
probable as they arose. Elinor, though she felt really interested in the welfare of Colonel Brandon, could not bestow
all the wonder on his going so suddenly away, which Mrs.
Jennings was desirous of her feeling; for besides that the circumstance did not in her opinion justify such lasting amazement or variety of speculation, her wonder was otherwise
disposed of. It was engrossed by the extraordinary silence of
her sister and Willoughby on the subject which they must
know to be peculiarly interesting to them all. As this silence
continued, everyday made it appear more strange and more
incompatible with the disposition of both. Why they should
not openly acknowledge to her mother and herself what their
constant behaviour to each other declared to have taken
place, Elinor could not imagine.

She could easily conceive that marriage might not be immediately in their power; for though Willoughby was inde-

pendent, there was no reason to believe him rich. His estate had been rated by Sir John at about six or seven hundred a year; but he lived at an expense to which that income could hardly be equal, and he had himself often complained of his poverty. But for this strange kind of secrecy maintained by them relative to their engagement, which in fact concealed nothing at all, she could not account; and it was so wholly contradictory to their general opinions and practice, that a doubt sometimes entered her mind of their being really engaged, and this doubt was enough to prevent her making any inquiry of Marianne.

Nothing could be more expressive of attachment to them all than Willoughby's behaviour. To Marianne it had all the distinguishing tenderness which a lover's heart could give, and to the rest of the family it was the affectionate attention of a son and a brother. The cottage seemed to be considered and loved by him as his home; many more of his hours were spent there than at Allenham; and if no general engagement collected them at the park, the exercise which called him out in the morning was almost certain of ending there, where the rest of the day was spent by himself at the side of Marianne, and by his favourite pointer at her feet.

One evening in particular, about a week after Colonel Brandon had left the country, his heart seemed more than usually open to every feeling of attachment to the objects around him; and on Mrs. Dashwood's happening to mention her design of improving the cottage in the spring, he warmly opposed every alteration of a place which affection had established as perfect with him.

"What!" he exclaimed. "Improve this dear cottage! No. *That* I will never consent to. Not a stone must be added to its walls, not an inch to its size if my feelings are regarded."

"Do not be alarmed," said Miss Dashwood, "nothing of the kind will be done; for my mother will never have money enough to attempt it."

"I am heartily glad of it," he cried. "May she always be poor if she can employ her riches no better."

"Thank you, Willoughby. But you may be assured that I would not sacrifice one sentiment of local attachment of yours, or of anyone whom I loved, for all the improvements in the world. Depend upon it that whatever unemployed sum may remain when I make up my accounts in the spring, I would even rather lay it uselessly by than dispose of it in a

manner so painful to you. But are you really so attached to
this place as to see no defect in it?"

"I am," said he. "To me it is faultless. Nay, more, I consider it as the only form of building in which happiness is attainable, and were I rich enough, I would instantly pull
Combe down and build it up again in the exact plan of this
cottage."

"With dark narrow stairs, and a kitchen that smokes, I
suppose," said Elinor.

"Yes," cried he in the same eager tone, "with all and everything belonging to it; in no one convenience or *in*convenience about it, should the least variation be perceptible.
Then, and then only, under such a roof, I might perhaps be
as happy at Combe as I have been at Barton."

"I flatter myself," replied Elinor, "that even under the disadvantage of better rooms and a broader staircase, you will
hereafter find your own house as faultless as you now do
this."

"There certainly are circumstances," said Willoughby,
"which might greatly endear it to me; but this place will always have one claim on my affection, which no other can
possibly share."

Mrs. Dashwood looked with pleasure at Marianne, whose
fine eyes were fixed so expressively on Willoughby, as
plainly denoted how well she understood him.

"How often did I wish," added he, "when I was at Allenham this time twelvemonth, that Barton cottage were inhab-
ited! I never passed within view of it without admiring its
situation and grieving that no one should live in it. How little did I then think that the very first news I should hear
from Mrs. Smith when I next came into the country would
be that Barton cottage was taken: and I felt an immediate
satisfaction and interest in the event, which nothing but a
kind of prescience of what happiness I should experience
from it can account for. Must it not have been so, Marianne?" speaking to her in a lowered voice. Then continuing
his former tone, he said, "And yet this house you would
spoil, Mrs. Dashwood? You would rob it of its simplicity by
imaginary improvement! And this dear parlour in which our
acquaintance first began, and in which so many happy hours
have been since spent by us together, you would degrade to
the condition of a common entrance, and everybody would
be eager to pass through the room which has hitherto con-

tained within itself, more real accommodation and comfort than any other apartment of the handsomest dimensions in the world could possibly afford."

Mrs. Dashwood again assured him that no alteration of the kind should be attempted.

"You are a good woman," he warmly replied. "Your promise makes me easy. Extend it a little farther, and it will make me happy. Tell me that not only your house will remain the same but that I shall ever find you and yours as unchanged as your dwelling and that you will always consider me with the kindness which has made everything belonging to you so dear to me."

The promise was readily given, and Willoughby's behaviour during the whole of the evening declared at once his affection and happiness.

"Shall we see you to-morrow to dinner?" said Mrs. Dashwood when he was leaving them. "I do not ask you to come in the morning, for we must walk to the park to call on Lady Middleton."

He engaged to be with them by four o'clock.

Chapter 15

MRS. DASHWOOD'S visit to Lady Middleton took place the next day, and two of her daughters went with her; but Marianne excused herself from being of the party under some trifling pretext of employment; and her mother, who concluded that a promise had been made by Willoughby the night before of calling on her while they were absent, was perfectly satisfied with her remaining at home.

On their return from the park they found Willoughby's curricle and servant in waiting at the cottage, and Mrs. Dashwood was convinced that her conjecture had been just. So far it was all as she had foreseen, but on entering the house she beheld what no foresight had taught her to expect. They were no sooner in the passage than Marianne came hastily out of the parlour apparently in violent affliction with her handkerchief at her eyes; and without noticing them ran upstairs. Surprised and alarmed they proceeded directly into

the room she had just quitted, where they found only
Willoughby, who was leaning against the mantel-piece with
his back towards them. He turned round on their coming in,
and his countenance showed that he strongly partook of the
emotion which overpowered Marianne.

"Is anything the matter with her?" cried Mrs. Dashwood
as she entered; "is she ill?"

"I hope not," he replied, trying to look cheerful; and with
a forced smile presently added, "It is I who may rather expect to be ill—for I am now suffering under a very heavy
disappointment!"

"Disappointment!"

"Yes, for I am unable to keep my engagement with you.
Mrs. Smith has this morning exercised the privilege of
riches upon a poor dependant cousin by sending me on business to London. I have just received my dispatches and
taken my farewell of Allenham; and by way of exhilaration
I am now come to take my farewell of you."

"To London!—and are you going this morning?"

"Almost this moment."

"This is very unfortunate. But Mrs. Smith must be
obliged; and her business will not detain you from us long
I hope."

He coloured as he replied, "You are very kind, but I have
no idea of returning into Devonshire immediately. My visits
to Mrs. Smith are never repeated within the twelvemonth."

"And is Mrs. Smith your only friend? Is Allenham the
only house in the neighbourhood to which you will be welcome? For shame, Willoughby. Can you wait for an invitation here?"

His colour increased; and with his eyes fixed on the
ground he only replied, "You are too good."

Mrs. Dashwood looked at Elinor with surprise. Elinor felt
equal amazement. For a few moments everyone was silent.
Mrs. Dashwood first spoke.

"I have only to add, my dear Willoughby, that at Barton
cottage you will always be welcome; for I will not press you
to return here immediately because you only can judge how
far *that* might be pleasing to Mrs. Smith; and on this head
I shall be no more disposed to question your judgment than
to doubt your inclination."

"My engagements at present," replied Willoughby confusedly, "are of such a nature—that—I dare not flatter myself—"

He stopped. Mrs. Dashwood was too much astonished to speak, and another pause succeeded. This was broken by Willoughby, who said with a faint smile, "It is folly to linger in this manner. I will not torment myself any longer by remaining among friends whose society it is impossible for me now to enjoy."

He then hastily took leave of them all and left the room. They saw him step into his carriage, and in a minute it was out of sight.

Mrs. Dashwood felt too much for speech and instantly quitted the parlour to give way in solitude to the concern and alarm which this sudden departure occasioned.

Elinor's uneasiness was at least equal to her mother's. She thought of what had just passed with anxiety and distrust. Willoughby's behaviour in taking leave of them, his embarrassment and affection of cheerfulness and, above all, his unwillingness to accept her mother's invitation, a backwardness so unlike a lover, so unlike himself, greatly disturbed her. One moment she feared that no serious design had ever been formed on his side and the next that some unfortunate quarrel had taken place between him and her sister; the distress in which Marianne had quitted the room was such as a serious quarrel could most reasonably account for, though when she considered what Marianne's love for him was, a quarrel seemed almost impossible.

But whatever might be the particulars of their separation, her sister's affliction was indubitable; and she thought with the tenderest compassion of that violent sorrow which Marianne was in all probability not merely giving way to as a relief but feeding and encouraging as a duty.

In about half an hour her mother returned, and though her eyes were red, her countenance was not uncheerful.

"Our dear Willoughby is now some miles from Barton, Elinor," said she as she sat down to work, "and with how heavy a heart does he travel?"

"It is all very strange. So suddenly to be gone! It seems but the work of a moment. And last night he was with us so happy, so cheerful, so affectionate? And now after only ten minutes notice—Gone too without intending to return! Something more than what he owned to us must have happened. He did not speak; he did not behave like himself. *You*

must have seen the difference as well as I. What can it be?
Can they have quarrelled? Why else should he have shown
such unwillingness to accept your invitation here?"

"It was not inclination that he wanted, Elinor; I could
plainly see *that*. He had not the power of accepting it. I have
thought it all over I assure you, and I can perfectly account
for everything that at first seemed strange to me as well as
to you."

"Can you indeed?"

"Yes. I have explained it to myself in the most satisfactory
way; but you, Elinor, who love to doubt where you can— It
will not satisfy *you*, I know; but you shall not talk *me* out of
my trust in it. I am persuaded that Mrs. Smith suspects his
regard for Marianne, disapproves of it (perhaps because she
has other views for him), and on that account is eager to get
him away; and that the business which she sends him off to
transact is invented as an excuse to dismiss him. This is
what I believe to have happened. He is moreover aware that
she *does* disapprove the connection; he dares not therefore at
present confess to her his engagement with Marianne; and
he feels himself obliged from his dependent situation to give
into her schemes and absent himself from Devonshire for a
while. You will tell me, I know, that this may or may *not*
have happened; but I will listen to no cavil unless you can
point out any other method of understanding the affair as
satisfactory as this. And now, Elinor, what have you to say?"

"Nothing, for you have anticipated my answer."

"Then you would have told me that it might or might not
have happened. Oh! Elinor, how incomprehensible are your
feelings! You had rather take evil upon credit than good.
You had rather look out for misery for Marianne and guilt
for poor Willoughby than an apology for the latter. You are
resolved to think him blameable because he took leave of us
with less affection than his usual behaviour has shown. And
is no allowance to be made for inadvertence or for spirits de-
pressed by recent disappointment? Are no probabilities to be
accepted merely because they are not certainties? Is nothing
due to the man whom we have all so much reason to love
and no reason in the world to think ill of? To the possibility
of motives unanswerable in themselves, though unavoidably
secret for a while? And, after all, what is it you suspect him
of?"

"I can hardly tell you myself. But suspicion of something

unpleasant is the inevitable consequence of such an alteration as we have just witnessed in him. There is great truth,
however, in what you have now urged of the allowances
which ought to be made for him, and it is my wish to be
candid in my judgment of everybody. Willoughby may undoubtedly have very sufficient reasons for his conduct, and
I will hope that he has. But it would have been more like
Willoughby to acknowledge them at once. Secrecy may be
advisable, but still I cannot help wondering at its being practised by him."

"Do not blame him, however, for departing from his character where the deviation is necessary. But you really do
admit the justice of what I have said in his defence? I am
happy, and he is acquitted."

"Not entirely. It may be proper to conceal their engagement (if they *are* engaged) from Mrs. Smith; and if that is
the case, it must be highly expedient for Willoughby to be
but little in Devonshire at present. But this is no excuse for
their concealing it from us."

"Concealing it from us! My dear child, do you accuse
Willoughby and Marianne of concealment? This is strange
indeed, when your eyes have been reproaching them everyday for incautiousness."

"I want no proof of their affection," said Elinor; "but of
their engagement I do."

"I am perfectly satisfied of both."

"Yet not a syllable has been said to you on the subject by
either of them."

"I have not wanted syllables where actions have spoken
so plainly. Has not his behaviour to Marianne and to all of
us for at least the last fortnight declared that he loved and
considered her as his future wife, and that he felt for us the
attachment of the nearest relation? Have we not perfectly
understood each other? Has not my consent been daily asked
by his looks, his manner, his attentive and affectionate respect? My Elinor, is it possible to doubt their engagement?
How could such a thought occur to you? How is it to be supposed that Willoughby, persuaded as he must be of your sister's love, should leave her, and leave her perhaps for
months, without telling her of his affection; that they should
part without a mutual exchange of confidence?"

"I confess," replied Elinor, "that every circumstance except *one* is in favour of their engagement; but that *one* is the

total silence of both on the subject, and with me it almost outweighs every other."

"How strange this is! You must think wretchedly indeed of Willoughby if after all that has openly passed between them you can doubt the nature of the terms on which they are together. Has he been acting a part in his behaviour to your sister all this time? Do you suppose him really indifferent to her?"

"No, I cannot think that. He must and does love her I am sure."

"But with a strange kind of tenderness if he can leave her with such indifference, such carelessness of the future as you attribute to him."

"You must remember, my dear mother, that I have never considered this matter as certain. I have had my doubts, I confess; but they are fainter than they were, and they may soon be entirely done away. If we find they correspond, every fear of mine will be removed."

"A mighty concession indeed! If you were to see them at the altar, you would suppose they were going to be married. Ungracious girl! But *I* require no such proof. Nothing in my opinion has ever passed to justify doubt; no secrecy has been attempted; all has been uniformly open and unreserved. You cannot doubt your sister's wishes. It must be Willoughby therefore whom you suspect. But why? Is he not a man of honour and feeling? Has there been any inconsistency on his side to create alarm? Can he be deceitful?"

"I hope not, I believe not," cried Elinor. "I love Willoughby, sincerely love him; and suspicion of his integrity cannot be more painful to yourself than to me. It has been involuntary, and I will not encourage it. I was startled, I confess, by the alteration in his manners this morning; he did not speak like himself and did not return your kindness with any cordiality. But all this may be explained by such a situation of his affairs as you have supposed. He had just parted from my sister, had seen her leave him in the greatest affliction; and if he felt obliged, from a fear of offending Mrs. Smith, to resist the temptation of returning here soon, and yet aware that by declining your invitation, by saying that he was going away for some time, he should seem to act an ungenerous, a suspicious part by our family, he might well be embarrassed and disturbed. In such a case, a plain and open avowal of his difficulties would have been more to his honour I think, as well as more consistent with his general character; but I will not raise objections against anyone's conduct on so illiberal a foundation as a difference in judgment from myself or a deviation from what I may think right and consistent."

"You speak very properly. Willoughby certainly does not deserve to be suspected. Though *we* have not known him long, he is no stranger in this part of the world; and who has ever spoken to his disadvantage? Had he been in a situation to act independently and marry immediately, it might have been odd that he should leave us without acknowledging everything to me at once; but this is not the case. It is an engagement in some respects not prosperously begun, for their marriage must be at a very uncertain distance; and even secrecy, as far as it can be observed, may now be very advisable."

They were interrupted by the entrance of Margaret; and Elinor was then at liberty to think over the representations of her mother, to acknowledge the probability of many, and hope for the justice of all.

They saw nothing of Marianne till dinner time, when she entered the room and took her place at the table without saying a word. Her eyes were red and swollen; and it seemed as if her tears were even then restrained with difficulty. She avoided the looks of them all, could neither eat nor speak, and after some time, on her mother's silently pressing her hand with tender compassion, her small degree of fortitude was quite overcome; she burst into tears and left the room.

This violent oppression of spirits continued the whole evening. She was without any power because she was without any desire of command over herself. The slightest mention of anything relative to Willoughby overpowered her in an instant; and though her family were most anxiously attentive to her comfort, it was impossible for them if they spoke at all to keep clear of every subject which her feelings connected with him.

Chapter 16

MARIANNE WOULD have thought herself very inexcusable had she been able to sleep at all the first night after parting from Willoughby. She would have been ashamed to look her family in the face the next morning had she not risen from her bed in more need of repose than when she lay down in it. But the feelings which made such composure a disgrace left her in no danger of incurring it. She was awake the whole night, and she wept the greatest part of it. She got up with a headache, was unable to talk, and unwilling to take any nourishment; giving pain every moment to her mother and sisters, and forbidding all attempt at consolation from either. Her sensibility was potent enough!

When breakfast was over she walked out by herself and wandered about the village of Allenham, indulging the recollection of past enjoyment and crying over the present reverse for the chief of the morning.

The evening passed off in the equal indulgence of feeling. She played over every favourite song that she had been used to play to Willoughby, every air in which their voices had been oftenest joined, and sat at the instrument gazing on every line of music that he had written out for her, till her heart was so heavy that no further sadness could be gained; and this nourishment of grief was every day applied. She spent whole hours at the pianoforte alternately singing and crying, her voice often totally suspended by her tears. In books too, as well as in music, she courted the misery which a contrast between the past and present was certain of giving. She read nothing but what they had been used to read together.

Such violence of affliction indeed could not be supported forever; it sunk within a few days into a calmer melancholy; but these employments to which she daily recurred, her solitary walks and silent meditations, still produced occasional effusions of sorrow as lively as ever.

No letter from Willoughby came, and none seemed expected by Marianne. Her mother was surprised, and Elinor again became uneasy. But Mrs. Dashwood could find explanations whenever she wanted them, which at least satisfied herself.

"Remember, Elinor," said she, "how very often Sir John fetches our letters himself from the post and carries them to it. We have already agreed that secrecy may be necessary, and we must acknowledge that it could not be maintained if their correspondence were to pass through Sir John's hands."

Elinor could not deny the truth of this, and she tried to find in it a motive sufficient for their silence. But there was one method so direct, so simple, and in her opinion so eligible of knowing the real state of the affair, and of instantly removing all mystery, that she could not help suggesting it to her mother.

"Why do you not ask Marianne at once," said she, "whether she is or is not engaged to Willoughby? From you, her mother, and so kind, so indulgent a mother, the question could not give offence. It would be the natural result of your affection for her. She used to be all unreserve and to you more especially."

"I would not ask such a question for the world. Supposing it possible that they are not engaged, what distress would not such an inquiry inflict! At any rate it would be most ungenerous. I should never deserve her confidence again after forcing from her a confession of what is meant at present to be unacknowledged to anyone. I know Marianne's heart. I know that she dearly loves me, and that I shall not be the last to whom the affair is made known, when circumstances make the revealment of it eligible. I would not attempt to force the confidence of anyone, of a child much less; because a sense of duty would prevent the denial which her wishes might direct."

Elinor thought this generosity overstrained, considering her sister's youth, and urged the matter further, but in vain; common sense, common care, common prudence, were all sunk in Mrs. Dashwood's romantic delicacy.

It was several days before Willoughby's name was mentioned before Marianne by any of her family; Sir John and Mrs. Jennings, indeed, were not so nice; their witticisms added pain to many a painful hour; but one evening Mrs. Dashwood, accidentally taking up a volume of Shakespeare, exclaimed:

"We have never finished *Hamlet,* Marianne; our dear Willoughby went away before we could get through it. We will

put it by, that when he comes again ... But it may be
months, perhaps, before *that* happens."

"Months!" cried Marianne, with strong surprise. "No—
nor many weeks."

Mrs. Dashwood was sorry for what she had said; but it
gave Elinor pleasure, as it produced a reply from Marianne
so expressive of confidence in Willoughby and knowledge
of his intentions.

One morning, about a week after his leaving the country,
Marianne was prevailed on to join her sisters in their usual
walk, instead of wandering away by herself. Hitherto she had
carefully avoided every companion in her rambles. If her sisters intended to walk on the downs, she directly stole away
towards the lanes; if they talked of the valley, she was as
speedy in climbing the hills, and could never be found when
the others set off. But at length she was secured by the exertions of Elinor, who greatly disapproved such continual seclu-
sion. They walked along the road through the valley, and
chiefly in silence, for Marianne's *mind* could not be controlled, and Elinor, satisfied with gaining one point, would
not then attempt more. Beyond the entrance of the valley,
where the country, though still rich, was less wild and more
open, a long stretch of the road which they had travelled on
first coming to Barton lay before them; and on reaching that
point, they stopped to look around them and examine a prospect which formed the distance of their view from the cottage, from a spot which they had never happened to reach in
any of their walks before.

Amongst the objects in the scene, they soon discovered an
animated one; it was a man on horseback riding towards
them. In a few minutes they could distinguish him to be a
gentleman; and in a moment afterwards Marianne rapturously exclaimed:

"It is he; it is indeed; I know it is!" and was hastening to
meet him, when Elinor cried out:

"Indeed, Marianne, I think you are mistaken. It is not
Willoughby. The person is not tall enough for him and has
not his air."

"He has, he has," cried Marianne. "I am sure he has. His
air, his coat, his horse. I knew how soon he would come."

She walked eagerly on as she spoke; and Elinor, to screen
Marianne from particularity, as she felt almost certain of its
not being Willoughby, quickened her pace and kept up with

her. They were soon within thirty yards of the gentleman. Marianne looked again; her heart sunk within her; and abruptly turning round, she was hurrying back, when the voices of both her sisters were raised to detain her; a third, almost as well known as Willoughby's, joined them in begging her to stop, and she turned round with surprise to see and welcome Edward Ferrars.

He was the only person in the world who could at that moment be forgiven for not being Willoughby, the only one who could have gained a smile from her; but she dispersed her tears to smile on *him,* and in her sister's happiness forgot for a time her own disappointment.

He dismounted, and giving his horse to his servant, walked back with them to Barton, whither he was purposely coming to visit them.

He was welcomed by them all with great cordiality, but especially by Marianne, who showed more warmth of regard in her reception of him than even Elinor herself. To Marianne, indeed, the meeting between Edward and her sister was but a continuation of that unaccountable coldness which she had often observed at Norland in their mutual behaviour. On Edward's side, more particularly, there was a deficiency of all that a lover ought to look and say on such an occasion. He was confused, seemed scarcely sensible of pleasure in seeing them, looked neither rapturous nor gay, said little but what was forced from him by questions, and distinguished Elinor by no mark of affection. Marianne saw and listened with increasing surprise. She began almost to feel a dislike of Edward; and it ended, as every feeling must end with her, by carrying back her thoughts to Willoughby, whose manners formed a contrast sufficiently striking to those of his brother elect.

After a short silence which succeeded the first surprise and inquiries of meeting, Marianne asked Edward if he came directly from London. No, he had been in Devonshire a fortnight.

"A fortnight!" she repeated, surprised at his being so long in the same county with Elinor without seeing her before.

He looked rather distressed as he added that he had been staying with some friends near Plymouth.

"Have you been lately in Sussex?" said Elinor.

"I was at Norland about a month ago."

"And how does dear, dear Norland look?" cried Marianne.

"Dear, dear Norland," said Elinor, "probably looks much as it always does at this time of year. The woods and walks thickly covered with dead leaves."

"Oh!" cried Marianne, "with what transporting sensations have I formerly seen them fall! How have I delighted as I walked to see them driven in showers about me by the wind! What feelings have they, the season, the air, altogether inspired! Now there is no one to regard them. They are seen only as a nuisance, swept hastily off, and driven as much as possible from the sight."

"It is not everyone," said Elinor, "who has your passion for dead leaves."

"No, my feelings are not often shared, not often understood. But *sometimes* they are." As she said this, she sank into a reverie for a few moments; but rousing herself again, "Now, Edward," said she, calling his attention to the prospect, "here is Barton valley. Look up it and be tranquil if you can. Look at those hills! Did you ever see their equals? To the left is Barton Park, amongst those woods and plantations. You may see one end of the house. And there, beneath that farthest hill which rises with such grandeur, is our cottage."

"It is a beautiful country," he replied; "but these bottoms must be dirty in winter."

"How can you think of dirt, with such objects before you?"

"Because," replied he, smiling, "among the rest of the objects before me, I see a very dirty lane."

"How strange!" said Marianne to herself as she walked on.

"Have you an agreeable neighbourhood here? Are the Middletons pleasant people?"

"No, not at all," answered Marianne; "we could not be more unfortunately situated."

"Marianne," cried her sister, "how can you say so? How can you be so unjust? They are a very respectable family, Mr. Ferrars, and towards us have behaved in the friendliest manner. Have you forgot, Marianne, how many pleasant days we have owed to them?"

"No," said Marianne in a low voice, "nor how many painful moments."

Elinor took no notice of this, and directing her attention to their visitor, endeavoured to support something like discourse with him by talking of their present residence, its conveniences, etc., extorting from him occasional questions and remarks. His coldness and reserve mortified her severely; she was vexed and half angry; but resolving to regulate her behaviour to him by the past rather than the present, she avoided every appearance of resentment or displeasure and treated him as she thought he ought to be treated from the family connection.

Chapter 17

MRS. DASHWOOD was surprised only for a moment at seeing him; for his coming to Barton was, in her opinion, of all things the most natural. Her joy and expressions of regard long outlived her wonder. He received the kindest welcome from her; and shyness, coldness, reserve, could not stand against such a reception. They had begun to fail him before he entered the house, and they were quite overcome by the captivating manners of Mrs. Dashwood. Indeed a man could not very well be in love with either of her daughters without extending the passion to her; and Elinor had the satisfaction of seeing him soon become more like himself. His affections seemed to reanimate towards them all, and his interest in their welfare again became perceptible. He was not in spirits however; he praised their house, admired its prospect, was attentive and kind; but still he was not in spirits. The whole family perceived it, and Mrs. Dashwood, attributing it to some want of liberality in his mother, sat down to table indignant against all selfish parents.

"What are Mrs. Ferrars's views for you at present, Edward?" said she when dinner was over and they had drawn round the fire; "are you still to be a great orator in spite of yourself?"

"No. I hope my mother is now convinced that I have no more talents than inclination for a public life!"

"But how is your fame to be established? For famous you *must* be to satisfy all your family; and with no inclination for expense, no affection for strangers, no profession, and no assurance, you may find it a difficult matter."

"I shall not attempt it. I have no wish to be distinguished; and I have every reason to hope I never shall. Thank Heaven! I cannot be forced into genius and eloquence."

"You have no ambition, I well know. Your wishes are all moderate."

"As moderate as those of the rest of the world, I believe. I wish as well as everybody else to be perfectly happy but like everybody else it must be in my own way. Greatness will not make me so."

"Strange if it would!" cried Marianne. "What have wealth or grandeur to do with happiness?"

"Grandeur has but little," said Elinor, "but wealth has much to do with it."

"Elinor, for shame!" said Marianne; "money can only give happiness where there is nothing else to give it. Beyond a competence, it can afford no real satisfaction as far as mere self is concerned."

"Perhaps," said Elinor, smiling, "we may come to the same point. *Your* competence and *my* wealth are very much alike, I dare say; and without them, as the world goes now, we shall both agree that every kind of external comfort must be wanting. Your ideas are only more noble than mine. Come, what is your competence?"

"About eighteen hundred or two thousand a year; not more than *that*."

Elinor laughed. "*Two* thousand a year! *One* is my wealth! I guessed how it would end."

"And yet two thousand a year is a very moderate income," said Marianne. "A family cannot well be maintained on a smaller. I am sure I am not extravagant in my demands. A proper establishment of servants, a carriage, perhaps two, and hunters, cannot be supported on less."

Elinor smiled again, to hear her sister describing so accurately their future expenses at Combe Magna.

"Hunters!" repeated Edward. "But why must you have hunters? Everybody does not hunt."

Marianne coloured as she replied, "But most people do."

"I wish," said Margaret, striking out a novel thought, "that somebody would give us all a large fortune apiece!"

"Oh that they would!" cried Marianne, her eyes sparkling with animation, and her cheeks glowing with the delight of such imaginary happiness.

"We are all unanimous in that wish, I suppose," said Elinor, "in spite of the insufficiency of wealth."

"Oh, dear!" cried Margaret, "how happy I should be! I wonder what I should do with it!"

Marianne looked as if she had no doubt on that point.

"I should be puzzled to spend a large fortune myself," said Mrs. Dashwood, "if my children were all to be rich without my help."

"You must begin your improvements on this house," observed Elinor, "and your difficulties will soon vanish."

"What magnificent orders would travel from this family to London," said Edward, "in such an event! What a happy day for booksellers, music-sellers, and print-shops! You, Miss Dashwood, would give a general commission for every new print of merit to be sent you; and as for Marianne, I know her greatness of soul; there would not be music enough in London to content her. And books! Thomson, Cowper, Scott—she would buy them all over and over again; she would buy up every copy, I believe, to prevent their falling into unworthy hands; and she would have every book that tells her how to admire an old twisted tree. Should not you, Marianne? Forgive me if I am very saucy. But I was willing to show you that I had not forgot our old disputes."

"I love to be reminded of the past, Edward. Whether it be melancholy or gay, I love to recall it; and you will never offend me by talking of former times. You are very right in supposing how my money would be spent—some of it, at least—my loose cash would certainly be employed in improving my collection of music and books."

"And the bulk of your fortune would be laid out in annuities on the authors or their heirs."

"No, Edward, I should have something else to do with it."

"Perhaps then you would bestow it as a reward on that person who wrote the ablest defence of your favourite maxim: that no one can ever be in love more than once in their life—for your opinion on that point is unchanged, I presume?"

"Undoubtedly. At my time of life opinions are tolerably fixed. It is not likely that I should now see or hear anything to change them."

"Marianne is as stedfast as ever, you see," said Elinor; "she is not at all altered."

"She is only grown a little more grave than she was."

"Nay, Edward," said Marianne, "*you* need not reproach me. You are not very gay yourself."

"Why should you think so!" replied he, with a sigh. "But gaiety never was a part of *my* character."

"Nor do I think it a part of Marianne's," said Elinor; "I should hardly call her a lively girl. She is very earnest, very eager in all she does; sometimes talks a great deal and always with animation; but she is not often really merry."

"I believe you are right," he replied, "and yet I have always set her down as a lively girl."

"I have frequently detected myself in such kind of mistakes," said Elinor, "in a total misapprehension of character in some point or other: fancying people so much more gay or grave, or ingenious or stupid than they really are, and I can hardly tell why or in what the deception originated. Sometimes one is guided by what they say of themselves, and very frequently by what other people say of them, without giving oneself time to deliberate and judge."

"But I thought it was right, Elinor," said Marianne, "to be guided wholly by the opinion of other people. I thought our judgments were given us merely to be subservient to those of our neighbours. This has always been your doctrine, I am sure."

"No, Marianne, never. My doctrine has never aimed at the subjection of the understanding. All I have ever attempted to influence has been the behaviour. You must not confound my meaning. I am guilty, I confess, of having often wished you to treat our acquaintance in general with greater attention; but when have I advised you to adopt their sentiments or conform to their judgment in serious matters?"

"You have not been able then to bring your sister over to your plan of general civility," said Edward to Elinor. "Do you gain no ground?"

"Quite the contrary," replied Elinor, looking expressively at Marianne.

"My judgment," he returned, "is all on your side of the question; but I am afraid my practice is much more on your sister's. I never wish to offend, but I am so foolishly shy that I often seem negligent when I am only kept back by my natural awkwardness. I have frequently thought that I must have been intended by nature to be fond of low company, I am so little at my ease among strangers of gentility!"

"Marianne has not shyness to excuse any inattention of hers," said Elinor.

"She knows her own worth too well for false shame," replied Edward. "Shyness is only the effect of a sense of inferiority in some way or other. If I could persuade myself that my manners were perfectly easy and graceful, I should not be shy."

"But you would still be reserved," said Marianne, "and that is worse."

Edward stared. "Reserved! Am I reserved, Marianne?"

"Yes, very."

"I do not understand you," replied he, colouring. "Reserved! How? In what manner? What am I to tell you? What can you suppose?"

Elinor looked surprised at his emotion, but trying to laugh off the subject, she said to him, "Do not you know my sister well enough to understand what she means? Do not you know she calls everyone reserved who does not talk as fast and admire what she admires as rapturously as herself?"

Edward made no answer. His gravity and thoughtfulness returned on him in their fullest extent, and he sat for some time silent and dull.

Chapter 18

ELINOR SAW, with great uneasiness, the low spirits of her friend. His visit afforded her but a very partial satisfaction, while his own enjoyment in it appeared so imperfect. It was evident that he was unhappy; she wished it were equally evident that he still distinguished her by the same affection which once she had felt no doubt of inspiring; but hitherto the continuance of his preference seemed very uncertain; and the reservedness of his manner towards her contradicted one moment what a more animated look had intimated the preceding one.

He joined her and Marianne in the breakfast-room the next morning before the others were down; and Marianne, who was always eager to promote their happiness as far as she could, soon left them to themselves. But before she was halfway upstairs she heard the parlour door open, and turning round, was astonished to see Edward himself come out.

"I am going into the village to see my horses," said he, "as you are not yet ready for breakfast; I shall be back again presently."

Edward returned to them with fresh admiration of the surrounding country; in his walk to the village, he had seen many parts of the valley to advantage; and the village itself, in a much higher situation than the cottage, afforded a general view of the whole, which had exceedingly pleased him. This was a subject which ensured Marianne's attention, and she was beginning to describe her own admiration of these scenes and to question him more minutely on the objects that had particularly struck him, when Edward interrupted her by saying, "You must not inquire too far, Marianne. Remember I have no knowledge in the picturesque, and I shall offend you by my ignorance and want of taste if we come to particulars. I shall call hills steep which ought to be bold; surfaces strange and uncouth which ought to be irregular and rugged; and distant objects out of sight which ought to be indistinct through the soft medium of a hazy atmosphere. You must be satisfied with such admiration as I can honestly give. I call it a very fine country: the hills are steep, the woods seem full of fine timber, and the valley looks comfortable and snug, with rich meadows and several neat farmhouses scattered here and there. It exactly answers my idea of a fine country because it unites beauty with utility, and I dare say it is a picturesque one too because you admire it; I can easily believe it to be full of rocks and promontories, grey moss and brushwood, but these are all lost on me. I know nothing of the picturesque."

"I am afraid it is but too true," said Marianne; "but why should you boast of it?"

"I suspect," said Elinor, "that to avoid one kind of affection, Edward here falls into another. Because he believes many people pretend to more admiration of the beauties of nature than they really feel and is disgusted with such pretensions, he affects greater indifference and less discrimination in viewing them himself than he possesses. He is fastidious and will have an affectation of his own."

"It is very true," said Marianne, "that admiration of landscape scenery is become a mere jargon. Everybody pretends to feel and tries to describe with the taste and elegance of him who first defined what picturesque beauty was. I detest jargon of every kind, and sometimes I have kept my feelings to myself because I could find no language to describe them in but what was worn and hackneyed out of all sense and meaning."

"I am convinced," said Edward, "that you really feel all the delight in a fine prospect which you profess to feel. But, in return, your sister must allow me to feel no more than I profess. I like a fine prospect, but not on picturesque principles. I do not like crooked, twisted, blasted trees. I admire them much more if they are tall, straight and flourishing. I do not like ruined, tattered cottages. I am not fond of nettles, or thistles, or heath blossoms. I have more pleasure in a snug farmhouse than a watch-tower, and a troop of tidy, happy villagers please me better than the finest banditti in the world."

Marianne looked with amazement at Edward, with compassion at her sister. Elinor only laughed.

The subject was continued no further; and Marianne remained thoughtfully silent till a new object suddenly engaged her attention. She was sitting by Edward, and in taking his tea from Mrs. Dashwood, his hand passed so directly before her as to make a ring, with a plait of hair in the centre, very conspicuous on one of his fingers.

"I never saw you wear a ring before, Edward," she cried. "Is that Fanny's hair? I remember her promising to give you some. But I should have thought her hair had been darker."

Marianne spoke inconsiderately what she really felt; but when she saw how much she had pained Edward, her own vexation at her want of thought could not be surpassed by his. He coloured very deeply, and giving a momentary glance at Elinor, replied, "Yes, it is my sister's hair. The setting always casts a different shade on it you know."

Elinor had met his eye, and looked conscious likewise. That the hair was her own, she instantaneously felt as well satisfied as Marianne; the only difference in their conclusions was that what Marianne considered as a free gift from her sister, Elinor was conscious must have been procured by some theft or contrivance unknown to herself. She was not in a humour, however, to regard it as an affront, and affecting to take no notice of what passed, by instantly talking of something else, she internally resolved henceforward to catch every opportunity of eyeing the hair and of satisfying herself, beyond all doubt, that it was exactly the shade of her own.

Edward's embarrassment lasted some time, and it ended in an absence of mind still more settled. He was particularly grave the whole morning. Marianne severely censured herself for what she had said; but her own forgiveness might have been more speedy had she known how little offence it had given her sister.

Before the middle of the day, they were visited by Sir John and Mrs. Jennings, who, having heard of the arrival of a gentleman at the cottage, came to take a survey of the guest. With the assistance of his mother-in-law, Sir John was not long in discovering that the name of Ferrars began with an F and this prepared a future mine of raillery against the devoted Elinor, which nothing but the newness of their acquaintance with Edward could have prevented from being immediately sprung. But, as it was, she only learned from some very significant looks how far their penetration, founded on Margaret's instructions, extended.

Sir John never came to the Dashwoods without either inviting them to dine at the park the next day or to drink tea with them that evening. On the present occasion, for the better entertainment of their visitor, towards whose amusement he felt himself bound to contribute, he wished to engage them for both.

"You *must* drink tea with us to-night," said he, "for we shall be quite alone; and to-morrow you must absolutely dine with us, for we shall be a large party."

Mrs. Jennings enforced the necessity. "And who knows but you may raise a dance," said she. "And that will tempt *you*, Miss Marianne."

"A dance!" cried Marianne. "Impossible! Who is to dance?"

"Who? Why yourselves and the Careys and Whitakers to be sure. What! You thought nobody could dance because a certain person that shall be nameless is gone!"

"I wish with all my soul," cried Sir John, "that Willoughby were among us again."

This, and Marianne's blushing, gave new suspicions to Edward. "And who is Willoughby?" said he in a low voice to Miss Dashwood, by whom he was sitting.

She gave him a brief reply. Marianne's countenance was

more communicative. Edward saw enough to comprehend not only the meaning of others but such of Marianne's expressions as had puzzled him before; and when their visitors left them, he went immediately round her and said in a whisper, "I have been guessing. Shall I tell you my guess?"

"What do you mean?"

"Shall I tell you?"

"Certainly." '

"Well then, I guess that Mr. Willoughby hunts."

Marianne was surprised and confused, yet she could not help smiling at the quiet archness of his manner, and after a moment's silence said,

"Oh! Edward! How can you? But the time will come I hope . . . I am sure you will like him."

"I do not doubt it," replied he, rather astonished at her earnestness and warmth; for had he not imagined it to be a joke for the good of her acquaintance in general, founded only on a something or a nothing between Mr. Willoughby and herself, he would not have ventured to mention it.

Chapter 19

EDWARD REMAINED a week at the cottage; he was earnestly pressed by Mrs. Dashwood to stay longer; but as if he were bent only on self-mortification, he seemed resolved to be gone when his enjoyment among his friends was at the height. His spirits during the last two or three days, though still very unequal, were greatly improved; he grew more and more partial to the house and environs, never spoke of going away without a sigh, declared his time to be wholly disengaged, even doubted to what place he should go when he left them; but still, go he must. Never had any week passed so quickly. He could hardly believe it to be gone. He said so repeatedly; other things he said too which marked the turn of his feelings and gave the lie to his actions. He had no pleasure at Norland; he detested being in town; but either to Norland or London he must go. He valued their kindness beyond anything, and his greatest happiness was in being with them. Yet he must leave them at the end of a week, in spite of their wishes and his own, and without any restraint on his time.

Elinor placed all that was astonishing in this way of acting to his mother's account; and it was happy for her that he had a mother whose character was so imperfectly known to her as to be the general excuse for everything strange on the part of her son. Disappointed, however, and vexed as she was, and sometimes displeased with his uncertain behaviour to herself, she was very well disposed on the whole to regard his actions with all the candid allowances and generous qualifications which had been rather more painfully extorted from her for Willoughby's service by her mother. His want of spirits, of openness, and of consistency, were most usually attributed to his want of independence and his better knowledge of Mrs. Ferrars's dispositions and designs. The shortness of his visit, the steadiness of his purpose in leaving them, originated in the same fettered inclination, the same inevitable necessity of temporizing with his mother. The old well-established grievance of duty against will, parent against child, was the cause of all. She would have been glad to know when these difficulties were to cease, this opposition was to yield; when Mrs. Ferrars would be reformed, and her son be at liberty to be happy. But from such vain wishes, she was forced to turn for comfort to the renewal of her confidence in Edward's affection, to the remembrance of every mark of regard in look or word which fell from him while at Barton, and above all to that flattering proof of it which he constantly wore round his finger.

"I think, Edward," said Mrs. Dashwood as they were at breakfast the last morning, "you would be a happier man if you had any profession to engage your time and give an interest to your plans and actions. Some inconvenience to your friends, indeed, might result from it: you would not be able to give them so much of your time. But (with a smile) you would be materially benefited in one particular at least: you would know where to go when you left them."

"I do assure you," he replied, "that I have long thought on this point, as you think now. It has been and is and probably will always be a heavy misfortune to me that I have had no necessary business to engage me, no profession to give me employment, or afford me anything like independence. But unfortunately my own nicety and the nicety of my friends have made me what I am: an idle, helpless being. We never could agree in our choice of a profession. I always preferred the church, as I still do. But that was not smart enough for my family. They recommended the army. That was a great deal too smart for me. The law was allowed to be genteel enough; many young men who had chambers in the Temple made a very good appearance in the first circles and drove about town in very knowing gigs. But I had no inclination for the law, even in this less abstruse study of it which my family approved. As for the navy, it had fashion on its side, but I was too old when the subject was first started to enter it; and at length, as there was no necessity for my having any profession at all, as I might be as dashing and expensive without a red coat on my back as with one, idleness was pronounced on the whole to be the most advantageous and honourable, and a young man of eighteen is not in general so earnestly bent on being busy as to resist the solicitations of his friends to do nothing. I was therefore entered at Oxford and have been properly idle ever since."

"The consequence of which, I suppose, will be," said Mrs. Dashwood, "since leisure has not promoted your own happiness, that your sons will be brought up to as many pursuits, employments, professions, and trades as Columella's."

"They will be brought up," said he in a serious accent, "to be as unlike myself as is possible. In feeling, in action, in condition, in everything."

"Come, come; this is all an effusion of immediate want of spirits, Edward. You are in a melancholy humour and fancy that anyone unlike yourself must be happy. But remember that the pain of parting from friends will be felt by everybody at times, whatever be their education or state. Know your own happiness. You want nothing but patience; or give it a more fascinating name: call it hope. Your mother will secure to you, in time, that independence you are so anxious for; it is her duty, and it will, it must ere long, become her happiness to prevent your whole youth from being wasted in discontent. How much may not a few months do?"

"I think," replied Edward, "that I may defy many months to produce any good to me."

This desponding turn of mind, though it could not be communicated to Mrs. Dashwood, gave additional pain to them all in the parting which shortly took place and left an uncomfortable impression on Elinor's feelings especially, which required some trouble and time to subdue. But as it was her determination to subdue it, and to prevent herself from appearing to suffer more than what all her family suffered on his going away, she did not adopt the method so judiciously employed by Marianne on a similar occasion to augment and fix her sorrow by seeking silence, solitude, and idleness. Their means were as different as their objects and equally suited to the advancement of each.

Elinor sat down to her drawing-table as soon as he was out of the house, busily employed herself the whole day, neither sought nor avoided the mention of his name, appeared to interest herself almost as much as ever in the general concerns of the family; and if by this conduct she did not lessen her own grief, it was at least prevented from unnecessary increase, and her mother and sisters were spared much solicitude on her account.

Such behaviour as this, so exactly the reverse of her own, appeared no more meritorious to Marianne than her own had seemed faulty to her. The business of self-command she settled very easily: with strong affections it was impossible; with calm ones it could have no merit. That her sister's affections *were* calm, she dared not deny, though she blushed to acknowledge it; and of the strength of her own, she gave a very striking proof by still loving and respecting that sister in spite of this mortifying conviction.

Without shutting herself up from her family, or leaving the house in determined solitude to avoid them, or lying awake the whole night to indulge meditation, Elinor found every day afforded her leisure enough to think of Edward and of Edward's behaviour in every possible variety which the different state of her spirits at different times could produce: with tenderness, pity, approbation, censure, and doubt. There were moments in abundance when, if not by the absence of her mother and sisters, at least by the nature of their employments, conversation was forbidden among them, and every effect of solitude was produced. Her mind was inevitably at liberty; her thoughts could not be chained elsewhere; and the past and the future, on a subject so interesting, must be before her, must force her attention, and engross her memory, her reflection, and her fancy.

From a reverie of this kind, as she sat at her drawing-table, she was roused one morning soon after Edward's leaving them by the arrival of company. She happened to be quite alone. The closing of the little gate at the entrance of the green court in front of the house drew her eyes to the window, and she saw a large party walking up to the door. Amongst them were Sir John and Lady Middleton and Mrs. Jennings, but there were two others, a gentleman and lady who were quite unknown to her. She was sitting near the window, and as soon as Sir John perceived her, he left the rest of the party to the ceremony of knocking at the door, and stepping across the turf, obliged her to open the casement to speak to him, though the space was so short between the door and the window as to make it hardly possible to speak at one without being heard at the other.

"Well," said he, "we have brought you some strangers. How do you like them?"

"Hush! They will hear you."

"Never mind if they do. It is only the Palmers. Charlotte is very pretty, I can tell you. You may see her if you look this way."

As Elinor was certain of seeing her in a couple of minutes without taking that liberty, she begged to be excused.

"Where is Marianne? Has she run away because we are come? I see her instrument is open."

"She is walking, I believe."

They were now joined by Mrs. Jennings, who had not patience enough to wait till the door was opened before she told *her* story. She came hallooing to the window, "How do you do, my dear? How does Mrs. Dashwood do? And where are your sisters? What! All alone! You will be glad of a little company to sit with you. I have brought my other son and daughter to see you. Only think of their coming so suddenly! I thought I heard a carriage last night while we were drinking our tea, but it never entered my head that it could be them. I thought of nothing but whether it might not be Colonel Brandon come back again; so I said to Sir John, I do think I hear a carriage; perhaps it is Colonel Brandon come back again"——

Elinor was obliged to turn from her in the middle of her story to receive the rest of the party; Lady Middleton introduced the two strangers; Mrs. Dashwood and Margaret came downstairs at the same time, and they all sat down to look at one another while Mrs. Jennings continued her story as she walked through the passage into the parlour attended by Sir John.

Mrs. Palmer was several years younger than Lady Middleton and totally unlike her in every respect. She was short and plump, had a very pretty face, and the finest expression of good humour in it that could possibly be. Her manners were by no means so elegant as her sister's, but they were much more prepossessing. She came in with a smile, smiled all the time of her visit except when she laughed, and smiled when she went away. Her husband was a grave-looking young man of five or six and twenty, with an air of more fashion and sense than his wife but of less willingness to please or be pleased. He entered the room with a look of self-consequence, slightly bowed to the ladies without speaking a word, and after briefly surveying them and their apartments, took up a newspaper from the table and continued to read it as long as he stayed.

Mrs. Palmer, on the contrary, who was strongly endowed by nature with a turn for being uniformly civil and happy, was hardly seated before her admiration of the parlour and everything in it burst forth.

"Well! What a delightful room this is! I never saw anything so charming! Only think, Mama, how it is improved since I was here last! I always thought it such a sweet place, ma'am! (Turning to Mrs. Dashwood.) But you have made it so charming! Only look, Sister, how delightful everything is! How I should like such a house for myself! Should not you, Mr. Palmer?"

Mr. Palmer made her no answer and did not even raise his eyes from the newspaper.

"Mr. Palmer does not hear me," said she, laughing; "he never does sometimes. It is so ridiculous!"

This was quite a new idea to Mrs. Dashwood; she had never been used to find wit in the inattention of anyone, and could not help looking with surprise at them both.

Mrs. Jennings, in the meantime, talked on as loud as she could and continued her account of their surprise the evening before on seeing their friends, without ceasing till everything was told. Mrs. Palmer laughed heartily at the recollection of their astonishment, and everybody agreed, two or three times over, that it had been quite an agreeable surprise.

"You may believe how glad we all were to see them," added Mrs. Jennings, leaning forwards towards Elinor and speaking in a low voice as if she meant to be heard by no one else, though they were seated on different sides of the room; "but, however, I can't help wishing they had not travelled quite so fast, nor made such a long journey of it, for they came all round by London upon account of some business, for you know (nodding significantly and pointing to her daughter) it was wrong in her situation. I wanted her to stay at home and rest this morning, but she would come with us; she longed so much to see you all!"

Mrs. Palmer laughed and said it would not do her any harm.

"She expects to be confined in February," continued Mrs. Jennings.

Lady Middleton could no longer endure such a conversation, and therefore exerted herself to ask Mr. Palmer if there was any news in the paper.

"No, none at all," he replied, and read on.

"Here comes Marianne," cried Sir John. "Now, Palmer, you shall see a monstrous pretty girl."

He immediately went into the passage, opened the front door, and ushered her in himself. Mrs. Jennings asked her as soon as she appeared if she had not been to Allenham; and Mrs. Palmer laughed so heartily at the question, as to show she understood it. Mr. Palmer looked up on her entering the room, stared at her some minutes, and then returned to his newspaper. Mrs. Palmer's eye was now caught by the drawings which hung round the room. She got up to examine them.

"Oh! dear, how beautiful these are! Well! How delightful! Do but look, Mama, how sweet! I declare they are quite charming; I could look at them forever." And then sitting down again, she very soon forgot that there were any such things in the room.

When Lady Middleton rose to go away, Mr. Palmer rose also, laid down the newspaper, stretched himself, and looked at them all round.

"My love, have you been asleep?" said his wife, laughing.

He made her no answer; and only observed after again examining the room, that it was very low pitched and that the ceiling was crooked. He then made his bow and departed with the rest.

Sir John had been very urgent with them all to spend the next day at the park. Mrs. Dashwood, who did not choose to dine with them oftener than they dined at the cottage, absolutely refused on her own account; her daughters might do

as they pleased. But they had no curiosity to see how Mr.
and Mrs. Palmer ate their dinner, and no expectation of pleasure from them in any other way. They attempted, therefore,
likewise to excuse themselves; the weather was uncertain
and not likely to be good. But Sir John would not be satisfied; the carriage should be sent for them and they must
come. Lady Middleton too, though she did not press their
mother, pressed them. Mrs. Jennings and Mrs. Palmer joined
their entreaties; all seemed equally anxious to avoid a family
party; and the young ladies were obliged to yield.

"Why should they ask us?" said Marianne as soon as they
were gone. "The rent of this cottage is said to be low; but
we have it on very hard terms if we are to dine at the park
whenever anyone is staying either with them or with us."

"They mean no less to be civil and kind to us now," said
Elinor, "by these frequent invitations than by those which
we received from them a few weeks ago. The alteration is
not in them if their parties are grown tedious and dull. We
must look for the change elsewhere."

Chapter 20

As THE Miss Dashwoods entered the drawing-room of the
park the next day at one door, Mrs. Palmer came running in
at the other, looking as good-humoured and merry as before.
She took them all most affectionately by the hand and expressed great delight in seeing them again.

"I am so glad to see you!" said she, seating herself between Elinor and Marianne, "for it is so bad a day I was
afraid you might not come, which would be a shocking
thing, as we go away again to-morrow. We must go, for the
Westons come to us next week you know. It was quite a sudden thing our coming at all, and I knew nothing of it till the
carriage was coming to the door, and then Mr. Palmer asked
me if I would go with him to Barton. He is so droll! He
never tells me anything! I am so sorry we cannot stay
longer; however we shall meet again in town very soon, I
hope."

They were obliged to put an end to such an expectation.

"Not go to town!" cried Mrs. Palmer with a laugh, "I shall be quite disappointed if you do not. I could get the nicest house in the world for you next door to ours in Hanover Square. You must come, indeed. I am sure I shall be very happy to chaperon you at any time till I am confined if Mrs. Dashwood should not like to go into public."

They thanked her, but were obliged to resist all her entreaties.

"Oh! my love," cried Mrs. Palmer to her husband, who just then entered the room; "you must help me persuade the Miss Dashwoods to go to town this winter."

Her love made no answer; and after slightly bowing to the ladies, began complaining of the weather.

"How horrid all this is!" said he. "Such weather makes everything and everybody disgusting. Dullness is as much produced within doors as without by rain. It makes one detest all one's acquaintance. What the devil does Sir John mean by not having a billiard room in his house? How few people know what comfort is! Sir John is as stupid as the weather."

The rest of the company soon dropped in.

"I am afraid, Miss Marianne," said Sir John, "you have not been able to take your usual walk to Allenham to-day."

Marianne looked very grave and said nothing.

"Oh! don't be so sly before us," said Mrs. Palmer; "for we know all about it, I assure you; and I admire your taste very much, for I think he is extremely handsome. We do not live a great way from him in the country, you know. Not above ten miles, I dare say."

"Much nearer thirty," said her husband.

"Ah! well! There is not much difference. I never was at his house, but they say it is a sweet pretty place."

"As vile a spot as I ever saw in my life," said Mr. Palmer.

Marianne remained perfectly silent, though her countenance betrayed her interest in what was said.

"Is it very ugly?" continued Mrs. Palmer. "Then it must be some other place that is so pretty I suppose."

When they were seated in the dining-room, Sir John observed with regret that they were only eight altogether.

"My dear," said he to his lady, "it is very provoking that we should be so few. Why did not you ask the Gilberts to come to us to-day?"

"Did not I tell you, Sir John, when you spoke to me about it before, that it could not be done? They dined with us last."

"You and I, Sir John," said Mrs. Jennings, "should not stand upon such ceremony."

"Then you would be very ill-bred," cried Mr. Palmer.

"My love, you contradict everybody," said his wife with her usual laugh. "Do you know that you are quite rude?"

"I did not know I contradicted anybody in calling your mother ill-bred."

"Aye, you may abuse me as you please," said the good-natured old lady; "you have taken Charlotte off my hands and cannot give her back again. So there I have the whip hand of you."

Charlotte laughed heartily to think that her husband could not get rid of her; and exultingly said she did not care how cross he was to her, as they must live together. It was impossible for anyone to be more thoroughly good-natured, or more determined to be happy than Mrs. Palmer. The studied indifference, insolence, and discontent of her husband gave her no pain: and when he scolded or abused her, she was highly diverted.

"Mr. Palmer is so droll!" said she in a whisper to Elinor. "He is always out of humour."

Elinor was not inclined, after a little observation, to give him credit for being so genuinely and unaffectedly ill-natured or ill-bred as he wished to appear. His temper might perhaps be a little soured by finding, like many others of his sex, that through some unaccountable bias in favour of beauty, he was the husband of a very silly woman; but she knew that this kind of blunder was too common for any sensible man to be lastingly hurt by it. It was rather a wish of distinction, she believed, which produced his contemptuous treatment of everybody and his general abuse of everything before him. It was the desire of appearing superior to other people. The motive was too common to be wondered at; but the means, however they might succeed by establishing his superiority in ill-breeding, were not likely to attach anyone to him except his wife.

"Oh! my dear Miss Dashwood," said Mrs. Palmer soon afterwards, "I have got such a favour to ask of you and your sister. Will you come and spend some time at Cleveland this Christmas? Now, pray do; and come while the Westons are with us. You cannot think how happy I shall be! It will be quite delightful!—— My love," applying to her husband, "don't you long to have the Miss Dashwoods come to Cleveland?"

"Certainly," he replied with a sneer, "I came into Devonshire with no other view."

"There now," said his lady, "you see Mr. Palmer expects you; so you cannot refuse to come."

They both eagerly and resolutely declined her invitation.

"But indeed you must and shall come. I am sure you will like it of all things. The Westons will be with us, and it will be quite delightful. You cannot think what a sweet place Cleveland is; and we are so gay now, for Mr. Palmer is always going about the country canvassing against the election; and so many people come to dine with us that I never saw before; it is quite charming! But, poor fellow! It is very fatiguing to him! For he is forced to make everybody like him."

Elinor could hardly keep her countenance as she assented to the hardship of such an obligation.

"How charming it will be," said Charlotte, "when he is in Parliament! Won't it? How I shall laugh! It will be so ridiculous to see all his letters directed to him with an M. P. But do you know, he says, he will never frank for me? He declares he won't. Don't you, Mr. Palmer?"

Mr. Palmer took no notice of her.

"He cannot bear writing, you know," she continued. "He says it is quite shocking."

"No," said he, "I never said anything so irrational. Don't palm all your abuses of language upon me."

"There now, you see how droll he is. This is always the way with him! Sometimes he won't speak to me for half a day together, and then he comes out with something so droll—all about anything in the world."

She surprised Elinor very much as they returned into the drawing-room by asking her whether she did not like Mr. Palmer excessively.

"Certainly," said Elinor, "he seems very agreeable."

"Well, I am so glad you do. I thought you would; he is so pleasant; and Mr. Palmer is excessively pleased with you and your sisters, I can tell you; and you can't think how disappointed he will be if you don't come to Cleveland. I can't imagine why you should object to it."

Elinor was again obliged to decline her invitation; and by

changing the subject, put a stop to her entreaties. She thought it probable that as they lived in the same county, Mrs. Palmer might be able to give some more particular account of Willoughby's general character than could be gathered from the Middletons' partial acquaintance with him; and she was eager to gain from anyone such a confirmation of his merits as might remove the possibility of fear for Marianne. She began by inquiring if they saw much of Mr. Willoughby at Cleveland and whether they were intimately acquainted with him.

"Oh! dear, yes; I know him extremely well," replied Mrs. Palmer. "Not that I ever spoke to him indeed, but I have seen him forever in town. Somehow or other I never happened to be staying at Barton while he was at Allenham. Mama saw him here once before, but I was with my uncle at Weymouth. However, I dare say we should have seen a great deal of him in Somersetshire if it had not happened very unluckily that we should never have been in the country together. He is very little at Combe, I believe; but if he were ever so much there, I do not think Mr. Palmer would visit him, for he is in the opposition you know, and besides it is such a way off. I know why you inquire about him very well; your sister is to marry him. I am monstrous glad of it, for then I shall have her for a neighbour you know."

"Upon my word," replied Elinor, "you know much more of the matter than I do if you have any reason to expect such a match."

"Don't pretend to deny it, because you know it is what everybody talks of. I assure you I heard of it in my way through town."

"My dear Mrs. Palmer!"

"Upon my honour I did. I met Colonel Brandon Monday morning in Bond Street just before we left town, and he told me of it directly."

"You surprise me very much. Colonel Brandon tell you of it! Surely you must be mistaken. To give such intelligence to a person who could not be interested in it, even if it were true, is not what I should expect Colonel Brandon to do."

"But I do assure you it was so, for all that, and I will tell you how it happened. When we met him, he turned back and walked with us; and so we began talking of my brother and sister, and one thing and another, and I said to him, 'So, Colonel, there is a new family come to Barton cottage, I hear, and mama sends me word they are very pretty, and that one of them is going to be married to Mr. Willoughby of Combe Magna. Is it true, pray? For of course you must know, as you have been in Devonshire so lately.' "

"And what did the Colonel say?"

"Oh! he did not say much; but he looked as if he knew it to be true, so from that moment I set it down as certain. It will be quite delightful, I declare! When is it to take place?"

"Mr. Brandon was very well I hope."

"Oh! yes, quite well; and so full of your praises, he did nothing but say fine things of you."

"I am flattered by his commendation. He seems an excellent man, and I think him uncommonly pleasing."

"So do I. He is such a charming man that it is quite a pity he should be so grave and so dull. Mama says *he* was in love with your sister too. I assure you it was a great compliment if he was, for he hardly ever falls in love with anybody."

"Is Mr. Willoughby much known in your part of Somersetshire?" said Elinor.

"Oh! yes, extremely well; that is, I do not believe many people are acquainted with him because Combe Magna is so far off; but they all think him extremely agreeable I assure you. Nobody is more liked than Mr. Willoughby wherever he goes, and so you may tell your sister. She is a monstrous lucky girl to get him, upon my honour; not but that he is much more lucky in getting her, because she is so very handsome and agreeable that nothing can be good enough for her. However I don't think her hardly at all handsomer than you, I assure you; for I think you both excessively pretty, and so does Mr. Palmer too I am sure, though we could not get him to own it last night."

Mrs. Palmer's information respecting Willoughby was not very material; but any testimony in his favour, however small, was pleasing to her.

"I am so glad we are got acquainted at last," continued Charlotte. "And now I hope we shall always be great friends. You can't think how much I longed to see you! It is so delightful that you should live at the cottage! Nothing can be like it to be sure! And I am so glad your sister is going to be well-married! I hope you will be a great deal at Combe Magna. It is a sweet place by all accounts."

"You have been long acquainted with Colonel Brandon, have not you?"

"Yes, a great while; ever since my sister married. He was a particular friend of Sir John's. I believe," she added in a low voice, "he would have been very glad to have had me if he could. Sir John and Lady Middleton wished it very much. But mama did not think the match good enough for me; otherwise Sir John would have mentioned it to the Colonel, and we should have been married immediately."

"Did not Colonel Brandon know of Sir John's proposal to your mother before it was made? Had he never owned his affection to yourself?"

"Oh! no; but if mama had not objected to it, I dare say he would have liked it of all things. He had not seen me then above twice, for it was before I left school. However, I am much happier as I am. Mr. Palmer is just the kind of man I like."

Chapter 21

THE PALMERS returned to Cleveland the next day, and the two families at Barton were again left to entertain each other. But this did not last long; Elinor had hardly got their last visitors out of her head, had hardly done wondering at Charlotte's being so happy without a cause, at Mr. Palmer's acting so simply with good abilities, and at the strange unsuitableness which often existed between husband and wife, before Sir John's and Mrs. Jennings's active zeal in the cause of society procured her some other new acquaintance to see and observe.

In a morning's excursion to Exeter they had met with two young ladies, whom Mrs. Jennings had the satisfaction of discovering to be her relations, and this was enough for Sir John to invite them directly to the park, as soon as their present engagements at Exeter were over. Their engagements at Exeter instantly gave way before such an invitation, and Lady Middleton was thrown into no little alarm on the return of Sir John by hearing that she was very soon to receive a visit from two girls whom she had never seen in her life, and of whose elegance, whose tolerable gentility even, she could have no proof; for the assurances of her husband and mother

on that subject went for nothing at all. Their being her relations too made it so much the worse; and Mrs. Jennings's attempts at consolation were therefore unfortunately founded
when she advised her daughter not to care about their being
so fashionable because they were all cousins and must put
up with one another. As it was impossible, however, now to
prevent their coming, Lady Middleton resigned herself to the
idea of it with all the philosophy of a well-bred woman, contenting herself with merely giving her husband a gentle reprimand on the subject five or six times every day.

The young ladies arrived; their appearance was by no
means ungenteel or unfashionable. Their dress was very
smart, their manners very civil, they were delighted with the
house and in raptures with the furniture, and they happened
to be so dotingly fond of children that Lady Middleton's
good opinion was engaged in their favour before they had
been an hour at the park. She declared them to be very
agreeable girls indeed, which for her ladyship was enthusiastic admiration. Sir John's confidence in his own judgment
rose with this animated praise, and he set off directly for the
cottage to tell the Miss Dashwoods of the Miss Steeles' arrival and to assure them of their being the sweetest girls in
the world. From such commendation as this, however, there
was not much to be learned; Elinor well knew that the
sweetest girls in the world were to be met with in every part
of England, under every possible variation of form, face,
temper, and understanding. Sir John wanted the whole family to walk to the park directly and look at his guests. Be-
nevolent, philanthropic man! It was painful to him even to
keep a third cousin to himself.

"Do come now," said he. "Pray come— You must come—
I declare you shall come— You can't think how you will
like them. Lucy is monstrous pretty and so good-humoured
and agreeable! The children are all hanging about her already as if she was an old acquaintance. And they both long
to see you of all things, for they have heard at Exeter that
you are the most beautiful creatures in the world; and I have
told them it is all very true, and a great deal more. You will
be delighted with them I am sure. They have brought the
whole coach full of playthings for the children. How can you
be so cross as not to come? Why they are your cousins, you
know, after a fashion. *You* are my cousins, and they are my
wife's; so you must be related."

But Sir John could not prevail. He could only obtain a promise of their calling at the park within a day or two, and then left them in amazement at their indifference, to walk home and boast anew of their attractions to the Miss Steeles, as he had been already boasting of the Miss Steeles to them.

When their promised visit to the park and consequent introduction to these young ladies took place, they found in the appearance of the eldest, who was nearly thirty, with a very plain and not a sensible face, nothing to admire; but in the other, who was not more than two or three and twenty, they acknowledged considerable beauty; her features were pretty, and she had a sharp quick eye and a smartness of air, which though it did not give actual elegance or grace, gave distinction to her person. Their manners were particularly civil, and Elinor soon allowed them credit for some kind of sense when she saw with what constant and judicious attentions they were making themselves agreeable to Lady Middleton. With her children they were in continual raptures, extolling their beauty, courting their notice, and humouring all their whims; and such of their time as could be spared from the importunate demands which this politeness made on it was spent in admiration of whatever her ladyship was doing, if she happened to be doing anything, or in taking patterns of some elegant new dress in which her appearance the day before had thrown them into unceasing delight. Fortunately for those who pay their court through such foibles, a fond mother, though in pursuit of praise for her children, the most rapacious of human beings, is likewise the most credulous; her demands are exorbitant; but she will swallow anything; and the excessive affection and endurance of the Miss Steeles towards her offspring were viewed therefore by Lady Middleton without the smallest surprise or distrust. She saw with maternal complacency all the impertinent incroachments and mischievous tricks to which her cousins submitted. She saw their sashes untied, their hair pulled about their ears, their work-bags searched, and their knives and scissors stolen away, and felt no doubt of its being a reciprocal enjoyment. It suggested no other surprise than that Elinor and Marianne should sit so composedly by, without claiming a share in what was passing.

"John is in such spirits to-day!" said she, on his taking Miss Steele's pocket handkerchief and throwing it out of window. "He is full of monkey tricks."

And soon afterwards, on the second boy's violently pinching one of the same lady's fingers, she fondly observed, "How playful William is!"

"And here is my sweet little Annamaria," she added, tenderly caressing a little girl of three years old, who had not made a noise for the last two minutes; "And she is always so gentle and quiet. Never was there such a quiet little thing!"

But unfortunately in bestowing these embraces, a pin in her ladyship's head-dress, slightly scratching the child's neck, produced from this pattern of gentleness such violent screams as could hardly be outdone by any creature professedly noisy. The mother's consternation was excessive; but it could not surpass the alarm of the Miss Steeles, and everything was done by all three, in so critical an emergency, which affection could suggest as likely to assuage the agonies of the little sufferer. She was seated in her mother's lap, covered with kisses, her wound bathed with lavender-water, by one of the Miss Steeles, who was on her knees to attend her, and her mouth stuffed with sugar plums by the other. With such a reward for her tears, the child was too wise to cease crying. She still screamed and sobbed lustily, kicked her two brothers for offering to touch her, and all their united soothings were ineffectual till Lady Middleton luckily remembering that in a scene of similar distress last week some apricot marmalade had been successfully applied for a bruised temple, the same remedy was eagerly proposed for this unfortunate scratch, and a slight intermission of screams in the young lady on hearing it gave them reason to hope that it would not be rejected. She was carried out of the room therefore in her mother's arms in quest of this medicine, and as the two boys chose to follow, though earnestly entreated by their mother to stay behind, the four young ladies were left in a quietness which the room had not known for many hours.

"Poor little creature!" said Miss Steele as soon as they were gone. "It might have been a very sad accident."

"Yet I hardly know how," cried Marianne, "unless it had been under totally different circumstances. But this is the usual way of heightening alarm, where there is nothing to be alarmed at in reality."

"What a sweet woman Lady Middleton is!" said Lucy Steele.

Marianne was silent; it was impossible for her to say what she did not feel, however trivial the occasion; and upon Elinor, therefore, the whole task of telling lies when politeness required it always fell. She did her best when thus called on by speaking of Lady Middleton with more warmth than she felt, though with far less than Miss Lucy.

"And Sir John too," cried the elder sister, "what a charming man he is!"

Here too Miss Dashwood's commendation, being only simple and just, came in without any éclat. She merely observed that he was perfectly good-humoured and friendly.

"And what a charming little family they have! I never saw such fine children in my life. I declare I quite dote upon them already, and indeed I am always distractedly fond of children."

"I should guess so," said Elinor with a smile, "from what I have witnessed this morning."

"I have a notion," said Lucy, "you think the little Middletons rather too much indulged; perhaps they may be the outside of enough; but it is so natural in Lady Middleton; and for my part, I love to see children full of life and spirits; I cannot bear them if they are tame and quiet."

"I confess," replied Elinor, "that while I am at Barton Park, I never think of tame and quiet children with any abhorrence."

A short pause succeeded this speech, which was first broken by Miss Steele, who seemed very much disposed for conversation, and who now said rather abruptly, "And how do you like Devonshire, Miss Dashwood? I suppose you were very sorry to leave Sussex."

In some surprise at the familiarity of this question, or at least of the manner in which it was spoken, Elinor replied that she was.

"Norland is a prodigious beautiful place, is not it?" added Miss Steele.

"We have heard Sir John admire it excessively," said Lucy, who seemed to think some apology necessary for the freedom of her sister.

"I think everyone *must* admire it," replied Elinor, "who ever saw the place; though it is not to be supposed that anyone can estimate its beauties as we do."

"And had you a great many smart beaux there? I suppose

you have not so many in this part of the world; for my part, I think they are a vast addition always."

"But why should you think," said Lucy, looking ashamed of her sister, "that there are not as many genteel young men in Devonshire as Sussex?"

"Nay, my dear, I'm sure I don't pretend to say that there an't. I'm sure there's a vast many smart beaux in Exeter; but you know, how could I tell what smart beaux there might be about Norland; and I was only afraid the Miss Dashwoods might find it dull at Barton if they had not so many as they used to have. But perhaps you young ladies may not care about the beaux and had as lief be without them as with them. For my part, I think they are vastly agreeable, provided they dress smart and behave civil. But I can't bear to see them dirty and nasty. Now there's Mr. Rose at Exeter, a prodigious smart young man, quite a beau, clerk to Mr. Simpson you know; and yet if you do but meet him of a morning, he is not fit to be seen. I suppose your brother was quite a beau, Miss Dashwood, before he married, as he was so rich?"

"Upon my word," replied Elinor, "I cannot tell you, for I do not perfectly comprehend the meaning of the word. But this I can say, that if he ever was a beau before he married, he is one still, for there is not the smallest alteration in him."

"Oh! dear! One never thinks of married men's being beaux; they have something else to do."

"Lord! Anne," cried her sister, "you can talk of nothing but beaux; you will make Miss Dashwood believe you think of nothing else." And then to turn the discourse, she began admiring the house and the furniture.

This specimen of the Miss Steeles was enough. The vulgar freedom and folly of the eldest left her no recommendation, and as Elinor was not blinded by the beauty of the shrewd look of the youngest to her want of real elegance and artlessness, she left the house without any wish of knowing them better.

Not so, the Miss Steeles. They came from Exeter well provided with admiration for the use of Sir John Middleton, his family, and all his relations, and no niggardly proportion was now dealt out to his fair cousins, whom they declared to be the most beautiful, elegant, accomplished, and agreeable girls they had ever beheld, and with whom they were particularly anxious to be better acquainted. And to be better ac-

quainted, therefore, Elinor soon found, was their inevitable
lot, for as Sir John was entirely on the side of the Miss
Steeles, their party would be too strong for opposition, and
that kind of intimacy must be submitted to which consists of
sitting an hour or two together in the same room almost every day. Sir John could do no more; but he did not know that
any more was required; to be together was, in his opinion,
to be intimate, and while his continual schemes for their
meeting were effectual, he had not a doubt of their being established friends.

To do him justice, he did everything in his power to promote their unreserve by making the Miss Steeles acquainted
with whatever he knew or supposed of his cousins' situations in the most delicate particulars; and Elinor had not
seen them more than twice, before the eldest of them wished
her joy on her sister's having been so lucky as to make a
conquest of a very smart beau since she came to Barton.

" 'Twill be a fine thing to have her married so young to be
sure," said she, "and I hear he is quite a beau and prodigious
handsome. And I hope you may have as good luck yourself
soon, but perhaps you may have a friend in the corner already."

Elinor could not suppose that Sir John would be more nice
in proclaiming his suspicions of her regard for Edward than
he had been with respect to Marianne; indeed it was rather
his favourite joke of the two, as being somewhat newer and
more conjectural; and since Edward's visit, they had never
dined together without his drinking to her best affections
with so much significancy and so many nods and winks as
to excite general attention. The letter *F* had been likewise invariably brought forward and found productive of such
countless jokes that its character as the wittiest letter in the
alphabet had been long established with Elinor.

The Miss Steeles, as she expected, had now all the benefit
of these jokes, and in the eldest of them they raised a curiosity to know the name of the gentleman alluded to, which,
though often impertinently expressed, was perfectly of a
piece with her general inquisitiveness into the concerns of
their family. But Sir John did not sport long with the curiosity which he delighted to raise, for he had at least as much
pleasure in telling the name as Miss Steele had in hearing it.

"His name is Ferrars," said he in a very audible whisper;
"but pray do not tell it, for it's a great secret."

"Ferrars!" repeated Miss Steele; "Mr. Ferrars is the happy man, is he? What! Your sister-in-law's brother, Miss Dashwood? A very agreeable young man to be sure; I know him very well."

"How can you say so, Anne?" cried Lucy, who generally made an amendment to all her sister's assertions. "Though we have seen him once or twice at my uncle's, it is rather too much to pretend to know him very well."

Elinor heard all this with attention and surprise. "And who was this uncle? Where did he live? How came they acquainted?" She wished very much to have the subject continued, though she did not choose to join in it herself; but nothing more of it was said, and for the first time in her life, she thought Mrs. Jennings deficient either in curiosity after petty information or in a disposition to communicate it. The manner in which Miss Steele had spoken of Edward increased her curiosity; for it struck her as being rather ill-natured, and suggested the suspicion of that lady's knowing, or fancying herself to know, something to his disadvantage. But her curiosity was unavailing, for no further notice was taken of Mr. Ferrars's name by Miss Steele when alluded to or even openly mentioned by Sir John.

Chapter 22

MARIANNE, who had never much toleration for anything like impertinence, vulgarity, inferiority of parts, or even difference of taste from herself, was at this time particularly ill-disposed from the state of her spirits to be pleased with the Miss Steeles, or to encourage their advances; and to the invariable coldness of her behaviour towards them, which checked every endeavour at intimacy on their side, Elinor principally attributed that preference of herself which soon became evident in the manners of both, but especially of Lucy, who missed no opportunity of engaging her in conversation or of striving to improve their acquaintance by an easy and frank communication of her sentiments.

Lucy was naturally clever; her remarks were often just and amusing; and as a companion for half an hour Elinor frequently found her agreeable; but her powers had received no aid from education: she was ignorant and illiterate, and her deficiency of all mental improvement, her want of information in the most common particulars, could not be concealed from Miss Dashwood in spite of her constant endeavour to appear to advantage. Elinor saw and pitied her for the neglect of abilities which education might have rendered so respectable; but she saw, with less tenderness of feeling, the thorough want of delicacy, of rectitude, and integrity of mind, which her attentions, her assiduities, her flatteries at the park betrayed; and she could have no lasting satisfaction in the company of a person who joined insincerity with ignorance, whose want of instruction prevented their meeting in conversation on terms of equality, and whose conduct towards others made every show of attention and deference towards herself perfectly valueless.

"You will think my question an odd one, I dare say," said Lucy to her one day as they were walking together from the park to the cottage; "but, pray, are you personally acquainted with your sister-in-law's mother, Mrs. Ferrars?"

Elinor *did* think the question a very odd one, and her countenance expressed it as she answered that she had never seen Mrs. Ferrars.

"Indeed!" replied Lucy; "I wonder at that, for I thought you must have seen her at Norland sometimes. Then perhaps you cannot tell me what sort of a woman she is?"

"No," returned Elinor, cautious of giving her real opinion of Edward's mother, and not very desirous of satisfying what seemed impertinent curiosity; "I know nothing of her."

"I am sure you think me very strange for inquiring about her in such a way," said Lucy, eyeing Elinor attentively as she spoke, "but perhaps there may be reasons— I wish I might venture; but, however, I hope you will do me the justice of believing that I do not mean to be impertinent."

Elinor made her a civil reply, and they walked on for a few minutes in silence. It was broken by Lucy, who renewed the subject again by saying with some hesitation, "I cannot bear to have you think me impertinently curious. I am sure I would rather do anything in the world than be thought so by a person whose good opinion is so well worth having as yours. And I am sure I should not have the smallest fear of trusting *you*; indeed I should be very glad of your advice how to manage in such an uncomfortable situation as I am;

but, however, there is no occasion to trouble *you*. I am sorry you do not happen to know Mrs. Ferrars."

"I am sorry I do *not*," said Elinor in great astonishment, "if it could be of any use to *you* to know my opinion of her. But really, I never understood that you were at all connected with that family, and therefore I am a little surprised, I confess, at so serious an inquiry into her character."

"I dare say you are, and I am sure I do not at all wonder at it. But if I dared tell you all, you would not be so much surprised. Mrs. Ferrars is certainly nothing to me at present, but the time *may* come—how soon it will come must depend upon herself—when we may be very intimately connected."

She looked down as she said this, amiably bashful, with only one side glance at her companion to observe its effect on her.

"Good heavens!" cried Elinor, "what do you mean? Are you acquainted with Mr. Robert Ferrars? Can you be?" And she did not feel much delighted with the idea of such a sister-in-law.

"No," replied Lucy, "not to Mr. *Robert* Ferrars. I never saw him in my life; but," fixing her eyes upon Elinor, "to his elder brother."

What felt Elinor at that moment? Astonishment that would have been as painful as it was strong had not an immediate disbelief of the assertion attended it. She turned towards Lucy in silent amazement, unable to divine the reason or object of such a declaration, and though her complexion varied, she stood firm in incredulity and felt in no danger of an hysterical fit or a swoon.

"You may well be surprised," continued Lucy; "for to be sure you could have had no idea of it before; for I dare say he never dropped the smallest hint of it to you or any of your family; because it was always meant to be a great secret, and I am sure has been faithfully kept so by me to this hour. Not a soul of all my relations know of it but Anne, and I never should have mentioned it to you if I had not felt the greatest dependence in the world upon your secrecy; and I really thought my behaviour in asking so many questions about Mrs. Ferrars must seem so odd that it ought to be explained. And I do not think Mr. Ferrars can be displeased when he knows I have trusted you, because I know he has the highest opinion in the world of all your family, and looks upon yourself and the other Miss Dashwoods quite as his own sisters." She paused.

Elinor for a few moments remained silent. Her astonishment at what she heard was at first too great for words; but at length forcing herself to speak, and to speak cautiously, she said with a calmness of manner which tolerably well concealed her surprise and solicitude, "May I ask if your engagement is of long standing?"

"We have been engaged these four years."

"Four years!"

"Yes."

Elinor, though greatly shocked, still felt unable to believe it.

"I did not know," said she, "that you were even acquainted till the other day."

"Our acquaintance, however, is of many years date. He was under my uncle's care, you know, a considerable while."

"Your uncle!"

"Yes, Mr. Pratt. Did you never hear him talk of Mr. Pratt?"

"I think I have," replied Elinor, with an exertion of spirits which increased with her increase of emotion.

"He was four years with my uncle, who lives at Longstaple, near Plymouth. It was there our acquaintance began, for my sister and me was often staying with my uncle, and it was there our engagement was formed, though not till a year after he had quitted as a pupil; but he was almost always with us afterwards. I was very unwilling to enter into it, as you may imagine, without the knowledge and approbation of his mother; but I was too young and loved him too well to be so prudent as I ought to have been. Though you do not know him so well as me, Miss Dashwood, you must have seen enough of him to be sensible he is very capable of making a woman sincerely attached to him."

"Certainly," answered Elinor, without knowing what she said; but after a moment's reflection she added, with revived security of Edward's honour and love and her companion's falsehood, "Engaged to Mr. Edward Ferrars! I confess myself so totally surprised at what you tell me that really—I beg your pardon; but surely there must be some mistake of person or name. We cannot mean the same Mr. Ferrars."

"We can mean no other," cried Lucy, smiling. "Mr. Edward Ferrars, the eldest son of Mrs. Ferrars of Park Street, and brother of your sister-in-law, Mrs. John Dashwood, is the person I mean; you must allow that *I* am not likely to be deceived as to the name of the man on who all my happiness depends."

"It is strange," replied Elinor in a most painful perplexity, "that I should never have heard him even mention your name."

"No. Considering our situation, it was not strange. Our first care has been to keep the matter secret. You knew nothing of me or my family, and therefore there could be no *occasion* for ever mentioning my name to you, and as he was always particularly afraid of his sister's suspecting anything, *that* was reason enough for his not mentioning it."

She was silent. Elinor's security sank; but her self-command did not sink with it.

"Four years you have been engaged," said she with a firm voice.

"Yes, and heaven knows how much longer we may have to wait. Poor Edward! It puts him quite out of heart." Then taking a small miniature from her pocket, she added, "To prevent the possibility of mistake, be so good as to look at this face. It does not do him justice to be sure, but yet I think you cannot be deceived as to the person it was drew for. I have had it above these three years."

She put it into her hands as she spoke, and when Elinor saw the painting, whatever other doubts her fear of a too hasty decision or her wish of detecting falsehood might suffer to linger in her mind, she could have none of its being Edward's face. She returned it almost instantly, acknowledging the likeness.

"I have never been able," continued Lucy, "to give him my picture in return, which I am very much vexed at, for he has been always so anxious to get it! But I am determined to sit for it the very first opportunity."

"You are quite in the right," replied Elinor calmly. They then proceeded a few paces in silence. Lucy spoke first.

"I am sure," said she, "I have no doubt in the world of your faithfully keeping this secret, because you must know of what importance it is to us not to have it reach his mother; for she would never approve of it, I dare say. I shall have no fortune, and I fancy she is an exceeding proud woman."

"I certainly did not seek your confidence," said Elinor;

"but you do me no more than justice in imagining that I may be depended on. Your secret is safe with me, but pardon me if I express some surprise at so unnecessary a communication. You must at least have felt that my being acquainted with it could not add to its safety."

As she said this, she looked earnestly at Lucy, hoping to discover something in her countenance, perhaps the falsehood of the greatest part of what she had been saying; but Lucy's countenance suffered no change.

"I was afraid you would think I was taking a great liberty with you," said she, "in telling you all this. I have not known you long to be sure, personally at least, but I have known you and all your family by description a great while; and as soon as I saw you, I felt almost as if you was an old acquaintance. Besides in the present case I really thought some explanation was due to you after my making such particular inquiries about Edward's mother; and I am so unfortunate that I have not a creature whose advice I can ask. Anne is the only person that knows of it, and she has no judgment at all; indeed she does me a great deal more harm than good, for I am in constant fear of her betraying me. She does not know how to hold her tongue, as you must perceive, and I am sure I was in the greatest fright in the world t'other day when Edward's name was mentioned by Sir John, lest she should out with it all. You can't think how much I go through in my mind from it altogether. I only wonder that I am alive after what I have suffered for Edward's sake these last four years. Everything in such suspense and uncertainty, and seeing him so seldom—we can hardly meet above twice a year. I am sure I wonder my heart is not quite broke."

Here she took out her handkerchief, but Elinor did not feel very compassionate.

"Sometimes," continued Lucy after wiping her eyes, "I think whether it would not be better for us both to break off the matter entirely." As she said this, she looked directly at her companion. "But then at other times I have not resolution enough for it. I cannot bear the thoughts of making him so miserable as I know the very mention of such a thing would do. And on my own account too—so dear as he is to me—I don't think I could be equal to it. What would you advise me to do in such a case, Miss Dashwood? What would you do yourself?"

"Pardon me," replied Elinor, startled by the question, "but

I can give you no advice under such circumstances. Your
own judgment must direct you."

"To be sure," continued Lucy after a few minutes silence
on both sides, "his mother must provide for him sometime
or other, but poor Edward is so cast down about it! Did not
you think him dreadful low-spirited when he was at Barton?
He was so miserable when he left us at Longstaple, to go to
you, that I was afraid you would think him quite ill."

"Did he come from your uncle's then, when he visited
us?"

"Oh! yes, he had been staying a fortnight with us. Did you
think he came directly from town?"

"No," replied Elinor, most feelingly sensible of every
fresh circumstance in favour of Lucy's veracity; "I remember he told us that he had been staying a fortnight with some
friends near Plymouth." She remembered too her own surprise at the time, at his mentioning nothing further of those
friends, at his total silence with respect even to their names.

"Did not you think him sadly out of spirits?" repeated
Lucy.

"We did indeed, particularly so when he first arrived."

"I begged him to exert himself for fear you should suspect
what was the matter; but it made him so melancholy, not being able to stay more than a fortnight with us and seeing me
so much affected. Poor fellow! I am afraid it is just the same
with him now, for he writes in wretched spirits. I heard from
him just before I left Exeter," taking a letter from her pocket
and carelessly showing the direction to Elinor. "You know
his hand, I dare say, a charming one it is; but that is not written so well as usual. He was tired, I dare say, for he had just
filled the sheet to me as full as possible."

Elinor saw that it *was* his hand, and she could doubt no
longer. The picture, she had allowed herself to believe,
might have been accidentally obtained; it might not have
been Edward's gift; but a correspondence between them by
letter could subsist only under a positive engagement, could
be authorized by nothing else; for a few moments she was
almost overcome—her heart sank within her, and she could
hardly stand; but exertion was indispensably necessary, and
she struggled so resolutely against the oppression of her
feelings that her success was speedy and for the time complete.

"Writing to each other," said Lucy, returning the letter

into her pocket, "is the only comfort we have in such long separations. Yes, *I* have one other comfort in his picture; but poor Edward has not even *that*. If he had but my picture, he says he should be easy. I gave him a lock of my hair set in a ring when he was at Longstaple last, and that was some comfort to him, he said, but not equal to a picture. Perhaps you might notice the ring when you saw him?"

"I did," said Elinor with a composure of voice under which was concealed an emotion and distress beyond anything she had ever felt before. She was mortified, shocked, confounded.

Fortunately for her, they had now reached the cottage, and the conversation could be continued no further. After sitting with them a few minutes, the Miss Steeles returned to the park, and Elinor was then at liberty to think and be wretched.

VOLUME II

Chapter 1

HOWEVER SMALL Elinor's general dependence on Lucy's veracity might be, it was impossible for her on serious reflection to suspect it in the present case, where no temptation could be answerable to the folly of inventing a falsehood of such a description. What Lucy had asserted to be true, therefore, Elinor could not, dared not longer doubt, supported as it was too on every side by such probabilities and proofs, and contradicted by nothing but her own wishes. Their opportunity of acquaintance in the house of Mr. Pratt was a foundation for the rest, at once indisputable and alarming; and Edward's visit near Plymouth, his melancholy state of mind, his dissatisfaction at his own prospects, his uncertain behaviour towards herself, the intimate knowledge of the Miss Steeles as to Norland and their family connections, which had often surprised her, the picture, the letter, the ring, formed altogether such a body of evidence as overcame every fear of condemning him unfairly, and established as a fact, which no partiality could set aside, his ill-treatment of herself. Her resentment of such behaviour, her indignation at having been its dupe, for a short time made her feel only for herself; but other ideas, other considerations soon arose. Had Edward been intentionally deceiving her? Had he feigned a regard for her which he did not feel? Was his engagement to Lucy an engagement of the heart? No, whatever it might once have been, she could not believe it such at present. His affection was all her own. She could not be deceived in that. Her mother, sisters, Fanny, all had been conscious of his regard for her at Norland; it was not an illusion of her own vanity. He certainly loved her. What a softener of the heart was this persuasion! How much could it not tempt her to forgive! He had been blameable, highly blameable, in remaining at Norland after he first felt her influence over him to be more than it ought to be. In that he could not be defended; but if he had injured her, how much more had he injured himself; if her case were pitiable, his was hopeless. His imprudence had made her miserable for a while; but it seemed to have deprived himself of all chance of ever being otherwise. She might in time regain tranquillity; but *he,* what had he to look forward to? Could he ever be tolerably happy with Lucy Steele? Could he, were his affection for herself out of the question, with his integrity, his delicacy, and well-informed mind, be satisfied with a wife like her: illiterate, artful, and selfish?

The youthful infatuation of nineteen would naturally blind him to everything but her beauty and good nature; but the four succeeding years—years which if rationally spent give such improvement to the understanding—must have opened his eyes to her defects of education; while the same period of time, spent on her side in inferior society and more frivolous pursuits, had perhaps robbed her of that simplicity which might once have given an interesting character to her beauty.

If in the supposition of his seeking to marry herself his difficulties from his mother had seemed great, how much greater were they now likely to be when the object of his engagement was undoubtedly inferior in connections and probably inferior in fortune to herself. These difficulties, indeed, with a heart so alienated from Lucy, might not press very hard upon his patience; but melancholy was the state of the person by whom the expectation of family opposition and unkindness could be felt as a relief!

As these considerations occurred to her in painful succession, she wept for him more than for herself. Supported by the conviction of having done nothing to merit her present unhappiness and consoled by the belief that Edward had done nothing to forfeit her esteem, she thought she could even now, under the first smart of the heavy blow, command herself enough to guard every suspicion of the truth from her mother and sisters. And so well was she able to answer her own expectations that when she joined them at dinner only two hours after she had first suffered the extinction of all her dearest hopes, no one would have supposed from the appearance of the sisters that Elinor was mourning in secret over obstacles which must divide her forever from the object of her love and that Marianne was internally dwelling on the perfections of a man of whose whole heart she felt thoroughly possessed, and whom she expected to see in every carriage which drove near their house.

The necessity of concealing from her mother and Marianne what had been entrusted in confidence to herself, though it obliged her to unceasing exertion, was no aggravation of Elinor's distress. On the contrary it was a relief to her to be spared the communication of what would give such affliction to them, and to be saved likewise from hearing that condemnation of Edward which would probably flow from the excess of their partial affection for herself, and which was more than she felt equal to support.

From their counsel or their conversation she knew she could receive no assistance; their tenderness and sorrow must add to her distress, while her self-command would neither receive encouragement from their example nor from their praise. She was stronger alone, and her own good sense so well supported her that her firmness was as unshaken, her appearance of cheerfulness as invariable, as with regrets so poignant and so fresh, it was possible for them to be.

Much as she had suffered from her first conversation with Lucy on the subject, she soon felt an earnest wish of renewing it; and this for more reasons than one. She wanted to hear many particulars of their engagement repeated again; she wanted more clearly to understand what Lucy really felt for Edward, whether there were any sincerity in her declaration of tender regard for him; and she particularly wanted to convince Lucy, by her readiness to enter on the matter again and her calmness in conversing on it, that she was no otherwise interested in it than as a friend, which she very much feared her involuntary agitation in their morning discourse must have left at least doubtful. That Lucy was disposed to be jealous of her appeared very probable; it was plain that Edward had always spoken highly in her praise, not merely from Lucy's assertion but from her venturing to trust her on so short a personal acquaintance with a secret so confessedly and evidently important. And even Sir John's joking intelligence must have had some weight. But indeed, while Elinor remained so well assured within herself of being really beloved by Edward, it required no other consideration of probabilities to make it natural that Lucy should be jealous; and that she was so, her very confidence was a proof. What other reason for the disclosure of the affair could there be but that Elinor might be informed by it of Lucy's superior claims on Edward and be taught to avoid him in future? She had little difficulty in understanding thus much of her rival's intentions; and while she was firmly resolved to act by her as every principle of honour and honesty directed, to combat her own affection for Edward and to see him as little as possible, she could not deny herself the comfort of endeavouring to convince Lucy that her heart was unwounded. And as she could now have nothing more painful to hear on the subject than had already been told, she did not mistrust her own ability of going through a repetition of particulars with composure.

But it was not immediately that an opportunity of doing so could be commanded, though Lucy was as well disposed as herself to take advantage of any that occurred; for the weather was not often fine enough to allow of their joining in a walk, where they might most easily separate themselves from the others; and though they met at least every other evening either at the park or cottage, and chiefly at the former, they could not be supposed to meet for the sake of conversation. Such a thought would never enter either Sir John or Lady Middleton's head, and therefore very little leisure was ever given for general chat, and none at all for particular discourse. They met for the sake of eating, drinking, and laughing together, playing at cards, or consequences, or any other game that was sufficiently noisy.

One or two meetings of this kind had taken place without affording Elinor any chance of engaging Lucy in private when Sir John called at the cottage one morning to beg in the name of charity that they would all dine with Lady Middleton that day, as he was obliged to attend the club at Exeter, and she would otherwise be quite alone except her mother and the two Miss Steeles. Elinor, who foresaw a fairer opening for the point she had in view in such a party as this was likely to be, more at liberty among themselves under the tranquil and well-bred direction of Lady Middleton than when her husband united them together in one noisy purpose, immediately accepted the invitation; Margaret, with her mother's permission, was equally compliant, and Marianne, though always unwilling to join any of their parties, was persuaded by her mother, who could not bear to have her seclude herself from any chance of amusement, to go likewise.

The young ladies went, and Lady Middleton was happily preserved from the frightful solitude which had threatened her. The insipidity of the meeting was exactly such as Elinor had expected; it produced not one novelty of thought or expression, and nothing could be less interesting than the whole of their discourse both in the dining parlour and drawing-room: to the latter, the children accompanied them, and while they remained there she was too well convinced of the impossibility of engaging Lucy's attention to attempt it. They quitted it only with the removal of the tea-things. The card-table was then placed, and Elinor began to wonder at herself for having ever entertained a hope of finding time for conversation at the park. They all rose up in preparation for a round game.

"I am glad," said Lady Middleton to Lucy, "you are not going to finish poor little Annamaria's basket this evening; for I am sure it must hurt your eyes to work fillagree by candlelight. And we will make the dear little love some amends for her disappointment to-morrow, and then I hope she will not much mind it."

This hint was enough; Lucy recollected herself instantly and replied, "Indeed you are very much mistaken, Lady Middleton; I am only waiting to know whether you can make your party without me or I should have been at my fillagree already. I would not disappoint the little angel for all the world, and if you want me at the card-table now, I am resolved to finish the basket after supper."

"You are very good; I hope it won't hurt your eyes. Will you ring the bell for some working-candles? My poor little girl would be sadly disappointed, I know, if the basket was not finished to-morrow, for though I told her it certainly would not, I am sure she depends upon having it done."

Lucy directly drew her work table near her and reseated herself with an alacrity and cheerfulness which seemed to infer that she could taste no greater delight than in making a fillagree basket for a spoiled child.

Lady Middleton proposed a rubber of Casino to the others. No one made any objection but Marianne, who, with her usual inattention to the forms of general civility, exclaimed, "Your ladyship will have the goodness to excuse *me;* you know I detest cards. I shall go to the pianoforte; I have not

touched it since it was tuned." And without further ceremony, she turned away and walked to the instrument.

Lady Middleton looked as if she thanked heaven that *she*
had never made so rude a speech.

"Marianne can never keep long from that instrument you
know, ma'am," said Elinor, endeavouring to smooth away
the offence; "and I do not much wonder at it, for it is the
very best toned pianoforte I ever heard."

The remaining five were now to draw their cards.

"Perhaps," continued Elinor, "if I should happen to cut
out, I may be of some use to Miss Lucy Steele in rolling her
papers for her; and there is so much still to be done to the
basket that it must be impossible I think for her labour sin-
gly to finish it this evening. I should like the work exceedingly if she would allow me a share in it."

"Indeed I shall be very much obliged to you for your
help," cried Lucy, "for I find there is more to be done to it
than I thought there was; and it would be a shocking thing
to disappoint dear Annamaria after all."

"Oh! that would be terrible indeed," said Miss Steele.
"Dear little soul, how I do love her!"

"You are very kind," said Lady Middleton to Elinor; "and
as you really like the work, perhaps you will be as well
pleased not to cut in till another rubber, or will you take
your chance now?"

Elinor joyfully profited by the first of these proposals; and
thus, by a little of that address which Marianne could never
condescend to practise, gained her own end and pleased
Lady Middleton at the same time. Lucy made room for her
with ready attention, and the two fair rivals were thus seated
side by side at the same table, and with the utmost harmony
engaged in forwarding the same work. The pianoforte, at
which Marianne, wrapped up in her own music and her own
thoughts, had by this time forgotten that anybody was in the
room besides herself, was luckily so near them, that Miss
Dashwood now judged she might safely, under the shelter of
its noise, introduce the interesting subject without any risk
of being heard at the card-table.

Chapter 2

IN A FIRM though cautious tone, Elinor thus began.

"I should be undeserving of the confidence you have honoured me with if I felt no desire for its continuance or no further curiosity on its subject. I will not apologize, therefore, for bringing it forward again."

"Thank you," cried Lucy warmly, "for breaking the ice; you have set my heart at ease by it, for I was somehow or other afraid I had offended you by what I told you that Monday."

"Offended me! How could you suppose so? Believe me," and Elinor spoke it with the truest sincerity, "nothing could be farther from my intention than to give you such an idea. Could you have a motive for the trust that was not honourable and flattering to me?"

"And yet I do assure you," replied Lucy, her little sharp eyes full of meaning, "there seemed to me to be a coldness and displeasure in your manner that made me quite uncomfortable. I felt sure that you was angry with me; and have been quarrelling with myself ever since for having took such a liberty as to trouble you with my affairs. But I am very glad to find it was only my own fancy, and that you do not really blame me. If you knew what a consolation it was to me to relieve my heart by speaking to you of what I am always thinking of every moment of my life, your compassion would make you overlook everything else I am sure."

"Indeed I can easily believe that it was a very great relief to you to acknowledge your situation to me, and be assured that you shall never have reason to repent it. Your case is a very unfortunate one; you seem to me to be surrounded with difficulties, and you will have need of all your mutual affection to support you under them. Mr. Ferrars, I believe, is entirely dependent on his mother."

"He has only two thousand pounds of his own; it would be madness to marry upon that, though for my own part, I could give up every prospect of more without a sigh. I have been always used to a very small income and could struggle with any poverty for him; but I love him too well to be the selfish means of robbing him, perhaps, of all that his mother might give him if he married to please her. We must wait, if may be, for many years. With almost every other man in the world, it would be an alarming prospect; but Edward's affection and constancy nothing can deprive me of, I know."

"That conviction must be everything to you; and he is undoubtedly supported by the same trust in yours. If the strength of your reciprocal attachment had failed, as between many people and under many circumstances it naturally would during a four years' engagement, your situation would have been pitiable indeed."

Lucy here looked up, but Elinor was careful in guarding her countenance from every expression that could give her words a suspicious tendency.

"Edward's love for me," said Lucy, "has been pretty well put to the test by our long, very long absence since we were first engaged, and it has stood the trial so well that I should be unpardonable to doubt it now. I can safely say that he has never gave me one moment's alarm on that account from the first."

Elinor hardly knew whether to smile or sigh at this assertion.

Lucy went on. "I am rather of a jealous temper too by nature, and from our different situations in life, from his being so much more in the world than me, and our continual separation, I was enough inclined for suspicion to have found out the truth in an instant if there had been the slightest alteration in his behaviour to me when we met, or any lowness of spirits that I could not account for, or if he had talked more of one lady than another, or seemed in any respect less happy at Longstaple than he used to be. I do not mean to say that I am particularly observant or quick-sighted in general, but in such a case I am sure I could not be deceived."

"All this," thought Elinor, "is very pretty; but it can impose upon neither of us."

"But what," said she after a short silence, "are your views? Or have you none but that of waiting for Mrs. Ferrars's death, which is a melancholy and shocking extremity? Is her son determined to submit to this, and to all the tediousness of the many years of suspense in which it may involve you, rather than run the risk of her displeasure for a while by owning the truth?"

"If we could be certain that it would be only for a while! But Mrs. Ferrars is a very headstrong, proud woman, and in her first fit of anger upon hearing it would very likely secure everything to Robert, and the idea of that, for Edward's sake, frightens away all my inclination for hasty measures."

"And for your own sake too, or you are carrying your disinterestedness beyond reason."

Lucy looked at Elinor again and was silent.

"Do you know Mr. Robert Ferrars?" asked Elinor.

"Not at all. I never saw him; but I fancy he is very unlike his brother—silly and a great coxcomb."

"A great coxcomb!" repeated Miss Steele, whose ear had caught those words by a sudden pause in Marianne's music. "Oh! they are talking of their favourite beaux, I dare say."

"No, sister," cried Lucy, "you are mistaken there; our favourite beaux are *not* great coxcombs."

"I can answer for it that Miss Dashwood's is not," said Mrs. Jennings, laughing heartily; "for he is one of the modestest, prettiest behaved young men I ever saw; but as for Lucy, she is such a sly little creature there is no finding out who *she* likes."

"Oh!" cried Miss Steele, looking significantly round at them, "I dare say Lucy's beau is quite as modest and pretty behaved as Miss Dashwood's."

Elinor blushed in spite of herself. Lucy bit her lip and looked angrily at her sister. A mutual silence took place for some time. Lucy first put an end to it by saying in a lower tone, though Marianne was then giving them the powerful protection of a very magnificent concerto, "I will honestly tell you of one scheme which has lately come into my head for bringing matters to bear; indeed I am bound to let you into the secret, for you are a party concerned. I dare say you have seen enough of Edward to know that he would prefer the church to every other profession; now my plan is that he should take orders as soon as he can, and then through your interest, which I am sure you would be kind enough to use out of friendship for him and I hope out of some regard to me, your brother might be persuaded to give him Norland living, which I understand is a very good one, and the present incumbent not likely to live a great while. That would be enough for us to marry upon, and we might trust to time and chance for the rest."

"I should be always happy," replied Elinor, "to show any

mark of my esteem and friendship for Mr. Ferrars; but do
not you perceive that my interest on such an occasion would
be perfectly unnecessary? He is brother to Mrs. John
Dashwood—*that* must be recommendation enough to her
husband."

"But Mrs. John Dashwood would not much approve of
Edward's going into orders."

"Then I rather suspect that my interest would do very little."

They were again silent for many minutes. At length Lucy
exclaimed with a deep sigh, "I believe it would be the wisest
way to put an end to the business at once by dissolving the
engagement. We seem so beset with difficulties on every
side that though it would make us miserable for a time, we
should be happier perhaps in the end. But you will not give
me your advice, Miss Dashwood?"

"No," answered Elinor with a smile which concealed very
agitated feelings, "on such a subject I certainly will not. You
know very well that my opinion would have no weight with
you unless it were on the side of your wishes."

"Indeed you wrong me," replied Lucy with great solemnity; "I know nobody of whose judgment I think so highly
as I do of yours; and I do really believe that if you was to
say to me, 'I advise you by all means to put an end to your
engagement with Edward Ferrars, it will be more for the
happiness of both of you,' I should resolve upon doing it immediately."

Elinor blushed for the insincerity of Edward's future wife
and replied, "This compliment would effectually frighten me
from giving any opinion on the subject had I formed one. It
raises my influence much too high; the power of dividing
two people so tenderly attached is too much for an indifferent person."

"'Tis because you are an indifferent person," said Lucy
with some pique and laying a particular stress on those
words, "that your judgment might justly have such weight
with me. If you could be supposed to be biassed in any respect by your own feelings, your opinion would not be
worth having."

Elinor thought it wisest to make no answer to this, lest
they might provoke each other to an unsuitable increase of
ease and unreserve; and was even partly determined never to
mention the subject again. Another pause therefore of many

minutes' duration succeeded this speech, and Lucy was still the first to end it.

"Shall you be in town this winter, Miss Dashwood?" said she with all her accustomary complacency.

"Certainly not."

"I am sorry for that," returned the other while her eyes brightened at the information, "it would have gave me such pleasure to meet you there! But I dare say you will go for all that. To be sure, your brother and sister will ask you to come to them."

"It will not be in my power to accept their invitation if they do."

"How unlucky that is! I had quite depended upon meeting you there. Anne and me are to go the latter end of January to some relations who have been wanting us to visit them these several years! But I only go for the sake of seeing Edward. He will be there in February, otherwise London would have no charms for me; I have not spirits for it."

Elinor was soon called to the card-table by the conclusion of the first rubber, and the confidential discourse of the two ladies was therefore at an end, to which both of them submitted without any reluctance, for nothing had been said on either side to make them dislike each other less than they had done before; and Elinor sat down to the card-table with the melancholy persuasion that Edward was not only without affection for the person who was to be his wife but that he had not even the chance of being tolerably happy in marriage, which sincere affection on *her* side would have given; for self-interest alone could induce a woman to keep a man to an engagement of which she seemed so thoroughly aware that he was weary.

From this time the subject was never revived by Elinor; and when entered on by Lucy, who seldom missed an opportunity of introducing it and was particularly careful to inform her confidante of her happiness whenever she received a letter from Edward, it was treated by the former with calmness and caution, and dismissed as soon as civility would allow; for she felt such conversations to be an indulgence which Lucy did not deserve and which were dangerous to herself.

The visit of the Miss Steeles at Barton Park was lengthened far beyond what the first invitation implied. Their favour increased; they could not be spared; Sir John would not hear of their going; and in spite of their numerous and long-arranged engagements in Exeter, in spite of the absolute necessity of their returning to fulfil them immediately, which was in full force at the end of every week, they were prevailed on to stay nearly two months at the park and to assist in the due celebration of that festival which requires a more than ordinary share of private balls and large dinners to proclaim its importance.

Chapter 3

THOUGH MRS. JENNINGS was in the habit of spending a large portion of the year at the houses of her children and friends, she was not without a settled habitation of her own. Since the death of her husband, who had traded with success in a less elegant part of the town, she had resided every winter in a house in one of the streets near Portman Square. Towards this home she began on the approach of January to turn her thoughts, and thither she one day abruptly, and very unexpectedly by them, asked the elder Miss Dashwoods to accompany her. Elinor, without observing the varying complexion of her sister and the animated look which spoke no indifference to the plan, immediately gave a grateful but absolute denial for both, in which she believed herself to be speaking their united inclinations. The reason alleged was their determined resolution of not leaving their mother at that time of the year. Mrs. Jennings received the refusal with some surprise and repeated her invitation immediately.

"Oh! Lord, I am sure your mother can spare you very well, and I *do* beg you will favour me with your company, for I've quite set my heart upon it. Don't fancy that you will be any inconvenience to me, for I shan't put myself at all out of my way for you. It will only be sending Betty by the coach, and I hope I can afford *that*. We three shall be able to go very well in my chaise; and when we are in town if you do not like to go wherever I do, well and good, you may always go with one of my daughters. I am sure your mother will not object to it; for I have had such good luck in getting my own children off my hands that she will think me a very fit person to have the charge of you; and if I don't get one of you at least well married before I have done with you, it shall not be my fault. I shall speak a good word for you to all the young men, you may depend upon it."

"I have a notion," said Sir John, "that Miss Marianne would not object to such a scheme if her elder sister would come into it. It is very hard indeed that she should not have a little pleasure because Miss Dashwood does not wish it. So I would advise you two to set off for town when you are tired of Barton, without saying a word to Miss Dashwood about it."

"Nay," cried Mrs. Jennings, "I am sure I shall be monstrous glad of Miss Marianne's company, whether Miss Dashwood will go or not; only the more the merrier say I, and I thought it would be more comfortable for them to be together because if they got tired of me, they might talk to one another and laugh at my odd ways behind my back. But one or the other, if not both of them, I must have. Lord bless me! How do you think I can live poking by myself, I who have been always used till this winter to have Charlotte with me. Come, Miss Marianne, let us strike hands upon the bargain, and if Miss Dashwood will change her mind by-and-by, why so much the better."

"I thank you, ma'am, sincerely thank you," said Marianne with warmth; "your invitation has insured my gratitude forever, and it would give me such happiness, yes almost the greatest happiness I am capable of, to be able to accept it. But my mother, my dearest, kindest mother—I feel the justice of what Elinor has urged, and if she were to be made less happy, less comfortable by our absence—Oh! no, nothing should tempt me to leave her. It should not, must not be a struggle."

Mrs. Jennings repeated her assurance that Mrs. Dashwood could spare them perfectly well; and Elinor, who now understood her sister and saw to what indifference to almost everything else she was carried by her eagerness to be with Willoughby again, made no further direct opposition to the plan, and merely referred it to her mother's decisions, from whom, however, she scarcely expected to receive any support in her endeavour to prevent a visit which she could not approve of for Marianne, and which on her own account she had particular reasons to avoid. Whatever Marianne was desirous of, her mother would be eager to promote; she could not expect to influence the latter to cautiousness of conduct in an affair respecting which she had never been able to inspire her with distrust; and she dared not explain the motive of her own disinclination for going to London. That Marianne, fastidious as she was, thoroughly acquainted with Mrs. Jennings' manners, and invariably disgusted by them, should overlook every inconvenience of that kind, should disregard whatever must be most wounding to her irritable feelings, in her pursuit of one object, was such a proof, so strong, so full of the importance of that object to her, as Elinor, in spite of all that had passed, was not prepared to witness.

On being informed of the invitation, Mrs. Dashwood, persuaded that such an excursion would be productive of much amusement to both her daughters, and perceiving through all her affectionate attention to herself how much the heart of Marianne was in it, would not hear of their declining the offer upon *her* account; insisted on their both accepting it directly, and then began to foresee with her usual cheerfulness a variety of advantages that would accrue to them all from this separation.

"I am delighted with the plan," she cried; "it is exactly what I could wish. Margaret and I shall be as much benefited by it as yourselves. When you and the Middletons are gone, we shall go on so quietly and happily together with our books and our music! You will find Margaret so improved when you come back again! And I have a little plan of alteration for your bedrooms too, which may now be performed without inconvenience to anyone. It is very right that you *should* go to town; I would have every young woman of your condition in life acquainted with the manners and amusements of London. You will be under the care of a motherly good sort of woman, of whose kindness to you I can have no doubt. And in all probability you will see your brother, and whatever may be his faults or the faults of his wife, when I consider whose son he is, I cannot bear to have you so wholly estranged from each other."

"Though with your usual anxiety for our happiness," said Elinor, "you have been obviating every impediment to the present scheme which occurred to you, there is still one objection which, in my opinion, cannot be so easily removed."

Marianne's countenance sank.

"And what," said Mrs. Dashwood, "is my dear prudent Elinor going to suggest? What formidable obstacle is she now to bring forward? Do not let me hear a word about the expense of it."

"My objection is this: though I think very well of Mrs. Jennings' heart, she is not a woman whose society can afford us pleasure or whose protection will give us consequence."

"That is very true," replied her mother; "but of her society, separately from that of other people, you will scarcely have anything at all, and you will almost always appear in public with Lady Middleton."

"If Elinor is frightened away by her dislike of Mrs. Jennings," said Marianne, "at least it need not prevent *my* accepting her invitation. I have no such scruples, and I am sure I could put up with every unpleasantness of that kind with very little effort."

Elinor could not help smiling at this display of indifference towards the manners of a person to whom she had often had difficulty in persuading Marianne to behave with tolerable politeness: and resolved within herself that if her sister persisted in going, she would go likewise, as she did not think it proper that Marianne should be left to the sole guidance of her own judgment or that Mrs. Jennings should be abandoned to the mercy of Marianne for all the comfort of her domestic hours. To this determination she was the more easily reconciled by recollecting that Edward Ferrars, by Lucy's account, was not to be in town before February; and that their visit, without any unreasonable abridgment, might be previously finished.

"I will have you *both* go," said Mrs. Dashwood; "these objections are nonsensical. You will have much pleasure in being in London and especially in being together; and if Elinor would ever condescend to anticipate enjoyment, she would foresee it there from a variety of sources; she would perhaps expect some from improving her acquaintance with her sister-in-law's family."

Elinor had often wished for an opportunity of attempting to weaken her mother's dependence on the attachment of Edward and herself, that the shock might be the less when the whole truth were revealed, and now on this attack, though almost hopeless of success, she forced herself to begin her design by saying as calmly as she could, "I like Edward Ferrars very much and shall always be glad to see him, but as to the rest of the family, it is a matter of perfect indifference to me whether I am ever known to them or not."

Mrs. Dashwood smiled and said nothing. Marianne lifted up her eyes in astonishment, and Elinor conjectured that she might as well have held her tongue.

After very little further discourse, it was finally settled that the invitation should be fully accepted. Mrs. Jennings received the information with a great deal of joy and many assurances of kindness and care; nor was it a matter of pleasure merely to her. Sir John was delighted; for to a man whose prevailing anxiety was the dread of being alone, the acquisition of two to the number of inhabitants in London was something. Even Lady Middleton took the trouble of being delighted, which was putting herself rather out of her way; and as for the Miss Steeles, especially Lucy, they had never been so happy in their lives as this intelligence made them.

Elinor submitted to the arrangement which counteracted her wishes with less reluctance than she had expected to feel. With regard to herself, it was now a matter of unconcern whether she went to town or not, and when she saw her mother so thoroughly pleased with the plan, and her sister exhilarated by it in look, voice, and manner, restored to all her usual animation and elevated to more than her usual gaiety, she could not be dissatisfied with the cause and would hardly allow herself to distrust the consequence.

Marianne's joy was almost a degree beyond happiness, so great was the perturbation of her spirits and her impatience to be gone. Her unwillingness to quit her mother was her only restorative to calmness; and at the moment of parting, her grief on that score was excessive. Her mother's affliction was hardly less, and Elinor was the only one of the three who seemed to consider the separation as anything short of eternal.

Their departure took place in the first week in January. The Middletons were to follow in about a week. The Miss Steeles kept their station at the park and were to quit it only with the rest of the family.

Chapter 4

ELINOR COULD not find herself in the carriage with Mrs. Jennings, and beginning a journey to London under her protection and as her guest, without wondering at her own situation, so short had their acquaintance with that lady been, so wholly unsuited were they in age and disposition, and so many had been her objections against such a measure only a few days before! But these objections had all, with that happy ardour of youth which Marianne and her mother equally shared, been overcome or overlooked; and Elinor, in spite of every occasional doubt of Willoughby's constancy, could not witness the rapture of delightful expectation which filled the whole soul and beamed in the eyes of Marianne without feeling how blank was her own prospect, how cheerless her own state of mind in the comparison, and how gladly she would engage in the solicitude of Marianne's situation to have the same animating object in view, the same possibility of hope. A short, a very short time, however, must now decide what Willoughby's intentions were; in all probability he was already in town. Marianne's eagerness to be gone declared her dependence on finding him there; and Elinor was resolved not only upon gaining every new light as to his character which her own observation or the intelligence of others could give her, but likewise upon watching his behaviour to her sister with such zealous attention as to ascertain what he was and what he meant, before many meetings had taken place. Should the result of her observations be unfavourable, she was determined at all events to open the eyes of her sister; should it be otherwise, her exertions would be of a different nature—she must then learn to avoid every selfish comparison and banish every regret which might lessen her satisfaction in the happiness of Marianne.

They were three days on their journey, and Marianne's behaviour as they travelled was a happy specimen of what her future complaisance and companionableness to Mrs. Jennings might be expected to be. She sat in silence almost all the way, wrapped in her own meditations, and scarcely ever voluntarily speaking except when any object of picturesque beauty within their view drew from her an exclamation of delight exclusively addressed to her sister. To atone for this conduct therefore, Elinor took immediate possession of their post of civility which she had assigned herself, behaved with the greatest attention to Mrs. Jennings, talked with her, laughed with her, and listened to her whenever she could; and Mrs. Jennings on her side treated them both with all possible kindness, was solicitous on every occasion for their ease and enjoyment, and only disturbed that she could not make them choose their own dinners at the inn nor extort a confession of their preferring salmon to cod, or boiled fowls to veal cutlets. They reached town by three o'clock the third day, glad to be released after such a journey from the confinement of a carriage, and ready to enjoy all the luxury of a good fire.

The house was handsome and handsomely fitted up, and the young ladies were immediately put in possession of a very comfortable apartment. It had formerly been Charlotte's, and over the mantelpiece still hung a landscape in coloured silks of her performance, in proof of her having spent seven years at a great school in town to some effect.

As dinner was not to be ready in less than two hours from their arrival, Elinor determined to employ the interval in writing to her mother and sat down for that purpose. In a few moments Marianne did the same. "*I* am writing home, Marianne," said Elinor; "had not you better defer your letter for a day or two?"

"I am *not* going to write to my mother," replied Marianne hastily and as if wishing to avoid any further inquiry. Elinor said no more; it immediately struck her that she must then be writing to Willoughby, and the conclusion which as instantly followed was that however mysteriously they might wish to conduct the affair, they must be engaged. This conviction, though not entirely satisfactory, gave her pleasure, and she continued her letter with greater alacrity. Marianne's was finished in a very few minutes; in length it could be no more than a note: it was then folded up, sealed, and directed with eager rapidity. Elinor thought she could distinguish a large *W* in the direction, and no sooner was it complete than Marianne, ringing the bell, requested the footman who answered it to get that letter conveyed for her to the two-penny post. This decided the matter at once.

Her spirits still continued very high, but there was a flutter in them which prevented their giving much pleasure to her sister, and this agitation increased as the evening drew on. She could scarcely eat any dinner, and when they afterwards returned to the drawing-room, seemed anxiously listening to the sound of every carriage.

It was a great satisfaction to Elinor that Mrs. Jennings, by being much engaged in her own room, could see little of what was passing. The tea-things were brought in, and already had Marianne been disappointed more than once by a rap at a neighbouring door when a loud one was suddenly heard which could not be mistaken for one at any other house. Elinor felt secure of its announcing Willoughby's approach, and Marianne, starting up, moved towards the door. Everything was silent; this could not be borne many seconds; she opened the door, advanced a few steps towards the stairs, and after listening half a minute, returned into the room in all the agitation which a conviction of having heard him would naturally produce; in the ecstasy of her feelings at that instant she could not help exclaiming, "Oh! Elinor, it is Willoughby, indeed it is!" and seemed almost ready to throw herself into his arms, when Colonel Brandon appeared.

It was too great a shock to be borne with calmness, and she immediately left the room. Elinor was disappointed too; but at the same time her regard for Colonel Brandon ensured his welcome with her, and she felt particularly hurt that a man so partial to her sister should perceive that she experienced nothing but grief and disappointment in seeing him. She instantly saw that it was not unnoticed by him, that he even observed Marianne as she quitted the room, with such astonishment and concern as hardly left him the recollection of what civility demanded towards herself.

"Is your sister ill?" said he.

Elinor answered in some distress that she was, and then talked of headaches, low spirits, and over fatigues; and of everything to which she could decently attribute her sister's behaviour.

He heard her with the most earnest attention, but seeming to recollect himself, said no more on the subject, and began directly to speak of his pleasure at seeing them in London, making the usual inquiries about their journey and the friends they had left behind.

In this calm kind of way, with very little interest on either side, they continued to talk, both of them out of spirits, and the thoughts of both engaged elsewhere. Elinor wished very much to ask whether Willoughby were then in town, but she was afraid of giving him pain by an inquiry after his rival; and at length, by way of saying something, she asked if he had been in London ever since she had seen him last. "Yes," he replied with some embarrassment, "almost ever since; I have been once or twice at Delaford for a few days, but it has never been in my power to return to Barton."

This, and the manner in which it was said, immediately brought back to her remembrance all the circumstances to his quitting that place, with the uneasiness and suspicions they had caused to Mrs. Jennings, and she was fearful that her question had implied much more curiosity on the subject than she had ever felt.

Mrs. Jennings soon came in. "Oh! Colonel," said she with her usual noisy cheerfullness, "I am monstrous glad to see you—sorry I could not come before—beg your pardon, but I have been forced to look about me a little and settle my matters; for it is a long while since I have been at home, and you know one has always a world of little odd things to do after one has been away for any time; and then I have had Cartwright to settle with— Lord, I have been as busy as a bee ever since dinner! But pray, Colonel, how came you to conjure out that I should be in town to-day?"

"I had the pleasure of hearing it at Mr. Palmer's, where I have been dining."

"Oh! you did; well, and how do they all do at their house? How does Charlotte do? I warrant you she is a fine size by this time."

"Mrs. Palmer appeared quite well, and I am commissioned to tell you that you will certainly see her to-morrow."

"Aye, to be sure, I thought as much. Well, Colonel, I have brought two young ladies with me, you see—that is, you see but one of them now, but there is another somewhere. Your friend Miss Marianne, too—which you will not be sorry to hear. I do not know what you and Mr. Willoughby will do between you about her. Aye, it is a fine thing to be young and handsome—worse luck for me. However I got a very good husband, and I don't know what the greatest beauty can do more. Ah! Poor man! He has been dead these eight years and better. But Colonel, where have you been to since we parted? And how does your business go on? Come, come, let's have no secrets among friends."

He replied with his accustomary mildness to all her inquiries, but without satisfying her in any. Elinor now began to make the tea, and Marianne was obliged to appear again.

After her entrance, Colonel Brandon became more thoughtful and silent than he had been before, and Mrs. Jennings could not prevail on him to stay long. No other visitor appeared that evening, and the ladies were unanimous in agreeing to go early to bed.

Marianne rose the next morning with recovered spirits and happy looks. The disappointment of the evening before seemed forgotten in the expectation of what was to happen that day. They had not long finished their breakfast before Mrs. Palmer's barouche stopped at the door, and in a few minutes she came laughing into the room, so delighted to see them all that it was hard to say whether she received most pleasure from meeting her mother or the Miss Dashwoods again; so surprised at their coming to town, though it was what she had rather expected all along; so angry at their accepting her mother's invitation after having declined her own, though at the same time she would never have forgiven them if they had not come!

"Mr. Palmer will be so happy to see you," said she; "what do you think he said when he heard of your coming with mama? I forget what it was now, but it was something so droll!"

After an hour or two spent in what her mother called comfortable chat, or in other words, in every variety of inquiry concerning all their acquaintance on Mrs. Jennings's side, and in laughter without cause on Mrs. Palmer's, it was proposed by the latter that they should all accompany her to some shops where she had business that morning, to which Mrs. Jennings and Elinor readily consented, as having likewise some purchases to make themselves; and Marianne, though declining it at first, was induced to go likewise.

Wherever they went, she was evidently always on the watch. In Bond Street especially, where much of their business lay, her eyes were in constant inquiry; and in whatever shop the party were engaged, her mind was equally abstracted from everything actually before them, from all that interested and occupied the others. Restless and dissatisfied everywhere, her sister could never obtain her opinion of any article of purchase however it might equally concern them both; she received no pleasure from anything; was only impatient to be at home again, and could with difficulty govern her vexation at the tediousness of Mrs. Palmer, whose eye was caught by everything pretty, expensive, or new; who was wild to buy all, could determine on none, and dawdled away her time in rapture and indecision.

It was late in the morning before they returned home; and no sooner had they entered the house than Marianne flew eagerly upstairs, and when Elinor followed, she found her turning from the table with a sorrowful countenance which declared that no Willoughby had been there.

"Has no letter been left here for me since we went out?" she said to the footman who then entered with the parcels. She was answered in the negative. "Are you quite sure of it?" she replied. "Are you certain that no servant, no porter has left any letter or note?"

The man replied that none had.

"How very odd!" said she in a low and disappointed voice as she turned away to the window.

"How odd indeed!" repeated Elinor within herself, regarding her sister with uneasiness. "If she had not known him to be in town she would not have written to him as she did; she would have written to Combe Magna; and if he is in town, how odd that he should neither come nor write! Oh! my dear mother, you must be wrong in permitting an engagement between a daughter so young, a man so little known, to be carried on in so doubtful, so mysterious a manner! *I* long to inquire, but how will *my* interference be borne!"

She determined after some consideration that if appearances continued many days longer as unpleasant as they now were, she would represent in the strongest manner to her mother the necessity of some serious inquiry into the affair.

Mrs. Palmer and two elderly ladies of Mrs. Jennings's intimate acquaintance, whom she had met and invited in the morning, dined with them. The former left them soon after tea to fulfill her evening engagements, and Elinor was obliged to assist in making a whist-table for the others. Marianne was of no use on these occasions, as she would never learn the game, but though her time was therefore at her own disposal, the evening was by no means more productive of pleasure to her than to Elinor, for it was spent in all the anxiety of expectation and the pain of disappointment. She sometimes endeavoured for a few minutes to read; but the book was soon thrown aside, and she returned to the more interesting employment of walking backwards and forwards across the room, pausing for a moment whenever she came to the window in hopes of distinguishing the long-expected rap.

Chapter 5

"IF THIS open weather holds much longer," said Mrs. Jennings when they met at breakfast the following morning, "Sir John will not like leaving Barton next week; 'tis a sad thing for sportsmen to lose a day's pleasure. Poor souls! I always pity them when they do; they seem to take it so much to heart."

"That is true," cried Marianne in a cheerful voice, and walking to the window as she spoke to examine the day. "I had not thought of *that*. This weather will keep many sportsmen in the country."

It was a lucky recollection; all her good spirits were restored by it. "It is charming weather for *them* indeed," she continued as she sat down to the breakfast table with a happy countenance. "How much they must enjoy it! But" (with a little return of anxiety) "it cannot be expected to last long. At this time of year, and after such a series of rain, we shall certainly have very little more of it. Frosts will soon set in and in all probability with severity. In another day or two perhaps; this extreme mildness can hardly last longer— nay, perhaps it may freeze to-night!"

"At any rate," said Elinor, wishing to prevent Mrs. Jennings from seeing her sister's thoughts as clearly as she did, "I dare say we shall have Sir John and Lady Middleton in town by the end of next week."

"Aye, my dear, I'll warrant you we do. Mary always has her own way."

"And now," silently conjectured Elinor, "she will write to Combe by this day's post."

But if she *did,* the letter was written and sent away with a privacy which eluded all her watchfulness to ascertain the fact. Whatever the truth of it might be, and far as Elinor was from feeling thorough contentment about it, yet while she saw Marianne in spirits, she could not be very uncomfortable herself. And Marianne was in spirits; happy in the mildness of the weather and still happier in her expectation of a frost.

The morning was chiefly spent in leaving cards at the houses of Mrs. Jennings's acquaintance to inform them of her being in town; and Marianne was all the time busy in observing the direction of the wind, watching the variations of the sky, and imagining an alteration in the air.

"Don't you find it colder than it was in the morning, Elinor? There seems to me a very decided difference. I can hardly keep my hands warm even in my muff. It was not so yesterday, I think. The clouds seem parting too; the sun will be out in a moment; and we shall have a clear afternoon."

Elinor was alternately diverted and pained; but Marianne persevered and saw every night in the brightness of the fire, and every morning in the appearance of the atmosphere, the certain symptoms of approaching frost.

The Miss Dashwoods had no greater reason to be dissatisfied with Mrs. Jennings's style of living and set of acquaintance than with her behaviour to themselves, which was invariably kind. Everything in her household arrangements was conducted on the most liberal plan, and excepting a few old city friends whom, to Lady Middleton's regret, she had never dropped, she visited no one to whom an introduction could at all discompose the feelings of her young companions. Pleased to find herself more comfortably situated in that particular than she had expected, Elinor was very willing to compound for the want of much real enjoyment from any of their evening parties, which, whether at home or abroad, formed only for cards, could have little to amuse her.

Colonel Brandon, who had a general invitation to the house, was with them almost every day; he came to look at Marianne and talk to Elinor, who often derived more satisfaction from conversing with him than from any other daily occurrence, but who saw at the same time with much concern his continued regard for her sister. She feared it was a strengthening regard. It grieved her to see the earnestness with which he often watched Marianne, and his spirits were certainly worse than when at Barton.

About a week after their arrival it became certain that Willoughby was also arrived. His card was on the table when they came in from the morning's drive.

"Good God!" cried Marianne, "he has been here while we were out." Elinor, rejoiced to be assured of his being in London, now ventured to say, "depend upon it he will call again to-morrow." But Marianne seemed hardly to hear her, and on Mrs. Jennings's entrance, escaped with the precious card.

This event, while it raised the spirits of Elinor, restored to those of her sister all, and more than all, their former agitation. From this moment her mind was never quiet; the expectation of seeing him every hour of the day made her unfit for anything. She insisted on being left behind the next morning when the others went out.

Elinor's thoughts were full of what might be passing in Berkeley Street during their absence; but a moment's glance at her sister when they returned was enough to inform her that Willoughby had paid no second visit there. A note was just then brought in and laid on the table.

"For me?" cried Marianne, stepping hastily forward.

"No, ma'am, for my mistress."

But Marianne, not convinced, took it instantly up.

"It is indeed for Mrs. Jennings; how provoking!"

"You are expecting a letter, then?" said Elinor, unable to be longer silent.

"Yes, a little—not much."

After a short pause, "You have no confidence in me, Marianne."

"Nay, Elinor, this reproach from *you*—you who have confidence in no one!"

"Me!" returned Elinor in some confusion; "indeed, Marianne, I have nothing to tell."

"Nor I," answered Marianne with energy, "our situations, then, are alike. We have neither of us anything to tell; you, because you communicate, and I, because I conceal nothing."

Elinor, distressed by this charge of reserve in herself, which she was not at liberty to do away, knew not how, under such circumstances, to press for greater openness in Marianne.

Mrs. Jennings soon appeared, and the note being given

her, she read it aloud. It was from Lady Middleton, announcing their arrival in Conduit Street the night before, and requesting the company of her mother and cousins the following evening. Business on Sir John's part and a violent cold on her own prevented their calling in Berkeley Street. The invitation was accepted: but when the hour of appointment drew near, necessary as it was in common civility to Mrs. Jennings that they should both attend her on such a visit, Elinor had some difficulty in persuading her sister to go, for still she had seen nothing of Willoughby; and therefore was not more indisposed for amusement abroad than unwilling to run the risk of his calling again in her absence.

Elinor found, when the evening was over, that disposition is not materially altered by a change of abode, for although scarcely settled in town, Sir John had contrived to collect around him nearly twenty young people and to amuse them with a ball. This was an affair, however, of which Lady Middleton did not approve. In the country an unpremeditated dance was very allowable; but in London, where the reputation of elegance was more important and less easily obtained, it was risking too much for the gratification of a few girls to have it known that Lady Middleton had given a small dance of eight or nine couples, with two violins and a mere sideboard collation.

Mr. and Mrs. Palmer were of the party; from the former, whom they had not seen before since their arrival in town, as he was careful to avoid the appearance of any attention to his mother-in-law and therefore never came near her, they received no mark of recognition on their entrance. He looked at them slightly without seeming to know who they were and merely nodded to Mrs. Jennings from the other side of the room. Marianne gave one glance round the apartment as she entered; it was enough, *he* was not there—and she sat down, equally ill-disposed to receive or communicate pleasure. After they had been assembled about an hour, Mr. Palmer sauntered towards the Miss Dashwoods to express his surprise on seeing them in town, though Colonel Brandon had been first informed of their arrival at his house, and he had himself said something very droll on hearing that they were to come.

"I thought you were both in Devonshire," said he.

"Did you?" replied Elinor.

"When do you go back again?"

"I do not know." And thus ended their discourse.

Never had Marianne been so unwilling to dance in her life as she was that evening, and never so much fatigued by the exercise. She complained of it as they returned to Berkeley Street.

"Aye, aye," said Mrs. Jennings, "we know the reason of all that very well; if a certain person, who shall be nameless, had been there, you would not have been a bit tired: and to say the truth it was not very pretty of him not to give you the meeting when he was invited."

"Invited!" cried Marianne.

"So my daughter Middleton told me, for it seems Sir John met him somewhere in the street this morning." Marianne said no more, but looked exceedingly hurt. Impatient in this situation to be doing something that might lead to her sister's relief, Elinor resolved to write the next morning to her mother, and hoped by awakening her fears for the health of Marianne to procure those inquiries which had been so long delayed; and she was still more eagerly bent on this measure by perceiving after breakfast on the morrow that Marianne was again writing to Willoughby, for she could not suppose it to be to any other person.

About the middle of the day, Mrs. Jennings went out by herself on business, and Elinor began her letter directly while Marianne, too restless for employment, too anxious for conversation, walked from one window to the other or sat down by the fire in melancholy meditation. Elinor was very earnest in her application to her mother, relating all that had passed, her suspicions of Willoughby's inconstancy, urging her by every plea of duty and affection to demand from Marianne an account of her real situation with respect to him.

Her letter was scarcely finished when a rap foretold a visitor, and Colonel Brandon was announced. Marianne, who had seen him from the window, and who hated company of any kind, left the room before he entered it. He looked more than usually grave, and though expressing satisfaction at finding Miss Dashwood alone, as if he had somewhat in particular to tell her, sat for some time without saying a word. Elinor, persuaded that he had some communication to make in which her sister was concerned, impatiently expected its opening. It was not the first time of her feeling the same kind of conviction; for more than once before, beginning with the observation of "your sister looks unwell to-day," or "your sister seems out of spirits," he had appeared on the point either of disclosing or of inquiring something particular about her. After a pause of several minutes, their silence was broken by his asking her in a voice of some agitation when he was to congratulate her on the acquisition of a brother? Elinor was not prepared for such a question, and having no answer ready was obliged to adopt the simple and common expedient of asking what he meant? He tried to smile as he replied, "Your sister's engagement to Mr. Willoughby is very generally known."

"It cannot be generally known," returned Elinor, "for her own family do not know it."

He looked surprised and said, "I beg your pardon, I am afraid my inquiry has been impertinent; but I had not supposed any secrecy intended, as they openly correspond, and their marriage is universally talked of."

"How can that be? By whom can you have heard it mentioned?"

"By many—by some of whom you know nothing, by others with whom you are most intimate, Mrs. Jennings, Mrs. Palmer, and the Middletons. But still I might not have believed it, for where the mind is perhaps rather unwilling to be convinced, it will always find something to support its doubts, if I had not when the servant let me in to-day, accidentally seen a letter in his hand, directed to Mr. Willoughby in your sister's writing. I came to inquire, but I was convinced before I could ask the question. Is everything finally settled? Is it impossible to—? But I have no right, and I could have no chance of succeeding. Excuse me, Miss Dashwood. I believe I have been wrong in saying so much, but I hardly know what to do, and on your prudence I have the strongest dependence. Tell me that it is all absolutely resolved on, that any attempt, that in short concealment, if concealment be possible, is all that remains."

These words, which conveyed to Elinor a direct avowal of his love for her sister, affected her very much. She was not immediately able to say anything, and even when her spirits were recovered, she debated for a short time on the answer it would be most proper to give. The real state of things between Willoughby and her sister was so little known to herself that in endeavouring to explain it, she might be as liable to say too much as too little. Yet as she was convinced that

Marianne's affection for Willoughby could leave no hope of Colonel Brandon's success, whatever the event of that affection might be, and at the same time wished to shield her conduct from censure, she thought it most prudent and kind, after some consideration, to say more than she really knew or believed. She acknowledged, therefore, that though she had never been informed by themselves of the terms on which they stood with each other, of their mutual affection she had no doubt, and of their correspondence she was not astonished to hear.

He listened to her with silent attention, and on her ceasing to speak rose directly from his seat, and after saying in a voice of emotion, "To your sister I wish all imaginable happiness; to Willoughby that he may endeavour to deserve her,"—took leave and went away.

Elinor derived no comfortable feelings from this conversation to lessen the uneasiness of her mind on other points; she was left, on the contrary, with a melancholy impression of Colonel Brandon's unhappiness, and was prevented even from wishing it removed, by her anxiety for the very event that must confirm it.

Chapter 6

NOTHING OCCURRED during the next three or four days to make Elinor regret what she had done in applying to her mother; for Willoughby neither came nor wrote. They were engaged about the end of that time to attend Lady Middleton to a party from which Mrs. Jennings was kept away by the indisposition of her youngest daughter; and for this party, Marianne, wholly dispirited, careless of her appearance, and seeming equally indifferent whether she went or stayed, prepared without one look of hope or one expression of pleasure. She sat by the drawing-room fire after tea till the moment of Lady Middleton's arrival, without once stirring from her seat or altering her attitude, lost in her own thoughts and insensible of her sister's presence; and when at last they were told that Lady Middleton waited for them at the door, she started as if she had forgotten that anyone was expected.

They arrived in due time at the place of destination, and as soon as the string of carriages before them would allow, alighted, ascended the stairs, heard their names announced from one landing-place to another in an audible voice, and entered a room splendidly lit up, quite full of company, and insufferably hot. When they had paid their tribute of politeness by curtesying to the lady of the house, they were permitted to mingle in the crowd and take their share of the heat and inconvenience, to which their arrival must necessarily add. After some time spent in saying little and doing less, Lady Middleton sat down to Casino, and as Marianne was not in spirits for moving about, she and Elinor luckily succeeding to chairs, placed themselves at no great distance from the table.

They had not remained in this manner long, before Elinor perceived Willoughby, standing within a few yards of them, in earnest conversation with a very fashionable-looking young woman. She soon caught his eye, and he immediately bowed, but without attempting to speak to her or to approach Marianne, though he could not but see her; and then continued his discourse with the same lady. Elinor turned involuntarily to Marianne to see whether it could be unobserved by her. At that moment she first perceived him, and her whole countenance glowing with sudden delight, she would have moved towards him instantly had not her sister caught hold of her.

"Good heavens!" she exclaimed, "he is there— He is there— Oh! why does he not look at me? Why cannot I speak to him?"

"Pray, pray be composed," cried Elinor, "and do not betray what you feel to everybody present. Perhaps he has not observed you yet."

This, however, was more than she could believe herself; and to be composed at such a moment was not only beyond the reach of Marianne, it was beyond her wish. She sat in an agony of impatience which affected every feature.

At last he turned round again and regarded them both; she started up, and pronouncing his name in a tone of affection, held out her hand to him. He approached, and addressing himself rather to Elinor than Marianne, as if wishing to avoid her eye, and determined not to observe her attitude, inquired in a hurried manner after Mrs. Dashwood, and asked how long they had been in town. Elinor was robbed of all presence of mind by such an address and was unable to say a word. But the feelings of her sister were instantly expressed. Her face was crimsoned over, and she exclaimed in a voice of the greatest emotion, "Good God! Willoughby, what is the meaning of this? Have you not received my letters? Will you not shake hands with me?"

He could not then avoid it, but her touch seemed painful to him, and he held her hand only for a moment. During all this time he was evidently struggling for composure. Elinor watched his countenance and saw its expression becoming more tranquil. After a moment's pause, he spoke with calmness.

"I did myself the honour of calling in Berkeley Street last Tuesday and very much regretted that I was not fortunate enough to find yourselves and Mrs. Jennings at home. My card was not lost, I hope."

"But have you not received my notes?" cried Marianne in the wildest anxiety. "Here is some mistake I am sure—some dreadful mistake. What can be the meaning of it? Tell me, Willoughby; for heaven's sake tell me, what is the matter?"

He made no reply; his complexion changed and all his embarrassment returned; but as if, on catching the eye of the young lady with whom he had been previously talking, he felt the necessity of instant exertion, he recovered himself again, and after saying, "Yes, I had the pleasure of receiving the information of your arrival in town, which you were so good as to send me," turned hastily away with a slight bow and joined his friend.

Marianne, now looking dreadfully white and unable to stand, sank into her chair, and Elinor, expecting every moment to see her faint, tried to screen her from the observation of others while reviving her with lavender-water.

"Go to him, Elinor," she cried as soon as she could speak, "and force him to come to me. Tell him I must see him again—must speak to him instantly. I cannot rest—I shall not have a moment's peace till this is explained—some dreadful misapprehension or other. Oh, go to him this moment."

"How can that be done? No, my dearest Marianne, you must wait. This is not a place for explanations. Wait only till to-morrow."

With difficulty, however, could she prevent her from following him herself; and to persuade her to check her agitation, to wait at least with the appearance of composure till she might speak to him with more privacy and more effect, was impossible; for Marianne continued incessantly to give way in a low voice to the misery of her feelings by exclamations of wretchedness. In a short time Elinor saw Willoughby quit the room by the door towards the staircase, and telling Marianne that he was gone, urged the impossibility of speaking to him again that evening as a fresh argument for her to be calm. She instantly begged her sister would entreat Lady Middleton to take them home, as she was too miserable to stay a minute longer.

Lady Middleton, though in the middle of a rubber, on being informed that Marianne was unwell, was too polite to object for a moment to her wish of going away, and making over her cards to a friend, they departed as soon as the carriage could be found. Scarcely a word was spoken during their return to Berkeley Street. Marianne was in a silent agony, too much oppressed even for tears; but as Mrs. Jennings was luckily not come home, they could go directly to their own room, where hartshorn restored her a little to herself. She was soon undressed and in bed, and as she seemed desirous of being alone, her sister then left her, and while she waited the return of Mrs. Jennings, had leisure enough for thinking over the past.

That some kind of engagement had subsisted between Willoughby and Marianne she could not doubt; and that Willoughby was weary of it seemed equally clear; for however Marianne might still feed her own wishes, *she* could not attribute such behaviour to mistake or misapprehension of any kind. Nothing but a thorough change of sentiment could account for it. Her indignation would have been still stronger than it was had she not witnessed that embarrassment which seemed to speak a consciousness of his own misconduct and prevented her from believing him so unprincipled as to have been sporting with the affections of her sister from the first, without any design that would bear investigation. Absence might have weakened his regard, and convenience might have determined him to overcome it, but that such a regard had formerly existed she could not bring herself to doubt.

As for Marianne, on the pangs which so unhappy a meeting must already have given her, and on those still more severe which might await her in its probable consequence, she could not reflect without the deepest concern. Her own situation gained in the comparison; for while she could *esteem* Edward as much as ever, however they might be divided in future, her mind might be always supported. But every circumstance that could embitter such an evil seemed uniting to heighten the misery of Marianne in a final separation from Willoughby—in an immediate and irreconcilable rupture with him.

Chapter 7

BEFORE THE housemaid had lit their fire the next day, or the sun gained any power over a cold gloomy morning in January, Marianne, only half dressed, was kneeling against one of the window-seats for the sake of all the little light she could command from it, and writing as fast as a continual flow of tears would permit her. In this situation, Elinor, roused from sleep by her agitation and sobs, first perceived her; and after observing her for a few moments with silent anxiety, said in a tone of the most considerate gentleness:

"Marianne, may I ask?"—

"No, Elinor," she replied, "ask nothing; you will soon know all."

The sort of desperate calmness with which this was said lasted no longer than while she spoke and was immediately followed by a return of the same excessive affliction. It was some minutes before she could go on with her letter, and the frequent bursts of grief which still obliged her at intervals to withhold her pen were proofs enough of her feeling how more than probable it was that she was writing for the last time to Willoughby.

Elinor paid her every quiet and unobtrusive attention in her power; and she would have tried to soothe and tranquillize her still more, had not Marianne entreated her, with all the eagerness of the most nervous irritability, not to speak to her for the world. In such circumstances, it was better for both that they should not be long together; and the restless state of Marianne's mind not only prevented her from remaining in the room a moment after she was dressed, but requiring at once solitude and continual change of place, made her wander about the house till breakfast time, avoiding the sight of everybody.

At breakfast she neither ate nor attempted to eat anything; and Elinor's attention was then all employed, not in urging her, not in pitying her, nor in appearing to regard her, but in endeavouring to engage Mrs. Jennings's notice entirely to herself.

As this was a favourite meal with Mrs. Jennings, it lasted a considerable time, and they were just setting themselves, after it, round the common working table when a letter was delivered to Marianne, which she eagerly caught from the servant, and turning of a deathlike paleness, instantly ran out of the room. Elinor, who saw as plainly by this as if she had seen the direction that it must come from Willoughby, felt immediately such a sickness at heart as made her hardly able to hold up her head, and sat in such a general tremor as made her fear it impossible to escape Mrs. Jennings's notice. That good lady, however, saw only that Marianne had received a letter from Willoughby, which appeared to her a very good joke, and which she treated accordingly, by hoping, with a laugh, that she would find it to her liking. Of Elinor's distress, she was too busily employed in measuring lengths of worsted for her rug to see anything at all; and calmly continuing her talk as soon as Marianne disappeared, she said:

"Upon my word I never saw a young woman so desperately in love in my life! *My* girls were nothing to her, and yet they used to be foolish enough; but as for Miss Marianne, she is quite an altered creature. I hope, from the bottom of my heart, he won't keep her waiting much longer, for it is quite grievous to see her look so ill and forlorn. Pray, when are they to be married?"

Elinor, though never less disposed to speak than at that moment, obliged herself to answer such an attack as this, and, therefore, trying to smile, replied, "And have you really, Ma'am, talked yourself into a persuasion of my sister's being engaged to Mr. Willoughby? I thought it had been only a joke, but so serious a question seems to imply more; and I must beg, therefore, that you will not deceive yourself any longer. I do assure you that nothing would surprise me more than to hear of their being going to be married."

"For shame, for shame, Miss Dashwood! How can you talk so! Don't we all know that it must be a match, that they were over head and ears in love with each other from the first moment they met? Did not I see them together in Devonshire every day and all day long; and did not I know that your sister came to town with me on purpose to buy wedding clothes? Come, come, this won't do. Because you are so sly about it yourself, you think nobody else has any senses; but it is no such thing, I can tell you, for it has been known all over town this ever so long. I tell everybody of it and so does Charlotte."

"Indeed, Ma'am," said Elinor very seriously, "you are mistaken. Indeed, you are doing a very unkind thing in spreading the report, and you will find that you have, though you will not believe me now."

Mrs. Jennings laughed again, but Elinor had not spirits to say more, and eager at all events to know what Willoughby had written, hurried away to their room, where on opening the door she saw Marianne stretched on the bed, almost choked by grief, one letter in her hand and two or three others lying by her. Elinor drew near, but without saying a word; and seating herself on the bed, took her hand, kissed her affectionately several times, and then gave way to a burst of tears, which at first was scarcely less violent than Marianne's. The latter, though unable to speak, seemed to feel all the tenderness of this behaviour, and after some time thus spent in joint affliction, she put all the letters into Elinor's hands; and then covering her face with her handkerchief, almost screamed with agony. Elinor, who knew that such grief, shocking as it was to witness it, must have its course, watched by her till this excess of suffering had somewhat spent itself, and then turning eagerly to Willoughby's letter, read as follows:

Bond Street, January.

MY DEAR MADAM,

I HAVE just had the honour of receiving your letter, for which I beg to return my sincere acknowledgments. I am much concerned to find there was anything in my behaviour last night that did not meet your approbation; and though I am quite at a loss to discover in what point I could be so unfortunate as to offend you, I entreat your forgiveness of what I can assure you to have been perfectly unintentional. I shall never reflect on my former acquaintance with your family in Devonshire without the most grateful pleasure, and flatter myself it will not be broken by any mistake or misapprehension of my actions. My esteem for your whole family is very sincere; but if I have been so unfortunate as to give rise to a belief of more than I felt or meant to express, I shall reproach myself for not having been more guarded in my professions of that esteem. That I should ever have meant more, you will allow to be impossible when you understand that my affections have been long engaged elsewhere; and it will not be many weeks, I believe, before this engagement is fulfilled. It is with great regret that I obey your commands of returning the letters with which I have been honoured from you, and the lock of hair which you so obligingly bestowed on me.

> I am, dear Madam,
> > Your most obedient
> > humble Servant,
>
> > > > JOHN WILLOUGHBY

With what indignation such a letter as this must be read by Miss Dashwood may be imagined. Though aware before she began it that it must bring a confession of his inconstancy and confirm their separation forever, she was not aware that such language could be suffered to announce it! nor could she have supposed Willoughby capable of departing so far from the appearance of every honourable and delicate feeling—so far from the common decorum of a gentleman as to send a letter so impudently cruel: a letter which, instead of bringing with his desire of a release any professions of regret, acknowledged no breach of faith, denied all peculiar affection whatever—a letter of which every line was an insult, and which proclaimed its writer to be deep in hardened villainy.

She paused over it for some time with indignant astonishment; then read it again and again; but every perusal only served to increase her abhorrence of the man, and so bitter were her feelings against him that she dared not trust herself to speak, lest she might wound Marianne still deeper by treating their disengagement not as a loss to her of any possible good but as an escape from the worst and most irremediable of all evils, a connection for life with an unprincipled man, as a deliverance the most real, a blessing the most important.

In her earnest meditations on the contents of the letter, on the depravity of that mind which could dictate it, and probably on the very different mind of a very different person who had no other connection whatever with the affair than what her heart gave him with everything that passed, Elinor forgot the immediate distress of her sister, forgot that she had three letters on her lap yet unread, and so entirely forgot how long she had been in the room that when on hearing a carriage drive up to the door, she went to the window to see who could be coming so unreasonably early; she was all astonishment to perceive Mrs. Jennings's chariot, which she knew had not been ordered till one. Determined not to quit Marianne, though hopeless of contributing at present to her ease, she hurried away to excuse herself from attending Mrs. Jennings on account of her sister being indisposed. Mrs. Jennings, with a thoroughly good-humoured concern for its cause, admitted the excuse most readily, and Elinor, after seeing her safe off, returned to Marianne, whom she found attempting to rise from the bed, and whom she reached just in time to prevent her from falling on the floor, faint and giddy from a long want of proper rest and food; for it was many days since she had any appetite and many nights since she had really slept; and now, when her mind was no longer supported by the fever of suspense, the consequence of all this was felt in an aching head, a weakened stomach, and a general nervous faintness. A glass of wine, which Elinor procured for her directly, made her more comfortable, and she was at last able to express some sense of her kindness by saying:

"Poor Elinor! How unhappy I make you!"

"I only wish," replied her sister, "there were anything I *could* do which might be of comfort to you."

This, as everything else would have been, was too much for Marianne, who could only exclaim in the anguish of her heart, "Oh! Elinor, I am miserable indeed," before her voice was entirely lost in sobs.

Elinor could no longer witness this torrent of unresisted grief in silence.

"Exert yourself, dear Marianne," she cried, "if you would not kill yourself and all who love you. Think of your mother; think of her misery while *you* suffer; for her sake you must exert yourself."

"I cannot, I cannot," cried Marianne; "leave me, leave me

if I distress you; leave me, hate me, forget me! But do not torture me so. Oh! how easy for those who have no sorrow of their own to talk of exertion! Happy, happy Elinor, *you* cannot have an idea of what I suffer."

"Do you call *me* happy, Marianne? Ah! if you knew! And can you believe me to be so, while I see you so wretched!"

"Forgive me, forgive me," throwing her arms round her sister's neck; "I know you feel for me; I know what a heart you have; but yet you are—you must be happy; Edward loves you—What, oh! what can do away such happiness as that?"

"Many, many circumstances," said Elinor solemnly.

"No, no, no," cried Marianne wildly, "he loves you and only you. You *can* have no grief."

"I can have no pleasure while I see you in this state."

"And you will never see me otherwise. Mine is a misery which nothing can do away."

"You must not talk so, Marianne. Have you no comforts? No friends? Is your loss such as leaves no opening for consolation? Much as you suffer now, think of what you would have suffered if the discovery of his character had been delayed to a later period, if your engagement had been carried on for months and months, as it might have been, before he chose to put an end to it. Every additional day of unhappy confidence on your side would have made the blow more dreadful."

"Engagement!" cried Marianne, "there has been no engagement."

"No engagement!"

"No, he is not so unworthy as you believe him. He has broken no faith with me."

"But he told you that he loved you?"

"Yes—no—never absolutely. It was every day implied, but never professedly declared. Sometimes I thought it had been, but it never was."

"Yet you wrote to him?"

"Yes—could that be wrong after all that had passed? But I cannot talk."

Elinor said no more, and turning again to the three letters which now raised a much stronger curiosity than before, directly ran over the contents of all. The first, which was what her sister had sent him on their arrival in town, was to this effect.

Berkeley Street, January.

How surprised you will be, Willoughby, on receiving this; and I think you will feel something more than surprise when you know that I am in town. An opportunity of coming hither, though with Mrs. Jennings, was a temptation we could not resist. I wish you may receive this in time to come here to-night, but I will not depend on it. At any rate I shall expect you to-morrow. For the present, adieu.

M. D.

Her second note, which had been written on the morning after the dance at the Middletons', was in these words:

I cannot express my disappointment in having missed you the day before yesterday, nor my astonishment at not having received any answer to a note which I sent you above a week ago. I have been expecting to hear from you, and still more to see you, every hour of the day. Pray call again as soon as possible and explain the reason of my having expected this in vain. You had better come earlier another time because we are generally out by one. We were last night at Lady Middleton's, where there was a dance. I have been told that you were asked to be of the party. But could it be so? You must be very much altered indeed since we parted if that could be the case and you not there. But I will not suppose this possible, and I hope very soon to receive your personal assurance of its being otherwise.

M. D.

The contents of her last note to him were these:

What am I to imagine, Willoughby, by your behaviour last night? Again I demand an explanation of it. I was prepared to meet you with the pleasure which our separation naturally produced, with the familiarity which our intimacy at Barton appeared to me to justify. I was repulsed indeed! I have passed a wretched night in endeavouring to excuse a conduct which can scarcely be called less than insulting; but though I have not yet been able to form any reasonable apology for your behaviour, I am perfectly ready to hear your justification of it. You have perhaps been misinformed or purposely deceived in something concerning me which may have lowered me in your opinion. Tell me what it is, explain the grounds on which you acted, and I shall be satisfied in being able to satisfy you. It would grieve me indeed to be obliged to think ill of you; but if I am to do it, if I am to learn that

you are not what we have hitherto believed you, that your regard for us all was insincere, that your behaviour to me was
intended only to deceive, let it be told as soon as possible.
My feelings are at present in a state of dreadful indecision;
I wish to acquit you, but certainty on either side will be ease
to what I now suffer. If your sentiments are no longer what
they were, you will return my notes and the lock of my hair
which is in your possession.

M. D.

That such letters, so full of affection and confidence,
could have been so answered, Elinor, for Willoughby's sake,
would have been unwilling to believe. But her condemnation
of him did not blind her to the impropriety of their having
been written at all; and she was silently grieving over the
imprudence which had hazarded such unsolicited proofs of
tenderness, not warranted by anything preceding, and most
severely condemned by the event, when Marianne, perceiving that she had finished the letter, observed to her that they
contained nothing but what anyone would have written in
the same situation.

"I felt myself," she added, "to be as solemnly engaged to
him as if the strictest legal covenant had bound us to each
other."

"I can believe it," said Elinor; "but unfortunately he did
not feel the same."

"He *did* feel the same, Elinor. For weeks and weeks he felt
it. I know he did. Whatever may have changed him now (and
nothing but the blackest art employed against me can have
done it), I was once as dear to him as my own soul could
wish. This lock of hair, which now he can so readily give up,
was begged of me with the most earnest supplication. Had
you seen his look, his manner, had you heard his voice at that
moment! Have you forgot the last evening of our being together at Barton? The morning that we parted, too! When he
told me that it might be many weeks before we meet again—
His distress—can I ever forget his distress!"

For a moment or two she could say no more; but when
this emotion had passed away, she added, in a firmer tone,
"Elinor, I have been cruelly used; but not by Willoughby."

"Dearest Marianne, who but himself? By whom can he
have been instigated?"

"By all the world rather than by his own heart. I could

rather believe every creature of my acquaintance leagued together to ruin me in his opinion than believe his nature capable of such cruelty. This woman of whom he writes—whoever she be—or anyone, in short, but your own dear self, mama, and Edward, may have been so barbarous to bely me. Beyond you three is there a creature in the world whom I would not rather suspect of evil than Willoughby, whose heart I know so well?"

Elinor would not contend and only replied, "Whoever may have been so detestably your enemy, let them be cheated of their malignant triumph, my dear sister, by seeing how nobly the consciousness of your own innocence and good intentions supports your spirits. It is a reasonable and laudable pride which resists such malevolence."

"No, no," cried Marianne, "misery such as mine has no pride. I care not who knows that I am wretched. The triumph of seeing me so may be open to all the world. Elinor, Elinor, they who suffer little may be proud and independent as they like, may resist insult or return mortification, but I cannot. I must feel—I must be wretched—and they are welcome to enjoy the consciousness of it that can."

"But for my mother's sake and mine—"

"I would do more than for my own. But to appear happy when I am so miserable— Oh! who can require it?"

Again they were both silent. Elinor was employed in walking thoughtfully from the fire to the window, from the window to the fire, without knowing that she received warmth from one or discerning objects through the other; and Marianne, seated at the foot of the bed, with her head leaning against one of its posts, again took up Willoughby's letter, and after shuddering over every sentence, exclaimed, "It is too much! Oh! Willoughby, Willoughby, could this be yours! Cruel, cruel—nothing can acquit you. Elinor, nothing can. Whatever he might have heard against me, ought he not to have suspended his belief? Ought he not to have told me of it, to have given me the power of clearing myself? 'The lock of hair (repeating it from the letter) which you so obligingly bestowed on me—' That is unpardonable. Willoughby, where was your heart when you wrote those words? Oh! barbarously insolent! Elinor, can he be justified?"

"No, Marianne, in no possible way."

"And yet this woman—who knows what her art may have been—how long it may have been premeditated, and how deeply contrived by her! Who is she? Who can she be? Whom did I ever hear him talk of as young and attractive among his female acquaintance? Oh! no one, no one. He talked to me only of myself."

Another pause ensued; Marianne was greatly agitated, and it ended thus:

"Elinor, I must go home. I must go and comfort mama. Cannot we be gone to-morrow?"

"To-morrow, Marianne!"

"Yes, why should I stay here? I came only for Willoughby's sake, and now who cares for me? Who regards me?"

"It would be impossible to go to-morrow. We owe Mrs. Jennings much more than civility, and civility of the commonest kind must prevent such a hasty removal as that."

"Well, then, another day or two perhaps; but I cannot stay here long; I cannot stay to endure the questions and remarks of all these people. The Middletons and Palmers—how am I to bear their pity? The pity of such a woman as Lady Middleton! Oh! what would *he* say to that!"

Elinor advised her to lie down again, and for a moment she did so; but no attitude could give her ease; and in restless pain of mind and body she moved from one posture to another, till growing more and more hysterical, her sister could with difficulty keep her on the bed at all and for some time was fearful of being constrained to call for assistance. Some lavender drops, however, which she was at length persuaded to take, were of use; and from that time till Mrs. Jennings returned, she continued on the bed quiet and motionless.

Chapter 8

MRS. JENNINGS came immediately to their room on her return, and without waiting to have her request of admittance answered, opened the door and walked in with a look of real concern.

"How do you do my dear?" said she in a voice of great compassion to Marianne, who turned away her face without attempting to answer.

"How is she, Miss Dashwood? Poor thing! She looks very bad. No wonder. Aye, it is but too true. He is to be married very soon—a good-for-nothing fellow! I have no patience with him. Mrs. Taylor told me of it half an hour ago, and she was told it by a particular friend of Miss Grey herself, else I am sure I should not have believed it; and I was almost ready to sink as it was. Well, said I, all I can say is that if it is true he has used a young lady of my acquaintance abominably ill, and I wish with all my soul his wife may plague his heart out. And so I shall always say, my dear, you may depend on it. I have no notion of men's going on in this way: and if ever I meet him again, I will give him such a dressing as he has not had this many a day. But there is one comfort, my dear Miss Marianne; he is not the only young man in the world worth having; and with your pretty face you will never want admirers. Well, poor thing! I won't disturb her any longer, for she had better have her cry out at once and have done with it. The Parrys and Sandersons luckily are coming to-night you know, and that will amuse her."

She then went away, walking on tiptoe out of the room as if she supposed her young friend's affliction could be increased by noise.

Marianne, to the surprise of her sister, determined on dining with them. Elinor even advised her against it, but "No, she would go down; she could bear it very well, and the bustle about her would be less." Elinor, pleased to have her governed for a moment by such a motive, though believing it hardly possible that she could sit out the dinner, said no more; and adjusting her dress for her as well as she could while Marianne still remained on the bed, was ready to assist her into the dining-room as soon as they were summoned to it.

When there, though looking most wretchedly, she ate more and was calmer than her sister had expected. Had she tried to speak, or had she been conscious of half Mrs. Jennings's well-meant but ill-judged attentions to her, this calmness could not have been maintained; but not a syllable escaped her lips, and the abstraction of her thoughts preserved her in ignorance of everything that was passing before her.

Elinor, who did justice to Mrs. Jennings's kindness, though its effusions were often distressing and sometimes almost ridiculous, made her those acknowledgments and returned her those civilities which her sister could not make or return for herself. Their good friend saw that Marianne was unhappy and felt that everything was due to her which might make her at all less so. She treated her, therefore, with all the indulgent fondness of a parent towards a favourite child on the last day of its holidays. Marianne was to have the best place by the fire, was to be tempted to eat by every delicacy in the house, and to be amused by the relation of all the news of the day. Had not Elinor, in the sad countenance of her sister, seen a check to all mirth, she could have been entertained by Mrs. Jennings's endeavours to cure a disappointment in love by a variety of sweetmeats and olives, and a good fire. As soon, however, as the consciousness of all this was forced by continual repetition on Marianne, she could stay no longer. With an hasty exclamation of misery and a sign to her sister not to follow her, she directly got up and hurried out of the room.

"Poor soul!" cried Mrs. Jennings, as soon as she was gone, "how it grieves me to see her! And I declare if she is not gone away without finishing her wine! And the dried cherries, too! Lord! Nothing seems to do her any good. I am sure if I knew of anything she would like, I would send all over the town for it. Well, it is the oddest thing to me that a man should use such a pretty girl so ill! But when there is plenty of money on one side and next to none on the other, Lord bless you! They care no more about such things!"

"The lady, then—Miss Grey I think you called her—is very rich?"

"Fifty thousand pounds, my dear. Did you ever see her? A smart, stylish girl they say, but not handsome. I remember her aunt very well. Biddy Henshawe; she married a very wealthy man. But the family are all rich together. Fifty thousand pounds! And by all accounts it won't come before it's wanted, for they say he is all to pieces. No wonder! Dashing about with his curricle and hunters! Well, it don't signify talking, but when a young man, be he who he will, comes and makes love to a pretty girl and promises marriage, he has no business to fly off from his word only because he grows poor and a richer girl is ready to have him. Why don't he in such a case sell his horses, let his house, turn off his servants, and make at thorough reform at once? I warrant you, Miss Marianne would have been ready to wait till matters came round. But that won't do nowadays; nothing in the way of pleasure can ever be given up by the young men of this age."

"Do you know what kind of a girl Miss Grey is? Is she said to be amiable?"

"I never heard any harm of her; indeed I hardly ever heard her mentioned; except that Mrs. Taylor did say this morning that one day Miss Walker hinted to her that she believed Mr. and Mrs. Ellison would not be sorry to have Miss Grey married, for she and Mrs. Ellison could never agree."

"And who are the Ellisons?"

"Her guardians, my dear. But now she is of age and may choose for herself; and a pretty choice she has made! What now," after pausing a moment, "your poor sister is gone to her own room I suppose to moan by herself. Is there nothing one can get to comfort her? Poor dear, it seems quite cruel to let her be alone. Well, by-and-by we shall have a few friends, and that will amuse her a little. What shall we play at? She hates whist I know, but is there no round game she cares for?"

"Dear Ma'am, this kindness is quite unnecessary. Marianne I dare say will not leave her room again this evening. I shall persuade her if I can to go early to bed, for I am sure she wants rest."

"Aye, I believe that will be best for her. Let her name her own supper and go to bed. Lord! No wonder she has been looking so bad and so cast down this last week or two, for this matter I suppose has been hanging over her head as long as that. And so the letter that came to-day finished it! Poor soul! I am sure if I had had a notion of it, I would not have joked her about it for all my money. But then you know, how should I guess such a thing? I made sure of its being nothing but a common love letter, and you know young people like to be laughed at about them. Lord! How concerned Sir John and my daughters will be when they hear it! If I had had my senses about me I might have called in Conduit Street in my way home and told them of it. But I shall see them to-morrow."

"It would be unnecessary, I am sure, for you to caution Mrs. Palmer and Sir John against ever naming Mr. Willoughby, or making the slightest allusion to what has passed, before my sister. Their own good-nature must point out to them the real cruelty of appearing to know anything about it when she is present; and the less that may ever be said to myself on the subject, the more my feelings will be spared, as you my dear madam will easily believe."

"Oh! Lord! Yes, that I do, indeed. It must be terrible for you to hear it talked of; and as for your sister, I am sure I would not mention a word about it to her for the world. You saw I did not all dinner time. No more would Sir John nor my daughters, for they are all very thoughtful and considerate; especially if I give them a hint, as I certainly will. For my part, I think the less that is said about such things, the better, the sooner 'tis blown over and forgot. And what good does talking ever do, you know?"

"In this affair it can only do harm; more so perhaps than in many cases of a similar kind, for it has been attended by circumstances which, for the sake of everyone concerned in it, make it unfit to become the public conversation. I must do *this* justice to Mr. Willoughby: he has broken no positive engagement with my sister."

"Law, my dear! Don't pretend to defend him. No positive engagement indeed! After taking her all over Allenham House and fixing on the very rooms they were to live in hereafter!"

Elinor, for her sister's sake, could not press the subject further, and she hoped it was not required of her for Willoughby's; since, though Marianne might lose much, he could gain very little by the enforcement of the real truth. After a short silence on both sides, Mrs. Jennings, with all her natural hilarity, burst forth again.

"Well, my dear, 'tis a true saying about an ill wind, for it will be all the better for Colonel Brandon. He will have her at last; aye, that he will. Mind me now if they an't married by Midsummer. Lord! How he'll chuckle over this news! I hope he will come to-night. It will be all to one a better match for your sister. Two thousand a year without debt or drawback—except the little love-child, indeed; aye, I had forgot her; but she may be 'prenticed out at small cost, and then what does it signify? Delaford is a nice place, I can tell you; exactly what I call a nice old-fashioned place, full of comforts and conveniences; quite shut in with great garden walls that are covered with the best fruit-trees in the country, and such a mulberry tree in one corner! Lord! How Charlotte and I did stuff the only time we were there! Then there is a dove-cote, some delightful stewponds, and a very pretty canal; and everything, in short, that one could wish for: and, moreover, it is close to the church and only a quarter of a mile from the turnpike road, so 'tis never dull, for if you only go and sit up in an old yew arbour behind the house, you may see all the carriages that pass along. Oh! 'tis a nice place! A butcher hard by in the village, and the parsonage house within a stone's throw. To my fancy, a thousand times prettier than Barton Park, where they are forced to send three miles for their meat and have not a neighbour nearer than your mother. Well, I shall spirit up the Colonel as soon as I can. One shoulder of mutton, you know, drives another down. If we *can* put Willoughby out of her head!"

"Aye, if we can but do *that,* ma'am," said Elinor, "we shall do very well with or without Colonel Brandon." And then rising, she went away to join Marianne, whom she found, as she expected, in her own room, leaning in silent misery over the small remains of a fire, which, till Elinor's entrance, had been her only light.

"You had better leave me," was all the notice that her sister received from her.

"I will leave you," said Elinor, "if you will go to bed." But this, from the momentary perverseness of impatient suffering, she at first refused to do. Her sister's earnest though gentle persuasion, however, soon softened her to compliance, and Elinor saw her lay her aching head on the pillow, and saw her, as she hoped, in a way to get some quiet rest before she left her.

In the drawing-room, whither she then repaired, she was soon joined by Mrs. Jennings with a wine-glass full of something in her hand.

"My dear," said she, entering, "I have just recollected that I have some of the finest old Constantia wine in the house that ever was tasted; so I have brought a glass of it for your sister. My poor husband! How fond he was of it! Whenever he had a touch of his old cholicky gout, he said it did him more good than anything else in the world. Do take it to your sister."

"Dear Ma'am," replied Elinor, smiling at the difference of the complaints for which it was recommended, "how good you are! But I have just left Marianne in bed, and, I hope, almost asleep; and as I think nothing will be of so much service to her as rest, if you will give me leave, I will drink the wine myself."

Mrs. Jennings, though regretting that she had not been five minutes earlier, was satisfied with the compromise; and Elinor, as she swallowed the chief of it, reflected that, though its good effects on a cholicky gout were, at present, of little importance to her, its healing powers on a disappointed heart might be as reasonably tried on herself as on her sister.

Colonel Brandon came in while the party were at tea, and by his manner of looking round the room for Marianne, Elinor immediately fancied that he neither expected nor wished to see her there, and, in short, that he was already aware of what occasioned her absence. Mrs. Jennings was not struck by the same thought; for soon after his entrance she walked across the room to the tea-table where Elinor presided, and whispered, "The Colonel looks as grave as ever you see. He knows nothing of it; do tell him, my dear."

He shortly afterwards drew a chair close to hers, and with a look which perfectly assured her of his good information, inquired after her sister.

"Marianne is not well," said she. "She has been indisposed all day, and we have persuaded her to go to bed."

"Perhaps, then," he hesitatingly replied, "what I heard this morning may be—there may be more truth in it than I could believe possible at first."

"What did you hear?"

"That a gentleman whom I had reason to think—in short, that a man whom I *knew* to be engaged—but how shall I tell you? If you know it already, as surely you must, I may be spared."

"You mean," answered Elinor with forced calmness, "Mr. Willoughby's marriage with Miss Grey. Yes, we *do* know it all. This seems to have been a day of general elucidation, for this very morning first unfolded it to us. Mr. Willoughby is unfathomable! Where did you hear it?"

"In a stationer's shop in Pall Mall, where I had business. Two ladies were waiting for their carriage, and one of them was giving the other an account of the intended match in a voice so little attempting concealment that it was impossible for me not to hear all. The name of Willoughby, John Willoughby, frequently repeated, first caught my attention, and what followed was a positive assertion that everything was now finally settled respecting his marriage with Miss Grey. It was no longer to be a secret. It would take place even within a few weeks, with many particulars of preparations and other matters. One thing, especially, I remember, because it served to identify the man still more: as soon as the ceremony was over, they were to go to Combe Magna, his seat in Somersetshire. My astonishment! But it would be impossible to describe what I felt. The communicative lady I learned on inquiry, for I stayed in the shop till they were gone, was a Mrs. Ellison, and that, as I have been since informed, is the name of Miss Grey's guardian."

"It is. But have you likewise heard that Miss Grey has fifty thousand pounds? In that, if in anything, we may find an explanation."

"It may be so; but Willoughby is capable—at least I think"—he stopped a moment, then added in a voice which seemed to distrust itself—"and your sister—how did she—"

"Her sufferings have been very severe. I have only to hope that they may be proportionably short. It has been, it is, a most cruel affliction. Till yesterday, I believe, she never doubted his regard; and even now, perhaps, but *I* am almost convinced that he never was really attached to her. He has been very deceitful! And in some point there seems a hardness of heart about him."

"Ah!" said Colonel Brandon, "there is, indeed! But your sister does not—I think you said so—she does not consider it quite as you do?"

"You know her disposition and may believe how eagerly she would still justify him if she could."

He made no answer; and soon afterwards, by the removal of the tea-things and the arrangement of the card parties, the subject was necessarily dropped. Mrs. Jennings, who had watched them with pleasure while they were talking, and who expected to see the effect of Miss Dashwood's communication, in such an instantaneous gaiety on Colonel Brandon's side as might have become a man in the bloom of youth, of hope and happiness, saw him, with amazement, remain the whole evening more serious and thoughtful than usual.

Chapter 9

FROM A NIGHT of more sleep than she had expected Marianne awoke the next morning to the same consciousness of misery in which she had closed her eyes.

Elinor encouraged her as much as possible to talk of what she felt; and before breakfast was ready, they had gone through the subject again and again, with the same steady conviction and affectionate counsel on Elinor's side, the same impetuous feelings and varying opinions on Marianne's, as before. Sometimes she could believe Willoughby to be as unfortunate and as innocent as herself, and at others, lost every consolation in the impossibility of acquitting him. At one moment she was absolutely indifferent to the observation of all the world, at another she would seclude herself from it forever, and at a third could resist it with energy. In one thing, however, she was uniform—when it came to the point in avoiding, where it was possible, the presence of Mrs. Jennings, and in a determined silence when obliged to endure it. Her heart was hardened against the belief of Mrs. Jennings's entering into her sorrows with any compassion.

"No, no, no, it cannot be," she cried; "she cannot feel. Her kindness is not sympathy; her good-nature is not tenderness. All that she wants is gossip, and she only likes me now because I supply it."

Elinor had not needed this to be assured of the injustice to which her sister was often led in her opinion of others by the irritable refinement of her own mind, and the too-great importance placed by her on the delicacies of a strong sensibility and the graces of a polished manner. Like half the rest of the world, if more than half there be that are clever and good, Marianne, with excellent abilities and an excellent disposition, was neither reasonable nor candid. She expected from other people the same opinions and feelings as her own, and she judged of their motives by the immediate effect of their actions on herself. Thus a circumstance occurred while the sisters were together in their own room after breakfast which sank the heart of Mrs. Jennings still lower in her estimation; because, through her own weakness, it chanced to prove a source of fresh pain to herself, though Mrs. Jennings were governed in it by an impulse of the utmost goodwill.

With a letter in her outstretched hand, and countenance gaily smiling from the persuasion of bringing comfort, she entered their room, saying,

"Now, my dear, I bring you something that I am sure will do you good."

Marianne heard enough. In one moment her imagination placed before her a letter from Willoughby full of tenderness and contrition, explanatory of all that had passed, satisfactory, convincing; and instantly followed by Willoughby himself, rushing eagerly into the room to enforce at her feet, by the eloquence of his eyes, the assurances of his letter. The work of one moment was destroyed by the next. The handwriting of her mother, never till then unwelcome, was before her; and in the acuteness of the disappointment which followed such an ecstasy of more than hope, she felt as if, till that instant, she had never suffered.

The cruelty of Mrs. Jennings no language, within her reach in her moments of happiest eloquence, could have expressed; and now she could reproach her only by the tears which streamed from her eyes with passionate violence; a reproach, however, so entirely lost on its object, that after many expressions of pity she withdrew, still referring her to the letter for comfort. But the letter, when she was calm enough to read it, brought little comfort. Willoughby filled every page. Her mother, still confident of their engagement, and relying as warmly as ever on his constancy, had only been roused, by Elinor's application, to entreat from Marianne greater openness towards them both; and this, with such tenderness towards her, such affection for Willoughby, and such a conviction of their future happiness in each other, that she wept with agony through the whole of it.

All her impatience to be at home again now returned; her mother was dearer to her than ever; dearer through the very excess of her mistaken confidence in Willoughby, and she was wildly urgent to be gone. Elinor, unable herself to determine whether it were better for Marianne to be in London or at Barton, offered no counsel of her own except of patience till their mother's wishes could be known; and at length she obtained her sister's consent to wait for that knowledge.

Mrs. Jennings left them earlier than usual; for she could not be easy till the Middletons and Palmers were able to grieve as much as herself; and positively refusing Elinor's offered attendance, went out alone for the rest of the morning. Elinor, with a very heavy heart, aware of the pain she was going to communicate, and perceiving by Marianne's letter how ill she had succeeded in laying any foundation for it, then sat down to write her mother an account of what had passed and entreat her directions for the future; while Marianne, who came into the drawing-room on Mrs. Jennings's going away, remained fixed at the table where Elinor wrote, watching the advancement of her pen, grieving over her for the hardship of such a task, and grieving still more fondly over its effect on her mother.

In this manner they had continued about a quarter of an hour when Marianne, whose nerves could not then bear any sudden noise, was startled by a rap at the door.

"Who can this be?" cried Elinor. "So early, too! I thought we *had* been safe."

Marianne moved to the window.

"It is Colonel Brandon!" said she with vexation. "We are never safe from *him.*"

"He will not come in, as Mrs. Jennings is from home."

"I will not trust to that," retreating to her own room. "A man who has nothing to do with his own time has no conscience in his intrusion on that of others."

The event proved her conjecture right, though it was founded on injustice and error; for Colonel Brandon *did* come in; and Elinor, who was convinced that solicitude for Marianne brought him thither, and who saw *that* solicitude in his disturbed and melancholy look, and in his anxious though brief inquiry after her, could not forgive her sister for esteeming him so lightly.

"I met Mrs. Jennings in Bond Street," said he after the first salutation, "and she encouraged me to come on; and I was the more easily encouraged because I thought it probable that I might find you alone, which I was very desirous of doing. My object—my wish—my sole wish in desiring it—I hope, I believe it is—is to be a means of giving comfort;—no, I must not say comfort—not present comfort—but conviction, lasting conviction to your sister's mind. My regard for her, for yourself, for your mother—will you allow me to prove it by relating some circumstances which nothing but a *very* sincere regard—nothing but an earnest desire of being useful—— I think I am justified—though where so many hours have been spent in convincing myself that I am right, is there not some reason to fear I may be wrong?" He stopped.

"I understand you," said Elinor. "You have something to tell me of Mr. Willoughby that will open his character further. Your telling it will be the greatest act of friendship that can be shown Marianne. *My* gratitude will be ensured immediately by any information tending to that end, and *hers* must be gained by it in time. Pray, pray let me hear it."

"You shall; and, to be brief, when I quitted Barton last October—but this will give you no idea—I must go farther back. You will find me a very awkward narrator, Miss Dashwood; I hardly know where to begin. A short account of myself, I believe, will be necessary, and it *shall* be a short one. On such a subject," sighing heavily, "I can have little temptation to be diffuse."

He stopped a moment for recollection, and then, with another sigh, went on.

"You have probably entirely forgotten a conversation—(it is not to be supposed that it could make any impression on you)—a conversation between us one evening at Barton Park—it was the evening of a dance—in which I alluded to a lady I had once known, as resembling, in some measure, your sister Marianne."

"Indeed," answered Elinor, "I have *not* forgotten it." He looked pleased by this remembrance and added, "If I am not deceived by the uncertainty, the partiality of tender recollection, there is a very strong resemblance between them as well in mind as person: the same warmth of heart, the same eagerness of fancy and spirits. This lady was one of my nearest relations, an orphan from her infancy, and under the guardianship of my father. Our ages were nearly the same, and from our earliest years we were playfellows and friends. I cannot remember the time when I did not love Eliza; and my affection for her as we grew up was such, as perhaps, judging from my present forlorn and cheerless gravity, you might think me incapable of having ever felt. Hers, for me, was, I believe, fervent as the attachment of your sister to Mr. Willoughby; and it was, though from a different cause, no less unfortunate. At seventeen she was lost to me forever. She was married—married against her inclination to my

brother. Her fortune was large, and our family estate much
encumbered. And this, I fear, is all that can be said for the
conduct of one who was at once her uncle and guardian. My
brother did not deserve her; he did not even love her. I had
hoped that her regard for me would support her under any
difficulty, and for some time it did; but at last the misery of
her situation, for she experienced great unkindness, overcame all her resolution, and though she had promised me
that nothing——but how blindly I relate? I have never told
you how this was brought on. We were within a few hours
of eloping together for Scotland. The treachery, or the folly,
of my cousin's maid betrayed us. I was banished to the
house of a relation far distant, and she was allowed no liberty, no society, no amusement, till my father's point was
gained. I had depended on her fortitude too far, and the blow
was a severe one; but had her marriage been happy, so
young as I then was, a few months must have reconciled me
to it, or at least I should not have now to lament it. This,
however, was not the case. My brother had no regard for
her; his pleasures were not what they ought to have been,
and from the first he treated her unkindly. The consequence
of this upon a mind so young, so lively, so inexperienced as
Mrs. Brandon's, was but too natural. She resigned herself at
first to all the misery of her situation; and happy had it been
if she had not lived to overcome those regrets which the remembrance of me occasioned. But can we wonder that with
such a husband to provoke inconstancy, and without a friend
to advise or restrain her (for my father lived only a few
months after their marriage, and I was with my regiment in
the East Indies), she should fall? Had I remained in England,
perhaps—but I meant to promote the happiness of both by
removing from her for years, and for that purpose had procured my exchange. The shock which her marriage had
given me," he continued in a voice of great agitation, "was
of trifling weight—was nothing—to what I felt when I
heard, about two years afterwards, of her divorce. It was *that*
which threw this gloom—even now the recollection of what
I suffered—"

He could say no more, and rising hastily walked for a few
minutes about the room. Elinor, affected by his relation and
still more by his distress, could not speak. He saw her concern, and coming to her, took her hand, pressed it, and

kissed it with grateful respect. A few minutes more of silent exertion enabled him to proceed with composure.

"It was nearly three years after this unhappy period before I returned to England. My first care when I *did* arrive was of course to seek for her; but the search was as fruitless as it was melancholy. I could not trace her beyond her first seducer, and there was every reason to fear that she had removed from him only to sink deeper in a life of sin. Her legal allowance was not adequate to her fortune nor sufficient for her comfortable maintenance, and I learned from my brother that the power of receiving it had been made over some months before to another person. He imagined, and calmly could he imagine it, that her extravagance and consequent distress had obliged her to dispose of it for some immediate relief. At last, however, and after I had been six months in England, I *did* find her. Regard for a former servant of my own who had since fallen into misfortune, carried me to visit him in a sponging-house, where he was confined for debt; and there, in the same house, under a similar confinement, was my unfortunate sister. So altered—so faded—worn down by acute suffering of every kind! Hardly could I believe the melancholy and sickly figure before me to be the remains of the lovely, blooming, healthful girl on whom I had once doted. What I endured in so beholding her—but I have no right to wound your feelings by attempting to describe it—I have pained you too much already. That she was, to all appearance in the last stage of a consumption, was—yes, in such a situation it was my greatest comfort. Life could do nothing for her beyond giving time for a better preparation for death; and that was given. I saw her placed in comfortable lodgings and under proper attendants; I visited her every day during the rest of her short life; I was with her in her last moments."

Again he stopped to recover himself; and Elinor spoke her feelings in an exclamation of tender concern at the fate of his unfortunate friend.

"Your sister, I hope, cannot be offended," said he, "by the resemblance I have fancied between her and my poor disgraced relation. Their fates, their fortunes, cannot be the same; and had the natural sweet disposition of the one been guarded by a firmer mind or a happier marriage, she might have been all that you will live to see the other be. But to what does all this lead? I seem to have been distressing you

for nothing. Ah! Miss Dashwood—a subject such as this—
untouched for fourteen years—it is dangerous to handle it at
all! I *will* be more collected, more concise. She left to my
care her only child, a little girl, the offspring of her first
guilty connection, who was then about three years old. She
loved the child and had always kept it with her. It was a valued, a precious trust to me; and gladly would I have discharged it in the strictest sense, by watching over her
education myself, had the nature of our situations allowed it;
but I had no family, no home; and my little Eliza was therefore placed at school. I saw her there whenever I could, and
after the death of my brother (which happened about five
years ago, and which left to me the possession of the family
property), she frequently visited me at Delaford. I called her
a distant relation, but I am well aware that I have in general
been suspected of a much nearer connection with her. It is
now three years ago (she had just reached her fourteenth
year) that I removed her from school to place her under the
care of a very respectable woman residing in Dorsetshire,
who had the charge of four or five other girls of about the
same time of life; and for two years I had every reason to be
pleased with her situation. But last February, almost a
twelvemonth back, she suddenly disappeared. I had allowed
her (imprudently, as it has since turned out), at her earnest
desire, to go to Bath with one of her young friends, who was
attending her father there for his health. I knew him to be a
very good sort of man, and I thought well of his daughter—
better than she deserved, for with a most obstinate and ill-
judged secrecy she would tell nothing, would give no clue,
though she certainly knew all. He, her father, a well-
meaning but not a quick-sighted man, could really, I believe,
give no information; for he had been generally confined to
the house while the girls were ranging over the town and
making what acquaintance they chose; and he tried to convince me, as thoroughly as he was convinced himself, of his
daughter's being entirely unconcerned in the business. In
short, I could learn nothing but that she was gone; all the
rest, for eight long months, was left to conjecture. What I
thought, what I feared, may be imagined; and what I suffered, too."

"Good heavens!" cried Elinor, "could it be—could Willoughby—"

"The first news that reached me of her," he continued,

"came in a letter from herself last October. It was forwarded to me from Delaford, and I received it on the very morning of our intended party to Whitwell; and this was the reason of my leaving Barton so suddenly, which I am sure must at the time have appeared strange to everybody, and which I believe gave offence to some. Little did Mr. Willoughby imagine, I suppose, when his looks censured me for incivility in breaking up the party, that I was called away to the relief of one whom he had made poor and miserable; but *had* he known it, what would it have availed? Would he have been less gay or less happy in the smiles of your sister? No, he had already done that which no man who *can* feel for another would do. He had left the girl whose youth and innocence he had seduced in a situation of the utmost distress, with no creditable home, no help, no friends, ignorant of his address! He had left her promising to return; he neither returned, nor wrote, nor relieved her."

"This is beyond everything!" exclaimed Elinor.

"His character is now before you: expensive, dissipated, and worse than both. Knowing all this as I have now known it many weeks, guess what I must have felt on seeing your sister as fond of him as ever, and on being assured that she was to marry him, guess what I must have felt for all your sakes. When I came to you last week and found you alone, I came determined to know the truth; though irresolute what to do when it *was* known. My behaviour must have seemed strange to you then; but now you will comprehend it. To suffer you all to be so deceived; to see your sister—but what could I do? I had no hope of interfering with success; and sometimes I thought your sister's influence might yet reclaim him. But now, after such dishonourable usage, who can tell what were his designs on her? Whatever they may have been, however, she may now, and hereafter doubtless *will*, turn with gratitude towards her own condition, when she compares it with that of my poor Eliza, when she considers the wretched and hopeless situation of this poor girl and pictures her to herself, with an affection for him as strong, still as strong as her own, and with a mind tormented by self-reproach which must attend her through life. Surely this comparison must have its use with her. She will feel her own sufferings to be nothing. They proceed from no misconduct and can bring no disgrace. On the contrary, every friend must be made still more her friend by them. Concern for her unhappiness and respect for her fortitude under it must strengthen every attachment. Use your own discretion, however, in communicating to her what I have told you. You must know best what will be its effect; but had I not seriously and from my heart believed it might be of service, might lessen her regrets, I would not have suffered myself to trouble you with this account of my family afflictions, with a recital which may seem to have been intended to raise myself at the expense of others."

Elinor's thanks followed this speech with grateful earnestness; attended, too, with the assurance of her expecting material advantage to Marianne from the communication of what had passed.

"I have been more pained," said she, "by her endeavours to acquit him than by all the rest; for it irritates her mind more than the most perfect conviction of his unworthiness can do. Now, though at first she will suffer much, I am sure she will soon become easier. Have you," she continued after a short silence, "ever seen Mr. Willoughby since you left him at Barton?"

"Yes," he replied gravely, "once I have. One meeting was unavoidable."

Elinor, startled by his manner, looked at him anxiously, saying:

"What? Have you met him to—"

"I could meet him in no other way. Eliza had confessed to me, though most reluctantly, the name of her lover; and when he returned to town, which was within a fortnight after myself, we met by appointment, he to defend, I to punish his conduct. We returned unwounded, and the meeting, therefore, never got abroad."

Elinor sighed over the fancied necessity of this; but to a man and a soldier she presumed not to censure it.

"Such," said Colonel Brandon after a pause, "has been the unhappy resemblance between the fate of mother and daughter! And so imperfectly have I discharged my trust!"

"Is she still in town?"

"No, as soon as she recovered from her lying-in, for I found her near her delivery, I removed her and her child into the country, and there she remains."

Recollecting, soon afterwards, that he was probably dividing Elinor from her sister, he put an end to his visit, receiving from her again the same grateful acknowledgments, and leaving her full of compassion and esteem for him.

Chapter 10

WHEN THE particulars of this conversation were repeated by Miss Dashwood to her sister, as they very soon were, the effect on her was not entirely such as the former had hoped to see. Not that Marianne appeared to distrust the truth of any part of it, for she listened to it all with the most steady and submissive attention, made neither objection nor remark, attempted no vindication of Willoughby, and seemed to show by her tears that she felt it to be impossible. But though this behaviour assured Elinor that the conviction of his guilt *was* carried home to her mind, though she saw with satisfaction the effect of it in her no longer avoiding Colonel Brandon when he called, in her speaking to him, even voluntarily speaking, with a kind of compassionate respect, and though she saw her spirits less violently irritated than before, she did not see her less wretched. Her mind did become settled, but it was settled in a gloomy dejection. She felt the loss of Willoughby's character yet more heavily than she had felt the loss of his heart; his seduction and desertion of Miss Williams, the misery of that poor girl, and the doubt of what his designs might *once* have been on herself, preyed altogether so much on her spirits that she could not bring herself to speak of what she felt even to Elinor; and brooding over her sorrows in silence gave more pain to her sister than could have been communicated by the most open and most frequent confession of them.

To give the feelings or the language of Mrs. Dashwood on receiving and answering Elinor's letter would be only to give a repetition of what her daughters had already felt and said: of a disappointment hardly less painful than Marianne's, and an indignation even greater than Elinor's. Long letters from her, quickly succeeding each other, arrived to tell all that she suffered and thought; to express her anxious solicitude for Marianne, and entreat she would bear up with fortitude under this misfortune. Bad indeed must the nature

of Marianne's affliction be when her mother could talk of
fortitude! Mortifying and humiliating must be the origin of
those regrets which *she* could wish her not to indulge!

Against the interest of her own individual comfort, Mrs.
Dashwood had determined that it would be better for Marianne to be anywhere at that time than at Barton, where everything within her view would be bringing back the past in
the strongest and most afflicting manner by constantly placing Willoughby before her such as she had always seen him
there. She recommended it to her daughters, therefore, by all
means not to shorten their visit to Mrs. Jennings; the length
of which, though never exactly fixed, had been expected by
all to comprise at least five or six weeks. A variety of occu-
pations, of objects, and of company, which could not be procured at Barton, would be inevitable there, and might yet,
she hoped, cheat Marianne at times into some interest beyond herself, and even into some amusement, much as the
idea of both might now be spurned by her.

From all danger of seeing Willoughby again, her mother
considered her to be at least equally safe in town as in the
country, since his acquaintance must now be dropped by all
who called themselves her friends. Design could never bring
them in each other's way; negligence could never leave them
exposed to a surprise; and chance had less in its favour in
the crowd of London than even in the retirement of Barton,
where it might force him before her while paying that visit
at Allenham on his marriage, which Mrs. Dashwood, from
foreseeing at first as a probable event, had brought herself to
expect as a certain one.

She had yet another reason for wishing her children to remain where they were; a letter from her son-in-law had told
her that he and his wife were to be in town before the middle of February, and she judged it right that they should
sometimes see their brother.

Marianne had promised to be guided by her mother's
opinion, and she submitted to it, therefore, without opposition, though it proved perfectly different from what she
wished and expected, though she felt it to be entirely wrong,
formed on mistaken grounds, and that by requiring her
longer continuance in London it deprived her of the only
possible alleviation of her wretchedness, the personal sympathy of her mother, and doomed her to such society and

such scenes as must prevent her ever knowing a moment's rest.

But it was a matter of great consolation to her that what brought evil to herself would bring good to her sister; and Elinor, on the other hand, suspecting that it would not be in her power to avoid Edward entirely, comforted herself by thinking that though their longer stay would therefore militate against her own happiness, it would be better for Marianne than an immediate return into Devonshire.

Her carefulness in guarding her sister from ever hearing Willoughby's name mentioned was not thrown away. Marianne, though without knowing it herself, reaped all its advantage; for neither Mrs. Jennings nor Sir John, nor even Mrs. Palmer herself, ever spoke of him before her. Elinor wished that the same forbearance could have extended towards herself, but that was impossible, and she was obliged to listen day after day to the indignation of them all.

Sir John could not have thought it possible. "A man of whom he had always had such reason to think well! Such a good-natured fellow! He did not believe there was a bolder rider in England! It was an unaccountable business. He wished him at the devil with all his heart. He would not speak another word to him, meet him where he might, for all the world! No, not if it were to be by the side of Barton covert, and they were kept waiting for two hours together. Such a scoundrel of a fellow! Such a deceitful dog! It was only the last time they met that he had offered him one of Folly's puppies! And this was the end of it!"

Mrs. Palmer, in her way, was equally angry. "She was determined to drop his acquaintance immediately, and she was very thankful that she had never been acquainted with him at all. She wished with all her heart Combe Magna was not so near Cleveland; but it did not signify, for it was a great deal too far off to visit; she hated him so much that she was resolved never to mention his name again, and she should tell everybody she saw how good-for-nothing he was."

The rest of Mrs. Palmer's sympathy was shown in procuring all the particulars in her power of the approaching marriage and communicating them to Elinor. She could soon tell at what coachmaker's the new carriage was building, by what painter Mr. Willoughby's portrait was drawn, and at what warehouse Miss Grey's clothes might be seen.

The calm and polite unconcern of Lady Middleton on the

occasion was a happy relief to Elinor's spirits, oppressed as they often were by the clamorous kindness of the others. It was a great comfort to her to be sure of exciting no interest in *one* person at least among their circle of friends; a great comfort to know that there was *one* who would meet her without feeling any curiosity after particulars or any anxiety for her sister's health.

Every qualification is raised at times by the circumstances of the moment to more than its real value; and she was sometimes worried down by officious condolence to rate good breeding as more indispensable to comfort than good nature.

Lady Middleton expressed her sense of the affair about once every day, or twice if the subject occurred very often, by saying, "It is very shocking indeed!" and by the means of this continual though gentle vent was able not only to see the Miss Dashwoods from the first without the smallest emotion, but very soon to see them without recollecting a word of the matter; and having thus supported the dignity of her own sex and spoken her decided censure of what was wrong in the other, she thought herself at liberty to attend to the interest of her own assemblies and therefore determined (though rather against the opinion of Sir John) that as Mrs. Willoughby would at once be a woman of elegance and fortune, to leave her card with her as soon as she married.

Colonel Brandon's delicate, unobtrusive inquiries were never unwelcome to Miss Dashwood. He had abundantly earned the privilege of intimate discussion of her sister's disappointment by the friendly zeal with which he had endeavoured to soften it, and they always conversed with confidence. His chief reward for the painful exertion of disclosing past sorrows and present humiliations was given in the pitying eye with which Marianne sometimes observed him and the gentleness of her voice whenever (though it did not often happen) she was obliged, or could oblige herself, to speak to him. *These* assured him that his exertion had produced an increase of goodwill towards himself, and *these* gave Elinor hopes of its being further augmented hereafter; but Mrs. Jennings, who knew nothing of all this, who knew only that the Colonel continued as grave as ever, and that she could neither prevail on him to make the offer himself nor commission her to make it for him, began, at the end of two days, to think that, instead of Midsummer, they would not be married till Michaelmas, and by the end of a week that it would not be a match at all. The good understanding between the Colonel and Miss Dashwood seemed rather to declare that the honours of the mulberry tree, the canal, and the yew arbour would all be made over to *her*; and Mrs. Jennings had for some time ceased to think at all of Mr. Ferrars.

Early in February, within a fortnight from the receipt of Willoughby's letter, Elinor had the painful office of informing her sister that he was married. She had taken care to have the intelligence conveyed to herself as soon as it was known that the ceremony was over, as she was desirous that Marianne should not receive the first notice of it from the public papers, which she saw her eagerly examining every morning.

She received the news with resolute composure, made no observation on it, and at first shed no tears; but after a short time they would burst out, and for the rest of the day, she was in a state hardly less pitiable than when she first learned to expect the event.

The Willoughbys left town as soon as they were married; and Elinor now hoped, as there could be no danger of her seeing either of them, to prevail on her sister, who had never yet left the house since the blow first fell, to go out again by degrees as she had done before.

About this time the two Miss Steeles, lately arrived at their cousin's house in Bartlett's Buildings, Holborn, presented themselves again before their more grand relations in Conduit and Berkeley Street, and were welcomed by them all with great cordiality.

Elinor only was sorry to see them. Their presence always gave her pain, and she hardly knew how to make a very gracious return to the overpowering delight of Lucy in finding her *still* in town.

"I should have been quite disappointed if I had not found you here *still*," said she repeatedly, with a strong emphasis on the word. "But I always thought I *should*. I was almost sure you would not leave London yet awhile; though you *told* me, you know, at Barton, that you should not stay above a *month*. But I thought at the time that you would most likely change your mind when it came to the point. It would have been such a great pity to have went away before your brother and sister came. And now to be sure you will be in no *hurry* to be gone. I am amazingly glad you did not keep to *your word*."

Elinor perfectly understood her and was forced to use all her self-command to make it appear that she did *not*.

"Well, my dear," said Mrs. Jennings, "and how did you travel?"

"Not in the stage, I assure you," replied Miss Steele with quick exultation; "we came post all the way and had a very smart beau to attend us. Mr. Davies was coming to town, and so we thought we'd join him in a post-chaise; and he behaved very genteelly, and paid ten or twelve shillings more than we did."

"Oh, oh!" cried Mrs. Jennings; "very pretty, indeed! And the Doctor is a single man, I warrant you."

"There now," said Miss Steele, affectedly simpering, "everybody laughs at me so about the Doctor, and I cannot think why. My cousins say they are sure I have made a conquest; but for my part I declare I never think about him from one hour's end to another. 'Lord! Here comes your beau, Nancy,' my cousin said t'other day when she saw him crossing the street to the house. 'My beau, indeed!' said I, 'I cannot think who you mean. The Doctor is no beau of mine.' "

" 'Aye, aye, that is very pretty talking. But it won't do. The Doctor is the man, I see.' "

" 'No, indeed!' " replied her cousin with affected earnestness, " 'and I beg you will contradict it if you ever hear it talked of.' "

Mrs. Jennings directly gave her the gratifying assurance that she certainly would *not,* and Miss Steele was made completely happy.

"I suppose you will go and stay with your brother and sister, Miss Dashwood, when they come to town," said Lucy, returning, after a cessation of hostile hints, to the charge.

"No, I do not think we shall."

"Oh, yes, I dare say you will."

Elinor would not humour her by further opposition.

"What a charming thing it is that Mrs. Dashwood can spare you both for so long a time together!"

"Long a time, indeed!" interposed Mrs. Jennings. "Why, their visit is but just begun!"

Lucy was silenced.

"I am sorry we cannot see your sister, Miss Dashwood,"

said Miss Steele. "I am sorry she is not well"; for Marianne had left the room on their arrival.

"You are very good. My sister will be equally sorry to miss the pleasure of seeing you; but she has been very much plagued lately with nervous headaches which make her unfit for company or conversation."

"Oh, dear, that is a great pity! But such old friends as Lucy and me!—I think she might see *us*; and I am sure we would not speak a word."

Elinor, with great civility, declined the proposal. Her sister was perhaps laid down upon the bed, or in her dressing gown, and therefore not able to come to them.

"Oh, if that's all," cried Miss Steele, "we can just as well go and see *her*."

Elinor began to find this impertinence too much for her temper; but she was saved the trouble of checking it by Lucy's sharp reprimand, which now, as on many occasions, though it did not give much sweetness to the manners of one sister, was of advantage in governing those of the other.

Chapter 11

AFTER SOME opposition, Marianne yielded to her sister's entreaties and consented to go out with her and Mrs. Jennings one morning for half an hour. She expressly conditioned, however, for paying no visits, and would do no more than accompany them to Gray's in Sackville Street, where Elinor was carrying on a negotiation for the exchange of a few old-fashioned jewels of her mother.

When they stopped at the door, Mrs. Jennings recollected that there was a lady at the other end of the street on whom she ought to call; and as she had no business at Gray's, it was resolved that while her young friends transacted theirs, she should pay her visit and return for them.

On ascending the stairs, the Miss Dashwoods found so many people before them in the room that there was not a person at liberty to attend to their orders; and they were obliged to wait. All that could be done was to sit down at that end of the counter which seemed to promise the quickest succession; one gentleman only was standing there, and it is probable that Elinor was not without hope of exciting his politeness to a quicker dispatch. But the correctness of his eye and the delicacy of his taste proved to be beyond his politeness. He was giving orders for a toothpick-case for himself, and till its size, shape, and ornaments were determined, all of which, after examining and debating for a quarter of an hour over every toothpick-case in the shop, were finally arranged by his own inventive fancy, he had no leisure to bestow any other attention on the two ladies than what was comprised in three or four very broad stares; a kind of notice which served to imprint on Elinor the remembrance of a person and face of strong, natural, sterling insignificance, though adorned in the first style of fashion.

Marianne was spared from the troublesome feelings of contempt and resentment on this impertinent examination of their features, and on the puppyism of his manner in deciding on all the different horrors of the different toothpick-cases presented to his inspection, by remaining unconscious of it all; for she was as well able to collect her thoughts within herself, and be as ignorant of what was passing around her, in Mr. Gray's shop, as in her own bedroom.

At last the affair was decided. The ivory, the gold, and the pearls all received their appointment, and the gentleman, having named the last day on which his existence could be continued without the possession of the toothpick-case, drew on his gloves with leisurely care; and bestowing another glance on the Miss Dashwoods, but such a one as seemed rather to demand than express admiration, walked off with a happy air of real conceit and affected indifference.

Elinor lost no time in bringing her business forward, and was on the point of concluding it when another gentleman presented himself at her side. She turned her eyes towards his face and found him with some surprise to be her brother.

Their affection and pleasure in meeting was just enough to make a very creditable appearance in Mr. Gray's shop. John Dashwood was really far from being sorry to see his sisters again; it rather gave them satisfaction; and his inquiries after their mother were respectful and attentive.

Elinor found that he and Fanny had been in town two days.

"I wished very much to call upon you yesterday," said he, "but it was impossible, for we were obliged to take Harry to see the wild beasts at Exeter Exchange; and we spent the rest of the day with Mrs. Ferrars. Harry was vastly pleased. *This* morning I had fully intended to call on you if I could possibly find a spare half hour, but one has always so much to do on first coming to town. I am come here to bespeak Fanny a seal. But to-morrow I think I shall certainly be able to call in Berkeley Street and be introduced to your friend Mrs. Jennings. I understand she is a woman of very good fortune. And the Middletons too, you must introduce me to *them.* As my mother-in-law's relations, I shall be happy to show them every respect. They are excellent neighbours to you in the country, I understand."

"Excellent indeed. Their attention to our comfort, their friendliness in every particular, is more than I can express."

"I am extremely glad to hear it; upon my word; extremely glad indeed. But so it ought to be; they are people of large fortune; they are related to you, and every civility and accommodation that can serve to make your situation pleasant might be reasonably expected. And so you are most comfortably settled in your little cottage and want for nothing! Edward brought us a most charming account of the place; the most complete thing of its kind, he said, that ever was, and you all seemed to enjoy it beyond anything. It was a great satisfaction to us to hear it, I assure you."

Elinor did feel a little ashamed of her brother, and was not sorry to be spared the necessity of answering him by the arrival of Mrs. Jennings's servant, who came to tell her that his mistress waited for them at the door.

Mr. Dashwood attended them downstairs, was introduced to Mrs. Jennings at the door of her carriage, and repeating his hope of being able to call on them the next day, took leave.

His visit was duly paid. He came with a pretence at an apology from their sister-in-law for not coming too; "but she was so much engaged with her mother that really she had no leisure for going anywhere." Mrs. Jennings, however, assured him directly that she should not stand upon ceremony, for they were all cousins, or something like it, and she should certainly wait on Mrs. John Dashwood very soon and bring her sisters to see her. His manners to *them,* though calm, were perfectly kind; to Mrs. Jennings most attentively civil; and on Colonel Brandon's coming in soon after himself, he eyed him with a curiosity which seemed to say that he only wanted to know him to be rich, to be equally civil to *him*.

After staying with them half an hour, he asked Elinor to walk with him to Conduit Street and introduce him to Sir John and Lady Middleton. The weather was remarkably fine, and she readily consented. As soon as they were out of the house, his inquiries began.

"Who is Colonel Brandon? Is he a man of fortune?"

"Yes, he has very good property in Dorsetshire."

"I am glad of it. He seems a most gentlemanlike man; and I think, Elinor, I may congratulate you on the prospect of a very respectable establishment in life."

"Me, brother! What do you mean?"

"He likes you. I observed him narrowly and am convinced of it. What is the amount of his fortune?"

"I believe about two thousand a year."

"Two thousand a year"; and then working himself up to a pitch of enthusiastic generosity, he added, "Elinor, I wish, with all my heart, it were *twice* as much, for your sake."

"Indeed, I believe you," replied Elinor, "but I am very sure that Colonel Brandon has not the smallest wish of marrying *me*."

"You are mistaken, Elinor; you are very much mistaken. A very little trouble on your side secures him. Perhaps just at present he may be undecided; the smallness of your fortune may make him hang back; his friends may all advise him against it. But some of those little attentions and encouragements which ladies can so easily give will fix him in spite of himself. And there can be no reason why you should not try for him. It is not to be supposed that any prior attachment on your side—in short, you know as to an attachment of that kind, it is quite out of the question; the objections are insurmountable—you have too much sense not to see all that. Colonel Brandon must be the man; and no civility shall be wanting on my part to make him pleased with you and your family. It is a match that must give universal satisfaction. In short, it is a kind of thing that," lowering his voice to an important whisper, "will be exceedingly welcome to *all parties*." Recollecting himself, however, he added, "That is, I mean to say—your friends are all truly anxious to see you well settled; Fanny particularly, for she has your interest very much at heart, I assure you. And her mother too, Mrs.

Ferrars, a very good-natured woman; I am sure it would give her great pleasure; she said as much the other day."

Elinor would not vouchsafe any answer.

"It would be something remarkable now," he continued, "something droll if Fanny should have a brother and I a sister settling at the same time. And yet it is not very unlikely."

"Is Mr. Edward Ferrars," said Elinor with resolution, "going to be married?"

"It is not actually settled, but there is such a thing in agitation. He has a most excellent mother. Mrs. Ferrars, with the utmost liberality, will come forward and settle on him a thousand a year, if the match takes place. The lady is the Hon. Miss Morton, only daughter of the late Lord Morton, with thirty thousand pounds. A very desirable connection on both sides, and I have not a doubt of its taking place in time. A thousand a year is a great deal for a mother to give away, to make over forever; but Mrs. Ferrars has a noble spirit. To give you another instance of her liberality: The other day, as soon as we came to town, aware that money could not be very plenty with us just now, she put bank-notes into Fanny's hands to the amount of two hundred pounds. And extremely acceptable it is, for we must live at a great expense while we are here."

He paused for her assent and compassion; and she forced herself to say,

"Your expenses both in town and country must certainly be considerable, but your income is a large one."

"Not so large, I dare say, as many people suppose. I do not mean to complain, however; it is undoubtedly a comfortable one, and I hope will in time be better. The enclosure of Norland Common, now carrying on, is a most serious drain. And then I have made a little purchase within this half year: East Kingham Farm; you must remember the place where old Gibson used to live. The land was so very desirable for me in every respect, so immediately adjoining my own property, that I felt it my duty to buy it. I could not have answered it to my conscience to let it fall into any other hands. A man must pay for his convenience, and it *has* cost me a vast deal of money."

"More than you think it really and intrinsically worth?"

"Why, I hope not that. I might have sold it again the next day for more than I gave; but with regard to the purchase-money, I might have been very unfortunate indeed, for the stocks were at that time so low that if I had not happened to have the necessary sum in my banker's hands, I must have sold out to very great loss."

Elinor could only smile.

"Other great and inevitable expenses too we have had on first coming to Norland. Our respected father, as you well know, bequeathed all the Stanhill effects that remained at Norland (and very valuable they were) to your mother. Far be it from me to repine at his doing so; he had an undoubted right to dispose of his own property as he chose. But, in consequence of it, we have been obliged to make large purchases of linen, china, etc. to supply the place of what was taken away. You may guess, after all these expenses, how very far we must be from being rich, and how acceptable Mrs. Ferrars's kindness is."

"Certainly," said Elinor; "and assisted by her liberality, I hope you may yet live to be in easy circumstances."

"Another year or two may do much towards it," he gravely replied, "but, however, there is still a great deal to be done. There is not a stone laid of Fanny's green-house, and nothing but the plan of the flower-garden marked out."

"Where is the green-house to be?"

"Upon the knoll behind the house. The old walnut trees are all come down to make room for it. It will be a very fine object from many parts of the park, and the flower-garden will slope down just before it, and be exceedingly pretty. We have cleared away all the old thorns that grew in patches over the brow."

Elinor kept her concern and her censure to herself; and was very thankful that Marianne was not present to share the provocation.

Having now said enough to make his poverty clear, and to do away the necessity of buying a pair of ear-rings for each of his sisters in his next visit at Gray's, his thoughts took a cheerfuller turn, and he began to congratulate Elinor on having such a friend as Mrs. Jennings.

"She seems a most valuable woman indeed. Her house, her style of living, all bespeak an exceeding good income; and it is an acquaintance that has not only been of great use to you hitherto but in the end may prove materially advantageous. Her inviting you to town is certainly a vast thing in your favour; and indeed, it speaks altogether so great a regard for you that in all probability when she dies you will not be forgotten. She must have a great deal to leave."

"Nothing at all, I should rather suppose, for she has only her jointure, which will descend to her children."

"But it is not to be imagined that she lives up to her income. Few people of common prudence will do *that*; and whatever she saves, she will be able to dispose of."

"And do you not think it more likely that she should leave it to her daughters than to us?"

"Her daughters are both exceedingly well married, and therefore I cannot perceive the necessity of her remembering them further. Whereas, in my opinion, by her taking so much notice of you and treating you in this kind of way, she has given you a sort of claim on her future consideration, which a conscientious woman would not disregard. Nothing can be kinder than her behaviour; and she can hardly do all this without being aware of the expectation she raises."

"But she raises none in those most concerned. Indeed, brother, your anxiety for our welfare and prosperity carries you too far."

"Why to be sure," said he, seeming to recollect himself, "people have little, have very little in their power. But, my dear Elinor, what is the matter with Marianne? She looks very unwell, has lost her colour, and is grown quite thin. Is she ill?"

"She is not well; she has had a nervous complaint on her for several weeks."

"I am sorry for that. At her time of life, anything of an illness destroys the bloom forever! Hers has been a very short one! She was as handsome a girl last September as any I ever saw—and as likely to attract the men. There was something in her style of beauty to please them particularly. I remember Fanny used to say that she would marry sooner and better than you did; not but what she is exceedingly fond of *you*, but so it happened to strike her. She will be mistaken, however. I question whether Marianne *now* will marry a man worth more than five or six hundred a year, at the utmost, and I am very much deceived if *you* do not do better. Dorsetshire! I know very little of Dorsetshire; but, my dear Elinor, I shall be exceedingly glad to know more of it; and I think I can answer for your having Fanny and myself among the earliest and best pleased of your visitors."

Elinor tried very seriously to convince him that there was

no likelihood of her marrying Colonel Brandon; but it was an expectation of too much pleasure to himself to be relinquished; and he was really resolved on seeking an intimacy with that gentleman and promoting the marriage by every possible attention. He had just compunction enough for having done nothing for his sisters himself to be exceedingly anxious that everybody else should do a great deal; and an offer from Colonel Brandon, or a legacy from Mrs. Jennings, was the easiest means of atoning for his own neglect.

They were lucky enough to find Lady Middleton at home, and Sir John came in before their visit ended. Abundance of civilities passed on all sides. Sir John was ready to like anybody, and though Mr. Dashwood did not seem to know much about horses, he soon set him down as a very good-natured fellow, while Lady Middleton saw enough of fashion in his appearance to think his acquaintance worth having; and Mr. Dashwood went away delighted with both.

"I shall have a charming account to carry to Fanny," said he as he walked back with his sister. "Lady Middleton is really a most elegant woman! Such a woman as I am sure Fanny will be glad to know. And Mrs. Jennings, too, an exceeding well-behaved woman, though not so elegant as her daughter. Your sister need not have any scruple even of visiting *her,* which, to say the truth, has been a little the case, and very naturally; for we only knew that Mrs. Jennings was the widow of a man who had got all his money in a low way; and Fanny and Mrs. Ferrars were both strongly prepossessed that neither she nor her daughters were such kind of women as Fanny would like to associate with. But now I can carry her a most satisfactory account of both."

Chapter 12

MRS. JOHN DASHWOOD had so much confidence in her husband's judgment that she waited the very next day both on Mrs. Jennings and her daughter; and her confidence was rewarded by finding even the former, even the woman with whom her sisters were staying, by no means unworthy her notice; and as for Lady Middleton, she found her one of the most charming women in the world!

Lady Middleton was equally pleased with Mrs. Dashwood. There was a kind of cold-hearted selfishness on both sides which mutually attracted them; and they sympathized with each other in an insipid propriety of demeanour and a general want of understanding.

The same manners, however, which recommended Mrs. John Dashwood to the good opinion of Lady Middleton did not suit the fancy of Mrs. Jennings, and to *her* she appeared nothing more than a little proud-looking woman of uncordial address, who met her husband's sisters without any affection, and almost without having anything to say to them; for of the quarter of an hour bestowed on Berkeley Street she sat at least seven minutes and a half in silence.

Elinor wanted very much to know, though she did not choose to ask, whether Edward was then in town; but nothing would have induced Fanny voluntarily to mention his name before her till able to tell her that his marriage with Miss Morton was resolved on, or till her husband's expectations on Colonel Brandon were answered, because she believed them still so very much attached to each other that they could not be too sedulously divided in word and deed on every occasion. The intelligence, however, which *she* would not give, soon flowed from another quarter. Lucy came very shortly to claim Elinor's compassion on being unable to see Edward, though he had arrived in town with Mr. and Mrs. Dashwood. He dared not come to Bartlett's Buildings for fear of detection, and though their mutual impatience to meet was not to be told, they could do nothing at present but write.

Edward assured them himself of his being in town within a very short time, by twice calling in Berkeley Street. Twice was his card found on the table when they returned from their morning's engagements. Elinor was pleased that he had called, and still more pleased that she had missed him.

The Dashwoods were so prodigiously delighted with the Middletons that, though not much in the habit of giving anything, they determined to give them—a dinner; and soon after their acquaintance began, invited them to dine in Harley Street, where they had taken a very good house for three months. Their sisters and Mrs. Jennings were invited likewise, and John Dashwood was careful to secure Colonel

Brandon, who, always glad to be where the Miss Dashwoods were, received his eager civilities with some surprise but much more pleasure. They were to meet Mrs. Ferrars; but Elinor could not learn whether her sons were to be of the party. The expectation of seeing *her,* however, was enough to make her interested in the engagement; for though she could now meet Edward's mother without that strong anxiety which had once promised to attend such an introduction, though she could now see her with perfect indifference as to her opinion of herself, her desire of being in company with Mrs. Ferrars, her curiosity to know what she was like, was as lively as ever.

The interest with which she thus anticipated the party was soon afterwards increased, more powerfully than pleasantly, by her hearing that the Miss Steeles were also to be at it.

So well had they recommended themselves to Lady Middleton, so agreeable had their assiduities made them to her, that though Lucy was certainly not elegant and her sister not even genteel, she was as ready as Sir John to ask them to spend a week or two in Conduit Street; and it happened to be particularly convenient to the Miss Steeles, as soon as the Dashwoods' invitation was known, that their visit should begin a few days before the party took place.

Their claims to the notice of Mrs. John Dashwood, as the nieces of the gentleman who for many years had had the care of her brother, might not have done much, however, towards procuring them seats at her table; but as Lady Middleton's guests they must be welcome; and Lucy, who had long wanted to be personally known to the family, to have a nearer view of their characters and her own difficulties, and to have an opportunity of endeavouring to please them, had seldom been happier in her life than she was on receiving Mrs. John Dashwood's card.

On Elinor its effect was very different. She began immediately to determine that Edward, who lived with his mother, must be asked, as his mother was, to a party given by his sister; and to see him for the first time after all that passed, in the company of Lucy! She hardly knew how she could bear it!

These apprehensions, perhaps, were not founded entirely on reason and certainly not at all on truth. They were relieved, however, not by her own recollection but by the good will of Lucy, who believed herself to be inflicting a severe disappointment when she told her that Edward certainly would not be in Harley Street on Tuesday, and even hoped to be carrying the pain still further by persuading her that he was kept away by that extreme affection for herself which he could not conceal when they were together.

The important Tuesday came that was to introduce the two young ladies to this formidable mother-in-law.

"Pity me, dear Miss Dashwood!" said Lucy as they walked up the stairs together—for the Middletons arrived so directly after Mrs. Jennings that they all followed the servant at the same time. "There is nobody here but you that can feel for me. I declare I can hardly stand. Good gracious! In a moment I shall see the person that all my happiness depends on—that is to be my mother!"

Elinor could have given her immediate relief by suggesting the possibility of its being Miss Morton's mother, rather than her own, whom they were about to behold; but instead of doing that, she assured her, and with great sincerity, that she did pity her—to the utter amazement of Lucy, who, though really uncomfortable herself, hoped at least to be an object of irrepressible envy to Elinor.

Mrs. Ferrars was a little, thin woman, upright, even to formality, in her figure, and serious, even to sourness, in her aspect. Her complexion was sallow; and her features small, without beauty, and naturally without expression; but a lucky contraction of the brow had rescued her countenance from the disgrace of insipidity by giving it the strong characters of pride and ill nature. She was not a woman of many words; for, unlike people in general, she proportioned them to the number of her ideas; and of the few syllables that did escape her, not one fell to the share of Miss Dashwood, whom she eyed with the spirited determination of disliking her at all events.

Elinor could not *now* be made unhappy by this behaviour. A few months ago it would have hurt her exceedingly; but it was not in Mrs. Ferrars's power to distress her by it now; and the difference of her manners to the Miss Steeles, a difference which seemed purposely made to humble her more, only amused her. She could not but smile to see the graciousness of both mother and daughter towards the very person—for Lucy was particularly distinguished—whom of all others, had they known as much as she did, they would have been most anxious to mortify; while she herself, who had comparatively no power to wound them, sat pointedly slighted by both. But while she smiled at a graciousness so misapplied, she could not reflect on the mean-spirited folly from which it sprung, nor observe the studied attentions with which the Miss Steeles courted its continuance, without thoroughly despising them all four.

Lucy was all exultation on being so honourably distinguished; and Miss Steele wanted only to be teased about Dr. Davies to be perfectly happy.

The dinner was a grand one, the servants were numerous, and everything bespoke the Mistress's inclination for show and the Master's ability to support it. In spite of the improvements and additions which they were making to the Norland estate, and in spite of its owner having once been within some thousand pounds of being obliged to sell out at a loss, nothing gave any symptom of that indigence which he had tried to infer from it; no poverty of any kind, except of conversation, appeared, but there the deficiency was considerable. John Dashwood had not much to say for himself that was worth hearing, and his wife had still less. But there was no peculiar disgrace in this, for it was very much the case with the chief of their visitors, who almost all laboured under one or other of these disqualifications for being agreeable: want of sense, either natural or improved; want of elegance, want of spirits, or want of temper.

When the ladies withdrew to the drawing-room after dinner this poverty was particularly evident, for the gentlemen *had* supplied the discourse with some variety: the variety of politics, enclosing land, and breaking horses—but then it was all over; and one subject only engaged the ladies till coffee came in, which was the comparative heights of Harry Dashwood and Lady Middleton's second son, William, who were nearly of the same age.

Had both the children been there the affair might have been determined too easily by measuring them at once; but as Harry only was present, it was all conjectural assertion on both sides, and everybody had a right to be equally positive in their opinion and to repeat it over and over again as often as they liked.

The parties stood thus:

The two mothers, though each really convinced that her own son was the tallest, politely decided in favour of the other.

The two grandmothers, with not less partiality but more sincerity, were equally earnest in support of their own descendant.

Lucy, who was hardly less anxious to please one parent than the other, thought the boys were both remarkably tall for their age and could not conceive that there could be the smallest difference in the world between them; and Miss Steele, with yet greater address, gave it as fast as she could in favour of each.

Elinor, having once delivered her opinion on William's side, by which she offended Mrs. Ferrars and Fanny still more, did not see the necessity of enforcing it by any further assertion; and Marianne, when called on for hers, offended them all by declaring that she had no opinion to give, as she had never thought about it.

Before her removing from Norland, Elinor had painted a very pretty pair of screens for her sister-in-law, which being now just mounted and brought home, ornamented her present drawing-room; and these screens, catching the eye of John Dashwood on his following the other gentlemen into the room, were officiously handed by him to Colonel Brandon for his admiration.

"These are done by my eldest sister," said he, "and you, as a man of taste, will, I dare say, be pleased with them. I do not know whether you ever happened to see any of her performances before, but she is in general reckoned to draw extremely well."

The Colonel, though disclaiming all pretensions to connoisseurship, warmly admired the screens, as he would have done anything painted by Miss Dashwood; and the curiosity of the others being of course excited, they were handed round for general inspection. Mrs. Ferrars, not aware of their being Elinor's work, particularly requested to look at them; and after they had received the gratifying testimony of Lady Middleton's approbation, Fanny presented them to her mother, considerately informing her at the same time that they were done by Miss Dashwood.

"Hum!" said Mrs. Ferrars. "Very pretty," and without regarding them at all returned them to her daughter.

Perhaps Fanny thought for a moment that her mother had been quite rude enough, for, colouring a little, she immediately said: "They are very pretty, ma'am, an't they?" But then again, the dread of having been too civil, too encouraging herself, probably came over her, for she presently added:

"Do you not think they are something in Miss Morton's style of painting, ma'am? *She does* paint most delightfully! How beautifully her last landscape is done!"

"Beautifully indeed! But *she* does everything well."

Marianne could not bear this. She was already greatly displeased with Mrs. Ferrars; and such ill-timed praise of another at Elinor's expense, though she had not any notion of what was principally meant by it, provoked her immediately to say with warmth:

"This is admiration of a very particular kind! What is Miss Morton to us? Who knows, or who cares, for her? It is Elinor of whom *we* think and speak."

And so saying, she took the screens out of her sister-in-law's hands to admire them herself as they ought to be admired.

Mrs. Ferrars looked exceedingly angry, and drawing herself up more stiffly than ever, pronounced in retort this bitter phillippic, "Miss Morton is Lord Morton's daughter."

Fanny looked very angry too, and her husband was all in a fright at his sister's audacity. Elinor was much more hurt by Marianne's warmth than she had been by what produced it; but Colonel Brandon's eyes, as they were fixed on Marianne, declared that he noticed only what was amiable in it: the affectionate heart which could not bear to see a sister slighted in the smallest point.

Marianne's feelings did not stop here. The cold insolence of Mrs. Ferrars's general behaviour to her sister, seemed to her to foretell such difficulties and distresses to Elinor as her own wounded heart taught her to think of with horror; and urged by a strong impulse of affectionate sensibility, she moved after a moment to her sister's chair, and putting one arm round her neck and one cheek close to hers, said in a low, but eager, voice:

"Dear, dear Elinor, don't mind them. Don't let them make *you* unhappy."

She could say no more; her spirits were quite overcome, and hiding her face on Elinor's shoulder, she burst into tears. Everybody's attention was called, and almost everybody was concerned. Colonel Brandon rose up and went to them without knowing what he did. Mrs. Jennings, with a very intelligent "Ah! poor dear," immediately gave her her salts; and

Sir John felt so desperately enraged against the author of this nervous distress that he instantly changed his seat to one close by Lucy Steele, and gave her, in a whisper, a brief account of the whole shocking affair.

In a few minutes, however, Marianne was recovered enough to put an end to the bustle and sit down among the rest, though her spirits retained the impression of what had passed the whole evening.

"Poor Marianne!" said her brother to Colonel Brandon in a low voice, as soon as he could secure his attention, "she has not such good health as her sister—she is very nervous—she has not Elinor's constitution; and one must allow that there is something very trying to a young woman who *has been* a beauty in the loss of her personal attractions. You would not think it, perhaps, but Marianne *was* remarkably handsome a few months ago; quite as handsome as Elinor. Now you see it is all gone."

Chapter 13

ELINOR'S CURIOSITY to see Mrs. Ferrars was satisfied. She had found in her everything that could tend to make a further connection between the families undesirable. She had seen enough of her pride, her meanness, and her determined prejudice against herself, to comprehend all the difficulties that must have perplexed the engagement and retarded the marriage of Edward and herself, had he been otherwise free; and she had seen almost enough to be thankful for her *own* sake that one greater obstacle preserved her from suffering under any other of Mrs. Ferrars's creation, preserved her from all dependence upon her caprice, or any solicitude for her good opinion. Or at least, if she did not bring herself quite to rejoice in Edward's being fettered to Lucy, she determined, that had Lucy been more amiable, she *ought* to have rejoiced.

She wondered that Lucy's spirits could be so very much elevated by the civility of Mrs. Ferrars; that her interest and her vanity should so very much blind her as to make the attention which seemed only paid her because she was *not*

Elinor appear a compliment to herself—or to allow her to derive encouragement from a preference only given her because her real situation was unknown. But that it was so had not only been declared by Lucy's eyes at the time, but was declared over again the next morning more openly, for at her particular desire, Lady Middleton set her down in Berkeley Street on the chance of seeing Elinor alone to tell her how happy she was.

The chance proved a lucky one, for a message from Mrs. Palmer soon after she arrived carried Mrs. Jennings away.

"My dear friend," cried Lucy as soon as they were by themselves, "I come to talk to you of my happiness. Could anything be so flattering as Mrs. Ferrars's way of treating me yesterday? So exceeding affable as she was! You know how I dreaded the thoughts of seeing her; but the very moment I was introduced, there was such an affability in her behaviour as really should seem to say she had quite took a fancy to me. Now was not it so? You saw it all, and was not you quite struck with it?"

"She was certainly very civil to you."

"Civil! Did you see nothing but only civility? I saw a vast deal more. Such kindness as fell to the share of nobody but me! No pride, no hauteur, and your sister just the same: all sweetness and affability!"

Elinor wished to talk of something else, but Lucy still pressed her to own that she had reason for her happiness; and Elinor was obliged to go on.

"Undoubtedly, if they had known your engagement," said she, "nothing could be more flattering than their treatment of you; but as that was not the case—"

"I guessed you would say so," replied Lucy quickly, "but there was no reason in the world why Mrs. Ferrars should seem to like me if she did not, and her liking me is everything. You shan't talk me out of my satisfaction. I am sure it will all end well, and there will be no difficulties at all to what I used to think. Mrs. Ferrars is a charming woman, and so is your sister. They are both delightful women indeed! I wonder I should never hear you say how agreeable Mrs. Dashwood was!"

To this, Elinor had no answer to make and did not attempt any.

"Are you ill, Miss Dashwood? You seem low— You don't speak; sure you an't well."

"I never was in better health."

"I am glad of it with all my heart, but really you did not look it. I should be so sorry to have *you* ill; you that have been the greatest comfort to me in the world! Heaven knows what I should have done without your friendship."

Elinor tried to make a civil answer, though doubting her own success. But it seemed to satisfy Lucy, for she directly replied:

"Indeed, I am perfectly convinced of your regard for me, and next to Edward's love, it is the greatest comfort I have. Poor Edward! But now there is one good thing: we shall be able to meet, and meet pretty often, for Lady Middleton's delighted with Mrs. Dashwood, so we shall be a good deal in Harley Street, I dare say, and Edward spends half his time with his sister. Besides, Lady Middleton and Mrs. Ferrars will visit now; and Mrs. Ferrars and your sister were both so good to say more than once they should always be glad to see me. They are such charming women! I am sure if ever you tell your sister what I think of her, you cannot speak too high."

But Elinor would not give her any encouragement to hope that she *should* tell her sister. Lucy continued:

"I am sure I should have seen it in a moment if Mrs. Ferrars had took a dislike to me. If she had only made me a formal curtsey, for instance, without saying a word, and never after had took any notice of me, and never looked at me in a pleasant way—you know what I mean—if I had been treated in that forbidding sort of way I should have gave it all up in despair. I could not have stood it. For where she *does* dislike, I know it is most violent."

Elinor was prevented from making any reply to this civil triumph by the door's being thrown open, the servant's announcing Mr. Ferrars, and Edward's immediately walking in.

It was a very awkward moment, and the countenance of each showed that it was so. They all looked exceedingly foolish; and Edward seemed to have as great an inclination to walk out of the room again as to advance farther into it. The very circumstance, in its unpleasantest form, which they would each have been most anxious to avoid, had fallen on them. They were not only all three together but were together without the relief of any other person. The ladies recovered themselves first. It was not Lucy's business to put herself forward, and the appearance of secrecy must still be kept up. She could therefore only *look* her tenderness, and after slightly addressing him, said no more.

But Elinor had more to do; and so anxious was she, for his sake and her own, to do it well that she forced herself, after a moment's recollection, to welcome him with a look and manner that were almost easy and almost open; and another struggle, another effort, still improved them. She would not allow the presence of Lucy, nor the consciousness of some injustice towards herself, to deter her from saying that she was happy to see him, and that she had very much regretted being from home when he called before in Berkeley Street. She would not be frightened from paying him those attentions which, as a friend and almost a relation, were his due, by the observant eyes of Lucy, though she soon perceived them to be narrowly watching her.

Her manners gave some reassurance to Edward, and he had courage enough to sit down; but his embarrassment still exceeded that of the ladies in a proportion which the case rendered reasonable though his sex might make it rare; for his heart had not the indifference of Lucy's, nor could his conscience have quite the ease of Elinor's.

Lucy, with a demure and settled air, seemed determined to make no contribution to the comfort of the others, and would not say a word; and almost everything that *was* said proceeded from Elinor, who was obliged to volunteer all the information about her mother's health, their coming to town, etc., which Edward ought to have inquired about but never did.

Her exertions did not stop here; for she soon afterwards felt herself so heroically disposed as to determine, under pretence of fetching Marianne, to leave the others by themselves; and she really did it, and *that* in the handsomest manner, for she loitered away several minutes on the landing-place with the most high-minded fortitude before she went to her sister. When that was once done, however, it was time for the raptures of Edward to cease; for Marianne's joy hurried her into the drawing-room immediately. Her pleasure in seeing him was like every other of her feelings, strong in itself and strongly spoken. She met him with a hand that would be taken and a voice that expressed the affection of a sister.

"Dear Edward!" she cried, "this is a moment of great happiness! This would almost make amends for everything!"

Edward tried to return her kindness as it deserved, but before such witnesses he dared not say half what he really felt. Again they all sat down, and for a moment or two all were silent, while Marianne was looking with the most speaking tenderness, sometimes at Edward and sometimes at Elinor, regretting only that their delight in each other should be checked by Lucy's unwelcome presence. Edward was the first to speak, and it was to notice Marianne's altered looks and express his fear of her not finding London agree with her.

"Oh! don't think of me!" she replied with spirited earnestness, though her eyes were filled with tears as she spoke. "Don't think of *my* health. Elinor is well, you see. That must be enough for us both."

This remark was not calculated to make Edward or Elinor more easy, nor to conciliate the good will of Lucy, who looked up at Marianne with no very benignant expression.

"Do you like London?" said Edward, willing to say anything that might introduce another subject.

"Not at all. I expected much pleasure in it, but I have found none. The sight of you, Edward, is the only comfort it has afforded; and thank Heaven! you are what you always were!"

She paused—no one spoke.

"I think, Elinor," she presently added, "we must employ Edward to take care of us in our return to Barton. In a week or two, I suppose, we shall be going; and, I trust, Edward will not be very unwilling to accept the charge."

Poor Edward muttered something, but what it was, nobody knew, not even himself. But Marianne, who saw his agitation and could easily trace it to whatever cause best pleased herself, was perfectly satisfied and soon talked of something else.

"We spent such a day, Edward, in Harley Street yesterday! So dull, so wretchedly dull! But I have much to say to you on that head which cannot be said now."

And with this admirable discretion did she defer the assurance of her finding their mutual relatives more disagreeable than ever, and of her being particularly disgusted with his mother, till they were more in private.

"But why were you not there, Edward? Why did you not come?"

"I was engaged elsewhere."

"Engaged! But what was that when such friends were to be met?"

"Perhaps, Miss Marianne," cried Lucy, eager to take some revenge on her, "you think young men never stand upon engagements if they have no mind to keep them, little as well as great."

Elinor was very angry, but Marianne seemed entirely insensible of the sting, for she calmly replied:

"Not so, indeed; for, seriously speaking, I am very sure that conscience only kept Edward from Harley Street. And I really believe he *has* the most delicate conscience in the world, the most scrupulous in performing every engagement however minute, and however it may make against his interest or pleasure. He is the most fearful of giving pain, of wounding expectation, and the most incapable of being selfish of anybody I ever saw. Edward, it is so and I will say it. What! Are you never to hear yourself praised! Then you must be no friend of mine, for those who will accept of my love and esteem must submit to my open commendation."

The nature of commendation in the present case, however, happened to be particularly ill-suited to the feelings of two thirds of her auditors, and was so very unexhilarating to Edward that he very soon got up to go away.

"Going so soon!" said Marianne, "my dear Edward, this must not be."

And drawing him a little aside, she whispered her persuasion that Lucy could not stay much longer. But even this encouragement failed, for he would go; and Lucy, who would have outstayed him had his visit lasted two hours, soon afterwards went away.

"What can bring her here so often!" said Marianne on her leaving them. "Could she not see that we wanted her gone! How teasing to Edward!"

"Why so? We were all his friends, and Lucy has been the longest known to him of any. It is but natural that he should like to see her as well as ourselves."

Marianne looked at her steadily, and said, "You know, Elinor, that this is a kind of talking which I cannot bear. If you only hope to have your assertion contradicted, as I must suppose to be the case, you ought to recollect that I am the last person in the world to do it. I cannot descend to be tricked out of assurances that are not really wanted."

She then left the room, and Elinor dared not follow her to

say more, for bound as she was by her promise of secrecy to Lucy, she could give no information that would convince Marianne, and painful as the consequences of her still continuing in an error might be, she was obliged to submit to it. All that she could hope was that Edward would not often expose her or himself to the distress of hearing Marianne's mistaken warmth, nor to the repetition of any other part of the pain that had attended their recent meeting—and this she had every reason to expect.

Chapter 14

WITHIN A FEW days after this meeting, the newspapers announced to the world that the Lady of Thomas Palmer, Esq. was safely delivered of a son and heir, a very interesting and satisfactory paragraph, at least to all those intimate connections who knew it before.

This event, highly important to Mrs. Jennings's happiness, produced a temporary alteration in the disposal of her time, and influenced in a like degree the engagements of her young friends, for as she wished to be as much as possible with Charlotte, she went thither every morning as soon as she was dressed and did not return till late in the evening; and the Miss Dashwoods, at the particular request of the Middletons, spent the whole of every day in Conduit Street. For their own comfort they would much rather have remained at least all the morning in Mrs. Jennings's house, but it was not a thing to be urged against the wishes of everybody. Their hours were therefore made over to Lady Middleton and the two Miss Steeles, by whom their company was in fact as little valued as it was professedly sought.

They had too much sense to be desirable companions to the former; and by the latter they were considered with a jealous eye as intruding on *their* ground and sharing the kindness which they wanted to monopolize. Though nothing could be more polite than Lady Middleton's behaviour to Elinor and Marianne, she did not really like them at all. Because they neither flattered herself nor her children, she could not believe them good-natured; and because they were fond of reading, she fancied them satirical, perhaps without exactly knowing what it was to be satirical, but *that* did not signify. It was censure in common use, and easily given.

Their presence was a restraint both on her and on Lucy. It checked the idleness of one and the business of the other. Lady Middleton was ashamed of doing nothing before them, and the flattery which Lucy was proud to think of and administer at other times she feared they would despise her for offering. Miss Steele was the least discomposed of the three by their presence, and it was in their power to reconcile her to it entirely. Would either of them only have given her a full and minute account of the whole affair between Marianne and Mr. Willoughby, she would have thought herself amply rewarded for the sacrifice of the best place by the fire after dinner, which their arrival occasioned. But this conciliation was not granted, for though she often threw out expressions of pity for her sister to Elinor, and more than once dropped a reflection on the inconstancy of beaux before Marianne, no effect was produced but a look of indifference from the former or of disgust in the latter. An effort even yet lighter might have made her their friend. Would they only have laughed at her about the Doctor! But so little were they, any more than the others, inclined to oblige her that if Sir John dined from home, she might spend a whole day without hearing any other raillery on the subject than what she was kind enough to bestow on herself.

All these jealousies and discontents, however, were so totally unsuspected by Mrs. Jennings that she thought it a delightful thing for the girls to be together, and generally congratulated her young friends every night on having escaped the company of a stupid old woman so long. She joined them sometimes at Sir John's and sometimes at her own house; but wherever it was, she always came in excellent spirits, full of delight and importance, attributing Charlotte's well-doing to her own care, and ready to give so exact, so minute, a detail of her situation as only Miss Steele had curiosity enough to desire. One thing *did* disturb her; and of that she made her daily complaint. Mr. Palmer maintained the common but unfatherly opinion among his sex of all infants being alike; and though she could plainly perceive at different times the most striking resemblance between this baby and every one of his relations on both sides, there was no convincing his father of it; no persuading him to believe that it was not exactly like every other baby of the same age; nor could he even be brought to acknowledge the simple proposition of its being the finest child in the world.

I come now to the relation of a misfortune which about this time befell Mrs. John Dashwood. It so happened that while her two sisters with Mrs. Jennings were first calling on her in Harley Street, another of her acquaintance had dropped in, a circumstance in itself not apparently likely to produce evil to her. But while the imaginations of other people will carry them away to form wrong judgments of our conduct and to decide on it by slight appearances, one's happiness must in some measure be always at the mercy of chance. In the present instance, this last-arrived lady allowed her fancy so far to outrun truth and probability that on merely hearing the name of the Miss Dashwoods and understanding them to be Mr. Dashwood's sisters, she immediately concluded them to be staying in Harley Street, and this misconstruction produced within a day or two afterwards cards of invitation for them, as well as for their brother and sister, to a small musical party at her house. The consequence of which was that Mrs. John Dashwood was obliged to submit not only to the exceedingly great inconvenience of sending her carriage for the Miss Dashwoods, but, what was still worse, must be subject to all the unpleasantness of appearing to treat them with attention; and who could tell that they might not expect to go out with her a second time? The power of disappointing them, it was true, must always be hers. But that was not enough, for when people are determined on a mode of conduct which they know to be wrong, they feel injured by the expectation of anything better from them.

Marianne had now been brought, by degrees, so much into the habit of going out every day that it was become a matter of indifference to her whether she went or not, and she prepared quietly and mechanically for every evening's engagement, though without expecting the smallest amusement from any, and very often without knowing till the last moment where it was to take her.

To her dress and appearance she was grown so perfectly indifferent as not to bestow half the consideration on it, during the whole of her toilette, which it received from Miss Steele in the first five minutes of their being together, when it was finished. Nothing escaped *her* minute observation and general curiosity; she saw everything and asked everything; was never easy till she knew the price of every part of Marianne's dress; could have guessed the number of her gowns altogether with better judgment than Marianne herself, and was not without hopes of finding out before they parted how much her washing cost per week, and how much she had every year to spend upon herself. The impertinence of these kind of scrutinies, moreover, was generally concluded with a compliment, which though meant as its *douceur,* was considered by Marianne as the greatest impertinence of all, for after undergoing an examination into the value and make of her gown, the colour of her shoes, and the arrangement of her hair, she was almost sure of being told that upon "her word she looked vastly smart, and she dared to say would make a great many conquests."

With such encouragement as this was she dismissed on the present occasion to her brother's carriage, which they were ready to enter five minutes after it stopped at the door, a punctuality not very agreeable to their sister-in-law, who had preceded them to the house of her acquaintance and was there hoping for some delay on their part that might inconvenience either herself or her coachman.

The events of the evening were not very remarkable. The party, like other musical parties, comprehended a great many people who had real taste for the performance, and a great many more who had none at all; and the performers themselves were, as usual, in their own estimation and that of their immediate friends the first private performers in England.

As Elinor was neither musical nor affecting to be so, she made no scruple of turning away her eyes from the grand pianoforte whenever it suited her, and unrestrained even by the presence of a harp and a violoncello, would fix them at pleasure on any other object in the room. In one of these excursive glances she perceived, among a group of young men, the very he who had given them a lecture on toothpick-cases at Gray's. She perceived him soon afterwards looking at herself and speaking familiarly to her brother, and had just determined to find out his name from the latter when they both came towards her, and Mr. Dashwood introduced him to her as Mr. Robert Ferrars.

He addressed her with easy civility and twisted his head into a bow which assured her as plainly as words could have done that he was exactly the coxcomb she had heard him described to be by Lucy. Happy had it been for her if her regard for Edward had depended less on his own merit than on the merit of his nearest relations! For then his brother's bow must have given the finishing stroke to what the ill-humour of his mother and sister would have begun. But while she wondered at the difference of the two young men, she did not find that the emptiness and conceit of the one put her at all out of charity with the modesty and worth of the other. Why they *were* different, Robert explained to her himself in the course of a quarter of an hour's conversation; for, talking of his brother and lamenting the extreme *gaucherie* which he really believed kept him from mixing in proper society, he candidly and generously attributed it much less to any natural deficiency than to the misfortune of a private education, while he himself, though probably without any particular, any material, superiority by nature, merely from the advantage of a public school, was as well fitted to mix in the world as any other man.

"Upon my soul," he added, "I believe it is nothing more, and so I often tell my mother when she is grieving about it. 'My dear Madam,' I always say to her, 'you must make yourself easy. The evil is now irremediable, and it has been entirely your own doing. Why would you be persuaded by my uncle, Sir Robert, against your own judgment to place Edward under private tuition at the most critical time of his life? If you had only sent him to Westminster as well as myself instead of sending him to Mr. Pratt's, all this would have been prevented.' This is the way in which I always consider the matter, and my mother is perfectly convinced of her error."

Elinor would not oppose his opinion, because, whatever might be her general estimation of the advantage of a public school, she could not think of Edward's abode in Mr. Pratt's family with any satisfaction.

"You reside in Devonshire, I think," was his next observation, "in a cottage near Dawlish."

Elinor set him right as to its situation, and it seemed rather surprising to him that anybody could live in Devonshire without living near Dawlish. He bestowed his hearty approbation, however, on their species of house.

"For my own part," said he, "I am excessively fond of a cottage; there is always so much comfort, so much elegance about them. And I protest, if I had any money to spare, I should buy a little land and build one myself within a short distance of London, where I might drive myself down at any time and collect a few friends about me and be happy. I advise everybody who is going to build, to build a cottage. My friend Lord Courtland came to me the other day on purpose to ask my advice, and laid before me three different plans of Bonomi's. I was to decide on the best of them. 'My dear Courtland,' said I, immediately throwing them all into the fire, 'do not adopt either of them, but by all means build a cottage.' And that, I fancy, will be the end of it.

"Some people imagine that there can be no accommodations, no space in a cottage; but this is all a mistake. I was last month at my friend Elliott's near Dartford. Lady Elliott wished to give a dance. 'But how can it be done?' said she. 'My dear Ferrars, do tell me how it is to be managed. There is not a room in this cottage that will hold ten couples, and where can the supper be?' *I* immediately saw that there could be no difficulty in it, so I said, 'My dear Lady Elliott, do not be uneasy. The dining-parlour will admit eighteen couples with ease; card-tables may be placed in the drawing-room; the library may be open for tea and other refreshments; and let the supper be set out in the saloon.' Lady Elliott was delighted with the thought. We measured the dining-room, and found it would hold exactly eighteen couples, and the affair was arranged precisely after my plan. So that, in fact, you see, if people do but know how to set about it, every comfort may be as well enjoyed in a cottage as in the most spacious dwelling."

Elinor agreed to it all, for she did not think he deserved the compliment of rational opposition.

As John Dashwood had no more pleasure in music than his eldest sister, his mind was equally at liberty to fix on anything else, and a thought struck him during the evening, which he communicated to his wife for her approbation when they got home. The consideration of Mrs. Dennison's mistake in supposing his sisters their guests had suggested the propriety of their being really invited to become such while Mrs. Jennings's engagements kept her from home. The expense would be nothing, the inconvenience not more; and it was altogether an attention which the delicacy of his conscience pointed out to be requisite to its complete enfranchisement from his promise to his father. Fanny was startled at the proposal.

"I do not see how it can be done," said she, "without affronting Lady Middleton, for they spend every day with her; otherwise I should be exceedingly glad to do it. You know I am always ready to pay them any attention in my power, as my taking them out this evening shows. But they are Lady Middleton's visitors. How can I ask them away from her?"

Her husband, but with great humility, did not see the force of her objection. "They had already spent a week in this manner in Conduit Street, and Lady Middleton could not be displeased at their giving the same number of days to such near relations."

Fanny paused a moment, and then, with fresh vigour, said:

"My love, I would ask them with all my heart if it was in my power. But I had just settled within myself to ask the Miss Steeles to spend a few days with us. They are very well-behaved, good kind of girls, and I think the attention is due to them, as their uncle did so very well by Edward. We can ask your sisters some other year, you know; but the Miss Steeles may not be in town any more. I am sure you will like them; indeed, you *do* like them, you know, very much already, and so does my mother; and they are such favourites with Harry!"

Mr. Dashwood was convinced. He saw the necessity of inviting the Miss Steeles immediately, and his conscience was pacified by the resolution of inviting his sisters another year; at the same time, however, slyly suspecting that another year would make the invitation needless by bringing Elinor to town as Colonel Brandon's wife and Marianne as *their* visitor.

Fanny, rejoicing in her escape and proud of the ready wit that had procured it, wrote the next morning to Lucy to request her company and her sister's for some days in Harley Street as soon as Lady Middleton could spare them. This was enough to make Lucy really and reasonably happy. Mrs. Dashwood seemed actually working for her, herself, cherishing all her hopes and promoting all her views! Such an opportunity of being with Edward and his family was, above all things, the most material to her interest, and such an invitation the most gratifying to her feelings! It was an advantage that could not be too gratefully acknowledged, nor too speedily made use of; and the visit to Lady Middleton, which had not before had any precise limits, was instantly discovered to have been always meant to end in two days time.

When the note was shown to Elinor, as it was within ten minutes after its arrival, it gave her for the first time some share in the expectations of Lucy; for such a mark of uncommon kindness, vouchsafed on so short an acquaintance, seemed to declare that the good will towards her arose from something more than merely malice against herself, and might be brought by time and address to do everything that Lucy wished. Her flattery had already subdued the pride of Lady Middleton and made an entry into the close heart of Mrs. John Dashwood; and these were effects that laid open the probability of greater.

The Miss Steeles removed to Harley Street, and all that reached Elinor of their influence there strengthened her expectation of the event. Sir John, who called on them more than once, brought home such accounts of the favour they were in as must be universally striking. Mrs. Dashwood had never been so much pleased with any young women in her life as she was with them, had given each of them a needle book made by some emigrant, called Lucy by her Christian name, and did not know whether she should ever be able to part with them.

VOLUME III

Chapter 1

MRS. PALMER was so well at the end of a fortnight that her mother felt it no longer necessary to give up the whole of her time to her, and contenting herself with visiting her once or twice a day, returned from that period to her own home and her own habits, in which she found the Miss Dashwoods very ready to reassume their former share.

About the third or fourth morning after their being thus resettled in Berkeley Street, Mrs. Jennings, on returning from her ordinary visit to Mrs. Palmer, entered the drawing-room, where Elinor was sitting by herself, with an air of such hurrying importance as prepared her to hear something wonderful, and giving her time only to form that idea, began directly to justify it by saying:

"Lord! My dear Miss Dashwood! Have you heard the news?"

"No, ma'am. What is it?"

"Something so strange! But you shall hear it all. When I got to Mr. Palmer's, I found Charlotte quite in a fuss about the child. She was sure it was very ill: it cried and fretted and was all over pimples. So I looked at it directly and, 'Lord! My dear,' says I, 'it is nothing in the world but the red-gum,' and nurse said just the same. But Charlotte, she would not be satisfied, so Mr. Donovan was sent for; and luckily he happened to be just come in from Harley Street, so he stepped over directly, and as soon as ever he saw the child, he said just as we did that it was nothing in the world but the red-gum, and then Charlotte was easy. And so, just as he was going away again, it came into my head, I am sure I do not know how I happened to think of it, but it came into my head to ask him if there was any news. So upon that, he smirked and simpered and looked grave and seemed to know something or other, and at last he said in a whisper, 'For fear any unpleasant report should reach the young ladies under your care as to their sister's indisposition, I think it advisable to say that I believe there is no great reason for alarm; I hope Mrs. Dashwood will do very well.' "

"What! Is Fanny ill?"

"That is exactly what I said, my dear. 'Lord!' says I, 'is Mrs. Dashwood ill?' So then it all came out; and the long and the short of the matter, by all I can learn, seems to be this. Mr. Edward Ferrars, the very young man I used to joke with you about (but, however, as it turns out, I am monstrous glad there never was anything in it), Mr. Edward Ferrars, it seems, has been engaged above this twelvemonth to my cousin Lucy! There's for you, my dear! And not a creature knowing a syllable of the matter except Nancy! Could you have believed such a thing possible? There is no great wonder in their liking one another; but that matters should be brought so forward between them and nobody suspect it! *That* is strange! I never happened to see them together, or I am sure I should have found it out directly. Well, and so this was kept a great secret for fear of Mrs. Ferrars, and neither she nor your brother or sister suspected a word of the matter—till this very morning, poor Nancy, who, you know, is a well-meaning creature but no conjurer, popped it all out. 'Lord!' thinks she to herself, 'they are all so fond of Lucy, to be sure they will make no difficulty about it'; and so away she went to your sister, who was sitting all alone at her carpet-work, little suspecting what was to come, for she had just been saying to your brother only five minutes before that she thought to make a match between Edward and some Lord's daughter or other, I forget who. So you may think what a blow it was to all her vanity and pride. She fell into violent hysterics immediately, with such screams as reached your brother's ears as he was sitting in his own dressing-room downstairs, thinking about writing a letter to his steward in the country. So up he flew directly, and a terrible scene took place, for Lucy was come to them by that time, little dreaming what was going on. Poor soul! I pity *her*. And I must say, I think she was used very hardly, for your sister scolded like any fury and soon drove her into a fainting fit. Nancy, she fell upon her knees and cried bitterly; and your brother, he walked about the room and said he did not know what to do. Mrs. Dashwood declared they

should not stay a minute longer in the house, and your
brother was forced to go down upon *his* knees too, to persuade her to let them stay till they had packed up their
clothes. *Then* she fell into hysterics again, and he was so
frightened that he would send for Mr. Donovan, and Mr.
Donovan found the house in all this uproar. The carriage
was at the door ready to take my poor cousins away, and
they were just stepping in as he came off, poor Lucy in such
a condition, he says, she could hardly walk, and Nancy, she
was almost as bad. I declare I have no patience with your
sister; and I hope with all my heart it will be a match in spite
of her. Lord! What a taking poor Mr. Edward will be in
when he hears of it! To have his love used so scornfully! For
they say he is monstrous fond of her, as well he may. I
should not wonder if he was to be in the greatest of passion!
And Mr. Donovan thinks just the same. He and I had a great
deal of talk about it; and the best of all is that he is gone
back again to Harley Street, that he may be within call when
Mrs. Ferrars is told of it, for she was sent for as soon as ever
my cousins left the house, for your sister was sure *she* would
be in hysterics too; and so she may, for what I care. I have
no pity for either of them. I have no notion of people's making such a to-do about money and greatness. There is no reason on earth why Mr. Edward and Lucy should not marry,
for I am sure Mrs. Ferrars may afford to do very well by her
son, and though Lucy has next to nothing herself, she knows
better than anybody how to make the most of everything;
and I dare say, if Mrs. Ferrars would only allow him five
hundred a year, she would make as good an appearance with
it as anybody else would with eight. Lord! How snug they
might live in such another cottage as yours—or a little
bigger—with two maids and two men; and I believe I could
help them to a housemaid, for my Betty has a sister out of
place that would fit them exactly."

Here Mrs. Jennings ceased, and as Elinor had had time
enough to collect her thoughts, she was able to give such an
answer and make such observations as the subject might naturally be supposed to produce. Happy to find that she was
not suspected of any extraordinary interest in it; that Mrs.
Jennings (as she had of late often hoped might be the case)
had ceased to imagine her at all attached to Edward; and
happy above all the rest in the absence of Marianne, she felt
very well able to speak of the affair without embarrassment

and to give her judgment, as she believed, with impartiality on the conduct of everyone concerned in it.

She could hardly determine what her own expectation of its event really was; though she earnestly tried to drive away the notion of its being possible to end otherwise at last than in the marriage of Edward and Lucy. What Mrs. Ferrars would say and do, though there could not be a doubt of its nature, she was anxious to hear; and still more anxious to know how Edward would conduct himself. For *him* she felt much compassion; for Lucy very little, and it cost her some pains to procure that little; for the rest of the party none at all.

As Mrs. Jennings could talk on no other subject, Elinor soon saw the necessity of preparing Marianne for its discussion. No time was to be lost in undeceiving her, in making her acquainted with the real truth, and in endeavouring to bring her to hear it talked of by others without betraying that she felt any uneasiness for her sister or any resentment against Edward.

Elinor's office was a painful one. She was going to remove what she really believed to be her sister's chief consolation: to give such particulars of Edward as she feared would ruin him forever in her good opinion, and to make Marianne, by a resemblance in their situations which to *her* fancy would seem strong, feel all her own disappointment over again. But unwelcome as such a task must be, it was necessary to be done, and Elinor therefore hastened to perform it.

She was very far from wishing to dwell on her own feelings or to represent herself as suffering much, any otherwise than as the self-command she had practised since her first knowledge of Edward's engagement might suggest a hint of what was practicable to Marianne. Her narration was clear and simple; and though it could not be given without emotion, it was not accompanied by violent agitation nor impetuous grief. *That* belonged rather to the hearer, for Marianne listened with horror and cried excessively. Elinor was to be the comforter of others in her own distresses no less than in theirs; and all the comfort that could be given by assurances of her own composure of mind, and a very earnest vindication of Edward from every charge but of imprudence, was readily offered.

But Marianne for some time would give credit to neither.

Edward seemed a second Willoughby; and acknowledging as Elinor did, that she *had* loved him most sincerely, could she feel less than herself! As for Lucy Steele, she considered her so totally unamiable, so absolutely incapable of attaching a sensible man, that she could not be persuaded at first to believe, and afterwards to pardon, any former affection of Edward for her. She would not even admit it to have been natural; and Elinor left her to be convinced that it was so by that which only could convince her: a better knowledge of mankind.

Her first communication had reached no farther than to state the fact of the engagement and the length of time it had existed. Marianne's feelings had then broken in and put an end to all regularity of detail, and for some time all that could be done was to soothe her distress, lessen her alarms, and combat her resentment. The first question on her side, which led to farther particulars, was:

"How long has this been known to you, Elinor? Has he written to you?"

"I have known it these four months. When Lucy first came to Barton Park last November, she told me in confidence of her engagement."

At these words, Marianne's eyes expressed the astonishment which her lips could not utter. After a pause of wonder, she exclaimed:

"Four months! Have you known of this four months?"

Elinor confirmed it.

"What! While attending me in all my misery has this been on your heart? And I have reproached you for being happy!"

"It was not fit that you should then know how much I was the reverse!"

"Four months!" cried Marianne again. "So calm! So cheerful! How have you been supported?"

"By feeling that I was doing my duty. My promise to Lucy obliged me to be secret. I owed it to her, therefore, to avoid giving any hint of the truth; and I owed it to my family and friends not to create in them a solicitude about me which it could not be in my power to satisfy."

Marianne seemed much struck.

"I have very often wished to undeceive yourself and my mother," added Elinor, "and once or twice I have attempted it; but without betraying my trust, I never could have convinced you."

"Four months! And yet you loved him!"

"Yes. But I did not love only him; and while the comfort of others were dear to me, I was glad to spare them from knowing how much I felt. Now I can think and speak of it with little emotion. I would not have you suffer on my account, for I assure you I no longer suffer materially myself. I have many things to support me. I am not conscious of having provoked the disappointment by any imprudence of my own, and I have borne it as much as possible without spreading it farther. I acquit Edward of all essential misconduct. I wish him very happy; and I am so sure of his always doing his duty that though now he may harbour some regret, in the end he must become so. Lucy does not want sense, and that is the foundation on which everything good may be built. And after all, Marianne, after all that is bewitching in the idea of a single and constant attachment and all that can be said of one's happiness depending entirely on any particular person, it is not meant—it is not fit—it is not possible that it should be so. Edward will marry Lucy; he will marry a woman superior in person and understanding to half her sex; and time and habit will teach him to forget that he ever thought another superior to *her*."

"If such is your way of thinking," said Marianne, "if the loss of what is most valued is so easily to be made up by something else, your resolution, your self-command, are perhaps a little less to be wondered at. They are brought more within my comprehension."

"I understand you. You do not suppose that I have ever felt much. For four months, Marianne, I have had all this hanging on my mind without being at liberty to speak of it to a single creature, knowing that it would make you and my mother most unhappy whenever it were explained to you, yet unable to prepare you for it in the least. It was told me, it was in a manner forced on me by the very person herself whose prior engagement ruined all my prospects, and told me, as I thought, with triumph. This person's suspicions, therefore, I have had to oppose by endeavouring to appear indifferent where I have been most deeply interested; and it has not been only once; I have had her hopes and exultation to listen to again and again. I have known myself to be divided from Edward forever, without hearing one circumstance that could make me less desire the connection. Nothing has proved him unworthy; nor has anything declared him indifferent to me. I have had to contend against the unkindness of his sister and the insolence of his mother, and have suffered the punishment of an attachment without enjoying its advantages. And all this has been going on at a time when, as you too well know, it has not been my only unhappiness. If you can think me capable of ever feeling, surely you may suppose that I have suffered *now*. The composure of mind with which I have brought myself at present to consider the matter, the consolation that I have been willing to admit, have been the effect of constant and painful exertion; they did not spring up of themselves; they did not occur to relieve my spirits at first. No, Marianne. *Then,* if I had not been bound to silence, perhaps nothing could have kept me entirely—not even what I owed to my dearest friends—from openly showing that I was *very* unhappy."

Marianne was quite subdued.

"Oh! Elinor," she cried, "you have made me hate myself forever. How barbarous have I been to you!—you who have been my only comfort, who have borne with me in all my misery, who have seemed to be only suffering for me! Is this my gratitude? Is this the only return I can make you? Because your merit cries out upon myself, I have been trying to do it away."

The tenderest caresses followed this confession. In such a frame of mind as she was now in, Elinor had no difficulty in obtaining from her whatever promise she required; and at her request, Marianne engaged never to speak of the affair to anyone with the least appearance of bitterness, to meet Lucy without betraying the smallest increase of dislike to her, and even to see Edward himself if chance should bring them together, without any diminution of her usual cordiality. These were great concessions; but where Marianne felt that she had injured, no reparation could be too much for her to make.

She performed her promise of being discreet, to admiration. She attended to all that Mrs. Jennings had to say upon the subject with an unchanging complexion, dissented from her in nothing, and was heard three times to say, "Yes, ma'am." She listened to her praise of Lucy with only moving from one chair to another, and when Mrs. Jennings talked of Edward's affection, it cost her only a spasm in her throat. Such advances towards heroism in her sister made Elinor feel equal to anything herself.

The next morning brought a further trial of it in a visit

from their brother, who came with a most serious aspect to talk over the dreadful affair and bring them news of his wife.

"You have heard, I suppose," said he with great solemnity as soon as he was seated, "of the very shocking discovery that took place under our roof yesterday."

They all looked their assent; it seemed too awful a moment for speech.

"Your sister," he continued, "has suffered dreadfully. Mrs. Ferrars too—in short it has been a scene of such complicated distress—but I will hope that the storm may be weathered without our being any of us quite overcome. Poor Fanny! She was in hysterics all yesterday. But I would not alarm you too much. Donovan says there is nothing materially to be apprehended; her constitution is a good one, and her resolution equal to anything. She has borne it all with the fortitude of an angel! She says she never shall think well of anybody again; and one cannot wonder at it after being so deceived! meeting with such ingratitude where so much kindness had been shown, so much confidence had been placed! It was quite out of the benevolence of her heart that she had asked these young women to her house, merely because she thought they deserved some attention, were harmless, well-behaved girls, and would be pleasant companions; for otherwise we both wished very much to have invited you and Marianne to be with us while your kind friend there was attending her daughter. And now to be so rewarded! 'I wish with all my heart,' says poor Fanny in her affectionate way, 'that we had asked your sisters instead of them.'"

Here he stopped to be thanked, which being done, he went on.

"What poor Mrs. Ferrars suffered when first Fanny broke it to her is not to be described. While she with the truest affection had been planning a most eligible connection for him, was it to be supposed that he could be all the time secretly engaged to another person? Such a suspicion could never have entered her head! If she suspected *any* prepossession elsewhere, it could not be in *that* quarter. '*There*, to be sure,' said she, 'I might have thought myself safe.' She was quite in an agony. We consulted together, however, as to what should be done, and at last she determined to send for Edward. He came. But I am sorry to relate what ensued. All that Mrs. Ferrars could say to make him put an end to the engagement, assisted too as you may well suppose by my arguments and Fanny's entreaties, was of no avail. Duty, affection, everything was disregarded. I never thought Edward so stubborn, so unfeeling before. His mother explained to him her liberal designs in case of his marrying Miss Morton; told him she would settle on him the Norfolk estate, which, clear of land-tax, brings in a good thousand a year; offered even, when matters grew desperate, to make it twelve hundred; and in opposition to this if he still persisted in this low connection, represented to him the certain penury that must attend the match. His own two thousand pounds she protested should be his all; she would never see him again; and so far would she be from affording him the smallest assistance that if he were to enter into any profession with a view of better support, she would do all in her power to prevent his advancing in it."

Here Marianne, in an ecstasy of indignation, clapped her hands together and cried, "Gracious God! Can this be possible!"

"Well may you wonder, Marianne," replied her brother, "at the obstinacy which could resist such arguments as these. Your exclamation is very natural."

Marianne was going to retort, but she remembered her promises and forbore.

"All this, however," he continued, "was urged in vain. Edward said very little, but what he did say was in the most determined manner. Nothing should prevail on him to give up his engagement. He would stand to it, cost him what it might."

"Then," cried Mrs. Jennings with blunt sincerity, no longer able to be silent, "he has acted like an honest man! I beg your pardon, Mr. Dashwood, but if he had done otherwise, I should have thought him a rascal. I have some little concern in the business, as well as yourself, for Lucy Steele is my cousin, and I believe there is not a better kind of girl in the world, nor one who more deserves a good husband."

John Dashwood was greatly astonished; but his nature was calm, not open to provocation, and he never wished to offend anybody, especially anybody of good fortune. He therefore replied, without any resentment:

"I would by no means speak disrespectfully of any relation of yours, madam. Miss Lucy Steele is, I dare say, a very deserving young woman, but in the present case, you know the connection must be impossible. And to have entered into a secret engagement with a young man under her uncle's care, the son of a woman especially of such very large fortune as Mrs. Ferrars, is perhaps altogether a little extraordinary. In short, I do not mean to reflect upon the behaviour of any person whom you have a regard for, Mrs. Jennings. We all wish her extremely happy, and Mrs. Ferrars's conduct throughout the whole has been such as every conscientious, good mother in like circumstances would adopt. It has been dignified and liberal. Edward has drawn his own lot, and I fear it will be a bad one."

Marianne sighed out her similar apprehension, and Elinor's heart wrung for the feelings of Edward while braving his mother's threats for a woman who could not reward him.

"Well, sir," said Mrs. Jennings, "and how did it end?"

"I am sorry to say, ma'am, in a most unhappy rupture: Edward is dismissed forever from his mother's notice. He left her house yesterday, but where he is gone, or whether he is still in town, I do not know, for *we* of course can make no inquiry."

"Poor young man! And what is to become of him?"

"What, indeed, ma'am! It is a melancholy consideration. Born to the prospect of such affluence! I cannot conceive a situation more deplorable. The interest of two thousand pounds—how can a man live on it! And when to that is added the recollection that he might, but for his own folly, within three months have been in the receipt of two thousand five hundred a year (for Miss Morton has thirty thousand pounds), I cannot picture to myself a more wretched condition. We must all feel for him, and the more so because it is totally out of our power to assist him."

"Poor young man!" cried Mrs. Jennings, "I am sure he should be very welcome to bed and board at my house, and so I would tell him if I could see him. It is not fit that he should be living about at his own charge now at lodgings and taverns."

Elinor's heart thanked her for such kindness towards Edward, though she could not forbear smiling at the form of it.

"If he would only have done as well by himself," said John Dashwood, "as all his friends were disposed to do by him, he might now have been in his proper situation, and would have wanted for nothing. But as it is, it must be out of anybody's power to assist him. And there is one thing more preparing against him which must be worse than all: his mother has determined, with a very natural kind of spirit, to settle *that* estate upon Robert immediately which might have been Edward's on proper conditions. I left her this morning with her lawyer, talking over the business."

"Well!" said Mrs. Jennings, "that is *her* revenge. Everybody has a way of their own. But I don't think mine would be to make one son independent because another had plagued me."

Marianne got up and walked about the room.

"Can anything be more galling to the spirit of a man," continued John, "than to see his younger brother in possession of an estate which might have been his own? Poor Edward! I feel for him sincerely."

A few minutes more spent in the same kind of effusion concluded his visit; and with repeated assurances to his sisters that he really believed there was no material danger in Fanny's indisposition, and that they need not therefore be very uneasy about it, he went away, leaving the three ladies unanimous in their sentiments on the present occasion, as far at least as it regarded Mrs. Ferrars's conduct, the Dashwoods', and Edward's.

Marianne's indignation burst forth as soon as he quitted the room, and as her vehemence made reserve impossible in Elinor and unnecessary in Mrs. Jennings, they all joined in a very spirited critique upon the party.

Chapter 2

MRS. JENNINGS was very warm in her praise of Edward's conduct, but only Elinor and Marianne understood its true merit. *They* only knew how little he had had to tempt him to be disobedient and how small was the consolation, beyond the consciousness of doing right, that could remain to him in the loss of friends and fortune. Elinor gloried in his integrity and Marianne forgave all his offences in compassion for his punishment. But though confidence between them was, by this public discovery, restored to its proper state, it was not a subject on which either of them were fond of dwelling when alone. Elinor avoided it upon principle, as tending to fix still more upon her thoughts, by the too warm, too positive assurances of Marianne, that belief of Edward's continued affection for herself which she rather wished to do away; and Marianne's courage soon failed her in trying to converse upon a topic which always left her more dissatisfied with herself than ever by the comparison it necessarily produced between Elinor's conduct and her own.

She felt all the force of that comparison; but not as her sister had hoped, to urge her to exertion now; she felt it with all the pain of continual self-reproach, regretted most bitterly that she had never exerted herself before; but it brought only the torture of penitence without the hope of amendment. Her mind was so much weakened that she still fancied present exertion impossible, and therefore it only dispirited her more.

Nothing new was heard by them for a day or two afterwards of affairs in Harley Street or Bartlett's Buildings. But though so much of the matter was known to them already that Mrs. Jennings might have had enough to do in spreading that knowledge further without seeking after more, she had resolved from the first to pay a visit of comfort and inquiry to her cousins as soon as she could; and nothing but the hindrance of more visitors than usual had prevented her going to them within that time.

The third day succeeding their knowledge of the particulars was so fine, so beautiful a Sunday as to draw many to Kensington Gardens, though it was only the second week in March. Mrs. Jennings and Elinor were of the number; but Marianne, who knew that the Willoughbys were again in town and had a constant dread of meeting them, chose rather to stay at home than venture into so public a place.

An intimate acquaintance of Mrs. Jennings joined them soon after they entered the gardens, and Elinor was not sorry that by her continuing with them and engaging all Mrs. Jennings's conversation she was herself left to quiet reflection. She saw nothing of the Willoughbys, nothing of Edward, and for some time nothing of anybody who could by any chance, whether grave or gay, be interesting to her. But at last she found herself, with some surprise, accosted by Miss Steele, who, though looking rather shy, expressed great satisfaction in meeting them; and on receiving encouragement from the particular kindness of Mrs. Jennings, left her own party for a short time to join theirs. Mrs. Jennings immediately whispered to Elinor,

"Get it all out of her, my dear. She will tell you anything if you ask. You see I cannot leave Mrs. Clarke."

It was lucky, however, for Mrs. Jennings's curiosity and Elinor's too that she would tell anything *without* being asked, for nothing would otherwise have been learned.

"I am so glad to meet you," said Miss Steele, taking her familiarly by the arm, "for I wanted to see you of all things in the world." And then lowering her voice:

"I suppose Mrs. Jennings has heard all about it. Is she angry?"

"Not at all, I believe, with you."

"That is a good thing. And Lady Middleton, is *she* angry?"

"I cannot suppose it possible that she should."

"I am monstrous glad of it. Good gracious! I have had such a time of it! I never saw Lucy in such a rage in my life. She vowed at first she would never trim me up a new bonnet, nor do anything else for me again so long as she lived; but now she is quite come to, and we are as good friends as ever. Look, she made me this bow to my hat and put in the feather last night. There now, *you* are going to laugh at me too. But why should not I wear pink ribbons? I do not care if it *is* the Doctor's favourite colour. I am sure, for my part, I should never have known he *did* like it better than any other colour if he had not happened to say so. My cousins have been so plaguing me! I declare sometimes I do not know which way to look before them."

She had wandered away to a subject on which Elinor had nothing to say and therefore soon judged it expedient to find her way back again to the first.

"Well, but Miss Dashwood," speaking triumphantly, "people may say what they choose about Mr. Ferrars's declaring he would not have Lucy, for it's no such a thing, I can tell you; and it's quite a shame for such ill-natured reports to be spread abroad. Whatever Lucy might think about it herself, you know, it was no business of other people to set it down for certain."

"I never heard anything of the kind hinted at before, I assure you," said Elinor.

"Oh! did not you? But it *was* said, I know very well, and

by more than one; for Miss Godby told Miss Sparks that no-body in their senses could expect Mr. Ferrars to give up a woman like Miss Morton, with thirty thousand pounds to her fortune, for Lucy Steele that had nothing at all; and I had it from Miss Sparks myself. And besides that, my cousin Rich-ard said himself that when it came to the point, he was afraid Mr. Ferrars would be off; and when Edward did not come near us for three days, I could not tell what to think myself; and I believe in my heart Lucy gave it all up for lost; for we came away from your brother's on Wednesday, and we saw nothing of him not all Thursday, Friday, and Saturday, and did not know what was become with him. Once Lucy thought to write to him, but then her spirit rose against that. However, this morning he came just as we came home from church; and then it all came out, how he had been sent for Wednesday to Harley Street and been talked to by his mother and all of them, and how he had declared be-fore them all that he loved nobody but Lucy, and nobody but Lucy would he have. And how he had been so worried by what passed that as soon as he had went away from his mother's house, he had got upon his horse and rid into the country somewhere or other; and how he had stayed about at an inn all Thursday and Friday, on purpose to get the better of it. And after thinking it all over and over again, he said, it seemed to him as if, now he had no fortune, and no noth-ing at all, it would be quite unkind to keep her on to the en-gagement because it must be for her loss, for he had nothing but two thousand pounds and no hope of anything else; and if he was to go into orders, as he had some thoughts, he could get nothing but a curacy, and how was they to live upon that? He could not bear to think of her doing no better, and so he begged, if she had the least mind for it, to put an end to the matter directly and leave him to shift for himself. I heard him say all this as plain as could possibly be. And it was entirely for *her* sake and upon *her* account that he said a word about being off, and not upon his own. I will take my oath he never dropped a syllable of being tired of her, or of wishing to marry Miss Morton, or anything like it. But, to be sure, Lucy would not give ear to such kind of talking; so she told him directly (with a great deal about sweet and love, you know, and all that— Oh, la! One can't repeat such kind of things you know) she told him directly, she had not the least mind in the world to be off, for she could live with him upon a trifle and how little soever he might have, she should be very glad to have it all, you know, or something of the kind. So then he was monstrous happy and talked on some time about what they should do, and they agreed he should take orders directly, and they must wait to be married till he got a living. And just then I could not hear any more, for my cousin called from below to tell me Mrs. Richardson was come in her coach and would take one of us to Kensington Gardens; so I was forced to go into the room and interrupt them to ask Lucy if she would like to go, but she did not care to leave Edward; so I just run upstairs and put on a pair of silk stockings and came off with the Richardsons."

"I do not understand what you mean by interrupting them," said Elinor; "you were all in the same room together, were you not?"

"No, indeed, not us. La! Miss Dashwood, do you think people make love when anybody else is by? Oh for shame! To be sure you must know better than that. (Laughing affectedly.)—No, no, they were shut up in the drawing-room together, and all I heard was only by listening at the door."

"How!" cried Elinor. "Have you been repeating to me what you only learned yourself by listening at the door? I am sorry I did not know it before, for I certainly would not have suffered you to give me particulars of a conversation which you ought not to have known yourself. How could you behave so unfairly by your sister?"

"Oh, la! There is nothing in *that.* I only stood at the door and heard what I could. And I am sure Lucy would have done just the same by me, for a year or two back, when Martha Sharpe and I had so many secrets together, she never made any bones of hiding in a closet, or behind a chimney-board, on purpose to hear what we said."

Elinor tried to talk of something else, but Miss Steele could not be kept beyond a couple of minutes from what was uppermost in her mind.

"Edward talks of going to Oxford soon," said she, "but now he is lodging at No.—, Pall Mall. What an ill-natured woman his mother is, an't she? And your brother and sister were not very kind! However, I shan't say anything against them to *you;* and to be sure they did send us home in their own chariot, which was more than I looked for. And for my part, I was all in a fright for fear your sister should ask us for the huswives she had gave us a day or two before; but, however, nothing was said about them, and I took care to keep mine out of sight. Edward have got some business at Oxford, he says; so he must go there for a time; and after *that*, as soon as he can light upon a Bishop, he will be ordained. I wonder what curacy he will get! Good gracious! (giggling as she spoke) I'd lay my life I know what my cousins will say when they hear of it. They will tell me I should write to the Doctor to get Edward the curacy of his new living. I know they will; but I am sure I would not do such a thing for all the world. 'La!' I shall say directly, 'I wonder how you could think of such a thing. *I* write to the Doctor, indeed!' "

"Well," said Elinor, "it is a comfort to be prepared against the worst. You have got your answer ready."

Miss Steele was going to reply on the same subject, but the approach of her own party made another more necessary.

"Oh, la! Here come the Richardsons. I had a vast deal more to say to you, but I must not stay away from them not any longer. I assure you they are very genteel people. He makes a monstrous deal of money, and they keep their own coach. I have not time to speak to Mrs. Jennings about it myself, but pray tell her I am quite happy to hear she is not in anger against us, and Lady Middleton the same; and if anything should happen to take you and your sister away, and Mrs. Jennings should want company, I am sure we should be very glad to come and stay with her for as long a time as she likes. I suppose Lady Middleton won't ask us any more this bout. Good-bye; I am sorry Miss Marianne was not here. Remember me kindly to her. La! If you have not got your spotted muslin on! I wonder you was not afraid of its being torn."

Such was her parting concern, for after this she had time only to pay her farewell compliments to Mrs. Jennings before her company was claimed by Mrs. Richardson; and Elinor was left in possession of knowledge which might feed her powers of reflection some time, though she had learned very little more than what had been already foreseen and foreplanned in her own mind. Edward's marriage with Lucy was as firmly determined on, and the time of its taking place remained as absolutely uncertain, as she had concluded it would be; everything depended, exactly after her expectation, on his getting that preferment, of which, at present, there seemed not the smallest chance.

As soon as they returned to the carriage, Mrs. Jennings was eager for information; but as Elinor wished to spread as little as possible intelligence that had in the first place been so unfairly obtained, she confined herself to the brief repetition of such simple particulars as she felt assured that Lucy, for the sake of her own consequence, would choose to have known. The continuance of their engagement, and the means that were to be taken for promoting its end, was all her communication; and this produced from Mrs. Jennings the following natural remark.

"Wait for his having a living! Aye, we all know how *that* will end; they will wait a twelvemonth, and finding no good comes of it, will set down upon a curacy of fifty pounds a year, with the interest of his two thousand pounds and what little matter Mr. Steele and Mr. Pratt can give her. Then they will have a child every year! And Lord help 'em! How poor they will be! I must see what I can give them towards furnishing their house. Two maids and two men indeed! As I talked of t'other day. No, no, they must get a stout girl of all works. Betty's sister would never do for them *now*."

The next morning brought Elinor a letter by the twopenny post from Lucy herself. It was as follows:

Bartlett's Buildings, March

I HOPE my dear Miss Dashwood will excuse the liberty I take of writing to her; but I know your friendship for me will make you pleased to hear such a good account of myself and my dear Edward after all the troubles we have went through lately; therefore will make no more apologies, but proceed to say that, thank God! though we have suffered dreadfully, we are both quite well now and as happy as we must always be in one another's love. We have had great trials and great persecutions; but, however, at the same time gratefully acknowledge many friends, yourself not the least among them, whose great kindness I shall always thankfully remember, as will Edward too, who I have told of it. I am sure you will be glad to hear, as likewise dear Mrs. Jennings, I spent two happy hours with him yesterday afternoon; he would not hear of our parting, though earnestly did I, as I thought my duty required, urge him to it for prudence sake, and would have parted forever on the spot, would he consent to it; but he said it should never be; he did not regard his mother's anger while he could have my affections; our prospects are not very bright, to be sure, but we must wait and hope for the best; he will be ordained shortly, and should it ever be in your power to recommend him to anybody that has a living to bestow, am very sure you will not forget us; and dear Mrs. Jennings too, trust she will speak a good word for us to Sir John, or Mr. Palmer, or any friend that may be able to assist us.—Poor Anne was much to blame for what she did, but she did it for the best, so I say nothing: hope Mrs. Jennings won't think it too much trouble to give us a call should she come this way any morning; 'twould be a great kindness, and my cousins would be proud to know her.—My paper reminds me to conclude; and begging to be most gratefully and respectfully remembered to her, and to Sir John, and Lady Middleton, and the dear children, when you chance to see them; and love to Miss Marianne,

I am, etc. etc.

As soon as Elinor had finished it, she performed what she concluded to be its writer's real design, by placing it in the hands of Mrs. Jennings, who read it aloud with many comments of satisfaction and praise.

"Very well indeed!—How prettily she writes!—Aye, that was quite proper to let him be off if he would. That was just like Lucy.—Poor soul! I wish I *could* get him a living with all my heart.—She calls me dear Mrs. Jennings, you see. She is a good-hearted girl as ever lived.—Very well, upon my word. That sentence is very prettily turned. Yes, yes, I will go and see her, sure enough. How attentive she is to think of everybody!—Thank you, my dear, for showing it me. It is as pretty a letter as ever I saw, and does Lucy's head and heart great credit."

Chapter 3

THE MISS DASHWOODS had now been rather more than two months in town, and Marianne's impatience to be gone increased every day. She sighed for the air, the liberty, the quiet of the country and fancied that if any place could give her ease, Barton must do it. Elinor was hardly less anxious than herself for their removal, and only so much less bent on its being affected immediately, as that she was conscious of the difficulties of so long a journey, which Marianne could not be brought to acknowledge. She began, however, seriously to turn her thoughts towards its accomplishment and had already mentioned their wishes to their kind hostess, who resisted them with all the eloquence of her good will, when a plan was suggested which, though detaining them from home yet a few weeks longer, appeared to Elinor altogether much more eligible than any other. The Palmers were to remove to Cleveland about the end of March for the Easter holidays; and Mrs. Jennings, with both her friends, received a very warm invitation from Charlotte to go with them. This would not in itself have been sufficient for the delicacy of Miss Dashwood; but it was inforced with so much real politeness by Mr. Palmer himself as, joined to the very great amendment of his manners towards them since her sister had been known to be unhappy, induced her to accept it with pleasure.

When she told Marianne what she had done, however, her first reply was not very auspicious.

"Cleveland!" she cried with great agitation. "No, I cannot go to Cleveland."

"You forget," said Elinor, gently, "that its situation is not ... that it is not in the neighbourhood of ..."

"But it is in Somersetshire. I cannot go into Somersetshire. There, where I looked forward to going ... No, Elinor, you cannot expect me to go there."

Elinor would not argue upon the propriety of overcoming such feelings; she only endeavoured to counteract them by working on others, and represented it, therefore, as a measure which would fix the time of her returning to that dear mother, whom she so much wished to see, in a more eligible, more comfortable manner, than any other plan could do, and perhaps without any greater delay. From Cleveland, which was within a few miles of Bristol, the distance to Barton was not beyond one day, though a long day's journey; and their mother's servant might easily come there to attend them down; and as there could be no occasion for their staying above a week at Cleveland, they might now be at home in little more than three weeks' time. As Marianne's affection

for her mother was sincere, it must triumph, with little difficulty, over the imaginary evil she had started.

Mrs. Jennings was so far from being weary of her guests
that she pressed them very earnestly to return with her again
from Cleveland. Elinor was grateful for the attention, but it
could not alter their design; and their mother's concurrence
being readily gained, everything relative to their return was
arranged as far as it could be; and Marianne found some relief in drawing up a statement of the hours that were yet to
divide her from Barton.

"Ah! Colonel, I do not know what you and I shall do
without the Miss Dashwoods," was Mrs. Jennings's address
to him when he first called on her after their leaving her was
settled; "for they are quite resolved upon going home from
the Palmers; and how forlorn we shall be when I come back!
Lord! We shall sit and gape at one another as dull as two
cats."

Perhaps Mrs. Jennings was in hopes, by this vigorous
sketch of their future ennui, to provoke him to make that offer which might give himself an escape from it; and if so,
she had soon afterwards good reason to think her object
gained; for on Elinor's moving to the window to take more
expeditiously the dimensions of a print, which she was going to copy for her friend, he followed her to it with a look
of particular meaning and conversed with her there for several minutes. The effect of his discourse on the lady too,
could not escape her observation, for though she was too
honourable to listen, and had even changed her seat, on purpose that she might *not* hear, to one close by the pianoforte
on which Marianne was playing, she could not keep herself
from seeing that Elinor changed colour, attended with agitation, and was too intent on what he said to pursue her employment. Still further in confirmation of her hopes, in the
interval of Marianne's turning from one lesson to another,
some words of the Colonel's inevitably reached her ear, in
which he seemed to be apologizing for the badness of his
house. This set the matter beyond a doubt. She wondered indeed at his thinking it necessary to do so, but supposed it to
be the proper etiquette. What Elinor said in reply she could
not distinguish, but judged from the motion of her lips that
she did not think *that* any material objection; and Mrs.
Jennings commended her in her heart for being so honest.
They then talked on for a few minutes longer without her

catching a syllable when another lucky stop in Marianne's performance brought her these words in the Colonel's calm voice:

"I am afraid it cannot take place very soon."

Astonished and shocked at so unlover-like a speech, she was almost ready to cry out, "Lord! What should hinder it?" but checking her desire, confined herself to this silent ejaculation.

"This is very strange! Sure he need not wait to be older."

This delay on the Colonel's side, however, did not seem to offend or mortify his fair companion in the least, for on their breaking up the conference soon afterwards and moving different ways, Mrs. Jennings very plainly heard Elinor say, and with a voice which showed her to feel what she said:

"I shall always think myself very much obliged to you."

Mrs. Jennings was delighted with her gratitude, and only wondered that after hearing such a sentence, the Colonel should be able to take leave of them as he immediately did, with the utmost sang-froid, and go away without making her any reply! She had not thought her old friend could have made so indifferent a suitor.

What had really passed between them was to this effect:

"I have heard," said he with great compassion, "of the injustice your friend Mr. Ferrars has suffered from his family; for if I understand the matter right, he has been entirely cast off by them for persevering in his engagement with a very deserving young woman. Have I been rightly informed? Is it so?"

Elinor told him that it was.

"The cruelty, the impolitic cruelty," he replied with great feeling, "of dividing, or attempting to divide, two young people long attached to each other, is terrible. Mrs. Ferrars does not know what she may be doing, what she may drive her son to. I have seen Mr. Ferrars two or three times in Harley Street and am much pleased with him. He is not a young man with whom one can be intimately acquainted in a short time, but I have seen enough of him to wish him well for his own sake, and as a friend of yours, I wish it still more. I understand that he intends to take orders. Will you be so good as to tell him that the living of Delaford, now just vacant, as I am informed by this day's post, is his if he think it worth his acceptance; but *that,* perhaps, so unfortunately circumstanced as he is now, it may be nonsense to appear to doubt; I only wish it were more valuable. It is a rectory, but a small one; the late incumbent, I believe, did not make more than 200 £ per annum; and though it is certainly capable of improvement, I fear, not to such an amount as to afford him a very comfortable income. Such as it is, however, my pleasure in presenting him to it will be very great. Pray assure him of it."

Elinor's astonishment at this commission could hardly have been greater had the Colonel been really making her an offer of his hand. The preferment, which only two days before she had considered as hopeless for Edward, was already provided to enable him to marry; and *she,* of all people in the world, was fixed on to bestow it! Her emotion was such as Mrs. Jennings had attributed to a very different cause; but whatever minor feelings less pure, less pleasing, might have a share in that emotion, her esteem for the general benevolence, and her gratitude for the particular friendship, which together prompted Colonel Brandon to this act, were strongly felt and warmly expressed. She thanked him for it with all her heart, spoke of Edward's principles and disposition with that praise which she knew them to deserve; and promised to undertake the commission with pleasure if it were really his wish to put off so agreeable an office to another. But at the same time she could not help thinking that no one could so well perform it as himself. It was an office, in short, from which, unwilling to give Edward the pain of receiving an obligation from *her,* she would have been very glad to be spared herself; but Colonel Brandon, on motives of equal delicacy declining it likewise, seemed so desirous of its being given through her means that she would not on any account make further opposition. Edward, she believed, was still in town, and fortunately she had heard his address from Miss Steele. She could undertake, therefore, to inform him of it in the course of the day. After this had been settled, Colonel Brandon began to talk of his own advantage in securing so respectable and agreeable a neighbour, and *then* it was that he mentioned with regret that the house was small and indifferent, an evil which Elinor, as Mrs. Jennings had supposed her to do, made very light of, at least as far as regarded its size.

"The smallness of the house," she said, "I cannot imagine any inconvenience to them, for it will be in proportion to their family and income."

By which the Colonel was surprised to find that *she* was considering Mr. Ferrars's marriage as the certain consequence of the presentation; for he did not suppose it possible that Delaford living could supply such an income as anybody in his style of life would venture to settle on—and he said so.

"This little rectory *can* do no more than make Mr. Ferrars comfortable as a bachelor; it cannot enable him to marry. I am sorry to say that my patronage ends with this; and my interest is hardly more extensive. If, however, by any unforeseen chance it should be in my power to serve him further, I must think very differently of him from what I now do if I am not as ready to be useful to him then, as I sincerely wish I could be at present. What I am now doing, indeed, seems nothing at all, since it can advance him so little towards what must be his principal, his only, object of happiness. His marriage must still be a distant good; at least, I am afraid it cannot take place very soon."

Such was the sentence which, when misunderstood, so justly offended the delicate feelings of Mrs. Jennings; but after this narration of what really passed between Colonel Brandon and Elinor while they stood at the window, the gratitude expressed by the latter on their parting may perhaps appear in general, not less reasonably excited, nor less properly worded than if it had arisen from an offer of marriage.

Chapter 4

"WELL, MISS DASHWOOD," said Mrs. Jennings, sagaciously smiling as soon as the gentleman had withdrawn, "I do not ask you what the Colonel has been saying to you; for though, upon my honour, I *tried* to keep out of hearing, I could not help catching enough to understand his business. And I assure you I never was better pleased in my life, and I wish you joy of it with all my heart."

"Thank you, ma'am," said Elinor. "It *is* a matter of great joy to me; and I feel the goodness of Colonel Brandon most sensibly. There are not many men who would act as he has

done. Few people who have so compassionate an heart! I
never was more astonished in my life."

"Lord! My dear, you are very modest! I an't the least astonished at it in the world, for I have often thought of late
there was nothing more likely to happen."

"You judged from your knowledge of the Colonel's general benevolence; but at least you could not foresee that the
opportunity would so very soon occur."

"Opportunity!" repeated Mrs. Jennings. "Oh! as to that,
when a man has once made up his mind to such a thing,
somehow or other he will soon find an opportunity. Well, my
dear, I wish you joy of it again and again; and if ever there
was a happy couple in the world, I think I shall soon know
where to look for them."

"You mean to go to Delaford after them, I suppose," said
Elinor with a faint smile.

"Aye, my dear, that I do, indeed. And as to the house being a bad one, I do not know what the Colonel would be at,
for it is as good a one as ever I saw."

"He spoke of its being out of repair."

"Well, and whose fault is that? Why don't he repair it?
Who should do it but himself?"

They were interrupted by the servant's coming in to announce the carriage being at the door; and Mrs. Jennings immediately preparing to go, said:

"Well, my dear, I must be gone before I have had half my
talk out. But, however, we may have it all over in the evening, for we shall be quite alone. I do not ask you to go with
me, for I dare say your mind is too full of the matter to care
for company; and besides, you must long to tell your sister
all about it."

Marianne had left the room before the conversation began.

"Certainly, ma'am, I shall tell Marianne of it; but I shall
not mention it at present to anybody else."

"Oh! very well," said Mrs. Jennings rather disappointed.
"Then you would not have me tell it Lucy, for I think of going as far as Holborn to-day."

"No, ma'am, not even Lucy, if you please. One day's delay will not be very material; and till I have written to Mr.
Ferrars, I think it ought not to be mentioned to anybody else.
I shall do *that* directly. It is of importance that no time
should be lost with him, for he will of course have much to
do relative to his ordination."

This speech at first puzzled Mrs. Jennings exceedingly. Why Mr. Ferrars was to be written to about it in such a hurry she could not immediately comprehend. A few moments' reflection, however, produced a very happy idea, and she exclaimed:

"Oh ho!—I understand you. Mr. Ferrars is to be the man. Well, so much the better for him. Aye, to be sure, he must be ordained in readiness; and I am very glad to find things are so forward between you. But, my dear, is not this rather out of character? Should not the Colonel write himself? Sure, he is the proper person."

Elinor did not quite understand the beginning of Mrs. Jennings's speech; neither did she think it worth inquiring into; and therefore only replied to its conclusion.

"Colonel Brandon is so delicate a man that he rather wished anyone to announce his intentions to Mr. Ferrars than himself."

"And so *you* are forced to do it. Well, *that* is an odd kind of delicacy! However, I will not disturb you (seeing her preparing to write). You know your own concerns best. So good-bye, my dear. I have not heard of anything to please me so well since Charlotte was brought to bed."

And away she went: but returning again in a moment,

"I have just been thinking of Betty's sister, my dear. I should be very glad to get her so good a mistress. But whether she would do for a lady's maid, I am sure I can't tell. She is an excellent housemaid and works very well at her needle. However, you will think of all that at your leisure."

"Certainly, ma'am," replied Elinor, not hearing much of what she said, and more anxious to be alone than to be mistress of the subject.

How she should begin, how she should express herself in her note to Edward, was now all her concern. The particular circumstances between them made a difficulty of that which to any other person would have been the easiest thing in the world; but she equally feared to say too much or too little, and sat deliberating over her paper with the pen in her hand till broken in on by the entrance of Edward himself.

He had met Mrs. Jennings at the door in her way to the carriage as he came to leave his farewell card; and she, after apologizing for not returning herself, had obliged him to en-

ter by saying that Miss Dashwood was above and wanted to
speak with him on very particular business.

Elinor had just been congratulating herself, in the midst of
her perplexity, that however difficult it might be to express
herself properly by letter, it was at least preferable to giving
the information by word of mouth, when her visitor entered,
to force her upon this greatest exertion of all. Her astonishment and confusion were very great on his so sudden appearance. She had not seen him before since his engagement
became public and therefore not since his knowing her to be
acquainted with it; which with the consciousness of what she
had been thinking of, and what she had to tell him, made her
feel particularly uncomfortable for some minutes. He too
was much distressed, and they sat down together in a most
promising state of embarrassment. Whether he had asked her
pardon for his intrusion on first coming into the room, he
could not recollect; but determining to be on the safe side,
he made his apology in form as soon as he could say anything after taking a chair.

"Mrs. Jennings told me," said he, "that you wished to
speak with me, at least I understood her so, or I certainly
should not have intruded on you in such a manner; though
at the same time, I should have been extremely sorry to
leave London without seeing you and your sister; especially
as it will most likely be some time—it is not probable that
I should soon have the pleasure of meeting you again. I go
to Oxford to-morrow."

"You would not have gone, however," said Elinor, recovering herself and determined to get over what she so much
dreaded as soon as possible, "without receiving our good
wishes, even if we had not been able to give them in person.
Mrs. Jennings was quite right in what she said. I have something of consequence to inform you of, which I was on the
point of communicating by paper. I am charged with a most
agreeable office, (breathing rather faster than usual as she
spoke). Colonel Brandon, who was here only ten minutes
ago, has desired me to say that, understanding you mean to
take orders, he has great pleasure in offering you the living
of Delaford, now just vacant, and only wishes it were more
valuable. Allow me to congratulate you on having so respectable and well-judging a friend, and to join in his wish
that the living—it is about two hundred a year—were much
more considerable and such as might better enable you

to—as might be more than a temporary accommodation to yourself—such, in short, as might establish all your views of happiness."

What Edward felt, as he could not say it himself, it cannot be expected that anyone else should say for him. He *looked* all the astonishment which such unexpected, such unthought-of information could not fail of exciting; but he said only these two words:

"Colonel Brandon!"

"Yes," continued Elinor, gathering more resolution as some of the worst was over, "Colonel Brandon means it as a testimony of his concern for what has lately passed—for the cruel situation in which the unjustifiable conduct of your family has placed you—a concern which I am sure Marianne, myself, and all your friends must share; and likewise as a proof of his high esteem for your general character and his particular approbation of your behaviour on the present occasion."

"Colonel Brandon give *me* a living! Can it be possible?"

"The unkindness of your own relations has made you astonished to find friendship anywhere."

"No," replied he with sudden consciousness, "not to find it in *you*; for I cannot be ignorant that to you, to your goodness, I owe it all. I feel it. I would express it if I could; but, as you well know, I am no orator."

"You are very much mistaken. I do assure you that you owe it entirely, at least almost entirely, to your own merit and Colonel Brandon's discernment of it. I have had no hand in it. I did not even know till I understood his design that the living was vacant; nor had it ever occurred to me that he might have had such a living in his gift. As a friend of mine, of my family, he may perhaps—indeed I know he *has,* still greater pleasure in bestowing it; but upon my word, you owe nothing to my solicitation."

Truth obliged her to acknowledge some small share in the action; but she was at the same time so unwilling to appear as the benefactress of Edward that she acknowledged it with hesitation, which probably contributed to fix that suspicion in his mind which had recently entered it. For a short time he sat deep in thought after Elinor had ceased to speak; at last, and as if it were rather an effort, he said:

"Colonel Brandon seems a man of great worth and respectability. I have always heard him spoken of as such, and your brother, I know, esteems him highly. He is undoubtedly a sensible man, and in his manners perfectly the gentleman."

"Indeed," replied Elinor, "I believe that you will find him, on further acquaintance, all that you have heard him to be; and as you will be such very near neighbours, (for I understand the parsonage is almost close to the mansion-house), it is particularly important that he *should* be all this."

Edward made no answer, but when she had turned away her head, gave her a look so serious, so earnest, so uncheerful, as seemed to say that he might hereafter wish the distance between the parsonage and the mansion-house much greater.

"Colonel Brandon, I think, lodges in St. James's Street," said he soon afterwards, rising from his chair.

Elinor told him the number of the house.

"I must hurry away, then, to give him those thanks which you will not allow me to give *you*, to assure him that he has made me a very, an exceedingly happy man."

Elinor did not offer to detain him; and they parted with a very earnest assurance on *her* side of her unceasing good wishes for his happiness in every change of situation that might befall him; on *his*, with rather an attempt to return the same good will, than the power of expressing it.

"When I see him again," said Elinor to herself as the door shut him out, "I shall see him the husband of Lucy."

And with this pleasing anticipation, she sat down to reconsider the past, recall the words, and endeavour to comprehend all the feelings of Edward; and, of course, to reflect on her own with discontent.

When Mrs. Jennings came home, though she returned from seeing people whom she had never seen before, and of whom, therefore, she must have a great deal to say, her mind was so much more occupied by the important secret in her possession than by anything else that she reverted to it again as soon as Elinor appeared.

"Well, my dear," she cried, "I sent you up the young man. Did not I do right? And I suppose you had no great difficulty. You did not find him very unwilling to accept your proposal?"

"No, ma'am; *that* was not very likely."

"Well, and how soon will he be ready? For it seems all to depend upon that."

"Really," said Elinor, "I know so little of these kind of

forms that I can hardly even conjecture as to the time or the preparation necessary; but I suppose two or three months will complete his ordination."

"Two or three months!" cried Mrs. Jennings; "Lord! my dear, how calmly you talk of it; and can the Colonel wait two or three months! Lord bless me! I am sure it would put *me* quite out of patience! And though one would be very glad to do a kindness by poor Mr. Ferrars, I do think it is not worth while to wait two or three months for him. Sure, somebody else might be found that would do as well, somebody that is in orders already."

"My dear ma'am," said Elinor, "what can you be thinking of? Why, Colonel Brandon's only object is to be of use to Mr. Ferrars."

"Lord bless you, my dear! Sure you do not mean to persuade me that the Colonel only marries you for the sake of giving ten guineas to Mr. Ferrars!"

The deception could not continue after this; and an explanation immediately took place by which both gained considerable amusement for the moment without any material loss of happiness to either, for Mrs. Jennings only exchanged one form of delight for another, and still without forfeiting her expectation of the first.

"Aye, aye, the parsonage is but a small one," said she after the first ebullition of surprise and satisfaction was over, "and very likely *may* be out of repair; but to hear a man apologizing, as I thought, for a house that to my knowledge has five sitting-rooms on the ground floor and, I think the housekeeper told me, could make up fifteen beds!— And to you too, that had been used to live in Barton cottage! It seemed quite ridiculous. But, my dear, we must touch up the Colonel to do something to the parsonage and make it comfortable for them before Lucy goes to it."

"But Colonel Brandon does not seem to have any idea of the living's being enough to allow them to marry."

"The Colonel is a ninny, my dear; because he has two thousand a year himself, he thinks that nobody else can marry on less. Take my word for it that if I am alive, I shall be paying a visit at Delaford Parsonage before Michaelmas; and I am sure I shan't go if Lucy an't there."

Elinor was quite of her opinion as to the probability of their not waiting for anything more.

Chapter 5

EDWARD, HAVING carried his thanks to Colonel Brandon, proceeded with his happiness to Lucy; and such was the excess of it by the time he reached Bartlett's Buildings that she was able to assure Mrs. Jennings, who called on her again the next day with her congratulations, that she had never seen him in such spirits before in her life.

Her own happiness and her own spirits were at least very certain; and she joined Mrs. Jennings most heartily in her expectation of their being all comfortably together in Delaford Parsonage before Michaelmas. So far was she, at the same time, from any backwardness to give Elinor that credit which Edward *would* give her that she spoke of her friendship for them both with the most grateful warmth, was ready to own all their obligation to her, and openly declared that no exertion for their good on Miss Dashwood's part, either present or future, would ever surprise her, for she believed her capable of doing anything in the world for those she really valued. As for Colonel Brandon, she was not only ready to worship him as a saint but was moreover truly anxious that he should be treated as one in all worldly concerns; anxious that his tithes should be raised to the utmost; and secretly resolved to avail herself at Delaford, as far as she possibly could, of his servants, his carriage, his cows, and his poultry.

It was now above a week since John Dashwood had called in Berkeley Street, and as since that time no notice had been taken by them of his wife's indisposition beyond one verbal inquiry, Elinor began to feel it necessary to pay her a visit. This was an obligation, however, which not only opposed her own inclination but which had not the assistance of any encouragement from her companions. Marianne, not contented with absolutely refusing to go herself, was very urgent to prevent her sister's going at all; and Mrs. Jennings, though her carriage was always at Elinor's service, so very much disliked Mrs. John Dashwood that not even her curiosity to see how she looked after the late discovery, nor her strong desire to affront her by taking Edward's part, could overcome her unwillingness to be in her company again. The consequence was that Elinor set out by herself to pay a visit for which no one could really have less inclination, and to run the risk of a tête-à-tête with a woman whom neither of the others had so much reason to dislike.

Mrs. Dashwood was denied; but before the carriage could turn from the house, her husband accidentally came out. He expressed great pleasure in meeting Elinor, told her that he had been just going to call in Berkeley Street, and assuring her that Fanny would be very glad to see her, invited her to come in.

They walked upstairs into the drawing-room. Nobody was there.

"Fanny is in her own room, I suppose," said he; "I will go to her presently, for I am sure she will not have the least objection in the world to seeing *you*. Very far from it indeed. *Now* especially there cannot be. But, however, you and Marianne were always great favourites. Why would not Marianne come?"

Elinor made what excuse she could for her.

"I am not sorry to see you alone," he replied, "for I have a good deal to say to you. This living of Colonel Brandon's—can it be true? Has he really given it to Edward? I heard it yesterday by chance and was coming to you on purpose to inquire further about it."

"It is perfectly true. Colonel Brandon has given the living of Delaford to Edward."

"Really! Well, this is very astonishing! No relationship! No connection between them! And now that livings fetch such a price! What was the value of this?"

"About two hundred a year."

"Very well—and for the next presentation to a living of that value—supposing the late incumbent to have been old and sickly and likely to vacate it soon—he might have got I dare say—fourteen hundred pounds. And how came he not to have settled that matter before this person's death? *Now* indeed it would be too late to sell it, but a man of Colonel Brandon's sense! I wonder he should be so improvident in a point of such common, such natural, concern! Well, I am convinced that there is a vast deal of inconsistency in almost every human character. I suppose, however, on recollection, that the case may probably be *this*. Edward is only to hold the living till the person to whom the Colonel has really sold the presentation is old enough to take it. Aye, aye, that is the fact, depend upon it."

Elinor contradicted it, however, very positively; and by relating that she had herself been employed in conveying the offer from Colonel Brandon to Edward, and therefore must understand the terms on which it was given, obliged him to submit to her authority.

"It is truly astonishing!" he cried after hearing what she said; "what could be the Colonel's motive?"

"A very simple one—to be of use to Mr. Ferrars."

"Well, well; whatever Colonel Brandon may be, Edward is a very lucky man! You will not mention the matter to Fanny, however; for though I have broke it to her, and she bears it vastly well, she will not like to hear it much talked of."

Elinor had some difficulty here to refrain from observing that she thought Fanny might have borne with composure an acquisition of wealth to her brother by which neither she nor her child could be possibly impoverished.

"Mrs. Ferrars," added he, lowering his voice to the tone becoming so important a subject, "knows nothing about it at present, and I believe it will be best to keep it entirely concealed from her as long as may be. When the marriage takes place, I fear she must hear of it all."

"But why should such precaution be used? Though it is not to be supposed that Mrs. Ferrars can have the smallest satisfaction in knowing that her son has money enough to live upon—for *that* must be quite out of the question; yet why, after her late behaviour, is she supposed to feel at all? She has done with her son; she has cast him off forever and has made all those over whom she had any influence cast him off likewise. Surely, after doing so, she cannot be imagined liable to any impression of sorrow or of joy on his account. She cannot be interested in anything that befalls him. She would not be so weak as to throw away the comfort of a child and yet retain the anxiety of a parent!"

"Ah! Elinor," said John, "your reasoning is very good, but it is founded on ignorance of human nature. When Edward's unhappy match takes place, depend upon it his mother will feel as much as if she had never discarded him; and therefore every circumstance that may accelerate that dreadful event must be concealed from her as much as possible. Mrs. Ferrars can never forget that Edward is her son."

"You surprise me; I should think it must nearly have escaped her memory by *this* time."

"You wrong her exceedingly. Mrs. Ferrars is one of the most affectionate mothers in the world."

Elinor was silent.

"We think *now*," said Mr. Dashwood after a short pause, "of *Robert*'s marrying Miss Morton."

Elinor, smiling at the grave and decisive importance of her brother's tone, calmly replied:

"The lady, I suppose, has no choice in the affair."

"Choice! How do you mean?"

"I only mean that I suppose from your manner of speaking it must be the same to Miss Morton whether she marry Edward or Robert."

"Certainly there can be no difference; for Robert will now to all intents and purposes be considered as the eldest son; and as to anything else, they are both very agreeable young men; I do not know that one is superior to the other."

Elinor said no more, and John was also for a short time silent. His reflections ended thus:

"Of *one* thing, my dear sister," kindly taking her hand and speaking in an awful whisper, "I may assure you; and I *will* do it because I know it must gratify you. I have good reason to think—indeed I have it from the best authority or I should not repeat it, for otherwise it would be very wrong to say anything about it—but I have it from the very best authority—not that I ever precisely heard Mrs. Ferrars say it herself, but her daughter *did,* and I have it from her—that in short, whatever objections there might be against a certain—a certain connection—you understand me—it would have been far preferable to her: it would not have given her half the vexation that *this* does. I was exceedingly pleased to hear that Mrs. Ferrars considered it in that light—a very gratifying circumstance, you know, to us all. 'It would have been beyond comparison,' she said, 'the least evil of the two, and she would be glad to compound *now* for nothing worse.' But, however, all that is quite out of the question—not to be thought of or mentioned—as to any attachment you know—it never could be—all that is gone by. But I thought I would just tell you of this because I knew how much it must please you. Not that you have any reason to regret, my dear Elinor. There is no doubt of your doing exceedingly well—quite as well, or better, perhaps, all things considered. Has Colonel Brandon been with you lately?"

Elinor had heard enough, if not to gratify her vanity and raise her self-importance, to agitate her nerves and fill her mind; and she was therefore glad to be spared from the necessity of saying much in reply herself, and from the danger of hearing anything more from her brother, by the entrance of Mr. Robert Ferrars. After a few moments' chat, John Dashwood, recollecting that Fanny was yet uninformed of his sister's being there, quitted the room in quest of her; and Elinor was left to improve her acquaintance with Robert, who, by the gay unconcern, the happy self-complacency of his manner while enjoying so unfair a division of his mother's love and liberality to the prejudice of his banished brother, earned only by his own dissipated course of life and that brother's integrity, was confirming her most unfavourable opinion of his head and heart.

They had scarcely been two minutes by themselves before he began to speak of Edward; for he too had heard of the living and was very inquisitive on the subject. Elinor repeated the particulars of it as she had given them to John; and their effect on Robert, though very different, was not less striking than it had been on *him*. He laughed most immoderately. The idea of Edward's being a clergyman and living in a small parsonage house diverted him beyond measure; and when to that was added the fanciful imagery of Edward reading prayers in a white surplice and publishing the banns of marriage between John Smith and Mary Brown, he could conceive nothing more ridiculous.

Elinor, while she waited in silence and immovable gravity the conclusion of such folly, could not restrain her eyes from being fixed on him with a look that spoke all the contempt it excited. It was a look, however, very well bestowed, for it relieved her own feelings and gave no intelligence to him. He was recalled from wit to wisdom, not by any reproof of hers but by his own sensibility.

"We may treat it as a joke," said he at last, recovering from the affected laugh which had considerably lengthened out the genuine gaiety of the moment, "but upon my soul, it is a most serious business. Poor Edward! He is ruined forever. I am extremely sorry for it, for I know him to be a very good-hearted creature, as well-meaning a fellow, perhaps, as any in the world. You must not judge of him, Miss Dashwood, from *your* slight acquaintance. Poor Edward! His manners are certainly not the happiest in nature. But we are not all born, you know, with the same powers, the same address. Poor fellow! To see him in a circle of strangers! To be sure it was pitiable enough! But, upon my soul, I believe he has as good a heart as any in the kingdom; and I declare and protest to you I never was so shocked in my life as when it all burst forth. I could not believe it. My mother was the first person who told me of it, and I, feeling myself called on to act with resolution, immediately said to her, 'My dear Madam, I do not know what you may intend to do on the occasion, but as for myself, I must say that if Edward does marry this young woman, *I* never will see him again.' That was what I said immediately. I was most uncommonly shocked indeed! Poor Edward! He has done for himself completely! Shut himself out forever from all decent society! But, as I directly said to my mother, I am not in the least surprised at it; from his style of education it was always to be expected. My poor mother was half frantic."

"Have you ever seen the lady?"

"Yes, once while she was staying in this house, I happened to drop in for ten minutes; and I saw quite enough of her. The merest awkward country girl, without style or elegance, and almost without beauty. I remember her perfectly. Just the kind of girl I should suppose likely to captivate poor Edward. I offered immediately, as soon as my mother related the affair to me, to talk to him myself and dissuade him from the match; but it was too late *then,* I found, to do anything; for unluckily, I was not in the way at first and knew nothing of it till after the breach had taken place, when it was not for me, you know, to interfere. But had I been informed of it a few hours earlier, I think it is most probable that something might have been on. I certainly should have represented it to Edward in a very strong light. 'My dear fellow,' I should have said, 'consider what you are doing. You are making a most disgraceful connection, and such a one as your family are unanimous in disapproving.' I cannot help thinking, in short, that means might have been found. But now it is all too late. He must be starved, you know, that is certain absolutely starved."

He had just settled this point with great composure when the entrance of Mrs. John Dashwood put an end to the subject. But though *she* never spoke of it out of her own family,

Elinor could see its influence on her mind in the something like confusion of countenance with which she entered and an attempt at cordiality in her behaviour to herself. She even proceeded so far as to be concerned to find that Elinor and her sister were so soon to leave town, as she had hoped to see more of them; an exertion in which her husband, who attended her into the room and hung enamoured over her accents, seemed to distinguish everything that was most affectionate and graceful.

Chapter 6

ONE OTHER short call in Harley Street, in which Elinor received her brother's congratulations on their travelling so far towards Barton without any expense and on Colonel Brandon's being to follow them to Cleveland in a day or two, completed the intercourse of the brother and sisters in town; and a faint invitation from Fanny to come to Norland whenever it should happen to be in their way, which of all things was the most unlikely to occur, with a more warm, though less public, assurance from John to Elinor of the promptitude with which he should come to see her at Delaford, was all that foretold any meeting in the country.

It amused her to observe that all her friends seemed determined to send her to Delaford; a place in which, of all others, she would now least choose to visit or wish to reside; for not only was it considered as her future home by her brother and Mrs. Jennings, but even Lucy, when they parted, gave her a pressing invitation to visit her there.

Very early in April and tolerably early in the day, the two parties from Hanover Square and Berkeley Street set out from their respective homes to meet by appointment on the road. For the convenience of Charlotte, and her child, they were to be more than two days on their journey, and Mr. Palmer, travelling more expeditiously with Colonel Brandon, was to join them at Cleveland soon after their arrival.

Marianne, few as had been her hours of comfort in London and eager as she had long been to quit it, could not, when it came to the point, bid adieu to the house in which she had for the last time enjoyed those hopes and that confidence in Willoughby which were now extinguished forever, without great pain. Nor could she leave the place in which Willoughby remained, busy in new engagements and new schemes in which *she* could have no share, without shedding many tears.

Elinor's satisfaction at the moment of removal was more positive. She had no such object for her lingering thoughts to fix on; she left no creature behind from whom it would give her a moment's regret to be divided forever; she was pleased to be free herself from the persecution of Lucy's friendship; she was grateful for bringing her sister away unseen by Willoughby since his marriage; and she looked forward with hope to what a few months of tranquillity at Barton might do towards restoring Marianne's peace of mind and confirming her own.

Their journey was safely performed. The second day brought them into the cherished, or the prohibited, county of Somerset, for as such was it dwelt on by turns in Marianne's imagination; and in the forenoon of the third they drove up to Cleveland.

Cleveland was a spacious, modern-built house situated on a sloping lawn. It had no park, but the pleasure-grounds were tolerably extensive; and like every other place of the same degree of importance, it had its open shrubbery and closer wood walk; a road of smooth gravel winding round a plantation led to the front; the lawn was dotted over with timber; the house itself was under the guardianship of the fir, the mountain ash, and the acacia; and a thick screen of them altogether, interspersed with tall Lombardy poplars, shut out the offices.

Marianne entered the house with a heart swelling with emotion from the consciousness of being only eighty miles from Barton, and not thirty from Combe Magna; and before she had been five minutes within its walls, while the others were busily helping Charlotte show her child to the housekeeper, she quitted it again, stealing away through the winding shrubberies, now just beginning to be in beauty, to gain a distant eminence; where, from its Grecian temple, her eye, wandering over a wide tract of country to the southeast, could fondly rest on the farthest ridge of hills in the horizon and fancy that from their summits Combe Magna might be seen.

In such moments of precious, of invaluable misery, she rejoiced in tears of agony to be at Cleveland; and as she returned by a different circuit to the house, feeling all the happy privilege of country liberty, of wandering from place to place in free and luxurious solitude, she resolved to spend almost every hour of every day while she remained with the Palmers in the indulgence of such solitary rambles.

She returned just in time to join the others as they quitted the house, on an excursion through its more immediate premises; and the rest of the morning was easily whiled away in lounging round the kitchen garden, examining the bloom upon its walls, and listening to the gardener's lamentations upon blights, in dawdling through the greenhouse, where the loss of her favourite plants, unwarily exposed and nipped by the lingering frost, raised the laughter of Charlotte, and in visiting her poultry-yard, where, in the disappointed hopes of her dairymaid, by hens forsaking their nests, or being stolen by a fox, or in the rapid decease of a promising young brood, she found fresh sources of merriment.

The morning was fine and dry, and Marianne, in her plan of employment abroad, had not calculated for any change of weather during their stay at Cleveland. With great surprise, therefore, did she find herself prevented by a settled rain from going out again after dinner. She had depended on a twilight walk to the Grecian temple and perhaps all over the grounds, and an evening merely cold or damp would not have deterred her from it; but a heavy and settled rain even *she* could not fancy dry or pleasant weather for walking.

Their party was small, and the hours passed quietly away. Mrs. Palmer had her child, and Mrs. Jennings her carpet-work; they talked of the friends they had left behind, arranged Lady Middleton's engagements, and wondered whether Mr. Palmer and Colonel Brandon would get farther than Reading that night. Elinor, however little concerned in it, joined in their discourse, and Marianne, who had the knack of finding her way in every house to the library, however it might be avoided by the family in general, so procured herself a book.

Nothing was wanting on Mrs. Palmer's side that constant and friendly good humour could do to make them feel themselves welcome. The openness and heartiness of her manner more than atoned for that want of recollection and elegance which made her often deficient in the forms of politeness; her kindness, recommended by so pretty a face, was engaging; her folly, though evident, was not disgusting because it was not conceited; and Elinor could have forgiven everything but her laugh.

The two gentlemen arrived the next day to a very late dinner, affording a pleasant enlargement of the party and a very welcome variety to their conversation, which a long morning of the same continued rain had reduced very low.

Elinor had seen so little of Mr. Palmer, and in that little had seen so much variety in his address to her sister and herself that she knew not what to expect to find him in his own family. She found him, however, perfectly the gentleman in his behaviour to all his visitors and only occasionally rude to his wife and her mother; she found him very capable of being a pleasant companion and only prevented from being so always by too great an aptitude to fancy himself as much superior to people in general as he must feel himself to be to Mrs. Jennings and Charlotte. For the rest of his character and habits, they were marked, as far as Elinor could perceive, with no traits at all unusual in his sex and time of life. He was nice in his eating, uncertain in his hours; fond of his child, though affecting to slight it; and idled away the mornings at billiards, which ought to have been devoted to business. She liked him, however, upon the whole much better than she had expected, and in her heart was not sorry that she could like him no more; not sorry to be driven by the observation of his epicurism, his selfishness, and his conceit, to rest with complacency on the remembrance of Edward's generous temper, simple taste, and diffident feelings.

Of Edward, or at least of some of his concerns, she now received intelligence from Colonel Brandon, who had been into Dorsetshire lately; and who, treating her at once as the disinterested friend of Mr. Ferrars and the kind confidante of himself, talked to her a great deal of the Parsonage of Delaford, described its deficiencies, and told her what he meant to do himself towards removing them. His behaviour to her in this, as well as in every other particular, his open pleasure in meeting her after an absence of only ten days, his readiness to converse with her, and his deference for her opinion might very well justify Mrs. Jennings's persuasion of his attachment, and would have been enough, perhaps, had not Elinor still, as from the first, believed Marianne his real favourite, to make her suspect it herself. But as it was, such a notion had scarcely ever entered her head except by Mrs. Jennings's suggestion; and she could not help believing herself the nicest observer of the two; she watched his eyes while Mrs. Jennings thought only of his behaviour; and while his looks of anxious solicitude on Marianne's feeling, in her head and throat, the beginning of an heavy cold, because unexpressed by words, entirely escaped the latter lady's observation; *she* could discover in them the quick feelings and needless alarm of a lover.

Two delightful twilight walks on the third and fourth evenings of her being there, not merely on the dry gravel to the shrubbery but all over the grounds, and especially in the most distant parts of them where there was something more of wildness than in the rest, where the trees were the oldest, and the grass was the longest and wettest, had—assisted by the still greater imprudence of sitting in her wet shoes and stockings—given Marianne a cold so violent as, though for a day or two trifled with or denied, would force itself by increasing ailments on the concern of everybody and the notice of herself. Prescriptions poured in from all quarters and as usual were all declined. Though heavy and feverish, with a pain in her limbs, a cough, and a sore throat, a good night's rest was to cure her entirely; and it was with difficulty that Elinor prevailed on her when she went to bed to try one or two of the simplest of the remedies.

Chapter 7

MARIANNE GOT up the next morning at her usual time; to every inquiry replied that she was better, and tried to prove herself so by engaging in her accustomary employments. But a day spent in sitting shivering over the fire with a book in her hand, which she was unable to read, or in lying weary and languid on a sofa, did not speak much in favour of her amendment; and when at last she went early to bed, more and more indisposed, Colonel Brandon was only astonished at her sister's composure who, though attending and nursing her the whole day against Marianne's inclination, and forcing proper medicines on her at night, trusted, like Marianne, to the certainty and efficacy of sleep and felt no real alarm.

A very restless and feverish night, however, disappointed the expectation of both; and when Marianne, after persisting in rising, confessed herself unable to sit up and returned voluntarily to her bed, Elinor was very ready to adopt Mrs. Jennings's advice of sending for the Palmers' apothecary.

He came, examined his patient, and though encouraging Miss Dashwood to expect that a very few days would restore her sister to health; yet, by pronouncing her disorder to have a putrid tendency and allowing the word "infection" to pass his lips, gave instant alarm to Mrs. Palmer on her baby's account. Mrs. Jennings, who had been inclined from the first to think Marianne's complaint more serious than Elinor, now looked very grave on Mr. Harris's report, and confirming Charlotte's fears and caution, urged the necessity of her immediate removal with her infant; and Mr. Palmer, though treating their apprehensions as idle, found the anxiety and importunity of his wife too great to be withstood. Her departure therefore was fixed on; and within an hour after Mr. Harris's arrival she set off with her little boy and his nurse for the house of a near relation of Mr. Palmer's who lived a few miles on the other side of Bath; whither her husband promised, at her earnest entreaty, to join her in a day or two; and whither she was almost equally urgent with her mother to accompany her. Mrs. Jennings, however, with a kindness of heart which made Elinor really love her, declared her resolution of not stirring from Cleveland as long as Marianne remained ill, and of endeavouring by her own attentive care to supply to her the place of the mother she had taken her from; and Elinor found her on every occasion a most willing and active helpmate, desirous to share in all her fatigues, and often by her better experience in nursing, of material use.

Poor Marianne, languid and low from the nature of her malady and feeling herself universally ill, could no longer hope that to-morrow would find her recovered; and the idea of what to-morrow would have produced, but for this unlucky illness, made every ailment more severe; for on that day they were to have begun their journey home; and attended the whole way by a servant of Mrs. Jennings, were to have taken their mother by surprise on the following forenoon. The little that she said was all in lamentation of this inevitable delay; though Elinor tried to raise her spirits and make her believe, as she *then* really believed herself, that it would be a very short one.

The next day produced little or no alteration in the state of the patient; she certainly was not better, and except that there was no amendment, did not appear worse. Their party was now further reduced; for Mr. Palmer, though very unwilling to go, as well from real humanity and good nature as from a dislike of appearing to be frightened away by his wife, was persuaded at last by Colonel Brandon to perform his promise of following her; and while he was preparing to go, Colonel Brandon himself, with a much greater exertion, began to talk of going likewise. Here, however, the kindness of Mrs. Jennings interposed most acceptably; for to send the Colonel away while his love was in so much uneasiness, on her sister's account, would be to deprive them both, she thought, of every comfort; and, therefore, telling him at once that his stay at Cleveland was necessary to herself, that she should want him to play at piquet of an evening while Miss Dashwood was above with her sister, etc., she urged him so strongly to remain that he, who was gratifying the first wish of his own heart by a compliance, could not long even affect to demur; especially as Mrs. Jennings's entreaty was warmly seconded by Mr. Palmer, who seemed to feel a relief to himself in leaving behind him a person so well able to assist or advise Miss Dashwood in any emergency.

Marianne was of course kept in ignorance of all these arrangements. She knew not that she had been the means of sending the owners of Cleveland away in about seven days from the time of their arrival. It gave her no surprise that she saw nothing of Mrs. Palmer; and as it gave her likewise no concern, she never mentioned her name.

Two days passed away from the time of Mr. Palmer's departure, and her situation continued, with little variation, the same. Mr. Harris, who attended her every day, still talked boldly of a speedy recovery, and Miss Dashwood was equally sanguine; but the expectation of the others was by no means so cheerful. Mrs. Jennings had determined very early in the seizure that Marianne would never get over it, and Colonel Brandon, who was chiefly of use in listening to Mrs. Jennings's forebodings, was not in a state of mind to resist their influence. He tried to reason himself out of fears which the different judgment of the apothecary seemed to render absurd; but the many hours of each day in which he was left entirely alone were but too favourable for the admission of every melancholy idea, and he could not expel from his mind the persuasion that he should see Marianne no more.

On the morning of the third day, however, the gloomy anticipations of both were almost done away; for when Mr. Harris arrived, he declared his patient materially better. Her pulse was much stronger, and every symptom more favourable than on the preceding visit. Elinor, confirmed in every pleasant hope, was all cheerfulness; rejoicing that in her letters to her mother, she had pursued her own judgment rather than her friend's, in making very light of the indisposition which delayed them at Cleveland; and almost fixing on the time when Marianne would be able to travel.

But the day did not close so auspiciously as it began. Towards the evening Marianne became ill again, growing more heavy, restless, and uncomfortable than before. Her sister, however, still sanguine, was willing to attribute the change to nothing more than the fatigue of having sat up to have her bed made; and carefully administering the cordials prescribed, saw her with satisfaction sink at last into a slumber from which she expected the most beneficial effects. Her sleep, though not so quiet as Elinor wished to see it, lasted a considerable time; and anxious to observe the result of it herself, she resolved to sit with her during the whole of it. Mrs. Jennings, knowing nothing of any change in the patient, went unusually early to bed; her maid, who was one of the principal nurses, was recreating herself in the housekeeper's room, and Elinor remained alone with Marianne.

The repose of the latter became more and more disturbed; and her sister, who watched with unremitting attention her continual change of posture and heard the frequent but inarticulate sounds of complaint which passed her lips, was almost wishing to rouse her from so painful a slumber, when Marianne, suddenly awakened by some accidental noise in the house, started hastily up, and with feverish wildness, cried out—

"Is mama coming?"

"Not yet," replied the other, concealing her terror and assisting Marianne to lie down again, "but she will be here, I hope, before it is long. It is a great way, you know, from hence to Barton."

"But she must not go round by London," cried Marianne in the same hurried manner, "I shall never see her if she goes by London."

Elinor perceived with alarm that she was not quite herself, and while attempting to soothe her, eagerly felt her pulse. It was lower and quicker than ever! And Marianne still talking wildly of mama, her alarm increased so rapidly as to determine her on sending instantly for Mr. Harris and dispatching a messenger to Barton for her mother. To consult with Colonel Brandon on the best means of effecting the latter was a thought which immediately followed the resolution of its performance; and as soon as she had rung up the maid to take her place by her sister, she hastened down to the drawing-room, where she knew he was generally to be found at a much later hour than the present.

It was no time for hesitation. Her fears and her difficulties were immediately before him. Her fears, he had no courage, no confidence to attempt the removal of; he listened to them in silent despondence; but her difficulties were instantly obviated; for with a readiness that seemed to speak the occasion, and the service prearranged in his mind, he offered himself as the messenger who should fetch Mrs. Dashwood. Elinor made no resistance that was not easily overcome. She thanked him with brief though fervent gratitude, and while he went to hurry off his servant with a message to Mr. Harris and an order for post-horses directly, she wrote a few lines to her mother.

The comfort of such a friend at that moment as Colonel Brandon—of such a companion for her mother—how gratefully was it felt!—a companion whose judgment would guide, whose attendance must relieve, and whose friendship might soothe her! As far as the shock of such a summons *could* be lessened to her, his presence, his manners, his assistance, would lessen it.

He, meanwhile, whatever he might feel, acted with all the firmness of a collected mind, made every necessary arrangement with the utmost dispatch, and calculated with exactness the time in which she might look for his return. Not a moment was lost in delay of any kind. The horses arrived even before they were expected, and Colonel Brandon, only pressing her hand with a look of solemnity, and a few words spoken too low to reach her ear, hurried into the carriage. It was then about twelve o'clock, and she returned to her sister's apartment to wait for the arrival of the apothecary and to watch by her the rest of the night. It was a night of almost equal suffering to both. Hour after hour passed away in sleepless pain and delirium on Marianne's side, and in the most cruel anxiety on Elinor's, before Mr. Harris appeared. Her apprehensions, once raised, paid by their excess for all her former security; and the servant who sat up with her, for she would not allow Mrs. Jennings to be called, only tortured her more by hints of what her mistress had always thought.

Marianne's ideas were still, at intervals, fixed incoherently on her mother; and whenever she mentioned her name, it gave a pang to the heart of poor Elinor, who, reproaching herself for having trifled with so many days of illness and wretched for some immediate relief, fancied that all relief might soon be in vain, that everything had been delayed too long, and pictured to herself her suffering mother arriving too late to see this darling child, or to see her rational.

She was on the point of sending again for Mr. Harris, or if *he* could not come, for some other advice, when the former—but not till after five o'clock—arrived. His opinion, however, made some little amends for his delay for though acknowledging a very unexpected and unpleasant alteration in his patient, he would not allow the danger to be material and talked of the relief which a fresh mode of treatment must procure, with a confidence which, in a lesser degree, was communicated to Elinor. He promised to call again in the course of three or four hours, and left both the patient and her anxious attendant more composed than he had found them.

With strong concern and with many reproaches for not being called to their aid did Mrs. Jennings hear in the morning of what had passed. Her former apprehensions, now with greater reason restored, left her no doubt of the event; and though trying to speak comfort to Elinor, her conviction of her sister's danger would not allow her to offer the comfort of hope. Her heart was really grieved. The rapid decay, the early death of a girl so young, so lovely as Marianne, must have struck a less interested person with concern. On Mrs. Jennings's compassion she had other claims. She had been for three months her companion, was still under her care, and she was known to have been greatly injured and long unhappy. The distress of her sister too, particularly a favourite, was before her; and as for their mother, when Mrs. Jennings considered that Marianne might probably be to *her* what Charlotte was to herself, her sympathy in *her* sufferings was very sincere.

Mr. Harris was punctual in his second visit; but he came to be disappointed in his hopes of what the last would produce. His medicines had failed; the fever was unabated; and Marianne only more quiet, not more herself, remained in an heavy stupor. Elinor, catching all, and more than all, his fears in a moment, proposed to call in further advice. But he judged it unnecessary; he had still something more to try, some fresh application, of whose success he was almost as confident as the last; and his visit concluded with encouraging assurances which reached the ear but could not enter the heart of Miss Dashwood. She was calm except when she thought of her mother, but she was almost hopeless; and in this state she continued till noon, scarcely stirring from her sister's bed, her thoughts wandering from one image of grief, one suffering friend to another, and her spirits oppressed to the utmost by the conversation of Mrs. Jennings, who scrupled not to attribute the severity and danger of this attack to the many weeks of previous indisposition which Marianne's disappointment had brought on. Elinor felt all the reasonableness of the idea, and it gave fresh misery to her reflections.

About noon, however, she began—but with a caution—a dread of disappointment which for some time kept her silent even to her friend—to fancy, to hope she could perceive a slight amendment in her sister's pulse; she waited, watched, and examined it again and again; and at last, with an agitation more difficult to bury under exterior calmness than all her foregoing distress, ventured to communicate her hopes. Mrs. Jennings, though forced on examination to acknowledge a temporary revival, tried to keep her young friend from indulging a thought of its continuance; and Elinor, conning over every injunction of distrust, told herself likewise not to hope. But it was too late. Hope had already entered; and feeling all its anxious flutter, she bent over her sister to watch—she hardly knew for what. Half an hour passed away, and the favourable symptom yet blessed her. Others even arose to confirm it. Her breath, her skin, her lips, all flattered Elinor with signs of amendment and Marianne fixed her eyes on her with a rational, though languid, gaze. Anxiety and hope now oppressed her in equal degrees and left her no moment of tranquillity till the arrival of Mr. Harris at four o'clock; when his assurances, his felicitations on a recovery in her sister even surpassing his expectation, gave her confidence, comfort, and tears of joy.

Marianne was in every respect materially better, and he declared her entirely out of danger. Mrs. Jennings, perhaps satisfied with the partial justification of her forebodings which had been found in their late alarm, allowed herself to trust in his judgment and admitted with unfeigned joy, and soon with unequivocal cheerfulness, the probability of an entire recovery.

Elinor could not be cheerful. Her joy was of a different kind and led to anything rather than to gaiety. Marianne restored to life, health, friends, and to her doting mother was an idea to fill her heart with sensations of exquisite comfort and expand it in fervent gratitude; but it led to no outward demonstrations of joy, no words, no smiles. All within Elinor's breast was satisfaction, silent and strong.

She continued by the side of her sister with little intermission the whole afternoon, calming every fear, satisfying every inquiry of her enfeebled spirits, supplying every succour, and watching almost every look and every breath. The possibility of a relapse would of course in some moments occur to remind her of what anxiety was; but when she saw on her frequent and minute examination that every symptom of recovery continued, and saw Marianne at six o'clock sink into a quiet, steady, and to all appearance comfortable sleep, she silenced every doubt.

The time was now drawing on when Colonel Brandon might be expected back. At ten o'clock, she trusted, or at least not much later, her mother would be relieved from the dreadful suspense in which she must now be travelling towards them. The Colonel too! Perhaps scarcely less an object of pity! Oh! how slow was the progress of time which yet kept them in ignorance!

At seven o'clock, leaving Marianne still sweetly asleep, she joined Mrs. Jennings in the drawing-room to tea. Of breakfast she had been kept by her fears, and of dinner by their sudden reverse, from eating much; and the present refreshment, therefore, with such feelings of content as she brought to it, was particularly welcome. Mrs. Jennings would have persuaded her at its conclusion to take some rest before her mother's arrival, and allow *her* to take her place by Marianne; but Elinor had no sense of fatigue, no capability of sleep at that moment about her, and she was not to be kept away from her sister an unnecessary instant. Mrs. Jennings, therefore, attending her upstairs into the sick chamber to satisfy herself that all continued right, left her there again to her charge and her thoughts, and retired to her own room to write letters and sleep.

The night was cold and stormy. The wind roared round the house, and the rain beat against the windows; but Elinor, all happiness within, regarded it not. Marianne slept through every blast, and the travellers—they had a rich reward in store for every present inconvenience.

The clock struck eight. Had it been ten, Elinor would have been convinced that at that moment she heard a carriage driving up to the house; and so strong was the persuasion that she *did*, in spite of the *almost* impossibility of their being already come, that she moved into the adjoining dressing-closet and opened a window-shutter to be satisfied of the truth. She instantly saw that her ears had not deceived her. The flaring lamps of a carriage were immediately in view. By their uncertain light she thought she could discern it to be drawn by four horses; and this, while it told the excess of her poor mother's alarm, gave some explanation to such unexpected rapidity.

Never in her life had Elinor found it so difficult to be calm as at that moment. The knowledge of what her mother must be feeling as the carriage stopped at the door—of her doubt—her dread—perhaps her despair!—and of what *she* had to tell!—with such knowledge it was impossible to be calm. All that remained to be done was to be speedy; and, therefore staying only till she could leave Mrs. Jennings's maid with her sister, she hurried downstairs.

The bustle in the vestibule as she passed along an inner lobby, assured her that they were already in the house. She rushed forwards towards the drawing-room—she entered it—and saw only Willoughby.

Chapter 8

ELINOR, STARTING back with a look of horror at the sight of him, obeyed the first impulse of her heart in turning instantly to quit the room; and her hand was already on the lock when its action was suspended by his hastily advancing and saying in a voice rather of command than supplication:

"Miss Dashwood, for half an hour—for ten minutes—I entreat you to stay."

"No, sir," she replied with firmness, "I shall *not* stay. Your business cannot be with *me*. The servants, I suppose, forgot to tell you that Mr. Palmer was not in the house."

"Had they told me," he cried with vehemence, "that Mr. Palmer and all his relations were at the devil, it would not have turned me from the door. My business is with you and only you."

"With me!" in the utmost amazement, "well, sir, be quick, and if you can, less violent."

"Sit down, and I will be both."

She hesitated; she knew not what to do. The possibility of Colonel Brandon's arriving and finding him there came across her. But she had promised to hear him, and her curiosity no less than her honour was engaged. After a moment's recollection, therefore, concluding that prudence required dispatch, and that her acquiescence would best promote it, she walked silently towards the table and sat down. He took the opposite chair, and for half a minute not a word was said by either.

"Pray be quick, sir," said Elinor impatiently. "I have no time to spare."

He was sitting in an attitude of deep meditation and seemed not to hear her.

"Your sister," said he with abruptness a moment afterwards, "is out of danger. I heard it from the servant. God be praised! But is it true? Is it really true?"

Elinor would not speak. He repeated the inquiry with yet greater eagerness.

"For God's sake, tell me, is she out of danger or is she not?"

"We hope she is."

He rose up and walked across the room.

"Had I known as much half an hour ago— But since I *am* here"—speaking with a forced vivacity as he returned to his seat—"what does it signify? For once, Miss Dashwood—it will be the last time, perhaps—let us be cheerful together. I am in a fine mood for gaiety. Tell me honestly"—a deeper glow overspreading his cheeks—"do you think me most a knave or a fool?"

Elinor looked at him with greater astonishment than ever. She began to think that he must be in liquor; the strangeness of such a visit and of such manners seemed no otherwise intelligible; and with this impression she immediately rose, saying:

"Mr. Willoughby, I advise you at present to return to Combe. I am not at leisure to remain with you longer. Whatever your business may be with me, it will be better recollected and explained to-morrow."

"I understand you," he replied with an expressive smile and a voice perfectly calm, "yes, I am very drunk. A pint of porter with my cold beef at Marlborough was enough to overset me."

"At Marlborough!" cried Elinor, more and more at a loss to understand what he would be at.

"Yes, I left London this morning at eight o'clock, and the only ten minutes I have spent out of my chaise since that time procured me a luncheon at Marlborough."

The steadiness of his manner, and the intelligence of his eye as he spoke, convincing Elinor that whatever other unpardonable folly might bring him to Cleveland, he was not brought there by intoxication, she said, after a moment's recollection:

"Mr. Willoughby, you *ought* to feel, and I certainly *do*— that after what has passed—your coming here in this manner and forcing yourself upon my notice requires a very particular excuse. What is it that you mean by it?"

"I mean," said he with serious energy, "if I can, to make you hate me one degree less than you do *now*. I mean to offer some kind of explanation, some kind of apology, for the past; to open my whole heart to you, and by convincing you that though I have been always a blockhead, I have not been always a rascal, to obtain something like forgiveness from Ma—from your sister."

"Is this the real reason of your coming?"

"Upon my soul it is," was his answer, with a warmth which brought all the former Willoughby to her remembrance, and in spite of herself made her think him sincere.

"If that is all, you may be satisfied already, for Marianne *does*—she has *long* forgiven you."

"Has she!" he cried in the same eager tone. "Then she has forgiven me before she ought to have done it. But she shall forgive me again, and on more reasonable grounds.— *Now* will you listen to me?"

Elinor bowed her assent.

"I do not know," said he, after a pause of expectation on her side and thoughtfulness on his own, "how *you* may have accounted for my behaviour to your sister, or what diabolical motive you may have imputed to me. Perhaps you will hardly think the better of me—it is worth the trial, however, and you shall hear everything. When I first became intimate in your family, I had no other intention, no other view in the acquaintance than to pass my time pleasantly while I was obliged to remain in Devonshire, more pleasantly than I had ever done before. Your sister's lovely person and interesting manners could not but please me; and her behaviour to me almost from the first was of a kind— It is astonishing, when I reflect on what it was and what *she* was, that my heart should have been so insensible! But at first, I must confess, my vanity only was elevated by it. Careless of her happiness, thinking only of my own amusement, giving way to feelings which I had always been too much in the habit of indulging, I endeavoured by every means in my power to make myself pleasing to her without any design of returning her affection."

Miss Dashwood, at this point turning her eyes on him with the most angry contempt, stopped him by saying:

"It is hardly worth-while, Mr. Willoughby, for you to relate, or for me to listen any longer. Such a beginning as this cannot be followed by anything. Do not let me be pained by hearing anything more on the subject."

"I insist on your hearing the whole of it," he replied. "My fortune was never large, and I had always been expensive, always in the habit of associating with people of better income than myself. Every year since my coming of age, or even before I believe, had added to my debts; and though the death of my old cousin, Mrs. Smith, was to set me free, yet that event being uncertain and possibly far distant, it had been for some time my intention to re-establish my circumstances by marrying a woman of fortune. To attach myself to your sister, therefore, was not a thing to be thought of; and with a meanness, selfishness, cruelty which no indignant, no contemptuous look, even of yours, Miss Dashwood, can ever reprobate too much, I was acting in this manner, trying to engage her regard without a thought of returning it. But one thing may be said for me; even in that horrid state of selfish vanity, I did not know the extent of the injury I meditated, because I did not *then* know what it was to love. But have I ever known it? Well may it be doubted; for had I really loved, could I have sacrificed my feelings to vanity, to avarice? Or what is more, could I have sacrificed hers? But I have done it. To avoid a comparative poverty which her affection and her society would have deprived of all its horrors, I have, by raising myself to affluence, lost everything that could make it a blessing."

"You did then," said Elinor, a little softened, "believe yourself at one time attached to her."

"To have resisted such attractions, to have withstood such tenderness! Is there a man on earth who could have done it! Yes, I found myself, by insensible degrees, sincerely fond of her; and the happiest hours of my life were what I spent with her when I felt my intentions were strictly honourable and my feelings blameless. Even *then*, however, when fully determined on paying my addresses to her, I allowed myself most improperly to put off from day to day the moment of doing it, from an unwillingness to enter into an engagement while my circumstances were so greatly embarrassed. I will not reason here, nor will I stop for *you* to expatiate on the absurdity, and the worse than absurdity, of scrupling to engage my faith where my honour was already bound. The event has proved that I was a cunning fool, providing with great circumspection for a possible opportunity of making myself contemptible and wretched forever. At last, however, my resolution was taken, and I had determined as soon as I could engage her alone to justify the attentions I had so invariably paid her, and openly assure her of an affection which I had already taken such pains to display. But in the interim—in the interim of the very few hours that were to pass before I could have an opportunity of speaking with her in private—a circumstance occurred—an unlucky circumstance, to ruin all my resolution and with it all my comfort. A discovery took place"—here he hesitated and looked down—"Mrs. Smith had somehow or other been informed, I imagine by some distant relation whose interest it was to deprive me of her favour, of an affair, a connection—but I need not explain myself further," he added, looking at her with a heightened colour and an inquiring eye—"your particular intimacy—you have probably heard the whole story long ago."

"I have," returned Elinor, colouring likewise and hardening her heart anew against any compassion for him, "I have heard it all. And how you will explain away any part of your guilt in that dreadful business, I confess is beyond my comprehension."

"Remember," cried Willoughby, "from whom you received the account. Could it be an impartial one? I acknowledge that her situation and her character ought to have been respected by me. I do not mean to justify myself, but at the same time cannot leave you to suppose that I have nothing to urge, that because she was injured she was irreproachable, and because *I* was a libertine, *she* must be a saint. If the violence of her passions, the weakness of her understanding—I do not mean, however, to defend myself. Her affection for me deserved better treatment, and I often, with great self-reproach, recall the tenderness which for a very short time had the power of creating any return. I wish—I heartily wish it had never been. But I have injured more than herself; and I have injured one whose affection for me (may I say it?) was scarcely less warm than hers; and whose mind— Oh! how infinitely superior!"

"Your indifference, however, towards that unfortunate girl—I must say it, unpleasant to me as the discussion of such a subject may well be—your indifference is no apology for your cruel neglect of her. Do not think yourself excused by any weakness, any natural defect of understanding on her side, in the wanton cruelty so evident on yours. You must have known that while you were enjoying yourself in Devonshire, pursuing fresh schemes, always gay, always happy, she was reduced to the extremest indigence."

"But upon my soul, I did *not* know it," he warmly replied; "I did not recollect that I had omitted to give her my direc-

tion; and common sense might have told her how to find it
out."

"Well, sir, and what said Mrs. Smith?"

"She taxed me with the offence at once, and my confusion
may be guessed. The purity of her life, the formality of her
notions, her ignorance of the world—everything was against
me. The matter itself I could not deny, and vain was every
endeavour to soften it. She was previously disposed, I believe, to doubt the morality of my conduct in general, and
was, moreover, discontented with the very little attention,
the very little portion of my time that I had bestowed on her
in my present visit. In short, it ended in a total breach. By
one measure I might have saved myself. In the height of her
morality, good woman! she offered to forgive the past if I
would marry Eliza. That could not be; and I was formally
dismissed from her favour and her house. The night following this affair—I was to go the next morning—was spent by
me in deliberating on what my future conduct should be.
The struggle was great, but it ended too soon. My affection
for Marianne, my thorough conviction of her attachment to
me—it was all insufficient to outweigh that dread of poverty,
or get the better of those false ideas of the necessity of
riches, which I was naturally inclined to feel and expensive
society had increased. I had reason to believe myself secure
of my present wife if I chose to address her, and I persuaded
myself to think that nothing else in common prudence remained for me to do. A heavy scene, however, awaited me
before I could leave Devonshire; I was engaged to dine with
you on that very day; some apology was therefore necessary
for my breaking the engagement. But whether I should write
this apology or deliver it in person was a point of long de-
bate. To see Marianne, I felt, would be dreadful, and I even
doubted whether I could see her again and keep to my resolution. In that point, however, I undervalued my own mag-
nanimity, as the event declared; for I went, I saw her, and
saw her miserable, and left her miserable—and left her hoping never to see her again."

"Why did you call, Mr. Willoughby?" said Elinor, re-
proachfully; "a note would have answered every purpose.
Why was it necessary to call?"

"It was necessary to my own pride. I could not bear to
leave the country in a manner that might lead you, or the rest
of the neighbourhood, to suspect any part of what had really

passed between Mrs. Smith and myself; and I resolved, therefore, on calling at the cottage in my way to Honiton. The sight of your dear sister, however, was really dreadful; and to heighten the matter, I found her alone. You were all gone I do not know where. I had left her only the evening before, so fully, so firmly resolved within myself on doing right! A few hours were to have engaged her to me forever; and I remember how happy, how gay were my spirits, as I walked from the cottage to Allenham, satisfied with myself, delighted with everybody! But in this, our last interview of friendship, I approached her with a sense of guilt that almost took from me the power of dissembling. Her sorrow, her disappointment, her deep regret when I told her that I was obliged to leave Devonshire so immediately—I never shall forget it—united too with such reliance, such confidence in me! Oh, God! What a hard-hearted rascal I was!"

They were both silent for a few moments. Elinor first spoke.

"Did you tell her that you should soon return?"

"I do not know what I told her," he replied impatiently; "less than was due to the past, beyond a doubt, and in all likelihood much more than was justified by the future. I cannot think of it. It won't do. Then came your dear mother to torture me further with all her kindness and confidence. Thank Heaven! it *did* torture me. I was miserable. Miss Dashwood, you cannot have an idea of the comfort it gives me to look back on my own misery. I owe such a grudge to myself for the stupid, rascally folly of my own heart that all my past sufferings under it are only triumph and exultation to me now. Well, I went, left all that I loved, and went to those to whom at best I was only indifferent. My journey to town—travelling with my own horses, and therefore so tediously—no creature to speak to—my own reflection so cheerful—When I looked forward everything so inviting!—When I looked back at Barton, the picture so soothing!—Oh! it was a blessed journey!"

He stopped.

"Well, sir," said Elinor, who, though pitying him, grew impatient for his departure, "and this is all?"

"All!— No, have you forgot what passed in town?—That infamous letter— Did she show it you?"

"Yes, I saw every note that passed."

"When the first of hers reached me (as it immediately did,

for I was in town the whole time), what I felt is, in the common phrase, not to be expressed; in a more simple one—perhaps too simple to raise any emotion—my feelings were very, very painful. Every line, every word was—in the hackneyed metaphor which their dear writer, were she here, would forbid—a dagger to my heart. To know that Marianne was in town was—in the same language—a thunderbolt. Thunderbolts and daggers! What a reproof would she have given me! Her taste, her opinions—I believe they are better known to me than my own, and I am sure they are dearer."

Elinor's heart, which had undergone many changes in the course of this extraordinary conversation, was now softened again; yet she felt it her duty to check such ideas in her companion as the last.

"This is not right, Mr. Willoughby. Remember that you are married. Relate only what in your conscience you think necessary for me to hear."

"Marianne's note, by assuring me that I was still as dear to her as in former days, that in spite of the many, many weeks we had been separated she was as constant in her own feelings and as full of faith in the constancy of mine as ever, awakened all my remorse. I say awakened because time and London, business and dissipation, had in some measure quieted it; and I had been growing a fine hardened villain, fancying myself indifferent to her, and choosing to fancy that she too must have become indifferent to me; talking to myself of our past attachment as a mere idle, trifling business, shrugging up my shoulders in proof of its being so, and silencing every reproach, overcoming every scruple, by secretly saying now and then, 'I shall be heartily glad to hear she is well married.' But this note made me know myself better. I felt that she was infinitely dearer to me than any other woman in the world, and that I was using her infamously. But everything was then just settled between Miss Grey and me. To retreat was impossible. All that I had to do was to avoid you both. I sent no answer to Marianne, intending by that means to preserve myself from her further notice; and for some time I was even determined not to call in Berkeley Street; but at last, judging it wiser to affect the air of a cool, common acquaintance than anything else, I watched you all safely out of the house one morning and left my name."

"Watched us out of the house!"

"Even so. You would be surprised to hear how often I watched you, how often I was on the point of falling in with you. I have entered many a shop to avoid your sight as the carriage drove by. Lodging as I did in Bond Street, there was hardly a day in which I did not catch a glimpse of one or other of you; and nothing but the most constant watchfulness on my side, a most invariably prevailing desire to keep out of your sight, could have separated us so long. I avoided the Middletons as much as possible, as well as everybody else who was likely to prove an acquaintance in common. Not aware of their being in town, however, I blundered on Sir John, I believe, the first day of his coming, and the day after I had called at Mrs. Jennings's. He asked me to a party, a dance at his house in the evening. Had he *not* told me as an inducement that you and your sister were to be there, I should have felt it too certain a thing to trust myself near him. The next morning brought another short note from Marianne, still affectionate, open, artless, confiding— everything that could make *my* conduct most hateful. I could not answer it. I tried, but could not frame a sentence. But I thought of her, I believe, every moment of the day. If you *can* pity me, Miss Dashwood, pity my situation as it was *then*. With my head and heart full of your sister, I was forced to play the happy lover to another woman! Those three or four weeks were worse than all. Well, at last, as I need not tell you, you were forced on me; and what a sweet figure I cut! What an evening of agony it was! Marianne, beautiful as an angel on one side, calling me Willoughby in such a tone! Oh! God! Holding out her hand to me, asking me for an explanation with those bewitching eyes fixed in such speaking solicitude on my face! And Sophia, jealous as the devil on the other hand, looking all that was— Well, it does not signify; it is over now. Such an evening! I ran away from you all as soon as I could; but not before I had seen Marianne's sweet face as white as death. *That* was the last, last look I ever had of her; the last manner in which she appeared to me. It was a horrid sight! Yet when I thought of her to-day as really dying, it was a kind of comfort to me to imagine that I knew exactly how she would appear to those who saw her last in this world. She was before me, constantly before me, as I travelled, in the same look and hue."

A short pause of mutual thoughtfulness succeeded. Willoughby, first rousing himself, broke it thus:

"Well, let me make haste and be gone. Your sister is certainly better, certainly out of danger?"

"We are assured of it."

"Your poor mother too! Doting on Marianne."

"But the letter, Mr. Willoughby, your own letter; have you anything to say about that?"

"Yes, yes, *that* in particular. Your sister wrote to me again, you know, the very next morning. You saw what she said. I was breakfasting at the Ellisons, and her letter, with some others, was brought to me there from my lodgings. It happened to catch Sophia's eye before it caught mine; and its size, the elegance of the paper, the handwriting altogether, immediately gave her a suspicion. Some vague report had reached her before of my attachment to some young lady in Devonshire, and what had passed within her observation the preceding evening had marked who the young lady was and made her more jealous than ever. Affecting that air of playfulness, therefore, which is delightful in a woman one loves, she opened the letter directly and read its contents. She was well paid for her impudence. She read what made her wretched. Her wretchedness I could have borne, but her passion—her malice— At all events it must be appeased. And in short, what do you think of my wife's style of letter-writing? Delicate—tender—truly feminine—was it not?"

"Your wife! The letter was in your own handwriting."

"Yes, but I had only the credit of servilely copying such sentences as I was ashamed to put my name to. The original was all her own, her own happy thoughts and gentle diction. But what could I do? We were engaged, everything in preparation, the day almost fixed. But I am talking like a fool. Preparation!—Day!—In honest words, her money was necessary to me, and in a situation like mine, anything was to be done to prevent a rupture. And after all, what did it signify to my character in the opinion of Marianne and her friends in what language my answer was couched? It must have been only to one end. My business was to declare myself a scoundrel, and whether I did it with a bow or a bluster was of little importance. 'I am ruined forever in their opinion' said I to myself. 'I am shut out forever from their society; they already think me an unprincipled fellow; this letter will only make them think me a blackguard one.' Such were my reasonings as, in a sort of desperate carelessness, I copied my wife's words and parted with the last relics of Marianne. Her three notes—unluckily they were all in my pocket-book, or I should have denied their existence and hoarded them forever—I was forced to put them up and could not even kiss them. And the lock of hair—that too I had always carried about me in the same pocket-book, which was now searched by Madam with the most ingratiating virulence—the dear lock—all, every memento, was torn from me."

"You are very wrong, Mr. Willoughby, very blameable," said Elinor, while her voice, in spite of herself, betrayed her compassionate emotion; "you ought not to speak in this way either of Mrs. Willoughby or my sister. You have made your own choice. It was not forced on you. Your wife has a claim to your politeness, to your respect, at least. She must be attached to you or she would not have married you. To treat her with unkindness, to speak of her slightingly is no atonement to Marianne, nor can I suppose it a relief to your own conscience."

"Do not talk to me of my wife," said he with a heavy sigh. "She does not deserve your compassion. She knew I had no regard for her when we married. Well, married we were, and came down to Combe Magna to be happy, and afterwards returned to town to be gay. And now do you pity me, Miss Dashwood? Or have I said all this to no purpose? Am I—be it only one degree—am I less guilty in your opinion than I was before? My intentions were not always wrong. Have I explained away any part of my guilt?"

"Yes, you have certainly removed something—a little. You have proved yourself, on the whole, less faulty than I had believed you. You have proved your heart less wicked, much less wicked. But I hardly know—the misery that you have inflicted—I hardly know what could have made it worse."

"Will you repeat to your sister when she is recovered what I have been telling you? Let me be a little lightened too in her opinion as well as in yours. You tell me that she has forgiven me already. Let me be able to fancy that a better knowledge of my heart, and of my present feelings, will draw from her a more spontaneous, more natural, more gentle, less dignified forgiveness. Tell her of my misery and my penitence. Tell her that my heart was never inconstant to her, and if you will, that at this moment she is dearer to me than ever."

"I will tell her all that is necessary to what may comparatively be called your justification. But you have not explained to me the particular reason of your coming now, nor how you heard of her illness."

"Last night in Drury Lane lobby I ran against Sir John Middleton, and when he saw who I was—for the first time these two months—he spoke to me. That he had cut me ever since my marriage, I had seen without surprise or resentment. Now, however, his good-natured, honest, stupid soul, full of indignation against me and concern for your sister, could not resist the temptation of telling me what he knew ought to, though probably he did not think it *would,* vex me horridly. As bluntly as he could speak it, therefore, he told me that Marianne Dashwood was dying of a putrid fever at Cleveland. A letter that morning received from Mrs. Jennings declared her danger most imminent—the Palmers all gone off in a fright, etc. I was too much shocked to be able to pass myself off as insensible even to the undiscerning Sir John. His heart was softened in seeing mine suffer; and so much of his ill-will was done away that when we parted, he almost shook me by the hand while he reminded me of an old promise about a pointer puppy. What I felt on hearing that your sister was dying—and dying too, believing me the greatest villain upon earth, scorning, hating me in her latest moments—for how could I tell what horrid projects might not have been imputed? *One* person I was sure would represent me as capable of anything. What I felt was dreadful! My resolution was soon made, and at eight o'clock this morning I was in my carriage. Now you know all."

Elinor made no answer. Her thoughts were silently fixed on the irreparable injury which too early an independence and its consequent habits of idleness, dissipation, and luxury, had made in the mind, the character, the happiness, of a man who, to every advantage of person and talents, united a disposition naturally open and honest, and a feeling, affectionate temper. The world had made him extravagant and vain. Extravagance and vanity had made him cold-hearted and selfish. Vanity, while seeking its own guilty triumph at the expense of another, had involved him in a real attachment which extravagance, or at least its offspring, necessity, had required to be sacrificed. Each faulty propensity, in leading him to evil, had led him likewise to punishment. The attachment from which against honour, against feeling, against every better interest he had outwardly torn himself, now, when no longer allowable, governed every thought; and the connection, for the sake of which he had, with little scruple, left her sister to misery, was likely to prove a source of unhappiness to himself of a far more incurable nature. From a reverie of this kind she was recalled at the end of some minutes by Willoughby, who, rousing himself from a reverie at least equally painful, started up in preparation for going, and said:

"There is no use in staying here; I must be off."

"Are you going back to town?"

"No, to Combe Magna. I have business there; from thence to town in a day or two. Good-bye."

He held out his hand. She could not refuse to give him hers; he pressed it with affection.

"And you *do* think something better of me than you did?" said he, letting it fall, and leaning against the mantel-piece as if forgetting he was to go.

Elinor assured him that she did; that she forgave, pitied, wished him well, was even interested in his happiness, and added some gentle counsel as to the behaviour most likely to promote it. His answer was not very encouraging.

"As to that," said he, "I must rub through the world as well as I can. Domestic happiness is out of the question. If, however, I am allowed to think that you and yours feel an interest in my fate and actions, it may be the means—it may put me on my guard—at least it will be something to live for. Marianne to be sure is lost to me forever. Were I even by any blessed chance at liberty again—"

Elinor stopped him with a reproof.

"Well," he replied, "once more good-bye. I shall now go away and live in dread of one event."

"What do you mean?"

"Your sister's marriage."

"You are very wrong. She can never be more lost to you than she is now."

"But she will be gained by someone else. And if that someone should be the very he whom of all others I could least bear— But I will not stay to rob myself of all your compassionate good will, by showing that where I have most injured I can least forgive. Good-bye. God bless you!"

And with these words, he almost ran out of the room.

Chapter 9

ELINOR, FOR some time after he left her, for some time even after the sound of his carriage had died away, remained too much oppressed by a crowd of ideas widely differing in themselves, but of which sadness was the general result, to think even of her sister.

Willoughby, he whom only half an hour ago she had abhorred as the most worthless of men, Willoughby, in spite of all his faults, excited a degree of commiseration for the sufferings produced by them, which made her think of him as now separated forever from her family with a tenderness, a regret, rather in proportion, as she soon acknowledged within herself, to his wishes than to his merits. She felt that his influence over her mind was heightened by circumstances which ought not in reason to have weight: by that person of uncommon attraction, that open, affectionate, and lively manner which it was no merit to possess; and by that still ardent love for Marianne, which it was not even innocent to indulge. But she felt that it was so, long, long before she could feel his influence less.

When at last she returned to the unconscious Marianne, she found her just awaking, refreshed by so long and sweet a sleep to the extent of her hopes. Elinor's heart was full. The past, the present, the future, Willoughby's visit, Marianne's safety, and her mother's expected arrival, threw her altogether into an agitation of spirits which kept off every indication of fatigue and made her only fearful of betraying herself to her sister. Short was the time, however, in which that fear could affect her, for within half an hour after Willoughby's leaving the house, she was again called downstairs by the sound of another carriage. Eager to save her mother from every unnecessary moment's horrible suspense, she ran immediately into the hall, and reached the outward door just in time to receive and support her as she entered it.

Mrs. Dashwood, whose terror as they drew near the house had produced almost the conviction of Marianne's being no

more, had no voice to inquire after her, no voice even for
Elinor; but *she,* waiting neither for salutation nor inquiry, instantly gave the joyful relief; and her mother, catching it
with all her usual warmth, was in a moment as much overcome by her happiness as she had been before by her fears.
She was supported into the drawing-room between her
daughter and her friend; and there shedding tears of joy,
though still unable to speak, embraced Elinor again and
again, turning from her at intervals to press Colonel
Brandon's hand, with a look which spoke at once her gratitude and her conviction of his sharing with herself in the
bliss of the moment. He shared it, however, in a silence even
greater than her own.

As soon as Mrs. Dashwood had recovered herself, to see
Marianne was her first desire; and in two minutes she was
with her beloved child, rendered dearer to her than ever by
absence, unhappiness, and danger. Elinor's delight, as she
saw what each felt in the meeting, was only checked by an
apprehension of its robbing Marianne of further sleep; but
Mrs. Dashwood could be calm, could be even prudent, when
the life of a child was at stake; and Marianne, satisfied in
knowing her mother was near her, and conscious of being
too weak for conversation, submitted readily to the silence
and quiet prescribed by every nurse around her. Mrs.
Dashwood *would* sit up with her all night, and Elinor, in
compliance with her mother's entreaty, went to bed. But the
rest, which one night entirely sleepless and many hours of
the most wearing anxiety seemed to make requisite, was
kept off by irritation of spirits. Willoughby, "poor Willoughby," as she now allowed herself to call him, was constantly
in her thoughts; she would not but have heard his vindication for the world, and now blamed, now acquitted herself
for having judged him so harshly before. But her promise of
relating it to her sister was invariably painful. She dreaded
the performance of it, dreaded what its effect on Marianne
might be; doubted whether after such an explanation she
could ever be happy with another; and for a moment wished
Willoughby a widower. Then, remembering Colonel Brandon, reproved herself, felt that to *his* sufferings and *his* constancy, far more than to his rival's, the reward of her sister
was due, and wished anything rather than Mrs. Willoughby's
death.

The shock of Colonel Brandon's errand at Barton had

been much softened to Mrs. Dashwood by her own previous alarm; for so great was her uneasiness about Marianne that she had already determined to set out for Cleveland on that very day, without waiting for any further intelligence, and had so far settled her journey before his arrival that the Careys were then expected every moment to fetch Margaret away, as her mother was unwilling to take her where there might be infection.

Marianne continued to mend every day, and the brilliant cheerfulness of Mrs. Dashwood's looks and spirits proved her to be, as she repeatedly declared herself, one of the happiest women in the world. Elinor could not hear the declaration nor witness its proofs without sometimes wondering whether her mother ever recollected Edward. But Mrs. Dashwood, trusting to the temperate account of her own disappointment which Elinor had sent her, was led away by the exuberance of her joy to think only of what would increase it. Marianne was restored to her from a danger in which, as she now began to feel, her own mistaken judgment in encouraging the unfortunate attachment to Willoughby had contributed to place her; and in her recovery she had yet another source of joy unthought of by Elinor. It was thus imparted to her as soon as any opportunity of private conference between them occurred.

"At last we are alone. My Elinor, you do not yet know all my happiness. Colonel Brandon loves Marianne. He has told me so himself."

Her daughter, feeling by turns both pleased and pained, surprised and not surprised, was all silent attention.

"You are never like me, dear Elinor, or I should wonder at your composure now. Had I sat down to wish for any possible good to my family, I should have fixed on Colonel Brandon's marrying one of you as the object most desirable. And I believe Marianne will be the most happy with him of the two."

Elinor was half inclined to ask her reason for thinking so, because satisfied that none founded on an impartial consideration of their age, characters, or feelings, could be given; but her mother must always be carried away by her imagination on any interesting subject; and, therefore, instead of an inquiry, she passed it off with a smile.

"He opened his whole heart to me yesterday as we travelled. It came out quite unawares, quite undesignedly. I, you may well believe, could talk of nothing but my child; he could not conceal his distress; I saw that it equalled my own, and he, perhaps thinking that mere friendship, as the world now goes, would not justify so warm a sympathy—or rather not thinking at all, I suppose—giving way to irresistible feelings, made me acquainted with his earnest, tender, constant, affection for Marianne. He has loved her, my Elinor, ever since the first moment of seeing her."

Here, however, Elinor perceived not the language, not the professions of Colonel Brandon, but the natural embellishments of her mother's active fancy, which fashioned everything delightful to her as it chose.

"His regard for her, infinitely surpassing anything that Willoughby ever felt or feigned, as much more warm, as more sincere or constant—whichever we are to call it—has subsisted through all the knowledge of dear Marianne's unhappy prepossession for that worthless young man! And without selfishness—without encouraging a hope! Could he have seen her happy with another? Such a noble mind! Such openness, such sincerity! No one can be deceived in *him*."

"Colonel Brandon's character," said Elinor, "as an excellent man is well-established."

"I know it is," replied her mother seriously, "or after such a warning, *I* should be the last to encourage such affection, or even to be pleased by it. But his coming for me as he did, with such active, such ready friendship, is enough to prove him one of the worthiest of men."

"His character, however," answered Elinor, "does not rest on *one* act of kindness to which his affection for Marianne, were humanity out of the case, would have prompted him. To Mrs. Jennings, to the Middletons, he has been long and intimately known; they equally love and respect him; and even my own knowledge of him, though lately acquired, is very considerable; and so highly do *I* value and esteem him, that if Marianne can be happy with him, I shall be as ready as yourself to think our connection the greatest blessing to us in the world. What answer did you give him? Did you allow him to hope?"

"Oh! my love, I could not then talk of hope to him or to myself. Marianne might at that moment be dying. But he did not ask for hope or encouragement. His was an involuntary confidence, an irrepressible effusion to a soothing friend, not an application to a parent. Yet after a time I *did* say, for at

first I was quite overcome, that if she lived, as I trusted she
might, my greatest happiness would lie in promoting their
marriage; and since our arrival, since our delightful security,
I have repeated it to him more fully, have given him every
encouragement in my power. Time, a very little time, I tell
him, will do everything. Marianne's heart is not to be wasted
forever on such a man as Willoughby. His own merits must
soon secure it."

"To judge from the Colonel's spirits, however, you have
not yet made him equally sanguine."

"No. He thinks Marianne's affection too deeply rooted for
any change in it under a great length of time, and even supposing her heart again free, is too diffident of himself to believe that with such a difference of age and disposition he
could ever attach her. There, however, he is quite mistaken.
His age is only so much beyond hers as to be an advantage,
as to make his character and principles fixed; and his disposition, I am well convinced, is exactly the very one to make
your sister happy. And his person, his manners too, are all in
his favour. My partiality does not blind me; he certainly is
not so handsome as Willoughby; but at the same time, there
is something much more pleasing in his countenance. There
was always a something, if you remember, in Willoughby's
eyes at times which I did not like."

Elinor could *not* remember it; but her mother, without
waiting for her assent, continued:

"And his manners, the Colonel's manners are not only
more pleasing to me than Willoughby's ever were, but they
are of a kind I well know to be more solidly attaching to
Marianne. Their gentleness, their genuine attention to other
people, and their manly unstudied simplicity is much more
accordant with her real disposition than the liveliness, often
artificial and often ill-timed, of the other. I am very sure myself that had Willoughby turned out as really amiable as he
has proved himself the contrary, Marianne would yet never
have been so happy with *him* as she will be with Colonel
Brandon."

She paused. Her daughter could not quite agree with her,
but her dissent was not heard and therefore gave no offence.

"At Delaford she will be within an easy distance of me,"
added Mrs. Dashwood, "even if I remain at Barton; and in
all probability—for I hear it is a large village—indeed there

certainly *must* be some small house or cottage close by that
would suit us quite as well as our present situation."

Poor Elinor! Here was a new scheme for getting her to
Delaford! But her spirit was stubborn.

"His fortune too! For at my time of life you know, everybody cares about *that*; and though I neither know nor desire
to know what it really is, I am sure it must be a good one."

Here they were interrupted by the entrance of a third person, and Elinor withdrew to think it all over in private, to
wish success to her friend, and yet in wishing it, to feel a
pang for Willoughby.

Chapter 10

MARIANNE'S ILLNESS, though weakening in its kind, had not
been long enough to make her recovery slow; and with
youth, natural strength, and her mother's presence in aid, it
proceeded so smoothly as to enable her to remove, within
four days after the arrival of the latter, into Mrs. Palmer's
dressing-room. When there, at her own particular request,
for she was impatient to pour forth her thanks to him for
fetching her mother, Colonel Brandon was invited to visit
her.

His emotion in entering the room, in seeing her altered
looks, and in receiving the pale hand which she immediately
held out to him, was such as, in Elinor's conjecture, must
arise from something more than his affection for Marianne
or the consciousness of its being known to others; and she
soon discovered in his melancholy eye and varying complexion as he looked at her sister the probable recurrence of
many past scenes of misery to his mind, brought back by
that resemblance between Marianne and Eliza already acknowledged and now strengthened by the hollow eye, the
sickly skin, the posture of reclining weakness, and the warm
acknowledgement of peculiar obligation.

Mrs. Dashwood, not less watchful of what passed than her
daughter, but with a mind very differently influenced, and
therefore watching to very different effect, saw nothing in
the Colonel's behaviour but what arose from the most simple

and self-evident sensations, while in the actions and words
of Marianne she persuaded herself to think that something
more than gratitude already dawned.

At the end of another day or two, Marianne growing visibly stronger every twelve hours, Mrs. Dashwood, urged
equally by her own and her daughter's wishes, began to talk
of removing to Barton. On *her* measures depended those of
her two friends; Mrs. Jennings could not quit Cleveland during the Dashwoods' stay, and Colonel Brandon was soon
brought, by their united request, to consider his own abode
there as equally determinate if not equally indispensable. At
his and Mrs. Jennings's united request in return, Mrs.
Dashwood was prevailed on to accept the use of his carriage
on her journey back for the better accommodation of her
sick child; and the Colonel, at the joint invitation of Mrs.
Dashwood and Mrs. Jennings, whose active good nature
made her friendly and hospitable for other people as well as
herself, engaged with pleasure to redeem it by a visit at the
cottage in the course of a few weeks.

The day of separation and departure arrived; and Marianne, after taking so particular and lengthened a leave of
Mrs. Jennings, one so earnestly grateful, so full of respect
and kind wishes as seemed due to her own heart from a secret acknowledgment of past inattention, and bidding Colonel Brandon farewell with the cordiality of a friend, was
carefully assisted by him into the carriage, of which he
seemed anxious that she should engross at least half. Mrs.
Dashwood and Elinor then followed, and the others were left
by themselves to talk of the travellers and feel their own
dullness till Mrs. Jennings was summoned to her chaise to
take comfort in the gossip of her maid for the loss of her two
young companions; and Colonel Brandon immediately afterwards took his solitary way to Delaford.

The Dashwoods were two days on the road, and Marianne
bore her journey on both without essential fatigue. Everything that the most zealous affection, the most solicitous
care, could do to render her comfortable was the office of
each watchful companion; and each found their reward in
her bodily ease and her calmness of spirits. To Elinor the observation of the latter was particularly grateful. She, who
had seen her week after week so constantly suffering, oppressed by anguish of heart which she had neither courage to
speak of nor fortitude to conceal, now saw with a joy which

no other could equally share an apparent composure of mind, which, in being the result as she trusted of serious reflection, must eventually lead her to contentment and cheerfulness.

As they approached Barton, indeed, and entered on scenes of which every field and every tree brought some peculiar, some painful recollection, she grew silent and thoughtful, and turning away her face from their notice, sat earnestly gazing through the window. But here Elinor could neither wonder nor blame; and when she saw, as she assisted Marianne from the carriage, that she had been crying, she saw only an emotion too natural in itself to raise anything less tender than pity, and in its unobtrusiveness entitled to praise. In the whole of her subsequent manner, she traced the direction of a mind awakened to reasonable exertion; for no sooner had they entered their common sitting-room than Marianne turned her eyes around it with a look of resolute firmness, as if determined at once to accustom herself to the sight of every object with which the remembrance of Willoughby could be connected. She said little, but every sentence aimed at cheerfulness; and though a sigh sometimes escaped her, it never passed away without the atonement of a smile. After dinner she would try her pianoforte. She went to it; but the music on which her eye first rested was an opera procured for her by Willoughby, containing some of their favourite duets, and bearing on its outward leaf her own name in his handwriting. That would not do. She shook her head, put the music aside, and after running over the keys for a minute, complained of feebleness in her fingers and closed the instrument again, declaring, however, with firmness as she did so, that she should in future practise much.

The next morning produced no abatement in these happy symptoms. On the contrary, with a mind and body alike strengthened by rest, she looked and spoke with more genuine spirit, anticipating the pleasure of Margaret's return, and talking of the dear family party which would then be restored, of their mutual pursuits and cheerful society as the only happiness worth a wish.

"When the weather is settled, and I have recovered my strength," said she, "we will take long walks together every day. We will walk to the farm at the edge of the down and see how the children go on; we will walk to Sir John's new

plantations at Barton Cross, and the Abbeyland; and we will
often go to the old ruins of the Priory and try to trace its
foundations as far as we are told they once reached. I know
we shall be happy. I know the summer will pass happily
away. I mean never to be later in rising than six, and from
that time till dinner I shall divide every moment between
music and reading. I have formed my plan and am determined to enter on a course of serious study. Our own library
is too well known to me to be resorted to for anything beyond mere amusement. But there are many works well worth
reading at the park; and there are others of more modern
production which I know I can borrow of Colonel Brandon.
By reading only six hours a day, I shall gain in the course
of a twelvemonth a great deal of instruction which I now
feel myself to want."

Elinor honoured her for a plan which originated so nobly
as this, though smiling to see the same eager fancy which
had been leading her to the extreme of languid indolence
and selfish repining, now at work in introducing excess into
a scheme of such rational employment and virtuous self-
control. Her smile, however, changed to a sigh when she
remembered that her promise to Willoughby was yet unful-
filled, and feared she had that to communicate which might
again unsettle the mind of Marianne and ruin at least for a
time this fair prospect of busy tranquillity. Willing therefore
to delay the evil hour, she resolved to wait till her sister's
health were more secure before she appointed it. But the resolution was made only to be broken.

Marianne had been two or three days at home before the
weather was fine enough for an invalid like herself to venture out. But at last a soft, genial morning appeared, such as
might tempt the daughter's wishes and the mother's confidence; and Marianne, leaning on Elinor's arm, was authorized to walk as long as she could without fatigue in the lane
before the house.

The sisters set out at a pace, slow as the feebleness of
Marianne in an exercise hitherto untried since her illness required; and they had advanced only so far beyond the house
as to admit a full view of the hill, the important hill behind,
when pausing with her eyes turned towards it, Marianne
calmly said,

"There, exactly there"—pointing with one hand—"on that

projecting mound—there I fell; and there I first saw Willoughby."

Her voice sank with the word, but presently reviving she added:

"I am thankful to find that I can look with so little pain on the spot! Shall we ever talk on that subject, Elinor?"— hesitatingly it was said—"or will it be wrong? I *can* talk of it now, I hope, as I ought to do."

Elinor tenderly invited her to be open.

"As for regret," said Marianne, "I have done with that as far as *he* is concerned. I do not mean to talk to you of what my feelings have been for him but what they are *now*. At present, if I could be satisfied on one point, if I could be allowed to think that he was not *always* acting a part, not *always* deceiving me; but above all, if I could be assured that he never was so *very* wicked as my fears have sometimes fancied him since the story of that unfortunate girl—"

She stopped. Elinor joyfully treasured her words as she answered:

"If you could be assured of that, you think you should be easy."

"Yes. My peace of mind is doubly involved in it; for not only is it horrible to suspect a person who has been what *he* has been to *me* of such designs, but what must it make me appear to myself? What in a situation like mine, but a most shamefully unguarded affection could expose me to—"

"How then," asked her sister, "would you account for his behaviour?"

"I would suppose him— Oh! how gladly would I suppose him only fickle, very, very fickle."

Elinor said no more. She was debating within herself on the eligibility of beginning her story directly or postponing it till Marianne were in stronger health; and they crept on for a few minutes in silence.

"I am not wishing him too much good," said Marianne at last with a sigh, "when I wish his secret reflections may be no more unpleasant than my own. He will suffer enough in them."

"Do you compare your conduct with his?"

"No. I compare it with what it ought to have been; I compare it with yours."

"Our situations have borne little resemblance."

"They have borne more than our conduct. Do not, my

dearest Elinor, let your kindness defend what I know your judgment must censure. My illness has made me think. It has given me leisure and calmness for serious recollection. Long before I was enough recovered to talk, I was perfectly able to reflect. I considered the past; I saw in my own behaviour since the beginning of our acquaintance with him last autumn nothing but a series of imprudence towards myself and want of kindness to others. I saw that my own feelings had prepared my sufferings and that my want of fortitude under them had almost led me to the grave. My illness, I well knew, had been entirely brought on by myself, by such negligence of my own health as I had felt even at the time to be wrong. Had I died, it would have been self-destruction. I did not know my danger till the danger was removed; but with such feelings as these reflections gave me, I wonder at my recovery, wonder that the very eagerness of my desire to live, to have time for atonement to my God and to you all, did not kill me at once. Had I died, in what peculiar misery should I have left you, my nurse, my friend, my sister! You, who had seen all the fretful selfishness of my latter days; who had known all the murmurings of my heart! How should I have lived in *your* remembrance! My mother too! How could you have consoled her! I cannot express my own abhorrence of myself. Whenever I looked towards the past, I saw some duty neglected or some failing indulged. Everybody seemed injured by me. The kindness, the unceasing kindness of Mrs. Jennings, I had repaid with ungrateful contempt. To the Middletons, the Palmers, the Steeles, to every common acquaintance even, I had been insolent and unjust; with a heart hardened against their merits, and a temper irritated by their very attention. To John, to Fanny, yes, even to them, little as they deserve, I had given less than their due. But you, you above all, above my mother, had been wronged by me. I, and only I, knew your heart and its sorrows; yet to what did it influence me? Not to any compassion that could benefit you or myself. Your example was before me; but to what avail? Was I more considerate of you and your comfort? Did I imitate your forbearance or lessen your restraints by taking any part in those offices of general complaisance or particular gratitude which you had hitherto been left to discharge alone? No not less when I knew you to be unhappy than when I had believed you at ease did I turn away from every exertion of duty or friendship; scarcely allowing sorrow to exist but with me, regretting only *that* heart which had deserted and wronged me, and leaving you, for whom I professed an unbounded affection, to be miserable for my sake."

Here ceased the rapid flow of her self-reproving spirit; and Elinor, impatient to soothe though too honest to flatter, gave her instantly that praise and support which her frankness and her contrition so well deserved. Marianne pressed her hand and replied:

"You are very good. The future must be my proof. I have laid down my plan, and if I am capable of adhering to it my feelings shall be governed and my temper improved. They shall no longer worry others nor torture myself. I shall now live solely for my family. You, my mother, and Margaret must henceforth be all the world to me; you will share my affections entirely between you. From you, from my home, I shall never again have the smallest incitement to move; and if I do mix in other society it will be only to show that my spirit is humbled, my heart amended, and that I can practise the civilities, the lesser duties of life, with gentleness and forbearance. As for Willoughby, to say that I shall soon or that I shall ever forget him would be idle. His remembrance can be overcome by no change of circumstances or opinions. But it shall be regulated; it shall be checked by religion, by reason, by constant employment."

She paused—and added in a lower voice, "If I could but know *his* heart, everything would become easy."

Elinor, who had now been for some time reflecting on the propriety or impropriety of speedily hazarding her narration, without feeling at all nearer decision than at first, heard this; and perceiving that as reflection did nothing, resolution must do all, soon found herself leading to the fact.

She managed the recital, as she hoped, with address; prepared her anxious listener with caution; related simply and honestly the chief points on which Willoughby grounded his apology; did justice to his repentance; and softened only his protestations of present regard. Marianne said not a word. She trembled; her eyes were fixed on the ground, and her lips became whiter than even sickness had left them. A thousand inquiries sprang up from her heart, but she dared not urge one. She caught every syllable with panting eagerness; her hand, unknowingly to herself, closely pressed her sister's, and tears covered her cheeks.

Elinor, dreading her being tired, led her towards home; and till they reached the door of the cottage, easily conjecturing what her curiosity must be though no question was suffered to speak it, talked of nothing but Willoughby and their conversation together, and was carefully minute in every particular of speech and look where minuteness could be safely indulged. As soon as they entered the house Marianne, with a kiss of gratitude and these two words just articulate through her tears, "Tell mama," withdrew from her sister nd walked slowly upstairs. Elinor would not attempt to disturb a solitude so reasonable as what she now sought; and with a mind anxiously prearranging its result, and a resolution of reviving the subject again, should Marianne fail to do it, she turned into the parlour to fulfil her parting injunction.

Chapter 11

MRS. DASHWOOD did not hear unmoved the vindication of her former favourite. She rejoiced in his being cleared from some part of his imputed guilt; she was sorry for him; she wished him happy. But the feelings of the past could not be recalled. Nothing could restore him with a faith unbroken, a character unblemished, to Marianne. Nothing could do away the knowledge of what the latter had suffered through his means, nor remove the guilt of his conduct towards Eliza. Nothing could replace him, therefore, in her former esteem, nor injure the interests of Colonel Brandon.

Had Mrs. Dashwood, like her daughter, heard Willoughby's story from himself, had she witnessed his distress and been under the influence of his countenance and his manner, it is probable that her compassion would have been greater. But it was neither in Elinor's power nor in her wish to rouse such feelings in another by her retailed explanation, as had at first been called forth in herself. Reflection had given calmness to her judgment and sobered her own opinion of Willoughby's deserts; she wished, therefore, to declare only the simple truth, and lay open such facts as were really due to his character without any embellishment of tenderness to lead the fancy astray.

In the evening, when they were all three together, Marianne began voluntarily to speak of him again; but that it was not without an effort, the restless, unquiet thoughtfulness in which she had been for some time previously sitting—her rising colour, as she spoke—and her unsteady voice, plainly showed.

"I wish to assure you both," said she, "that I see everything as you can desire me to do."

Mrs. Dashwood would have interrupted her instantly with soothing tenderness had not Elinor, who really wished to hear her sister's unbiassed opinion, by an eager sign engaged her silence. Marianne slowly continued:

"It is a great relief to me—what Elinor told me this morning. I have now heard exactly what I wished to hear." For some moments her voice was lost; but recovering herself, she added, and with greater calmness than before, "I am now perfectly satisfied, I wish for no change. I never could have been happy with him, after knowing, as sooner or later I must have known, all this. I should have had no confidence, no esteem. Nothing could have done it away to my feelings."

"I know it; I know it," cried her mother. "Happy with a man of libertine practices! With one who had so injured the peace of the dearest of our friends and the best of men! No, my Marianne has not a heart to be made happy with such a man! Her conscience, her sensitive conscience, would have felt all that the conscience of her husband ought to have felt."

Marianne sighed and repeated, "I wish for no change."

"You consider the matter," said Elinor, "exactly as a good mind and a sound understanding must consider it; and I dare say, you perceive, as well as myself, not only in this but in many other circumstances, reason enough to be convinced that your marriage must have involved you in many certain troubles and disappointments in which you would have been poorly supported by an affection, on his side, much less certain. Had you married, you must have been always poor. His expensiveness is acknowledged even by himself, and his whole conduct declares that self-denial is a word hardly understood by him. His demands and your inexperience together on a small, very small income, must have brought on distresses which would not be the *less* grievous to you from having been entirely unknown and unthought of before. *Your* sense of honour and honesty would have led you, I know, when aware of your situation, to attempt all the economy that would appear to you possible; and perhaps, as long as your frugality retrenched only on your own comfort, you might have been suffered to practise it, but beyond that— And how little could the utmost of your single management do to stop the ruin which had begun before your marriage?— Beyond *that,* had you endeavoured, however reasonably, to abridge *his* enjoyments, is it not to be feared that instead of prevailing on feelings so selfish to consent to it, you would have lessened your own influence on his heart and made him regret the connection which had involved him in such difficulties?"

Marianne's lips quivered, and she repeated the word "Selfish?" in a tone that implied: "Do you really think him selfish?"

"The whole of his behaviour," replied Elinor, "from the beginning to the end of the affair has been grounded on selfishness. It was selfishness which first made him sport with your affections; which afterwards, when his own were engaged, made him delay the confession of it, and which finally carried him from Barton. His own enjoyment, or his own ease, was in every particular his ruling principle."

"It is very true. *My* happiness never was his object."

"At present," continued Elinor, "he regrets what he has done. And why does he regret it? Because he finds it has not answered towards himself. It has not made him happy. His circumstances are now unembarrassed. He suffers from no evil of that kind; and he thinks only that he has married a woman of a less amiable temper than yourself. But does it thence follow that had he married you he would have been happy? The inconveniences would have been different. He would then have suffered under the pecuniary distresses which, because they are removed, he now reckons as nothing. He would have had a wife of whose temper he could make no complaint, but he would have been always necessitous, always poor; and probably would soon have learned to rank the innumerable comforts of a clear estate and good income as of far more importance, even to domestic happiness, than the mere temper of a wife."

"I have not a doubt of it," said Marianne, "and I have nothing to regret, nothing but my own folly."

"Rather say your mother's imprudence, my child," said Mrs. Dashwood; "*she* must be answerable."

Marianne would not let her proceed; and Elinor, satisfied that each felt their own error, wished to avoid any survey of the past that might weaken her sister's spirits; she, therefore, pursuing the first subject, immediately continued,

"*One* observation may, I think, be fairly drawn from the whole of the story: that all Willoughby's difficulties have arisen from the first offence against virtue in his behaviour to Eliza Williams. That crime has been the origin of every lesser one and of all his present discontents."

Marianne assented most feelingly to the remark; and her mother was led by it to an enumeration of Colonel Brandon's injuries and merits, warm as friendship and design could unitedly dictate. Her daughter did not look, however, as if much of it were heard by her.

Elinor, according to her expectation, saw on the two or three following days that Marianne did not continue to gain strength as she had done; but while her resolution was unsubdued, and she still tried to appear cheerful and easy, her sister could safely trust to the effect of time upon her health.

Margaret returned, and the family were again all restored to each other, again quietly settled at the cottage, and if not pursuing their usual studies with quite so much vigour as when they first came to Barton, at least planning a vigorous prosecution of them in future.

Elinor grew impatient for some tidings of Edward. She had heard nothing of him since her leaving London, nothing new of his plans, nothing certain even of his present abode. Some letters had passed between her and her brother in consequence of Marianne's illness; and in the first of John's there had been this sentence: "We know nothing of our unfortunate Edward and can make no inquiries on so prohibited a subject, but conclude him to be still at Oxford"; which was all the intelligence of Edward afforded her by the correspondence, for his name was not even mentioned in any of the succeeding letters. She was not doomed, however, to be long in ignorance of his measures.

Their man-servant had been sent one morning to Exeter on business; and when, as he waited at table, he had satisfied the inquiries of his mistress as to the event of his errand, this was his voluntary communication:

"I suppose you know, ma'am, that Mr. Ferrars is married."

Marianne gave a violent start, fixed her eyes upon Elinor, saw her turning pale, and fell back in her chair in hysterics. Mrs. Dashwood, whose eyes, as she answered the servant's inquiry, had intuitively taken the same direction, was shocked to perceive by Elinor's countenance how much she really suffered, and in a moment afterwards, alike distressed by Marianne's situation, knew not on which child to bestow her principal attention.

The servant, who saw only that Miss Marianne was taken ill, had sense enough to call one of the maids, who, with Mrs. Dashwood's assistance, supported her into the other room. By that time Marianne was rather better, and her mother, leaving her to the care of Margaret and the maid, returned to Elinor, who, though still much disordered, had so far recovered the use of her reason and voice as to be just beginning an inquiry of Thomas as to the source of his intelligence. Mrs. Dashwood immediately took all that trouble on herself; and Elinor had the benefit of the information without the exertion of seeking it.

"Who told you that Mr. Ferrars was married, Thomas?"

"I see Mr. Ferrars myself, ma'am, this morning in Exeter, and his lady too, Miss Steele as was. They was stopping in a chaise at the door of the New London Inn as I went there with a message from Sally at the park to her brother, who is one of the post-boys. I happened to look up as I went by the chaise, and so I see directly it was the youngest Miss Steele; so I took off my hat, and she knew me and called to me, and inquired after you, ma'am, and the young ladies, especially Miss Marianne, and bid me I should give her compliments and Mr. Ferrars's, their best compliments and service, and how sorry they was they had not time to come on and see you, but they was in a great hurry to go forwards, for they was going farther down for a little while, but howsoever, when they come back, they'd make sure to come and see you."

"But did she tell you she was married, Thomas?"

"Yes, ma'am. She smiled, and said how she had changed her name since she was in these parts. She was always a very affable and free-spoken young lady, and very civil behaved. So, I made free to wish her joy."

"Was Mr. Ferrars in the carriage with her?"

"Yes, ma'am, I just see him leaning back in it, but he did not look up; he never was a gentleman such for talking."

Elinor's heart could easily account for his not putting himself forward; and Mrs. Dashwood probably found the same explanation.

"Was there no one else in the carriage?"

"No, ma'am, only they two."

"Do you know where they came from?"

"They come straight from town, as Miss Lucy—Mrs. Ferrars told me."

"And are going farther westward?"

"Yes, ma'am, but not to bide long. They will soon be back again, and then they'd be sure and call here."

Mrs. Dashwood now looked at her daughter; but Elinor knew better than to expect them. She recognized the whole of Lucy in the message and was very confident that Edward would never come near them. She observed in a low voice to her mother that they were probably going down to Mr. Pratt's, near Plymouth.

Thomas's intelligence seemed over. Elinor looked as if she wished to hear more.

"Did you see them off before you came away?"

"No, ma'am, the horses was just coming out, but I could not bide any longer; I was afraid of being late."

"Did Mrs. Ferrars look well?"

"Yes, ma'am, she said how she was very well; and to my mind she was always a very handsome young lady, and she seemed vastly contented."

Mrs. Dashwood could think of no other question, and Thomas and the table-cloth, now alike needless, were soon afterwards dismissed. Marianne had already sent to say that she should eat nothing more. Mrs. Dashwood's and Elinor's appetites were equally lost, and Margaret might think herself very well off that with so much uneasiness as both her sisters had lately experienced, so much reason as they had often had to be careless of their meals, she had never been obliged to go without her dinner before.

When the dessert and the wine were arranged, and Mrs. Dashwood and Elinor were left by themselves, they remained long together in a similarity of thoughtfulness and silence. Mrs. Dashwood feared to hazard any remark and ventured not to offer consolation. She now found that she had erred in relying on Elinor's representation of herself; and justly concluded that everything had been expressly softened at the time to spare her from an increase of unhap-

piness, suffering as she then had suffered for Marianne. She
found that she had been misled by the careful, the considerate attention of her daughter, to think the attachment, which
once she had so well understood, much slighter in reality
than she had been wont to believe, or than it was now
proved to be. She feared that under this persuasion she had
been unjust, inattentive, nay, almost unkind to her Elinor;
that Marianne's affliction, because more acknowledged,
more immediately before her, had too much engrossed her
tenderness and led her away to forget that in Elinor she
might have a daughter suffering almost as much, certainly
with less self-provocation and greater fortitude.

Chapter 12

ELINOR NOW found the difference between the expectation
of an unpleasant event, however certain the mind may be
told to consider it, and certainty itself. She now found that
in spite of herself, she had always admitted a hope while
Edward remained single that something would occur to prevent his marrying Lucy; that some resolution of his own,
some mediation of friends, or some more eligible opportunity of establishment for the lady would arise to assist the
happiness of all. But he was now married, and she condemned her heart for the lurking flattery which so much
heightened the pain of the intelligence.

That he should be married so soon, before (as she imagined) he could be in orders, and consequently before he
could be in possession of the living, surprised her a little at
first. But she soon saw how likely it was that Lucy, in her
self-provident care, in her haste to secure him, should overlook everything but the risk of delay. They were married,
married in town, and now hastening down to her uncle's.
What had Edward felt on being within four miles of Barton, on seeing her mother's servant, on hearing Lucy's message!

They would soon, she supposed, be settled at Delaford.
Delaford—that place in which so much conspired to give her
an interest; which she wished to be acquainted with and yet

desired to avoid. She saw them in an instant in their parsonage house; saw in Lucy the active, contriving manager, uniting at once a desire of smart appearance with the utmost frugality, and ashamed to be suspected of half her economical practices; pursuing her own interest in every thought, courting the favour of Colonel Brandon, of Mrs. Jennings, and of every wealthy friend. In Edward, she knew not what she saw, nor what she wished to see; happy or unhappy, nothing pleased her; she turned away her head from every sketch of him.

Elinor flattered herself that someone of their connections in London would write to them to announce the event and give further particulars, but day after day passed off and brought no letter, no tidings. Though uncertain that anyone were to blame, she found fault with every absent friend. They were all thoughtless or indolent.

"When do you write to Colonel Brandon, ma'am?" was an inquiry which sprung from the impatience of her mind to have something going on.

"I wrote to him, my love, last week, and rather expect to see than to hear from him again. I earnestly pressed his coming to us and should not be surprised to see him walk in to-day or to-morrow or any day."

This was gaining something, something to look forward to. Colonel Brandon *must* have some information to give.

Scarcely had she so determined it, when the figure of a man on horseback drew her eyes to the window. He stopped at their gate. It was a gentleman; it was Colonel Brandon himself. Now she should hear more, and she trembled in expectations of it. But—it was *not* Colonel Brandon—neither his air—nor his height. Were it possible, she should say it must be Edward. She looked again. He had just dismounted; she could not be mistaken—it *was* Edward. She moved away and sat down. "He comes from Mr. Pratt's purposely to see us. I *will* be calm; I *will* be mistress of myself."

In a moment she perceived that the others were likewise aware of the mistake. She saw her mother and Marianne change colour; saw them look at herself and whisper a few sentences to each other. She would have given the world to be able to speak and to make them understand that she hoped no coolness, no slight, would appear in their behaviour to him; but she had no utterance, and was obliged to leave all to their own discretion.

Not a syllable passed aloud. They all waited in silence for the appearance of their visitor. His footsteps were heard along the gravel path; in a moment he was in the passage; and in another he was before them.

His countenance, as he entered the room, was not too happy, even for Elinor. His complexion was white with agitation, and he looked as if fearful of his reception and conscious that he merited no kind one. Mrs. Dashwood, however, conforming, as she trusted, to the wishes of that daughter by whom she then meant in the warmth of her heart to be guided in everything, met him with a look of forced complacency, gave him her hand, and wished him joy.

He coloured and stammered out an unintelligible reply. Elinor's lips had moved with her mother's, and when the moment of action was over, she wished that she had shaken hands with him too. But it was then too late, and with a countenance meaning to be open, she sat down again and talked of the weather.

Marianne had retreated as much as possible out of sight to conceal her distress; and Margaret, understanding some part but not the whole of the case, thought it incumbent on her to be dignified, and therefore took a seat as far from him as she could and maintained a strict silence.

When Elinor had ceased to rejoice in the dryness of the season, a very awful pause took place. It was put an end to by Mrs. Dashwood, who felt obliged to hope that he had left Mrs. Ferrars very well. In a hurried manner he replied in the affirmative.

Another pause.

Elinor, resolving to exert herself, though fearing the sound of her own voice, now said:

"Is Mrs. Ferrars at Longstaple?"

"At Longstaple!" he replied with an air of surprise. "No, my mother is in town."

"I meant," said Elinor, taking up some work from the table, "to inquire after Mrs. *Edward* Ferrars."

She dared not look up; but her mother and Marianne both turned their eyes on him. He coloured, seemed perplexed, looked doubtingly, and after some hesitation, said,

"Perhaps you mean—my brother—you mean Mrs.—Mrs. *Robert* Ferrars."

"Mrs. Robert Ferrars!" was repeated by Marianne and her mother in an accent of the utmost amazement; and though

Elinor could not speak, even *her* eyes were fixed on him with the same impatient wonder. He rose from his seat and walked to the window, apparently from not knowing what to do; took up a pair of scissors that lay there, and while spoiling both them and their sheath by cutting the latter to pieces as he spoke, said in a hurried voice:

"Perhaps you do not know—you may not have heard that my brother is lately married to—to the youngest—to Miss Lucy Steele."

His words were echoed with unspeakable astonishment by all but Elinor, who sat with her head leaning over her work, in a state of such agitation as made her hardly know where she was.

"Yes," said he, "they were married last week and are now at Dawlish."

Elinor could sit it no longer. She almost ran out of the room, and as soon as the door was closed, burst into tears of joy, which at first she thought would never cease. Edward, who had till then looked anywhere rather than at her, saw her hurry away, and perhaps saw—or even heard—her emotion; for immediately afterwards he fell into a reverie which no remarks, no inquiries, no affectionate address of Mrs. Dashwood could penetrate; and at last, without saying a word, quitted the room and walked out towards the village— leaving the others in the greatest astonishment and perplexity on a change in his situation, so wonderful and so sudden; a perplexity which they had no means of lessening but by their own conjectures.

Chapter 13

UNACCOUNTABLE, however, as the circumstances of his release might appear to the whole family, it was certain that Edward was free: and to what purpose that freedom would be employed was easily predetermined by all; for after experiencing the blessings of *one* imprudent engagement, contracted without his mother's consent, as he had already done for more than four years, nothing less could be expected of him in the failure of *that* than the immediate contraction of another.

His errand at Barton, in fact, was a simple one. It was only to ask Elinor to marry him; and considering that he was not altogether inexperienced in such a question, it might be strange that he should feel so uncomfortable in the present case as he really did, so much in need of encouragement and fresh air.

How soon he had walked himself into the proper resolution, however, how soon an opportunity of exercising it occurred, in what manner he expressed himself, and how he was received, need not be particularly told. This only need be said: that when they all sat down to table at four o'clock, about three hours after his arrival, he had secured his lady, engaged her mother's consent, and was not only in the rapturous profession of the lover, but in the reality of reason and truth, one of the happiest of men. His situation indeed was more than commonly joyful. He had more than the ordinary triumph of accepted love to swell his heart and raise his spirits. He was released without any reproach to himself from an entanglement which had long formed his misery, from a woman whom he had long ceased to love; and elevated at once to that security with another, which he must have thought of almost with despair as soon as he had learned to consider it with desire. He was brought, not from doubt or suspense, but from misery to happiness; and the change was openly spoken in such a genuine, flowing, grateful cheerfulness as his friends had never witnessed in him before.

His heart was now open to Elinor, all its weaknesses, all its errors confessed, and his first boyish attachment to Lucy treated with all the philosophic dignity of twenty-four.

"It was a foolish, idle inclination on my side," said he, "the consequence of ignorance of the world and want of employment. Had my mother given me some active profession when I was removed at eighteen from the care of Mr. Pratt, I think—nay, I am sure it would never have happened; for though I left Longstaple with what I thought, at the time, a most unconquerable preference for his niece, yet had I then had any pursuit, any object to engage my time and keep me at a distance from her for a few months, I should very soon have outgrown the fancied attachment, especially by mixing more with the world, as in such a case I must have done. But instead of having anything to do, instead of having any profession chosen for me, or being allowed to choose any myself, I returned home to be completely idle; and for the first twelvemonth afterwards, I had not even the nominal employment which belonging to the university would have given me; for I was not entered at Oxford till I was nineteen. I had therefore nothing in the world to do but to fancy myself in love; and as my mother did not make my home in every respect comfortable, as I had no friend, no companion in my brother, and disliked new acquaintance, it was not unnatural for me to be very often at Longstaple, where I always felt myself at home and was always sure of a welcome; and accordingly I spent the greatest part of my time there from eighteen to nineteen: Lucy appeared everything that was amiable and obliging. She was pretty, too. At least I thought so *then,* and I had seen so little of other women that I could make no comparisons and see no defects. Considering everything, therefore, I hope, foolish as our engagement was, foolish as it has since in every way been proved, it was not at the time an unnatural or an inexcusable piece of folly."

The change which a few hours had wrought in the minds and the happiness of the Dashwoods was such—so great—as promised them all the satisfaction of a sleepless night. Mrs. Dashwood, too happy to be comfortable, knew not how to love Edward nor praise Elinor enough, how to be enough thankful for his release without wounding his delicacy, nor how at once to give them leisure for unrestrained conversation together and yet enjoy, as she wished, the sight and society of both.

Marianne could speak *her* happiness only by tears. Comparisons would occur; regrets would arise; and her joy, though sincere as her love for her sister, was of a kind to give her neither spirits nor language.

But Elinor— How are *her* feelings to be described? From the moment of learning that Lucy was married to another, that Edward was free, to the moment of his justifying the hopes which had so instantly followed, she was everything by turns but tranquil. But when the second moment had passed, when she found every doubt, every solicitude removed, compared her situation with what so lately it had been, saw him honourably released from his former engagement, saw him instantly profiting by the release to address herself and declare an affection as tender, as constant as she

had ever supposed it to be, she was oppressed, she was overcome by her own felicity; and happily disposed as is the human mind to be easily familiarized with any change for the
better, it required several hours to give sedateness to her
spirits or any degree of tranquillity to her heart.

Edward was now fixed at the cottage at least for a week;
for whatever other claims might be made on him, it was impossible that less than a week should be given up to the enjoyment of Elinor's company, or suffice to say half that was
to be said of the past, the present, and the future; for though
a very few hours spent in the hard labour of incessant talking will dispatch more subjects than can really be in common between any two rational creatures, yet with lovers it is
different. Between *them* no subject is finished, no communication is even made, till it has been made at least twenty
times over.

Lucy's marriage, the unceasing and reasonable wonder
among them all, formed of course one of the earliest discus-
sions of the lovers; and Elinor's particular knowledge of
each party made it appear to her in every view as one of the
most extraordinary and unaccountable circumstances she had
ever heard. How they could be thrown together, and by what
attraction Robert could be drawn on to marry a girl of whose
beauty she had herself heard him speak without any admiration, a girl, too, already engaged to his brother, and on
whose account that brother had been thrown off by his
family—it was beyond her comprehension to make out. To
her own heart it was a delightful affair; to her imagination
it was even a ridiculous one; but to her reason, her judgment, it was completely a puzzle.

Edward could only attempt an explanation by supposing
that perhaps at first accidentally meeting, the vanity of the
one had been so worked on by the flattery of the other as to
lead by degrees to all the rest. Elinor remembered what Robert had told her in Harley Street of his opinion of what his
own mediation in his brother's affairs might have done if applied to in time. She repeated it to Edward.

"*That* was exactly like Robert," was his immediate observation. "And *that*," he presently added, "might perhaps be in
his head when the acquaintance between them first began.
And Lucy perhaps at first might think only of procuring his
good offices in my favour. Other designs might afterwards
arise."

How long it had been carrying on between them, however, he was equally at a loss with herself to make out; for at Oxford, where he had remained by choice ever since his quitting London, he had had no means of hearing of her but from herself; and her letters to the very last were neither less frequent nor less affectionate than usual. Not the smallest suspicion, therefore, had ever occurred to prepare him for what followed; and when at last it burst on him in a letter from Lucy herself, he had been for some time, he believed, half stupified between the wonder, the horror, and the joy of such a deliverance. He put the letter into Elinor's hands.

"DEAR SIR,

BEING very sure I have long lost your affections, I have thought myself at liberty to bestow my own on another, and have no doubt of being as happy with him as I once used to think I might be with you; but I scorn to accept a hand while the heart was another's. Sincerely wish you happy in your choice, and it shall not be my fault if we are not always good friends, as our near relationship now makes proper. I can safely say I owe you no ill-will and am sure you will be too generous to do us any ill offices. Your brother has gained my affections entirely, and as we could not live without one another, we are just returned from the altar and are now on our way to Dawlish for a few weeks, which place your dear brother has great curiosity to see; but thought I would first trouble you with these few lines, and shall always remain,

Your sincere well-wisher, friend, and sister,

LUCY FERRARS

I have burnt all your letters and will return your picture the first opportunity. Please to destroy my scrawls, but the ring with my hair you are very welcome to keep."

Elinor read and returned it without any comment.

"I will not ask your opinion of it as a composition," said Edward. "For worlds would not I have had a letter of hers seen by *you* in former days. In a sister it is bad enough, but in a wife! How I have blushed over the pages of her writing! And I believe I may say that since the first half-year of our foolish—business—this is the only letter I ever received from her of which the substance made me any amends for the defect of the style."

"However it may have come about," said Elinor after a

pause; "they are certainly married. And your mother has brought on herself a most appropriate punishment. The independence she settled on Robert through resentment against you has put it in his power to make his own choice; and she has actually been bribing one son with a thousand a year to do the very deed which she disinherited the other for intending to do. She will hardly be less hurt, I suppose, by Robert's marrying Lucy than she would have been by your marrying her."

"She will be more hurt by it, for Robert always was her favourite. She will be more hurt by it, and on the same principle will forgive him much sooner."

In what state the affair stood at present between them, Edward knew not, for no communication with any of his family had yet been attempted by him. He had quitted Oxford within four and twenty hours after Lucy's letter arrived, and with only one object before him, the nearest road to Barton, had had no leisure to form any scheme of conduct with which that road did not hold the most intimate connection. He could do nothing till he were assured of his fate with Miss Dashwood; and by his rapidity in seeking *that* fate, it is to be supposed, in spite of the jealousy with which he had once thought of Colonel Brandon, in spite of the modesty with which he rated his own deserts and the politeness with which he talked of his doubts, he did not upon the whole expect a very cruel reception. It was his business, however, to say that he *did*, and he said it very prettily. What he might say on the subject a twelvemonth after must be referred to the imagination of husbands and wives.

That Lucy had certainly meant to deceive, to go off with a flourish of malice against him in her message by Thomas, was perfectly clear to Elinor; and Edward himself, now thoroughly enlightened on her character, had no scruple in believing her capable of the utmost meanness of wanton ill nature. Though his eyes had been long opened, even before his acquaintance with Elinor began, to her ignorance and a want of liberality in some of her opinions, they had been equally imputed by him to her want of education; and till her last letter reached him, he had always believed her to be a well-disposed, good-hearted girl and thoroughly attached to himself. Nothing but such a persuasion could have prevented his putting an end to an engagement which, long before the discovery of it laid him open to his mother's anger, had been a continual source of disquiet and regret to him.

"I thought it my duty," said he, "independent of my feelings, to give her the option of continuing the engagement or not when I was renounced by my mother and stood to all appearance without a friend in the world to assist me. In such a situation as that, where there seemed nothing to tempt the avarice or the vanity of any living creature, how could I suppose, when she so earnestly, so warmly insisted on sharing my fate, whatever it might be, that anything but the most disinterested affection was her inducement? And even now I cannot comprehend on what motive she acted, or what fancied advantage it could be to her to be fettered to a man for whom she had not the smallest regard, and who had only two thousand pounds in the world. She could not foresee that Colonel Brandon would give me a living."

"No, but she might suppose that something would occur in your favour, that your own family might in time relent. And at any rate she lost nothing by continuing the engagement, for she has proved that it fettered neither her inclination nor her actions. The connection was certainly a respectable one and probably gained her consideration among her friends; and if nothing more advantageous occurred, it would be better for her to marry *you* than be single."

Edward was of course immediately convinced that nothing could have been more natural than Lucy's conduct, nor more self-evident than the motive of it.

Elinor scolded him harshly, as ladies always scold the imprudence which compliments themselves, for having spent so much time with them at Norland when he must have felt his own inconstancy.

"Your behaviour was certainly very wrong," said she, "because, to say nothing of my own conviction, our relations were all led away by it to fancy and expect *what*, as you were *then* situated, could never be."

He could only plead an ignorance of his own heart and a mistaken confidence in the force of his engagement.

"I was simple enough to think that because my *faith* was plighted to another there could be no danger in my being with you; and that the consciousness of my engagement was to keep my heart as safe and sacred as my honour. I felt that I admired you, but I told myself it was only friendship; and

till I began to make comparisons between yourself and Lucy,
I did not know how far I was got. After that, I suppose, I
was wrong in remaining so much in Sussex, and the arguments with which I reconciled myself to the expediency of
it were no better than these: The danger is my own; I am
doing no injury to anybody but myself."

Elinor smiled, and shook her head.

Edward heard with pleasure of Colonel Brandon's being
expected at the cottage, as he really wished not only to be
better acquainted with him, but to have an opportunity of
convincing him that he no longer resented his giving him the
living of Delaford, "Which, at present," said he, "after
thanks so ungraciously delivered as mine were on the occasion, he must think I have never forgiven him for offering."

Now he felt astonished himself that he had never yet been
to the place. But so little interest had he taken in the matter
that he owed all his knowledge of the house, garden, and
glebe, extent of the parish, condition of the land, and rate of
the tithes to Elinor herself, who had heard so much of it
from Colonel Brandon, and heard it with so much attention
as to be entirely mistress of the subject.

One question after this only remained undecided between
them; one difficulty only was to be overcome. They were
brought together by mutual affection with the warmest approbation of their real friends; their intimate knowledge of
each other seemed to make their happiness certain; and they
only wanted something to live upon. Edward had two thousand pounds, and Elinor one, which, with Delaford living,
was all that they could call their own; for it was impossible
that Mrs. Dashwood should advance anything, and they were
neither of them quite enough in love to think that three hundred and fifty pounds a year would supply them with the
comforts of life.

Edward was not entirely without hopes of some favourable change in his mother towards him, and on *that* he rested
for the residue of their income. But Elinor had no such dependence; for since Edward would still be unable to marry
Miss Morton, and his choosing herself had been spoken of in
Mrs. Ferrars's flattering language as only a lesser evil than
his choosing Lucy Steele, she feared that Robert's offence
would serve no other purpose than to enrich Fanny.

About four days after Edward's arrival, Colonel Brandon
appeared, to complete Mrs. Dashwood's satisfaction, and to

give her the dignity of having for the first time since her living at Barton more company with her than her house would hold. Edward was allowed to retain the privilege of first comer, and Colonel Brandon therefore walked every night to his old quarters at the park, from whence he usually returned in the morning early enough to interrupt the lovers' first tête-à-tête before breakfast.

A three weeks' residence at Delaford, where, in his evening hours at least, he had little to do but to calculate the disproportion between thirty-six and seventeen, brought him to Barton in a temper of mind which needed all the improvement in Marianne's looks, all the kindness of her welcome, and all the encouragement of her mother's language, to make it cheerful. Among such friends, however, and such flattery, he did revive. No rumour of Lucy's marriage had yet reached him; he knew nothing of what had passed; and the first hours of his visit were consequently spent in hearing and in wondering. Everything was explained to him by Mrs. Dashwood, and he found fresh reason to rejoice in what he had done for Mr. Ferrars, since eventually it promoted the interest of Elinor.

It would be needless to say that the gentlemen advanced in the good opinion of each other as they advanced in each other's acquaintance, for it could not be otherwise. Their resemblance in good principles and good sense, in disposition and manner of thinking, would probably have been sufficient to unite them in friendship without any other attraction; but their being in love with two sisters, and two sisters fond of each other, made that mutual regard inevitable and immediate which might otherwise have waited the effect of time and judgment.

The letters from town, which a few days before would have made every nerve in Elinor's body thrill with transport, now arrived to be read with less emotion than mirth. Mrs. Jennings wrote to tell the wonderful tale, to vent her honest indignation against the jilting girl, and pour forth her compassion towards poor Mr. Edward, who, she was sure, had quite doted upon the worthless hussy, and was now, by all accounts almost brokenhearted at Oxford.—"I do think," she continued, "nothing was ever carried on so sly; for it was but two days before, Lucy called and sat a couple of hours with me. Not a soul suspected anything of the matter, not even Nancy, who, poor soul! came crying to me the day after

in a great fright for fear of Mrs. Ferrars, as well as not
knowing how to get to Plymouth; for Lucy, it seems, bor-
rowed all her money before she went off to be married,
on purpose we suppose to make a show with, and poor Nancy
had not seven shillings in the world; so I was very glad to
give her five guineas to take her down to Exeter, where she
thinks of staying three or four weeks with Mrs. Burgess in
hopes, as I tell her, to fall in with the Doctor again. And I
must say that Lucy's crossness not to take her along with
them in the chaise is worse than all. Poor Mr. Edward! I cannot get him out of my head, but you must send for him to
Barton, and Miss Marianne must try to comfort him."

Mr. Dashwood's strains were more solemn. Mrs. Ferrars
was the most unfortunate of women. Poor Fanny had suffered agonies of sensibility; and he considered the existence
of each, under such a blow, with grateful wonder. Robert's
offence was unpardonable, but Lucy's was infinitely worse.
Neither of them was ever again to be mentioned to Mrs.
Ferrars; and even if she might hereafter be induced to forgive her son, his wife should never be acknowledged as her
daughter, nor be permitted to appear in her presence. The secrecy with which everything had been carried on between
them was rationally treated as enormously heightening the
crime because, had any suspicion of it occurred to the others, proper measures would have been taken to prevent the
marriage; and he called on Elinor to join with him in regretting that Lucy's engagement with Edward had not rather
been fulfilled than that she should thus be the means of
spreading misery further in the family. He thus continued:

"Mrs. Ferrars has never yet mentioned Edward's name,
which does not surprise us; but to our great astonishment,
not a line has been received from him on the occasion. Perhaps, however, he is kept silent by his fear of offending, and
I shall, therefore, give him a hint by a line to Oxford that his
sister and I both think a letter of proper submission from
him, addressed perhaps to Fanny, and by her shown to her
mother, might not be taken amiss; for we all know the tenderness of Mrs. Ferrars's heart, and that she wishes for nothing so much as to be on good terms with her children."

This paragraph was of some importance to the prospects
and conduct of Edward. It determined him to attempt a reconciliation, though not exactly in the manner pointed out by
their brother and sister.

"A letter of proper submission!" repeated he; "would they have me beg my mother's pardon for Robert's ingratitude to *her* and breach of honour to *me*? I can make no submission. I am grown neither humble nor penitent by what has passed. I am grown very happy, but that would not interest. I know of no submission that *is* proper for me to make."

"You may certainly ask to be forgiven," said Elinor, "because you have offended; and I should think you might *now* venture so far as to profess some concern for having ever formed the engagement which drew on you your mother's anger."

He agreed that he might.

"And when she has forgiven you, perhaps a little humility may be convenient while acknowledging a second engagement almost as imprudent in *her* eyes as the first."

He had nothing to urge against it, but still resisted the idea of a letter of proper submission; and, therefore, to make it easier to him, as he declared a much greater willingness to make mean concessions by word of mouth than on paper, it was resolved that instead of writing to Fanny, he should go to London and personally entreat her good offices in his favour. "And if they really *do* interest themselves," said Marianne in her new character of candour, "in bringing about a reconciliation, I shall think that even John and Fanny are not entirely without merit."

After a visit on Colonel Brandon's side of only three or four days, the two gentlemen quitted Barton together. They were to go immediately to Delaford, that Edward might have some personal knowledge of his future home and assist his patron and friend in deciding on what improvements were needed to it; and from thence, after staying there a couple of nights, he was to proceed on his journey to town.

Chapter 14

AFTER A PROPER resistance on the part of Mrs. Ferrars, just so violent and so steady as to preserve her from that reproach which she always seemed fearful of incurring, the reproach of being too amiable, Edward was admitted to her presence and pronounced to be again her son.

Her family had of late been exceedingly fluctuating. For many years of her life she had had two sons; but the crime and annihilation of Edward a few weeks ago had robbed her of one; the similar annihilation of Robert had left her for a fortnight without any; and now, by the resuscitation of Edward, she had one again.

In spite of his being allowed once more to live, however, he did not feel the continuance of his existence secure till he had revealed his present engagement; for the publication of that circumstance, he feared, might give a sudden turn to his constitution and carry him off as rapidly as before. With apprehensive caution, therefore, it was revealed, and he was listened to with unexpected calmness. Mrs. Ferrars at first reasonably endeavoured to dissuade him from marrying Miss Dashwood by every argument in her power; told him that in Miss Morton he would have a woman of higher rank and larger fortune; and enforced the assertion by observing that Miss Morton was the daughter of a nobleman with thirty thousand pounds, while Miss Dashwood was only the daughter of a private gentleman with no more than *three*; but when she found that, though perfectly admitting the truth of her representation, he was by no means inclined to be guided by it, she judged it wisest from the experience of the past to submit; and therefore, after such an ungracious delay as she owed to her own dignity, and as served to prevent every suspicion of good will, she issued her decree of consent to the marriage of Edward and Elinor.

What she would engage to do towards augmenting their income was next to be considered; and here it plainly appeared that though Edward was now her only son, he was by no means her eldest; for while Robert was inevitably endowed with a thousand pounds a year, not the smallest objection was made against Edward's taking orders for the sake of two hundred and fifty at the utmost; nor was anything promised either for the present or in future beyond the ten thousand pounds, which had been given with Fanny.

It was as much, however, as was desired, and more than was expected by Edward and Elinor; and Mrs. Ferrars herself, by her shuffling excuses, seemed the only person surprised at her not giving more.

With an income quite sufficient to their wants thus secured to them, they had nothing to wait for after Edward was in possession of the living but the readiness of the house, to which Colonel Brandon, with an eager desire for the accommodation of Elinor, was making considerable improvements; and after waiting some time for their completion, after experiencing as usual a thousand disappointments and delays from the unaccountable dilatoriness of the workmen, Elinor, as usual, broke through the first positive resolution of not marrying till everything was ready, and the ceremony took place in Barton church early in the autumn.

The first month after their marriage was spent with their friend at the mansion-house, from whence they could superintend the progress of the parsonage and direct everything as they liked on the spot; could choose papers, project shrubberies, and invent a sweep. Mrs. Jennings's prophecies, though rather jumbled together, were chiefly fulfilled; for she was able to visit Edward and his wife in their parsonage by Michaelmas, and she found in Elinor and her husband, as she really believed, one of the happiest couples in the world. They had, in fact, nothing to wish for but the marriage of Colonel Brandon and Marianne, and rather better pasturage for their cows.

They were visited on their first settling by almost all their relations and friends. Mrs. Ferrars came to inspect the happiness which she was almost ashamed of having authorized; and even the Dashwoods were at the expense of a journey from Sussex to do them honour.

"I will not say that I am disappointed, my dear sister," said John as they were walking together one morning before the gates of Delaford House, "*that* would be saying too much, for certainly you have been one of the most fortunate young women in the world, as it is. But, I confess, it would give me great pleasure to call Colonel Brandon brother. His property here, his place, his house, everything in such respectable and excellent condition! And his woods! I have not seen such timber anywhere in Dorsetshire as there is now standing in Delaford Hanger! And though, perhaps, Marianne may not seem exactly the person to attract him, yet I think it would altogether be advisable for you to have them now frequently staying with you; for as Colonel Brandon seems a great deal at home, nobody can tell what may happen, for when people are much thrown together and see little of anybody else—and it will always be in your power to set her off to advantage, and so forth—in short, you may as well give her a chance. You understand me."

But though Mrs. Ferrars *did* come to see them, and always treated them with the make-believe of decent affection, they were never insulted by her real favour and preference. *That* was due to the folly of Robert and the cunning of his wife; and it was earned by them before many months had passed away. The selfish sagacity of the latter, which had at first drawn Robert into the scrape, was the principal instrument of his deliverance from it; for her respectful humility, assiduous attentions, and endless flatteries, as soon as the smallest opening was given for their exercise, reconciled Mrs. Ferrars to his choice, and re-established him completely in her favour.

The whole of Lucy's behaviour in the affair, and the prosperity which crowned it, therefore, may be held forth as a most encouraging instance of what an earnest, an unceasing attention to self-interest, however its progress may be apparently obstructed, will do in securing every advantage of fortune, with no other sacrifice than that of time and conscience. When Robert first sought her acquaintance and privately visited her in Bartlett's Buildings, it was only with the view imputed to him by his brother. He merely meant to persuade her to give up the engagement; and as there could be nothing to overcome but the affection of both, he naturally expected that one or two interviews would settle the matter. In that point, however, and that only, he erred; for though Lucy soon gave him hopes that his eloquence would convince her in *time,* another visit, another conversation, was always wanted to produce this conviction. Some doubts always lingered in her mind when they parted, which could only be removed by another half-hour's discourse with himself. His attendance was by this means secured, and the rest followed in course. Instead of talking of Edward, they came gradually to talk only of Robert, a subject on which he had always more to say than on any other, and in which she soon betrayed an interest even equal to his own; and, in short, it became speedily evident to both that he had entirely supplanted his brother. He was proud of his conquest, proud of tricking Edward, and very proud of marrying privately without his mother's consent. What immediately followed is known. They passed some months in great happiness at Dawlish; for she had many relations and old acquaintance to

cut, and he drew several plans for magnificent cottages; and
from thence returning to town, procured the forgiveness of
Mrs. Ferrars by the simple expedient of asking it, which, at
Lucy's instigation, was adopted. The forgiveness at first, indeed, as was reasonable, comprehended only Robert; and
Lucy, who had owed his mother no duty and therefore could
have transgressed none, still remained some weeks long un-
pardoned. But perseverance in humility of conduct and messages, in self-condemnation for Robert's offence, and
gratitude for the unkindness she was treated with, procured
her in time the haughty notice which overcame her by its
graciousness, and led soon afterwards by rapid degrees to
the highest state of affection and influence. Lucy became as
necessary to Mrs. Ferrars as either Robert or Fanny; and
while Edward was never cordially forgiven for having once
intended to marry her, and Elinor, though superior to her in
fortune and birth, was spoken of as an intruder, *she* was in
everything considered, and always openly acknowledged, to
be a favourite child. They settled in town, received very liberal assistance from Mrs. Ferrars, were on the best terms
imaginable with the Dashwoods; and setting aside the jealousies and ill will continually subsisting between Fanny and
Lucy, in which their husbands of course took a part, as well
as the frequent domestic disagreements between Robert and
Lucy themselves, nothing could exceed the harmony in
which they all lived together.

What Edward had done to forfeit the right of eldest son
might have puzzled many people to find out; and what Robert had done to succeed to it might have puzzled them still
more. It was an arrangement, however, justified in its effects
if not in its cause; for nothing ever appeared in Robert's
style of living or of talking to give a suspicion of his regretting the extent of his income as either leaving his brother too
little or bringing himself too much; and if Edward might be
judged from the ready discharge of his duties in every particular, from an increasing attachment to his wife and his
home, and from the regular cheerfulness of his spirits, he
might be supposed no less contented with his lot, no less
free from every wish of an exchange.

Elinor's marriage divided her as little from her family as
could well be contrived without rendering the cottage at Barton entirely useless; for her mother and sisters spent much
more than half their time with her. Mrs. Dashwood was act-

ing on motives of policy as well as pleasure in the frequency of her visits at Delaford; for her wish of bringing Marianne and Colonel Brandon together was hardly less earnest, though rather more liberal, than what John had expressed. It was now her darling object. Precious as was the company of her daughter to her, she desired nothing so much as to give up its constant enjoyment to her valued friend; and to see Marianne settled at the mansion-house was equally the wish of Edward and Elinor. They each felt his sorrow and their own obligations, and Marianne, by general consent, was to be the reward of all.

With such a confederacy against her, with a knowledge so intimate of his goodness, with a conviction of his fond attachment to herself, which at last, though long after it was observable to everybody else, burst on her—what could she do?

Marianne Dashwood was born to an extraordinary fate. She was born to discover the falsehood of her own opinions, and to counteract by her conduct her most favourite maxims. She was born to overcome an affection formed so late in life as at seventeen, and with no sentiment superior to strong esteem and lively friendship, voluntarily to give her hand to another—and *that* other, a man who had suffered no less than herself under the event of a former attachment, whom, two years before, she had considered too old to be married, and who still sought the constitutional safeguard of a flannel waistcoat!

But so it was. Instead of falling a sacrifice to an irresistible passion, as once she had fondly flattered herself with expecting, instead of remaining even forever with her mother and finding her only pleasures in retirement and study, as afterwards in her more calm and sober judgment she had determined on, she found herself at nineteen submitting to new attachments, entering on new duties, placed in a new home, a wife, the mistress of a family, and the patroness of a village.

Colonel Brandon was now as happy as all those who best loved him believed he deserved to be; in Marianne he was consoled for every past affliction; her regard and her society restored his mind to animation and his spirits to cheerfulness; and that Marianne found her own happiness in forming his was equally the persuasion and delight of each observing friend. Marianne could never love by halves; and her whole heart became, in time, as much devoted to her husband as it had once been to Willoughby.

Willoughby could not hear of her marriage without a pang; and his punishment was soon afterwards complete in the voluntary forgiveness of Mrs. Smith, who, by stating his marriage with a woman of character as the source of her clemency, gave him reason for believing that had he behaved with honour towards Marianne, he might at once have been happy and rich. That his repentance of misconduct, which thus brought its own punishment, was sincere, need not be doubted; nor that he long thought of Colonel Brandon with envy and of Marianne with regret. But that he was forever inconsolable, that he fled from society, or contracted an habitual gloom of temper, or died of a broken heart, must not be depended on; for he did neither. He lived to exert, and frequently to enjoy himself. His wife was not always out of humour, nor his home always uncomfortable; and in his breed of horses and dogs, and in sporting of every kind, he found no inconsiderable degree of domestic felicity.

For Marianne, however, in spite of his incivility in surviving her loss—he always retained that decided regard which interested him in everything that befell her, and made her his secret standard of perfection in woman; and many a rising beauty would be slighted by him in after-days as bearing no comparison with Mrs. Brandon.

Mrs. Dashwood was prudent enough to remain at the cottage without attempting a removal to Delaford; and fortunately for Sir John and Mrs. Jennings, when Marianne was taken from them, Margaret had reached an age highly suitable for dancing and not very ineligible for being supposed to have a lover.

Between Barton and Delaford there was that constant communication which strong family affection would naturally dictate; and among the merits and the happiness of Elinor and Marianne, let it not be ranked as the least considerable, that though sisters, and living almost within sight of each other, they could live without disagreement between themselves, or producing coolness between their husbands.

SELECTED BIBLIOGRAPHY

WORKS BY JANE AUSTEN

Sense and Sensibility, 1811 Novel (Signet Classic 0451–524195)
Pride and Prejudice, 1813 Novel (Signet Classic 0451–523652)
Mansfield Park, 1814 Novel (Signet Classic 0451–525019)
Emma, 1816 Novel (Signet Classic 0451–523067)
Northanger Abbey, 1818 Novel (Signet Classic 0451–523725)
Persuasion, 1818 Novel (Signet Classic 0451–522893)
Sanditon, fragment of a novel
The Watsons, fragment of a novel

SELECTED BIOGRAPHY AND CRITICISM

Austen-Leigh. J. E. *A Memoir of Jane Austen.* ed. by R. W. Chapman. London and New York: Oxford University Press, 1926.

Brown, Lloyd W. *Bits of Ivory. Narrative Techniques in Jane Austen's Fiction.* Baton Rouge: Louisiana State University Press, 1973.

Bush, Douglas. *Jane Austen.* Masters of World Literature Series. New York: Macmillan, 1975.

Butler, Marilyn. *Jane Austen and the War of Ideas.* Oxford: Clarendon Press; New York: Oxford University Press, 1975.

Craik, W. A. *Jane Austen: The Six Novels.* New York: Barnes & Noble, 1965.

Duckworth, Alistair M. *The Improvement of the Estate: A Study of Jane Austen's Novels.* Baltimore: Johns Hopkins Press, 1971.

Halperin, John, ed. *Jane Austen: Bicentenary Essays.* New York and London: Cambridge University Press, 1975.

Jenkins, Elizabeth. *Jane Austen: A Biography.* 1939; rpt. London: Gollancz, 1958.

Lascelles, Mary. *Jane Austen and Her Art.* 1939; rpt. London: Oxford University Press, 1963.

Laski, Marghanita. *Jane Austen and Her World.* New York: Viking Press, 1969.

Litz, A. Walton. *Jane Austen: A Study of Her Artistic Development.* New York: Oxford University Press, 1965.

McMaster, Juliet, ed. *Jane Austen's Achievement. Papers delivered at the Jane Austen Bicentennial Conferences at the University of Alberta.* London and Basingstoke: Macmillan, 1976.

Murdrick, Marvin. *Jane Austen: Irony as Defense and Discovery*. Princeton, N.J.: Princeton University Press; London: Oxford University Press, 1952.

Pinion, F. B. *A Jane Austen Companion: A Critical Survey and Reference Book*. London: Macmillan, 1973.

Southam, B.C., ed. *Critical Essays on Jane Austen*. London: Routledge & Kegan Paul, 1968.

———, ed. *Jane Austen: The Critical Heritage*. New York: Barnes & Noble, 1968.

Trilling, Lionel. *"Mansfield Park." Partisan Review,* 21 (1954), 429–511. Rpt. in his *The Opposing Self: Nine Essays in Criticism*. New York: Viking Press, 1955.

Watt, Ian, ed. *Jane Austen: A Collection of Critical Essays*. Englewood Cliffs, N.J.: Prentice-Hall, 1963.

Weinsheimer, Joel, ed. *Jane Austen Today*. Athens, Ga.: The University of Georgia Press, 1975.

Wiesenfarth, Joseph. *The Errand of Form: An Essay of Jane Austen's Art*. New York: Fordham University Press, 1967.

A Note on the Text

The text is based on the second edition of *Sense and Sensibility,* which was revised by Miss Austen and published in 1813. Typographical errors have been corrected; punctuation and archaic spellings have been brought into conformity with modern English usage.

READ THE TOP 25 SIGNET CLASSICS

TO ORDER CALL: 1-800-788-6262

"Aunt Hope says you can't be our daddy."

His gaze swung back to Hope. "Did she, now?"

"Yeah." Harper took a quick, audible breath. "But she also said we can get a puppy instead."

"I said we'll see."

"Okay, yeah," Harper admitted, engaging Hope in a stare down. "But that's almost the same thing as yes."

Hope held the child's glare with an unflinching one of her own. "I made no promises, Harper."

Walker's chuckle interrupted the staring match. "Wise woman."

And now she was locked in a silent contest of wills with him. Their gazes held a long, silent beat. An unspoken message passed between them, but Hope couldn't quite decipher the meaning.

Walker broke eye contact first.

"Ready to move in to your new home?" The words were directed at the twins, but Hope felt them in the depths of her soul.

Eight words, spoken in that rich, masculine baritone, and the carefully constructed life she'd envisioned for herself with the twins morphed into something new. Something different.

And for the first time in her life, unrealized dreams seemed possible.

Renee Ryan grew up in a Florida beach town where she learned to surf, sort of. With a degree from FSU, she explored career opportunities at a Florida theme park and a modeling agency and even taught high school economics. She currently lives with her husband in Nebraska, and many have mistaken their overweight cat for a small bear. You may contact Renee at reneeryan.com, on Facebook or on Twitter, @reneeryanbooks.

Books by Renee Ryan

Love Inspired

Thunder Ridge
Surprise Christmas Family

Village Green
Claiming the Doctor's Heart
The Doctor's Christmas Wish

Love Inspired Historical

Charity House
The Marshal Takes a Bride
Hannah's Beau
Loving Bella
The Lawman Claims His Bride
Charity House Courtship
The Outlaw's Redemption
Finally a Bride

Visit the Author Profile page at Harlequin.com for more titles.

Surprise
Christmas Family

Renee Ryan

LOVE INSPIRED
INSPIRATIONAL ROMANCE

LOVE INSPIRED®
INSPIRATIONAL ROMANCE

ISBN-13: 978-1-335-48852-7

Surprise Christmas Family

Love Inspired
22 Adelaide St. West, 40th Floor
Toronto, Ontario M5H 4E3, Canada
www.Harlequin.com

Printed in U.S.A.

And he said unto me, My grace is sufficient
for thee: for my strength is made perfect
in weakness. Most gladly therefore
will I rather glory in my infirmities,
that the power of Christ may rest upon me.
—*2 Corinthians* 12:9

For the girls: Barb, Donna, Jenna and Shirley,
a multitalented foursome that helped me
through some really tough times.
I love you, sister-chicks!

Chapter One

She was *not* stalking him, Hope Jeffries assured herself. Nothing so sneaky. She was simply confirming she'd found the right man. It was a risk, coming to his place of employment. But confronting him at a hospital was safer than showing up at his private residence.

Enough stalling. She was ready.

Hope unbuckled her seat belt, then checked her bag for the custody papers she'd had her attorney draw up last week. There they were, waiting for one final signature.

After a quick glance in the rearview mirror, she swiveled around to face the precious cargo sitting in the back seat. "Ready to go, girls?"

Two identical faces of dread stared back at her. Hope hated seeing the twins upset.

You're doing this for them.

For Harper and Kennedy. Her five-year-old nieces had become her world. Hope desperately wanted to make their lives as easy as possible, especially after the ordeal of losing their mother to cancer barely three months ago. The Lord had given Hope an unexpected blessing out of tragedy. She would not squander this chance to do right by the sister she'd failed in so many ways.

"This won't take long." She increased the wattage on her smile by a million. "We'll be in and out in a flash."

Giving them no chance to argue, she climbed out of the rental car and stepped into Thunder Ridge, Colorado, founded in 1899. The sign at the edge of town claimed a population of 15,128 and an oxygen-stealing elevation of 9,111 feet.

For a moment, Hope simply stood there and drank in the scene. Wow, just…wow. The Christmas season had arrived with an explosion of sparkles and bright colors. Fat, lazy snowflakes fell over the heavily decorated buildings of Main Street. Wreaths adorned the old-world style streetlamps, while miles and miles of garland hung from every available ledge, roofline and storefront window.

"Beautiful," she whispered. It was as if she'd been dropped in the middle of a live-action postcard designed to lure tourists.

Hope was definitely lured.

Thunder Ridge was a far cry from New York City. What must it be like to live here year-round? Pretty awesome, she guessed. The girls could be happy here. Hope prayed it didn't come to that.

I can't lose them, Lord. Her heart tripped at the thought. *I just can't.*

She might not have a choice.

Drawing in a deep, calming breath, she shifted her attention to the mountains looming on the horizon. They stood like dark, ominous guardians watching over what belonged to them. Hope could almost hear them say, "Intruder beware."

Now she was being fanciful. Dr. Hope Jeffries was never fanciful. As a college professor of Economics on track for tenure at Columbia University, she preferred practical theories to fairy tales.

One final look at the winter wonderland and she stepped back to the car. She helped the girls out of their car seats, then guided them onto the shoveled pavement of the hospital's parking lot.

"Let's do this." She used her most cheerful voice, remembering the advice their child psychologist had given Hope. Dr. Stephens had warned her that the girls took their cues from her.

Apparently not today. Instead of returning smiles, Hope received a chorus of pitiful sighs. Taking their tiny hands in hers, she steered the twins toward the sidewalk that led to the hospital's main entrance. They followed along in brooding silence.

"Aunt Hope? Do we *have* to go inside with you?" Kennedy glanced longingly over her shoulder, then shared a determined look with her sister. "Can't we wait in the car?"

"Absolutely not."

"If Mommy was here, she'd let us."

The disturbing thought had Hope gaping at her niece. "That can't possibly be true."

"It is so," Harper said. "We used to stay in the car all the time."

Hope prayed her niece was exaggerating. Surely Charity wouldn't have left her daughters in her beat-up VW Bug while she did, well, whatever called for her to fly solo. The possible activities were too numerous and, frankly, too frightening to contemplate. It was moments like these that Hope regretted the years of estrangement from her sister.

"Please, Aunt Hope," Kennedy whined. "Can't we sit in the car? You can lock us in. We won't try to get out. We know better."

"You're not waiting in the car."

"You might look like our Mommy," Harper said, hands on her hips. "But you don't act like her."

Her niece was correct. In terms of behavior, Hope had never been like her identical twin. There were times she wished she could be more carefree like Charity. Not this time. "You're coming with me, and that's the end of it."

Their crestfallen expressions nearly broke her heart. The twins had been through a lot of upheaval since Charity had shown up on Hope's doorstep. If this horrifying insight into their lives was true, their ordeal had started long before their mother had been diagnosed with breast cancer. *Oh, Charity, why didn't you come to me sooner?*

"Tell you what," she said, reaching for a compromise that would satisfy all three of them. "Once I'm finished with my—" she paused again "—errand, we'll stop in that sweetshop we passed this morning and get something fun to eat."

Kennedy's face lit up. "You mean, like, maybe some candy?"

"Maybe," Hope hedged, thinking a bribe probably wasn't the right way to go.

The girls looked at each other. In silent twin code, they communicated something only they understood, then nodded. "Okay," they said in unison.

Calling it a win, Hope squeezed each of their hands and set out for the hospital's entrance. She didn't like including the girls. She'd rather not have brought them to Colorado at all. But with their mother gone three months now, she was the only family they had left. Or rather the only family they knew.

That could change soon.

She wasn't ready.

What if Walker Evans wasn't a good guy? What if the private detective Hope had hired had missed something? The man had been pretty vague about the doctor's past, focusing mainly on the most recent few years.

This was a mistake.

Hope shouldn't have come to Thunder Ridge. She'd been too quick to act on her attorney's advice. She started to turn around, then stopped herself. She'd dragged the twins this far. She had to see this through. For their sake.

Keep telling yourself that. Admit it, professor, you're curious.

She was so curious.

How much did Walker Evans know about his daughters? She still fumed over the story Charity had told her right before she succumbed to the cancer. There'd been an impromptu Las Vegas wedding, and then a forced annulment when the selfish cad had discovered his new wife was pregnant. Hope couldn't imagine anyone being so heartless. She'd vowed to make him pay for what he'd done to her sister. Unfortunately, Charity died a handful of days after her confession, leaving Hope with more questions and very few answers.

She'd begun her search immediately following Charity's funeral. How many Walker Evanses could there be? More than she would have expected, but she'd eventually found the right man. He was an emergency room doctor working the night shift at Thunder Ridge Hospital. He came from a large, close-knit family that included lots of siblings, several dogs and rambling houses with white picket fences.

Just then, she spotted Dr. Evans standing inside the emergency room's entrance.

Hope's feet ground to a halt. She'd found her man. Oh my...

His black hair curled at the tips, and those eyes, the shape so familiar, so similar to the ones that stared out of Harper and Kennedy's sweet faces. Hope swallowed back a ridiculous sigh as she watched him, head bent, speaking to a little boy with his arm in a sling. In full doctor-mode, he alternated his attention between the child and his parents, who responded with nods and smiles. Lots of smiles.

It was clear the man was well-liked. By at least three people.

Hope sorted through the mass of emotions raging through her. There was surprise, worry, a little awe and fear. So much fear, it brought a sting to the back of her eyes. Maybe he would decide to step up. Five years was plenty of time to change a mind.

Maybe she was being overly pessimistic. Maybe the man would sign over custody without a fight. He'd abandoned his pregnant wife. That spoke volumes about his character. Didn't it?

As if sensing her gaze on him, he wrapped up his conversation with the family, straightened to his full height of six foot three and turned his head in her direction. Their eyes met through the plate glass window. And…

Boom.

That's inconvenient, she thought.

She reminded herself that Harper and Kennedy were her first—her only—priority. And if all went according to plan, they would no longer be her nieces.

They would be her daughters.

Walker couldn't help noticing the woman lurking behind a large potted plant just outside the hospital's main entrance. Kind of hard not to notice her. She was looking straight at him. Her stare was unwavering, unfriendly and, if he were honest with himself, unsettling. He couldn't imagine what he'd done to warrant such blatant hostility from a complete stranger. He'd never met her before. He'd have remembered those almond-shaped eyes and all that wheat-colored hair hanging past her shoulders in thick, unruly waves.

His stomach did a fast, unexpected roll. He hadn't been this intrigued by a woman since…

He refused to let his mind finish the thought.

Still, the instant masculine interest was as unwelcome as it was unexpected. It made him feel itchy, sad and slightly empty inside. No, not today. He wasn't going to relive the past, not even in the privacy of his own thoughts. He shoved aside the agonizing memories clawing for release and focused on the woman glaring at him.

Locked in their silent battle of wills, he attempted a neutral smile.

Mystery woman did not return the gesture.

In fact, her spine straightened. It was obvious she didn't like him. *Really* didn't like him. People usually liked him. A good bedside manner was part of the job.

She moved past the plants, and…whoa. Walker's breath caught in his throat. Mystery woman was not alone. She had two very wide-eyed little girls with her. They were identical in size and coloring and were absolutely adorable.

Walker guessed the twins were somewhere around four, maybe five years old. They wore matching red coats with shiny gold buttons marching down the front. Plaid knit caps had been positioned over their sleek dark hair at a jaunty angle.

Something deep and miserable washed over him. A familiar twinge of sorrow came next, giving him a hard pang in the center of his chest. Walker had come so close to happiness, and had actually had it for nearly a year, but then the Lord had cruelly ripped it away from him in a handful of hours. All that he had left was foggy memories, a lot of pain and something that had started as sorrow, but was becoming bitterness as each year passed.

He shook away the depressing insight as mother and daughters entered the building hand in hand in hand.

They drew closer, until Walker got a good look at the children's faces. His heart took another hit. Their eyes were a familiar pale blue. He'd seen those same eyes every day of his life. Whenever he looked in the mirror.

But that couldn't be.

The trio stopped a few feet in front of him. Walker rubbed a hand over his face, took another, longer look at the evidence staring back at him and accepted the truth.

The twins had his eyes.

Chapter Two

Hope witnessed the exact moment the good doctor made the family connection. The recognition was there in his frozen stance and stunned expression.

Clearly, she'd thrown him off balance. Or rather, the twins had. Hope had been right to approach him this morning.

As the man's gaze bounced from twin to twin, his shocked silence stretched into the uncomfortable. Shifted the power in Hope's favor. She pressed her advantage, reminding herself that this man might have—probably—abandoned his family. "Are you Dr. Evans? Dr. Walker Evans?"

She heard the disdain in her voice and nearly apologized. She wasn't usually so rude. But then she remembered what he'd done to her sister and, consequently, the twins. Hope had every reason to be antagonistic.

"That's right. I'm Dr. Evans. Are you, or—" with lightning speed, his gaze shifted from Harper to Kennedy, then settled back on Hope once again "—one of the girls, ill?"

"No, no. No!"

A faint smile crossed his lips. "One 'no' will do."

Hope frowned. She hadn't expected him to act so much

like a, well, like a doctor. Then again, it was his profession. "The twins and I are perfectly healthy."

He visibly relaxed. In the next instant, he tensed up again. His body language wasn't guarded, exactly, but neither was it especially friendly. Did he recognize her, or rather—Charity?

"So," he began. "You're here because...?"

"I, that is, *we*..." Hope trailed off, not quite sure how to continue. Clearly, she hadn't prepared enough for this part of her plan. She'd expected recognition, denial, something. Anything but confusion.

"Okay. Let's try a different approach." He spoke with a gentle assertiveness that probably endeared him to his patients. "We've established who I am, and that none of you are sick, but I still don't know who you are or why you've come to my ER."

Right.

"I'm Hope. Hope *Jeffries*." She enunciated her last name, waiting for some sign of recognition on his part.

None came, only more masculine bafflement that seemed a little too genuine to pass off as an act. It was possible Charity hadn't told him she had a twin sister, and so he wasn't making the connection. *Too many questions, not enough answers*, Hope thought. Or maybe he hadn't heard her clearly.

"Jeffries," she repeated.

Still nothing.

Something wasn't right. The man had married a woman with the same last name as Hope. Not just any woman, either, but Hope's identical twin. They shared matching features, except for a few cosmetic differences.

But no, not a single hint of recognition.

Hope considered her next move. She should probably

introduce the twins. "This is Harper—" she touched the little girl's shoulder "—and this is Kennedy."

"Pleased to meet you, Miss Harper and Miss Kennedy." He smiled down at the girls with genuine warmth.

They grinned back.

"I have to say, you look very festive in your red coats," he said, clearly comfortable conversing with young children. "Santa would approve. You can trust me on this. The jolly old man and I are friends."

"Really? You know Santa?"

"Absolutely."

Hope's lips twisted at a wry angle. She supposed his assertion wasn't a complete lie. He did dress up as the jolly old man every Christmas season at the homeless shelter. The investigator had given her that information with a smirk and eye roll.

"Santa and I spoke just the other day," he continued with a straight face. "It's a busy season for him, you know, but he always makes time for his friends."

The girls giggled, clearly charmed.

The feeling seemed mutual. Walker couldn't stop smiling at the twins. He remarked on their hats, which began an extensive dissertation from Harper, with occasional commentary from Kennedy, about their shopping trip to Macy's after the Thanksgiving parade.

As if mesmerized by the story, he leaned over, planted his hands on his knees and simply let the girls chatter away.

"Wow," he said when they wound down. "I can't imagine a better day. A parade *and* a shopping trip."

"Don't forget ice-skating," Kennedy reminded him. "We went ice-skating, too."

"Excellent." He swiveled his gaze up to Hope, stood tall and then stole her breath with a wink. "Well done."

Hope's plan was unraveling at her feet. The girls weren't supposed to warm up to their father so quickly. And he wasn't supposed to be putting them at ease with such effortless skill. Hope was debating how to wrestle back control of the situation when a gust of frigid air swept into the foyer.

"Why don't we get the three of you out of the cold?" Walker connected his gaze with Hope's. "And you can tell me why you're here."

"All right." Hope guided the girls deeper inside the building. She wasn't sure what she was going to say, or even do, but it didn't seem right to keep the twins standing in a draft while she decided her next step.

Battling a wave of doubt, she realized she needed to speak with the man alone.

As if reading her mind, he asked the twins, "Do either of you like to draw?"

"Not really." Harper responded for both girls. "But we like to color."

"Then you're in luck. We have coloring books and crayons in the first floor waiting room. Let's see if we can get you set up."

Five minutes later Walker had the twins sitting at a child-sized table, their coats on the back of their chairs, each with a coloring book and box of crayons in front of them.

"I'm going to have a quick word with your mother right in there." He pointed to a glassed-in room that overlooked the waiting area.

"But—" Kennedy's eyebrows scrunched together "—she's not—"

Hope cut off her niece with a quick shake of her head. "We won't be long."

"Okay." Shrugging, the girls went to work flipping

through their individual books. Each stopped at a picture of a cartoon princess appearing in deep conversation with a frog.

As they began transforming the blank picture into colorful masterpieces, Hope took the lead. Walker followed close on her heels. Her stomach roiled at the mix of rubbing alcohol and antiseptic wafting around them. She hated that scent. It brought her back to Charity's final days. Why had she chosen a hospital for this confrontation?

The memory of her sister's fast decline hit Hope like a physical blow. She was instantly transported back to that cold, sanitized hospital room where the social worker told her it was time to call in hospice.

In a cruel twist of fate, the day she'd moved Charity into her apartment near the university had also been the girls' fifth birthday. Charity had rallied for the celebration, but all Hope could recall from that day was the bold red scarf wrapped around her sister's head and her thin, gaunt face.

Hope took in a breath. A mistake, as another dose of that horrible scent filled her nostrils. She lowered her head so her companion wouldn't see her reaction.

Once inside the glass-enclosed room, he wasted no time getting to the point. "Well, Hope *Jeffries*." He added the same emphasis on her last name as she'd used moments before. "You seem to know me, while I'm having a difficult time placing you. Tell me how we met."

"You don't remember?"

"Should I?"

She brushed the hair off her forehead, gave him a good, long look at her face and waited for him to make the connection. A heavy silence fell between them.

A beat passed. Then two. By the third, he crossed his arms over his chest and set a broad shoulder against the wall beside him. "So, we're back to that, are we? I have several skills, Mrs. Jeffries. Mind reading is not one of them."

"I'm not married." For some reason, she felt it important to correct him on that point.

He acknowledged this with a single nod. "All right, *Ms.* Jeffries. Who are you and want do you want from me?"

He was clearly losing patience with her. She was losing patience with herself.

"I thought…" She shook her head. "I wasn't expecting you to…" She broke off again, drew in a deep breath and tried again. "You really don't recognize my face?"

"Evidently, this is some sort of game for you." He dropped all signs of affability. "I'm at the end of a long shift and I'm not in the mood to play, so I'll ask again. Who are you?"

"You're asking the wrong question."

"What question should I be asking?"

She sighed. "It doesn't matter who I am, but rather who *they* are." She waved her hand in the general direction of the waiting room where the girls were absorbed in their coloring.

"All right." He studied the twins with a long, considering look. "Who are they?"

"You really can't guess?"

"So—" he shoved a hand through his hair "—we're back to the game-playing."

"I assure you, Dr. Evans, this is no game for me, or for the twins."

"Then tell me who they are."

"Harper and Kennedy are your daughters."

Walker resumed leaning against the wall, grinding his teeth in irritation and thinking cynically that Hope Jeffries had seemed so normal. How had he failed to detect the crazy beneath that polished facade?

There was another possibility. Maybe this was some sort of prank one of his siblings had cooked up to shock him out of his predictable routine. All of them, except for his brother working in Africa, had been pushing Walker to join the living again, even going so far as to insist he shake things up a bit.

He was sufficiently shaken.

"Who sent you?"

"No one sent me." She blinked rapidly, and if he wasn't mistaken, tears were welling up in her eyes, almost as if he'd offended her with his question.

Walker wasn't buying the innocent act.

Her claim was too ridiculous to be real, not to mention impossible. He would remember fathering twins. No one was that forgetful. Thinking through her potential collaborators, he decided his oldest sister was the most likely candidate. "Did Quinn put you up to this?"

"I don't know anyone named Quinn." She said this without making direct eye contact.

Walker narrowed his eyes. "Remy?"

"I assure you, Dr. Evans, no one *put me up* to this." Her lips flattened in a grim line. "I sought you out this morning with one goal in mind. To introduce you to your daughters."

Walker shook his head. His mother had been wild about soap operas. Any child growing up in her home had been forced to watch the ridiculous shows a time or two. Walker knew this particular story line. A beautiful, mysterious stranger—she was always beautiful and mysterious—arrives in town claiming one of the male leads fathered her child. Amnesia was often a secondary plotline.

The situation was almost comical.

Except, Walker was not amused. "You've had your fun, Ms. Jeffries, but your little joke has gone on long enough."

"I did not travel all this way to make a joke." Her manner stopped just short of combative.

Walker was feeling fairly antagonistic himself. "Then why are you here?"

"I told you."

He attempted to stare a lie out of her.

She held steady under his gaze, not a flinch, barely a blink. Oh, she was good.

A very unpleasant thought occurred to Walker. This woman seemed to have intimate knowledge of his routine, enough to know where he would be this morning. Granted, he was a creature of habit. Anyone could figure out his schedule after minimal observation. Clearly, Ms. Jeffries had been watching him, following him, or had hired someone for the task.

Alarming, to say the least.

He should be afraid. But for some inexplicable reason he wasn't. He was, however, furious she'd targeted him. The woman was about to learn that Walker Evans was no easy mark.

He went on the offense. "How long have you been stalking me?"

"I have not been stalking you."

"No?" He pushed from the wall and moved to tower over her. Not hard to do. She was a good five inches shorter. "You somehow found out where I work and the hours I clock in and out on a regular basis. Then, you show up at the end of my shift so that you could make this ridiculous claim. That is, by its very definition, stalking."

"I suppose, from your point of view, it would seem that way."

"You…*suppose*?" The word came out in an angry

growl. It took all his willpower not to walk her out of the building. "What would you call it?"

Her attention dropped to the floor, but not before Walker saw the sliver of guilt moving through her gaze. "There was nothing sketchy about my behavior."

"Only all of it."

"All right, yes, I made it my business to discover as much as I could about you. I did it for the twins' sake." She jerked her head up, looking as fierce as any mother he'd met through the years. "They are my first—my *only*—priority."

She genuinely appeared to care for the girls. Walker was almost impressed. Almost, but not quite. "Not sure teaching them how to stalk a man is in their best interest. Notice how I keep using that word. *Stalk.*"

Instead of backing down, she reacted with a show of temper. "Try to look at this from my perspective. I needed to know if you were worthy of meeting Harper and Kennedy."

"Those girls are not my daughters." He couldn't put a fine enough point on that.

Mouth grim, she pivoted to look out into the waiting room. Pressing her palm flat against the wall of glass, she sighed heavily, then dropped her hand by her side. "This isn't how our conversation was supposed to go."

"What did you expect? Did you think you could just show up here, make your outrageous claim and then have me fall in line because the twins and I share the same eye color?"

"The resemblance is much stronger than that."

He didn't disagree. But Walker knew better than to say as much. "How did you pick me? No, let me guess. You did a Google search for men with dark hair, blue eyes and a healthy bank account."

"This is not about money."

Walker frowned at the sight of those two adorable little girls coloring with focused resolve. Their tiny, identical scowls reminded him of his brother Brent at that age, so determined, so focused on their task. He detected a hint of sadness about them, too, and that just slayed him.

They were sweet and innocent, and nothing like their scheming mother. Walker felt a pang of sorrow for the girls, wishing, in that moment, that they really were his daughters. He'd nearly been a father once. The Lord had taken that from him, as well.

Walker hardened his heart and turned to their mother. "How long did it take you to find a man that looked enough like the twins to put your scam into motion?"

"You want to know how I found you? I did an internet search. And, yes, I used Google. I also hired a private detective to fill in the blanks."

"You…wait, what? You hired a private detective?" Shocked into momentary silence, Walker stared at her. The woman really was crazy. How else could he explain hiring an investigator to zero in on her mark? Had she chosen Walker because he was a lonely widower who buried his grief in work, work and then even more work?

That seemed overly cruel. Something didn't add up here, something that kept nagging at the back of his brain. "Why me?"

"Harper and Kennedy deserve to know their father, and before you start denying you're him—" she swung her purse off her shoulder "—I have proof."

Other than a DNA test, maybe a pair of birth certificates, which couldn't possibly exist, there was nothing she could show Walker that would corroborate her absurd claim. "All right, I'll bite. Show me this so-called proof."

"Gladly." With a jerk of her wrist, she unzipped the

black bag, rummaged around, then pulled out a thin manila folder. "Here. What do you have to say for yourself now?"

Walker took the document she shoved into his hand and lowered his head. "It's a marriage certificate, issued on—" he recited a date not quite six years ago "—by the state of Nevada."

"The ceremony was conducted in a Las Vegas wedding chapel."

Las Vegas? How did the Marriage Capital of the World play into her scam?

"Take a look at the signature right there." She jabbed her finger at the groom's name, her palm covering the area where the bride had signed.

Walker blinked at the sight of his own name scrawled in a bold, familiar flourish. Where had he seen that handwriting?

"That's my name. But not my signature." He set the certificate on a nearby table. "Your private detective steered you to the wrong man."

"How many Walker Bartholomew Evans do you think there are in North America?"

"No idea."

"Seven."

"So many?"

"The groom claimed he was an ER doctor. You are the only medical doctor with your same name."

"Let me point out, Ms. Jeffries, the large flaw in your story." Walker kept his voice measured, although he was feeling anything but calm. "I've never been to Las Vegas."

He'd married Rachel surrounded by two hundred of their closest family and friends at Thunder Ridge Community Church. The day had been bright and sunny, the perfect start to the rest of their lives. Walker had been full of optimism. He'd said his vows in front of God, naively believing He would bless the marriage for many years to come.

"Now you're just being difficult, Dr. Evans. Take a look at this." She reached inside the folder again. This time, she pulled out an 8x10 glossy photograph. "Visual proof you were in Las Vegas at the time of the wedding."

Walker studied the image of a smiling couple surrounded by large urns overflowing with ugly, plastic flower arrangements. The bride bore a remarkable likeness to the woman glaring at him. There were differences, most of which could be explained away by the passage of time. There was another explanation, of course, but that conversation was for later.

For now, Walker switched his attention to the groom.

A knot of disappointment tangled in his gut. What had possessed Brent to participate in a tacky Las Vegas wedding?

And, yeah, there was no denying the groom was Brent, grinning like a loon, eyes suspiciously unfocused. He stood next to an equally glassy-eyed woman that resembled Hope Jeffries, and yet not really. Walker bounced his gaze between the flesh-and-blood woman glaring at him and the bride in the photo.

He reached for the marriage certificate again, snatching it up before she could object, and studied the bride's signature. *Charity Jeffries.*

Well, well, well.

His unexpected visitor wasn't crazy, after all.

Walker couldn't say the same for his brother. What had Brent been thinking, signing Walker's name instead of his own on a marriage license?

It seemed unnecessarily petty, even considering their strained relationship at the time.

What had Brent hoped to gain?

He'd lost far more than he'd won by sticking it to Walker, namely five years as a father to those beautiful little girls. Walker glanced at the duo, looked back at the date on the certificate. "When did you say the twins were born?"

"They turned five in July of this year."

"What day?"

"The tenth."

Walker did the math. Harper and Kennedy had arrived in the world exactly forty-one weeks and three days following Brent's marriage to Charity. The numbers added up.

Setting aside the document, he watched the girls through the glass. Even the way they colored reminded Walker of his brother. It wasn't out of the realm of possibility that Brent had had a quickie Vegas wedding. But to marry a woman, then abandon her and their daughters? That wasn't in his brother's DNA. Speaking of DNA, although Walker didn't doubt Brent was the father of those precious girls, a test would have to be taken to prove paternity.

Before all that, Brent had some serious explaining to do.

Walker returned his attention to the wedding picture. He thought back to the year listed on the marriage certificate. His brother had experienced unspeakable tragedy, which could explain his erratic behavior and bad choices.

"Well?" Hope's voice brought Walker back to the immediate problem at hand. "Do you still deny paternity?"

"I take it you have birth certificates, as well?"

She looked away. "Of course."

"That's not me in the photograph."

And that wasn't her in the picture, either. Which brought up a host of questions that Walker decided to save until they'd sorted out this unfortunate case of mistaken identity. "Wait here."

"You're *leaving*?" She sounded as outraged as she looked, all wide-eyed and furious. "Just like that?"

"I'm not leaving. I have something tucked away in my cubicle that you need to see. I would take you with me, but one of us has to stay here and watch the girls."

She glanced at the twins, then back at him, her eyes wary. "I don't think it's a good idea to let you—"

"Trust me." He touched her arm, willing her to see that he, unlike her, never lied. And he certainly didn't play games. "You're going to want to see this."

Her eyebrows slammed together. "What could you possibly have to show me?"

"Proof that I'm not the twins' father."

Chapter Three

Hope stared after Walker's retreating back, a sharp pain in her heart, the sensation cinching tighter and tighter. She wasn't an anxious person by nature, but she couldn't seem to stand still while he retrieved his supposed proof. She paced in a circle, wondering, worrying and wanting to jump out of her own skin. She had the right man.

He was the girls' father. Her proof was solid. What sort of evidence could he have that would possibly refute hers?

She paused at the plate glass window. The twins were completely absorbed in their task, heads bent in deep concentration, totally unaware of the drama playing out between their father and aunt.

The vice around her heart tightened. Hope loved Harper and Kennedy as if they were her own. The emotion ran deep, all the way down to the cellular level. If Walker didn't want them in his life, no problem, she wasn't here to change his mind. She would happily adopt them and take them back to New York. All she needed was his notarized signature on the custody papers.

When it came to family, the twins were all she had now. *Please, Lord, let him give them to me without a fight.* For a prayer, it wasn't especially wordy. Admittedly, she was rusty. She hadn't prayed since Charity died. The Lord had remained silent then. Maybe he wouldn't answer this time, either.

No use making assumptions. Hope was not giving up her quest for custody, and that was that. She would hound Walker until he admitted he was the twins' father. She would get him to sign over custody and continue on with her life free of guilt, knowing she'd done the right thing by coming here.

The masculine clearing of a throat announced his return.

With renewed resolve, Hope spun around to face him. What she saw surprised her. His eyes were filled with silent apology and a surprising amount of commiseration. An infuriating combination. Hope immediately bristled, dropping her gaze before he could see her reaction. It was only then that she noticed he held a silver picture frame in his hand.

"What's that?"

"A family portrait." He pressed the frame in her hands. "Take a look."

Her fingers automatically curled around the cold metal. "I don't see what a family picture has to do—"

"Look at the photograph, really look, then we'll talk."

Frowning, she studied the outdoor image of four men, brothers clearly, and two women, obviously their sisters. The siblings had been caught in a casual moment, appearing more candid than posed.

As the insanely gorgeous faces smiled at her, Hope's heart filled with a mix of dread and longing. Respect. Love. Support. She could see it all written in the collective body language. Unmistakable affection was there as well, in the positioning of hands randomly set on shoulders or arms slung around waists. The very essence of family had been captured in a single click of the camera's shutter and was too genuine to be explained away by chance.

Panic lodged in Hope's throat, stealing her ability to breathe.

The twins were related to these people. They were their family.

I'm going to lose them.

She couldn't bear the thought.

"Take a closer look at the people in the picture. That's me," Walker said, "right there, in the middle. The man on my right is Casey. He's the oldest and is a former military pilot with his own private cargo company. He also owns a coffee shop in town." He let that sink in a minute before adding, "The man on Casey's left is McCoy, a local photographer and artist. That's Quinn." He pointed to the taller of the two women. "She owns a sweetshop and tearoom in town. Our sister Remy is a veterinarian."

Quinn and Remy, the people he'd assumed had sent Hope to play a joke on him. The Evans siblings felt comfortable enough to play pranks on one another. Something moved deep inside her, a yearning so strong her knees threatened to buckle.

The twins were a part of this large, happy family. They belonged to them.

Hope had never belonged to anyone. Her father hadn't wanted her or Charity after their mother died, instead choosing to travel as a missionary to the Middle East. Even her sister hadn't wanted a relationship with Hope, saying she was too hung up on rules to be any fun. She'd spent her entire life on the outside looking in, always wishing for something just out of reach.

"And, finally," Walker said, still guiding her through the photograph, "the man on the far left, there—" he placed his fingertip on the image and tapped twice "—that's my brother Brent. Take a good, long look at him."

Hope did as he instructed, a sick feeling in the pit of her stomach.

"Brent—" Walker tapped the image again "—is the man you're looking for."

"But—" Hope swallowed "—your name is on the marriage certificate."

"I have no idea why my brother signed my name instead of his own. And believe me, he will answer for his behavior." He tried to take the picture. Hope held on to it and continued focusing on Brent Evans. "My brother is the man in the wedding photograph, not me. Brent is the father of your twins."

Her cheeks burned hot with humiliation. She'd made a colossal error. "I don't know what to say."

"It was a logical mistake," he allowed. "Brent and I are only eighteen months apart. We look a lot alike, and—"

"—could be twins."

He acknowledged this with a nod. "Others have said the same. But if you look closely, there are obvious differences."

She saw them now. Walker was taller by an inch and a half, maybe two. He was slightly leaner in build. His hair had more wave. Brent had a small scar over his left eye. There were more, but she didn't need to catalog them to know she'd made a terrible error in judgment.

Hope considered herself a practical woman. She could admit when she made a mistake. And she'd just made a big one. She returned the picture and said, "I was wrong."

"Yes, you were."

"In my defense, the evidence was strong."

"Except for one glaring detail." His voice held a note of censure.

Hope prickled. "How was I supposed to know your brother signed your name?"

"Now who's being difficult, *Ms*. Jeffries? I'm referring to something more obvious. You bore Brent's children. You had to know I wasn't the right man on first sight."

Hope sighed. Time to come clean. "I'm not the twins' mother."

"I figured that out already."

"Their mother was my identical twin sister."

"Yep, figured that one out, as well." His lips twisted at a sardonic angle. "Why not admit the truth at the beginning of our meeting? Why lie?"

"I didn't lie, exactly."

"A lie by omission is still a lie. Or as my brother-in-law is fond of saying, a half-truth is a whole lie."

Walker's brother-in-law wasn't wrong. Hope could feel the girls slipping away from her. Harper and Kennedy had uncles and aunts and cousins. What could she offer that compared to a large, extended family?

Her unconditional love and stability and so much more. This wasn't over.

"You led me to believe you were their mother."

She started to argue. But in the next breath, the fight left her. "I was wrong to do that."

How many times would she have to say that to gain absolution? As many as it took, she decided, knowing she had to make this right for the twins.

"We finally agree on something." She expected him to give her a much-deserved lecture. But instead, he added, "I prefer we were on the same page going forward, as well."

"Me, too." She meant every word.

He gave her a wide, boyish grin.

That smile. It made the man appear even more approachable than before, and really, really likeable. Hope didn't want to like Walker Evans. Technically, he was still the enemy.

What must he think of her?

She'd come to Thunder Ridge, guns blazing, making her accusations and…wait. So, she'd confronted the wrong Dr. Evans. Nothing had really changed, had it? The twins' father had walked away from his pregnant wife. Hope could still win custody. All she needed was a legally binding, notarized signature from Brent Evans and probably a DNA test. She needed to call her lawyer.

She also needed to speak with Brent Evans. "Would you be willing to introduce me to the twins' father?"

His smile dropped. "That's going to be a problem."

"Dr. Evans, please—"

"Call me Walker."

She nodded. "Walker, won't you reconsider?"

"You don't understand. It's not that I don't *want* to introduce the twins to Brent." He took her hand, gave it a gentle squeeze, held on. "It's that I *can't*."

Hope didn't want to be soothed by Walker's touch. But she was. "I…don't understand." And then she thought that maybe she did. "Is he incapacitated, or…ill?"

Were the twins about to lose another parent? The Lord couldn't be that cruel.

"It's nothing like that. Brent is fine. Unfortunately, he's currently out of the country."

"Is he on vacation?" she queried.

"It's a bit more honorable than that." Walker gave her hand another squeeze. "Brent is in Africa working for Doctors Without Borders."

The twins' father was in Africa? Dumbfounded by Walker's revelation, Hope clenched her jaw so hard her teeth ached from the pressure. It was too much to believe, and yet too ludicrous to be anything but true.

Africa. The word swirled around in her brain, nagging at her, shaming her for all the ugly thoughts she'd had about Walker Evans—a man who volunteered at a homeless shelter—and his brother, a man working for an international humanitarian organization. Both would look better in front of a judge in family court than a single woman with no family who taught Economics in New York City at a fancy private college.

Of all the scenarios Hope had conjured in her mind, learning that their father was working for Doctors Without Borders didn't make the top ten. It hadn't even made the list.

I'm going to lose the girls.

She breathed in slowly, catching a whiff of antiseptic that was uncomfortably strong. For a shocking moment, she thought she was going to be sick.

Hold it together.

The effort drained Hope of any remaining scraps of dignity. Images of Brent Evans administering medical care to the sick and impoverished sent another jolt of shame through her. Fear soon followed. Would a man like that openly deny his daughters?

Possibly. Her own father had done just that.

Hope's surroundings slowly came into focus, and she realized Walker still held her hand. His touch speared warmth up her arm and slammed into her heart. She should free her hand from his grip. She couldn't seem to move. The physical connection grounded her.

Frustration, urgency, embarrassment—the emotions knotted inside her. All those hours of research and the money spent on a private detective had brought her no closer to adopting her nieces.

"I see I've rendered you speechless." Walker's voice lacked any sign of condemnation. One more piece of evidence that proved he was the better person.

Hope shut her eyes a moment, wincing at the thought of her open hostility. "I don't know what to say—" she opened her eyes "—except I'm sorry for how I approached you."

"No worries." His blue eyes filled with compassion and understanding. It was the kind of look Hope had received from her sister's doctors whenever they presented bad news.

Walker Evans must be really great with his patients. Hope had to look away to catch her breath. When she returned her gaze, he was smiling, softly, kindly. The grain of black stubble on his jaw only managed to make him seem more approachable. Not some superhero with a medical degree. Just a regular guy with a bit more training than most men.

He let go of her hand.

The lack of contact left her feeling empty.

"If it helps," he said, taking a small step back, "I'm experiencing my own shock over the situation. I can't begin to imagine what was in my brother's head six years ago." Something in his gaze said he had a few guesses.

Hope would like to hear them. But first, she had her own admission to make. "I could say the same for my sister." Had her sister been completely honest with her about the twins' father? "Charity and I really never understood each other."

"An oddity for identical twins."

Hope didn't disagree. She and Charity had always been one step off. Yes, they'd been sisters, siblings, but never really close. "There was love between us, of course. It's just, our personalities were so different. We never had that twin connection I see in Harper and Kennedy."

Walker glanced at the wedding photograph, then looked back at Hope. "Now that, I believe."

They shared a smile, Hope's far more somber than the one Walker wore. She closed her eyes and sighed, regretting *so* much.

How she missed her sister and all the lost years they could never get back. The previous eight months had passed too quickly. The focus had been on Charity's illness and taking care of the twins rather than restoring their fractured relationship. Honest conversations had been rare. They'd made amends, but there hadn't been enough time to reconcile completely. Again, Hope wondered if Charity had been completely forthright about the twins' father.

She hated doubting her sister when Charity wasn't able to defend herself.

Sighing, Hope touched the photograph, carefully tracing the woman who was the polar opposite of her in every way but looks. "Everyone adored Charity. She was the outgoing twin."

She'd been almost childlike in her need for fun, perhaps even thoughtless in her pursuit of a good time. But Charity had brought Harper and Kennedy into the world when she could have made other choices.

For that alone, Hope could forgive her sister any mistakes she made as a mother. "Your brother and my sister made two beautiful children."

"I couldn't agree more. Look at that." Walker waggled his finger in the space between them. "We've agreed a second time. If we keep this up, we might actually become friends."

Hope's cheeks heated at the lighthearted comment. "I wouldn't go that far."

He chuckled.

Her heart pinged.

What would it be like to call this man a friend? It wasn't out of the realm of possibility. Their lives were connected now, tethered by two gorgeous little girls born three days, one week and nine months after a spontaneous Las Vegas wedding.

"The twins have been through a lot of turmoil in their short lives." Shifting slightly, she watched them. They were still coloring, but the squirming had begun. Hope calculated five minutes more and they would come looking for her. And she was only a smidge closer to finding their father. "What am I going to do?"

"Now who's asking the wrong question?"

"I'm sorry?"

"The question is…what are *we* going to do?" Walker stepped closer. Hope could feel his heat rolling over her like a warm, healing summer breeze. "I'm not your enemy, Hope. We're in this together."

And just like that, her resentment evaporated, replaced by an odd thrill of something she couldn't quite pinpoint. Relief, maybe? She might be back at square one, but she wasn't alone anymore. It was an unfamiliar, heady feeling, and one she didn't dare trust.

"I have to wonder why you came looking for the twins' father alone. Why didn't your sister join you?"

Hope started at the question, then realized Walker didn't know Charity was dead.

"I'm assuming something happened to her."

The man was perceptive. Under different circumstances, Hope would consider that an attractive character trait, but now it only made her sad. "My sister died recently."

His face softened in sympathy. "I'm sorry."

She was painfully aware that those two, simple words were exactly what she needed to hear. Had Walker offered empty platitudes, Hope would have closed herself off completely. But her usual defenses were crumbling under his gentle manner.

"How did she die?"

She hadn't spoken of Charity's passing with anyone besides the girls, and even then only in the most careful, gentle way.

Had Hope been feeling less wretched over the way she'd approached Walker, she would have brushed aside his question. Instead, she found herself saying, "She died of breast cancer three months ago."

"That's rough." Walker said nothing more, probably waiting for her to continue. At least he didn't attempt to touch her again.

"Charity showed up on my doorstep this past February, her daughters in tow. Until that day, I had no idea she was a mother."

"None?"

She looked away, feeling the guilt all over again. Why hadn't she tried to contact her sister through the years? Why had she allowed Charity to hold a grudge over who-knew-what? Hope still didn't know what had possessed her sister to cut all ties with her.

"We'd been estranged for years," she admitted. "Every one of which melted away the moment I laid eyes on her. She looked so beat down. When she shared the terrible news of her diagnosis, I never thought the cancer would be fatal."

"I'm sorry." Walker touched her then, nothing more than a brush of his fingertips across the back of her hand. The need to lean on him was a jolt Hope felt all the way down to her toes.

If she gave in to it, she would shatter.

"I could give you all sorts of clichés to ease your pain," he said, quickly looking away, swallowing a few times, as if trying to pull himself together. Then, blinking rapidly, he glanced back at her, deep sadness swirling in his gaze. "But there are some losses words never heal."

He sounded as if he spoke from personal experience. Had he lost someone he loved? The private investigator hadn't mentioned anything about a death of a spouse or girlfriend. Hope was coming to realize he hadn't been as thorough as she'd paid him to be, as evidenced by her approaching the wrong man. And now this, the genuine understanding that seemed far too real to be fake.

"Thank you." Her voice sounded as broken as she felt.

This man was a stranger, but a sympathetic one. He was also a man with a shared stake in the situation. The twins were his nieces, too. This moment of solidarity could very easily turn adversarial if she wasn't careful.

Hope needed Walker as an ally. Perhaps if she appealed to the healer in him, he would work with her.

"The doctors discovered the cancer too late. It all happened so quickly." Now that she started, the words spilled out of her in a rush. "After years of no communication, not even a text, there she was, on my doorstep, my sister. My twin. Asking me for help. I welcomed her back into my life without question. And her daughters. Harper and Kennedy are—"

"Hold that thought." Walker's sudden interruption had her nearly choking on her words. His quick "Hey, kiddos" shook Hope to the core.

How much had they heard?

Moving quickly, she rushed forward and dropped in front of them. "Perfect timing." She smoothed her expression into a pleasant smile. "We're just finishing up."

Neither girl responded. They were too busy staring up at Walker, eyes wide with adoration. Hope couldn't blame them. He'd turned his smile on the children and, well, *wow*. The man had a killer smile. Hope's heart lifted, sighed.

"What's that?" Kennedy pointed up to his neck.

"What? This old thing?" His smile turned into a playful grin. "It's called a stethoscope."

"The doctors used one of those on my mom." Harper studied the instrument with keen interest. "We weren't allowed to touch it, not ever."

"You can touch this one." Walker unwrapped the instrument from around his neck and lowered to his haunches. "It's used for listening to heartbeats. Go on. Touch it." He held the instrument closer to the girls. "You won't break it."

Both reached out tentatively. Harper's hand touched the black tubes first. Kennedy's followed a second later.

"These are the earpieces." Walker pointed to the identical ends. "They go into your—"

"Ears!" the girls shouted simultaneously.

"Exactly, and this is the chest-piece."

"That goes on your heart," Harper told him with no small amount of pride.

"Right again. Want to take a quick listen?"

Two pairs of eyes swung up to Hope. "Can we?"

"Of course."

"Who wants to go first?"

Kennedy answered a split second before her sister. "Me."

"Okay." Walker placed the earpieces in the girl's ears. "Can you hear my heartbeat? It sounds like lub-dub, lub-dub, lub-dub."

"I hear it!" Kennedy shouted the words.

"I want to try." Harper bounced on her toes. "Let me try."

Walker gave the excited child a turn.

With a sinking sensation in the pit of her stomach, Hope watched the interaction between uncle and nieces. Walker was really good with the girls. It had taken Hope weeks to win them over like that.

To be fair, she'd never been around children before Charity had shown up on her doorstep. Dr. Stephens had assured Hope that a bit of awkwardness was to be expected.

She was being too hard on herself. What did it matter how she and the twins had started? They were close now. For all intents and purposes, she was their mother.

Lesson over, Walker wrapped the stethoscope back around his own neck.

Now that the ice had been broken, Harper and Kennedy couldn't stop talking. The conversation turned to one of their favorite topics since arriving in Thunder Ridge. "Do you know how to build a snowman?"

"Do I know how to build a snowman?" Walker's voice held a note of amused irony. "You, my little friend, are in the presence of a master craftsman."

"Really?"

"I have skills, kiddo, taught to me by my older brother, a man world-renowned for his ice sculptures."

"I bet I'm better," Kennedy said, her little chin lifted at a proud angle.

Hope blinked at her niece. Kennedy knew how to build snowmen? That was news to her. With Charity's illness, then the onslaught of the summer months, and then setting the girls up in school, there hadn't been much time for playing in the snow. Okay, none.

"I like your confidence, kid." Walker patted Kennedy on the shoulder.

"I'm good, too," Harper said, rushing to stand next Kennedy, nearly knocking over her sister in the process. "I'm even better than her."

The girls scowled at each other. A little pushing ensued. Before full-on mutiny broke out, Walker smoothly stepped between them. Shifting them apart with a gentle nudge on each of their shoulders, he eyed the girls with a mix of amusement and affection. "There's a way to settle this."

Again, the girls spoke as one. "How?"

"We build a snowman."

"Can we do it now?"

"Now could be a problem." Walker made a grand show of looking around him, his movements exaggerated. "I'm currently out of snow."

Harper giggled. "Not here, silly."

"Well, we do have a park at the center of town with lots and lots of the white stuff." He swiveled a questioning gaze at Hope. "You game?"

He wanted to build a snowman, now? As in, this morning? "I was thinking we would touch base with your brother first. Then, maybe, you know—" she shrugged "—go from there."

"Ah." Walker checked the chunky watch on his wrist. "It's the middle of the afternoon in Zimbabwe. He may be out in the field or in surgery or, well, you get the idea."

"Oh." She couldn't keep the disappointment out of her voice.

"Tell you what, I'll send a quick text asking him to get in touch with me, stat."

Hope breathed a sigh of relief. "I would really appreciate that."

"Okay." There was a moment of hesitation, but then he

pulled out his cell phone and began tapping on the screen. His thumbs worked at lightning speed. He paused, studied the phone, then went back to typing out his message.

At last, he looked up. "Want to take a look before I press send?"

"Please."

He handed Hope the phone. She lowered her head, read quickly. The message was short and to the point.

Brent, we need to talk ASAP. A situation has arisen that requires your immediate attention.

"A—" Hope glanced at the girls "—situation?"

Walker followed the direction of her gaze. "Some things are better not put in a text."

He was right, of course. But still. Harper and Kennedy were too precious to be summed up as a *situation*.

"Hope." Walker touched her shoulder. "Do you have a revision you'd like to make?"

She reread the text, shook her head. "No." She handed over the phone. "It's good."

"Okay." Eyes never leaving hers, Walker touched the screen. An electronic whooshing sound indicated the text had been sent. "Now, we wait."

"We wait."

They continued staring at each other, neither moving, neither looking away.

"In the meantime—" A slow smile spread across Walker's face. Oh, that smile. "—what do you say we build a snowman?"

Hope sighed. Spending the morning in a field of snow with the twins' uncle wasn't a terrible idea. It would give her a chance to get to know Walker better, maybe get some information about his brother.

What could possibly go wrong?

"Sure. Let's do it."

Chapter Four

Walker went through a dozen emotions before settling on relief. The appearance of Hope and the twins meant he wouldn't have to fill his morning with frantic activity in an effort to forget. He wouldn't have to trudge home to an empty house or pray exhaustion took over before memories flooded his mind.

There were days when he found them comforting, but mostly they just made him sad. His family was right. He needed to let Rachel go. To what end? Peace of mind, yes, but who would remember her if not him? She'd been an orphan. No parents, no siblings, only Walker. He couldn't let her death relegate her to obscurity.

Shaking off a rush of melancholy, he put on a brave face and escorted the Jeffries back the way they came. The automatic doors slid open and the four of them stepped into the crisp Colorado morning air. The twins kept up an excited chatter. Their aunt remained silent, even when Harper asked if they could stop for hot chocolate before playing in the snow.

The suggestion gave Walker an idea, one that would make next steps go smoothly, at least for him. "I know just the place. Quinn's Sweet Shop is a block off the park."

"Quinn?" Hope's face scrunched in concentration, as if trying to remember where she'd heard the name. "Oh, Quinn. The older of your two sisters, the business owner not the vet."

"That's her." He gave Hope what he hoped was a nonthreatening smile. "The shop won't be open yet, but she'll be there. I'll give her a quick call to let her know we're coming. If you get there before me, knock on the front door. She'll let you in."

One of the girls stopped him with a tug on his arm. "You're not riding in our car?"

"I have a few things to finish up here first." Her little face fell and to Walker's horror, she looked like she was about to cry. "Hey, now, Kennedy, I'll be there. I promise."

She sniffled then, eyes wide, angled her head slightly to the left. "You know I'm Kennedy?"

"Well, sure."

"Most people can't tell us apart." This, from Harper, with equal amounts of awe.

Walker couldn't help but point out the obvious. "You, my little friend, will soon learn I'm not most people."

Time to start the process of bringing Harper and Kennedy into the Evans family fold. "I have a set of twin nieces a few years older than you. They're identical, just like you, but I can tell them apart."

The next few minutes were spent in a whirlwind of questions about Walker's nieces, then buckling the girls in the back seat of Hope's rental. He straightened, caught her eye over the top of the car. "I'll meet you at the store." He rattled off the address. "Twenty minutes, tops."

"We'll be there."

Hands stuffed in his pockets, Walker watched Hope drive out of the parking lot and then turn in the direction of Main Street.

As he made his way back inside the hospital, he mentally reviewed the events of the morning. It didn't take him long to come to the conclusion that Hope Jeffries hadn't been completely honest with him. She claimed she'd come to Thunder Ridge simply to introduce her nieces to their father.

That wasn't the only reason. She wanted something else. He had a few ideas what that was, and none of them boded well for Brent or the rest of the family.

But he was getting ahead of himself. Best to let the woman think she had the upper hand. In the meantime, Walker would get to know his nieces better. His throat caught on a breath and all he could think was that those sweet little girls were his nieces. Family. His family.

No way to predict how Brent would react to the news that he was a father of twins. But now that Walker had met Harper and Kennedy, he wasn't going to let them go without a fight. A plan began forming in his brain.

First step: gather more information.

After changing out of his scrubs, Walker grabbed the rest of his gear and a few necessary items for building a spectacular snowman. He arrived outside Quinn's shop with five minutes to spare. He cut the engine of his SUV and ran through what he knew about the twins, their mother and their aunt.

Not very much.

Walker didn't even know where Hope and the girls lived, or what Hope did for a living. He figured some sort of fancy, designer job. The woman had city written all over her. She was also successful, or at least comfortable enough to purchase fancy coats for herself and the twins.

Money wasn't her motivation. Unless she'd spent her last dime on those coats, and...

He was speculating.

No decision needed to be made until he spoke with Brent, which could prove more problematic than he'd let on. Walker pulled out his phone, checked for incoming texts. Nothing. He wasn't surprised.

Walker had been telling the truth when he told Hope that communication between the brothers was difficult. Sometimes it was due to technology. Brent chose to work in some of the remotest regions in Africa. But there was another reason, mostly Walker's fault.

Calculating the time difference, he sent another text. This one briefer than the last, only two words. Call me.

No response.

Walker opened his contacts next, scrolled to the *Q*s, then pressed on his sister's name. Quinn answered on the second ring. "What do you want?"

"Is that how you greet your favorite brother?"

"At the moment, you are most definitely not my favorite brother."

"*Good morning, Walker.* How hard is that?"

"Fine. *Good morning, Walker.*" She still sounded distracted, and he could hear the sound of machines coupled with incomprehensible chatter in the background. "Now, what do you want? I'm elbow-deep in melting chocolate."

"Pull yourself away and let me in the shop."

"And why would I do that?"

"I promised hot chocolate to a woman and two very sweet little girls." Walker climbed out of his car, then shouldered the door shut behind him. "Help me out, okay?"

"I...wait. Are you on a date?"

His stomach dipped. "It's not a date."

Silence met the statement.

Quinn's shock wasn't unexpected. It was no secret that Walker hadn't even looked at another woman, much less gone on a date since Rachel's death. He'd blamed work, but those who knew him best suspected he was using that as an excuse to hide from the world. They were correct. "Open the shop, Quinn. It's important."

"All right, all right. But this better be good."

He thought of Hope and the twins. "It is."

The next words out of Quinn's mouth were, "Alexa, disconnect."

The line went dead.

"Goodbye to you, too, sis." Shaking his head, Walker stuffed his phone into his back pocket and stepped onto the sidewalk. He caught sight of Hope and the twins hurrying toward him.

Well, Harper and Kennedy hurried. Hope moved at a more sedate pace.

When the twins saw him, they broke out in a run. Walker was working on zero hours of sleep, but the sight of those girls rushing to meet him energized him as no cup of coffee could.

He crouched, automatically opening his arms as if he'd been greeting them this way since they could toddle. Without an ounce of hesitation, Harper and Kennedy rushed into his embrace. The scent of baby shampoo filled his nose.

He set the girls at arm's length and smiled.

They grinned back. This easy familiarity outside the hospital wasn't typical for him, and he sensed it wasn't for them either. The sadness in them recognized the sadness in him. Loss had a way of drawing grief-stricken souls to each other. Walker had spent years pushing people away and keeping his distance from personal connections. For some reason he didn't feel the need to do either with these children.

Had the Lord brought the twins into Walker's life for a reason?

Hope came up behind the twins. She stopped in the middle of a single ray of sunlight. Her hair took on a golden glow, giving her an ethereal look. Her moss green eyes were radiant and full of an emotion Walker couldn't define. Love for the girls, but also concern, or maybe that was trepidation? She hadn't seemed afraid before. Angry, wary, a little hostile, but not afraid.

Was she worried Brent would take the girls away from her? Walker took a harder look at Hope Jeffries. She'd taken a risk coming here. Why?

That was the million-dollar question. For all he knew, she was gathering information about Brent and his family to use against them in a custody battle. She wouldn't win. Brent was their father. She was only their aunt. A DNA test would settle the matter.

But he was getting ahead of himself again. Hope could do the right thing. She could also make a lot of trouble for Brent.

Not on Walker's watch. "Thanks for coming," he said.

"I always keep my promises."

Good to know.

She ran her gaze over him. "You changed clothes."

"Scrubs aren't the best choice for rolling around in the snow."

"I suppose not." Something came and went in her eyes before she switched her attention to the building behind him, her eyes narrowing. "The shop looks closed."

"Quinn is in the back." He looked over his shoulder and saw his sister making her way through the darkened store. "Here she comes now."

While they waited for Walker's sister, Hope took a closer look at her surroundings, taking note of the nearby businesses. Most had charming, almost whimsical names.

The Wash and Spins, a sort of laundromat and dance studio hybrid; The Slippery Slope, a ski shop that could use a bit more Christmas decorations; a restaurant called Señor O'Malley's. What an odd name. She tried to imagine what sort of food they served.

She returned her gaze to Quinn's Sweet Shop. The type of business was self-explanatory.

Any minute now, the twins would meet Walker's sister, who was their aunt and yet another person who could take them away from Hope.

She watched as a slim silhouette worked the locks of the shop's glass door. The form was covered in flickering shadows, making it difficult for Hope to make out the woman's features. But when the door swung open and the store owner stepped into the light, one glance told Hope this was Walker's sister Quinn.

She had the same dark hair and blue, blue eyes as her brother and the twins. It wasn't just the color, but the shape, as well. The features were similar, as were the full lips. That was some strong DNA, Hope thought. A test would be superfluous. She would ask for one anyway.

Walker made the introductions. "Quinn, this is Hope Jeffries."

"Pleased to meet you, Hope Jeffries."

"Likewise."

The apron that covered Quinn's black wool pants and pale pink sweater had streaks of flour and what looked like melted chocolate. A big, shiny diamond ring hung from a sturdy-looking chain around her neck. The smile she gave Hope was reminiscent of her brother's. She directed that welcoming grin onto the girls, winning points with Hope for speaking to them directly. "And who might you be?"

"I'm Kennedy. And this is my twin sister, Harper. We're five."

Quinn's smile widened. "What a great age. I have twin girls. They're a little older than you, almost seven." She angled her head. "I adore your hats."

"Aunt Hope bought them for us."

"Your aunt has excellent taste." She aimed a wink in Hope's direction.

Kennedy tugged on Quinn's apron. "You look like Dr. Walker."

Quinn eyed her brother, her gaze serious. "That's because I'm Dr. Walker's older, wiser sister." She continued looking at him then shifted her gaze to Hope, her eyes slightly narrowed. "What do you say we get out of this cold and you can tell me how you know my brother?"

"We just met him this morning."

"Is that so?" She held his gaze. "I smell a story."

"You'll get it," Walker promised, not quite meeting his sister's eyes. "Right now, the twins want hot chocolate, and everyone knows you make the best in town."

"This is true." She offered a hand to Harper, then the other to Kennedy. "Come with me."

They reached out to her without question and let her guide them into the store.

Walker waved Hope inside ahead of him. She started forward, navigated the first step, then swung back around. With him still at street level, they were nearly eye to eye. She could see the different shades of blue in his eyes and the lines of fatigue at the edges. The grooves were deep, as if he'd been operating without sufficient sleep for a very long time.

Some strange instinct nearly had her lifting her hand to smooth away that mix of sadness and bafflement in his eyes. Hope resisted, barely. She understood his confusion, even sympathized. She'd had months to process the reality of her sister's quick wedding, and all that came after. Walker had only found out less than an hour ago.

"The twins don't know why we're in town," she told him. "I'd like it to stay that way, at least until I have a chance to speak with their father."

"Hope. We're on the same side."

"What side is that?"

"The twins'."

She sighed. "I've insulted you. That wasn't my intent. I just wanted to make sure you understood the fragile nature of the situation."

"Look. I know this is a big ask. But you're going to have to trust me." Frustration sounded in his voice, and showed in the way he pressed his thumb and forefinger to the bridge of his nose. "Can you do that?"

"I…" She paused, then nodded slowly. "Yes. I can." *For now.*

"Thank you."

A moment of solidarity passed between them.

Before she did something crazy, like reach out to him, she spun around and stepped into the pleasant scent of chocolate and sugar.

Quinn had stopped in the middle of the shop. Hands on her knees, she was currently leaning down and addressing the twins directly. "Now that I know your names, tell me, who wants hot chocolate?"

Two little hands shot in the air.

"Me, too." Quinn walked to one of the walls and pressed several buttons. Soon the interior of the store was bathed in a soft, golden glow. The twins gasped in delight.

Hope did the same. The decor was decidedly French, with pink and brown the dominating colors. Shelves loaded with a variety of gift baskets lined the wall behind a waist-high counter. The display cases were filled with every kind of confection any self-respecting sweet lover could ever want. "I adore your shop."

Smiling, Quinn moved to an industrial-looking machine and started working a series of knobs and switches. "It's a labor of love."

"I can tell." Hope spun in a circle, not sure what called to her most. The baskets of chocolate, the colorful macarons or the chocolate-covered popcorn. Her mouth watered. "The girls and I thought about stopping in here yesterday, but we wanted cupcakes, so we went to the bakery down the street instead."

"I'm sorry to hear that." Quinn's voice held zero judgment, but the stiffness in her shoulders indicated disappointment. "I make cupcakes, too."

"So I see." Hope moved closer to the display case and studied the selections. "Are those as good as they look?"

"Better." Walker drew alongside her.

"You know, Harper and Kennedy—" Quinn reached for an empty mug as she spoke "—you girls look a lot like my daughters."

"Do they like to make snowmen?" Harper wanted to know.

"Absolutely. We take our snowmen very seriously in this family." An unspoken question was in the look she shot Walker. "Maybe my brother will bring you over to my house this weekend and you can see what I mean."

"Can we, Aunt Hope?"

"We'll see."

Before either could object, Quinn was directing the twins toward a darling, kid-size table. She set a steaming mug in front of each girl. "Blow on it, it's hot."

Harper did as she requested. Kennedy, however, was too busy frowning in her mug to obey. "She has more marshmallows than I do."

"No, she doesn't," Quinn corrected in the gentle manner of a mother used to little girls arguing over marshmallows. "You each have seven."

Kennedy counted—out loud—only relenting once she discovered she had the promised seven.

"Here." Quinn handed Walker a mug. "You're officially on duty. Watch the girls while Hope and I have a little chat in the back."

Walker bounced his gaze between Hope and his sister. "I don't think that's a good idea."

"It's okay," Hope told him. "Really."

"Be right back." Quinn linked arms with Hope and drew her through a set of swinging double doors that led into the shop's massive kitchen. A team of employees hovered over workstations. Not a single person glanced in their direction. Complicated looking machines whirred, while giant mixers churned at a slow and steady pace.

All in all, a successful business in motion. A very loud successful business. Hope could hardly hear herself think.

Quinn took up a position near a large plate glass window, her back to the shop, which allowed Hope a direct line of sight to where Walker sat at the small table with the twins. The man should look ridiculous in that tiny little chair with his knees up to his chin. He looked perfectly at home, as if he'd had tea parties—or rather, hot chocolate parties—on a regular basis. Something like affection swept through her. "He's good with them."

Quinn glanced over her shoulder, sighed softly. There was sadness in the sound. When she turned around there was also the look of a protective big sister in her stance, something Hope would never have a chance to practice on Charity's behalf. Now she was sad.

"Walker has always had a knack with kids." Quinn's

eyes never left Hope's face. "Even before he marri—" she cleared her throat "—before he became an ER doctor."

Hope had questions. Unfortunately, Quinn had questions, as well, and didn't waste time voicing them. "What's going on between you and Walker?"

"It's complicated."

"Most things are when a woman shows up with two little girls that look like my brother, and every bit like my own daughters, save for a slight difference in hair color. So, I'm going to ask again, what's going on between you and Walker?"

Hope shifted from one foot to the other. She hadn't expected an interrogation. The Evans were proving kind, but also formidable. If they closed ranks on her...no. She wasn't going to go there just yet. "Your brother and I only met this morning."

All signs of patience disappeared, replaced with a slight stiffening of shoulders. The worried expression was back, as well. "I see."

"I don't think you do."

"I heard the girls call you Aunt Hope. Where's their mother?"

"Dead." The word came out hard and a little cold, a perfect companion to the emotion spreading through her heart. She'd lost all sense of polite behavior. Hope hadn't come to Thunder Ridge to be thrown on the defensive. She'd come because Charity could not.

As if understanding her pain, Quinn's expression softened. "I'm sorry for your loss."

Thrown off guard, again, she forced out a response through tight lips. "Thank you."

"I'm going to speak plainly, and I ask that you do the same."

Hope nodded.

"Is Walker..." Quinn let her words trail off, spun around, frowned at the sight of her brother laughing over something one of the twins just said. "I can't believe I'm asking you this, because it seems so out of character, and the timing is pretty close to impossible, but is Walker the father of those girls out there?"

"No."

Quinn's relief was palpable.

"Your brother Brent is their father."

"Walker Bartholomew Evans. A word, if you please. Now."

Walker met his sister's eyes. The look she leveled on him supplied all the information he needed. Quinn knew about Brent and the twins.

Setting down his mug, he told the girls, "Be right back," and then stood.

He passed Hope halfway across the shop. In that moment, when their eyes met and held, he knew. He knew, as sure as he knew his own name, that Hope Jeffries had come to Thunder Ridge with a plan firmly in place, one that would put them on opposite sides of a fight.

A shame, he thought. He possibly could have grown to like her. The thought felt like a betrayal to the woman he'd promised to love until death do us part.

"You told Quinn about Brent, your sister and the twins."

"She knows enough."

"How did she take the news?"

"About the same as you, with equal amounts of shock and a weird sort of acceptance." She eyed him thoughtfully. "Why is that? What aren't you telling me about your brother?"

"No idea what you mean," Walker hedged. No good would come from sharing too much information.

After shooting her a final glance, he joined his sister in the kitchen, then motioned her to follow him to her private office where they couldn't be overheard. An unnecessary precaution due to the high volume of noise, but Walker wasn't taking any chances. Brent deserved a chance to do the right thing before the gossip started.

Walker waited for Quinn to enter the room, then shut the door behind him.

"So," Quinn began. "Are we absolutely sure Brent is the father?"

"Pretty much." He rattled off the wedding date, followed up with the girls' birthday approximately nine months later. "He'll need to take a DNA test, but that'll prove more a formality. Hope has proof. I've seen it."

"Okay, okay." She blew out a breath. "Okay."

"This is a good thing, Quinn. The twins are amazing."

"Yeah, yeah, I know, of course. You're right. I just need a moment to process all of this." Drawing in a deep breath, she rubbed the back of her neck. "How long have you known?"

"For about—" he checked the time on his watch "—an hour and a half."

His answer seemed to shock her. "I'm confused. Why did Hope contact you?"

"It's complicated."

"Hmm." Quinn eyed him closely. "You're hiding something."

Walker quickly filled her in on what he knew. Which was, admittedly, not much. "I'll get the rest out of Hope this morning."

Quinn didn't seem to hear him. She was too busy tapping her fingertip on her chin and looking off into the distance. "We need to call a family meeting."

"Agreed." The siblings congregated at Quinn's every

Sunday afternoon following church. But Sunday was too many days away.

"I'll set it up for later tonight. Say, seven." Quinn pulled her cell phone from a pocket in her apron. "Will you be able to attend?" she asked without looking up from the screen.

"I'm off the next two nights."

"Excellent."

While she typed, Walker added, "I've reached out to Brent, twice. He hasn't replied."

"Not surprised."

Walker wasn't either. Regret was an uncomfortable emotion.

"I'll reach out, too." Quinn's fingers slowed. "Okay, done."

A second later, a ding indicated Walker had a new group text. He pulled out his phone, read the message. Typical Quinn. She'd been cryptic, but insistent. Emergency family meeting, 7:00 p.m., my house. No excuses except broken bones or death.

Responses came in at a rapid pace, ranging from I'll be there to What's up? To Casey's Are you kidding me right now? I have a hot date tonight!

Quinn answered: I said NO EXCUSES unless you are broken or dead. You will be both if you don't show up.

Walker snorted. "Way to tap into your softer side."

"That was my softer side." Grinning, she stuffed her phone into the back pocket of her jeans. "You should bring Hope and the twins. The girls can play with Sinclair and Skylar while we discuss next steps."

"That's the plan." When Walker returned to the main area of the shop, the girls were finished drinking their hot chocolate. "Ready to build a snowman?"

Kennedy clapped her hands. "Can he be as tall as you?"

"We might want to start with something a little more manageable."

"Okay, if you say so."

Walker grinned. Apparently, hot chocolate made little girls agreeable. Women too, because Hope dutifully followed them out of the shop without a single argument.

The twins launched into a popular children's song about building snowmen. Their voices rang with pure joy, if a bit off-key. Their enthusiasm was infectious, the kind of ease that came from childhood innocence and the resiliency of youth.

Walker couldn't deny wanting a little of that innocence, knowing he'd never be able to capture what he'd lost. Scripture spoke of having the faith of a child. Faith. Trust that the Lord was in control. Walker had once carried that in his heart. He'd cut himself off from personal relationships beyond family for so long he'd nearly forgotten how to feel much of anything beyond getting from one minute to the next.

Harper skipped beside him. Taking his hand, she asked, "Are we there yet?"

"Almost." He spoke to Hope over the child's head. "Quinn called a family meeting for tonight. She wants to tell the rest of our siblings about…you know. I'd like you to be there."

She nodded.

"The twins can play with Quinn's daughters while we all talk."

"Oh, I—" she went silent a moment "—I suppose that will be all right."

"Come on," Kennedy urged. "You're going too slow."

Seeing their destination at last, the twins rushed into the park, singing and laughing and kicking up snow.

Walker attempted to pick up his pace, but Hope stopped

him with a touch to his arm. "I'm not sure the girls have ever made a snowman before." She glanced toward them, worry creasing across her brow. "I don't know why they lied."

"They wanted to impress an adult. It's common with children their age, especially after suffering a traumatic loss."

"How do you know that?"

"My job is to diagnose. I can't do that if I don't listen to what patients tell me, and what they leave out." The girls called his name. He called back, "On my way."

Trotting over, he knelt beside them, then scooped up a handful of snow, packing, testing, rolling it around in his palms.

Kennedy leaned over his arm. "What are you doing?"

"Seeing what kind of snow we have to work with. Good news—" he rolled the ball around in his hand "—it's perfect."

He added more snow, kept packing until the tiny clump was perfectly round.

With the twins mimicking him, Walker kept adding snow to his. By the time the mound was too big to hold, the girls had given up on their attempts and were watching him with wide eyes.

"All right." He set the snowball on the ground. "Let's roll."

Chapter Five

Hope hung back, torn between joining the fun and simply watching Walker and the twins. The snowball that had once fit in his gloved palm quickly grew to the size of a large boulder.

Apparently, the man did know what he was doing.

The atmosphere among the trio was full of cheer, joyful even. Hope hadn't seen the twins this happy in months, maybe ever. She felt a slight relaxing of her body. Drawing in a slow, careful breath, she let the scent of pine trees and freshly fallen snow fill her nose.

Standing here, in what she guessed was the beating heart of Thunder Ridge, was like being wrapped in a festive Christmas present. Bows, garland, wreaths and ribbon dominated every available space. The gazebo nestled on the edge of the park also had tiny fairy lights and silver bells.

She spun in a circle, taking it all in, falling in love with the scene, the town. She slammed her eyes shut against the longing that spread through her. Christmas, family, how she missed them. But that made no sense. How could she miss something she never really had?

Opening her eyes, she shouted over the girls' laughter. "That is going to be one big snowman."

Walker gave her a pointed look. "You going to get over here and help?"

Hope took a step in his direction, paused. It wasn't that she didn't want to join the fun. It was that she didn't know how. She'd spent her life watching from the sidelines, alone and unnoticed. She was a thinker. Losing herself in her head had become comfortable, normal, safe, a barrier between her and the unknown world.

"You know—" Walker made a grand show of struggling under the weight of the now insanely large snowball "—this would go smoother with an extra pair of hands."

"On my way."

She tugged on her gloves and took a step. But when she heard a dog barking, she stopped cold.

An enormous, absolutely gorgeous Saint Bernard came into view. The excited animal danced at the feet of his owner, a tall man dressed in dark-washed jeans and a blue ski jacket. A camera with a large lens hung from his neck. He moved with long, languid strides, the pace slow and lazy, as if he had nowhere special to be. Hope thought she recognized him but needed a closer look to be certain.

Walker paused mid-roll, and then pointed to the newcomers. "Stop right there."

Man and dog ignored him.

"I mean it." Walker glared at the other man. "Control your beast."

Said beast performed a high-kick dance in place, its face full of goofy dog joy.

"My girl is harmless as they come, aren't you, baby?" The man kissed the dog's head, then aimed a narrow-eyed glance at the emerging snowman. "And you're doing that all wrong. I taught you better. Put your shoulders into it."

"Stay back, McCoy." Walker lifted his palm in the air. "Leave this to the experts."

"Since you asked so nicely." The dog owner—McCoy— let the excited animal off her leash.

She did two fast spins, impressive considering her size, and then sped across the park, clumps of snow flying in her wake. Walker intercepted the animal before she got near the twins. The dog greeted him with a doggy dance and loud, happy barks.

"There she is. There's my sweet girl." Walker reached down and framed the dog's face in his hands. "When you gonna leave your mean owner and come live with me?"

The Saint Bernard barked at him.

"I know we'll be very happy together." He kissed the animal on the snout.

Not to be outdone, the dog reared up on her hind legs, planted her large paws on his shoulders and slurped her big pink tongue across his face.

He laughed. "Yuck."

She repeated the public display of affection.

"Yeah, yeah, I love you, too. Now get off me, you big doofus." He calmed the dog down with soft, soothing words and gentle strokes. "Come meet my friends."

Hope had a moment of sheer terror when he started guiding the dog toward the twins. But the dog followed Walker at a slow, sedate pace, behaving more like a pampered house cat than a dog the size of a small horse.

Walker told the animal to drop. She immediately did as commanded, grinning up at him as if he were her long lost love.

Walker motioned the twins closer. They were clearly nervous, but also filled with anticipation. Hope knew the feeling. She'd always wanted a dog, the bigger and sloppier the better. It hadn't been possible. A dog required a yard, which came with a house, which meant her father would have had to stay in the States and care for his daughters.

He'd chosen mission work abroad over his family.

That memory had no place here. So, Hope focused on watching Walker show the twins how to pet the dog. "You want to follow the direction her fur grows. Like this. Yes, perfect, that's it. Good girl, Bertha," he praised the dog for sitting still. "Try again, Harper. Excellent. Now you, Kennedy."

Caught up in the sweet moment, Hope laid a hand on her heart. She drew in a tight breath, and then sighed it back out. Thoughts of "what if" ran through her mind.

Captured by the possibility, she forgot that Bertha came with an owner. "Hey," he said, approaching her.

Hope started. "Oh, sorry. I…" She concentrated on calming her breath. "Hello. I didn't see you standing there."

"I can be stealthy." The smile he gave her brought back the image of the Evans siblings in the silver picture frame.

"You're Walker's brother. The…artist?"

"Sculptor, actually. And photographer." He pointed to the camera slung around his neck.

"I remember now. Your name is McCoy."

"That's me."

Three Evans siblings down, two to go. No, make that three if she counted Brent.

"And now I'm feeling as if I missed the opening of a Broncos game and we're deep in the second quarter. You are…?"

"I'm Hope. Hope Jeffries."

"Well, Hope. Hope Jeffries. Pleased to meet you."

He stuck out his hand, a slightly flirty smile on his lips. He had the Evanses' stunning good looks, but unlike when

Walker looked at her like that, she felt nothing. No hitch in her breathing. No ping in her heart.

Realizing he was waiting for her to take his hand, she pressed her palm against his, and again, no spark, no visceral response like the first time she'd touched Walker's hand. Or every other time they connected physically. A brush of fingers, a touch to her arm.

She pulled free of McCoy's grip.

He shifted his stance slightly and glanced over at the scene playing out with Walker, Bertha and the twins. After a moment, he turned back and zeroed in on Hope's face. "You're a friend of Walker's?"

"Not really," she admitted, then gave him what was becoming her standard line. "We just met this morning."

"He seems pretty friendly with your...daughters?" He asked the question in the same tentative way she'd asked about his profession.

She answered him with equal brevity. "Nieces."

"Ah."

Silence fell over them. She tried not to fidget or fill the awkward moment with words. Just as well. McCoy's attention remained glued to his brother and the twins.

He angled his head, contemplated the scene another moment, then turned back to Hope. "You know, when I first entered the park, I thought Walker was playing with my nieces."

"I—I'm sorry, did you call Harper and Kennedy your nieces?"

How did he know? Wow, Quinn worked fast. She must have contacted her siblings as soon as Hope left her office.

"I'm not talking about *your* nieces. But mine. Sinclair and Skylar are bigger than your girls, probably because they're older. Maybe. I don't know much about kids, which could explain why I think they all look alike." He laughed, sobered a second later, narrowed his eyes. "Maybe…"

Hope opened her mouth, shut it. She didn't know how to respond to McCoy's obvious confusion. Of course the two sets of twins looked alike. They were cousins. That wasn't something she could just blurt out. Or could she?

McCoy didn't seem to notice her silent battle. "Speaking of Quinn, that reminds me, she sent me a text this morning. I ignored it." He shrugged. "She's always sending texts. We call her the social chairman of the family."

Hope laughed.

"Excuse me a minute." He pulled out his phone, thumbed it to life and then studied the screen. "Huh."

He tapped a quick reply, then returned the phone to his back pocket. His eyebrows slammed together. "Would you look at that, Walker is actually smiling."

Hope followed the direction of his gaze. Walker was, indeed, smiling. Why would that be such a shock?

With a quick, effortless move, McCoy whipped the camera up to his face. A series of clicks followed, then several more. Hope studied the scene, wondering what he was capturing.

And then she knew. Walker and the twins.

Her heart pinged. This wasn't the first time she'd felt the sensation. She didn't like it any more now than she had the first time.

Walker had dropped to his knees, laughing. Kennedy clung to his back like a koala bear. Harper was on the ground still petting Bertha with slow, careful strokes.

The three of them looked like a family, a happy, functional, normal family. And McCoy Evans was capturing the moment with his camera.

He continued clicking away, completely unaware of

how Hope was reacting. She could feel the twins slipping away with each shutter of the camera.

What have I done? She should have never brought Harper and Kennedy to Thunder Ridge with her. She should have made the trip alone.

Too late.

No. No, it wasn't. Brent could deny they were his daughters. Hope could still win custody.

But would Walker and his siblings happily hand them over to her without a fight? Possibly, maybe…but not likely.

By the time McCoy lowered the camera, she was in a full panic.

"As much as I've enjoyed meeting you, I have an appointment in—" he glanced at the chunky black watch on his wrist "—five minutes ago. Sorry, gotta go."

McCoy whistled one long shrill note through his fingertips. Bertha hopped to her feet, swung away from Harper without actually touching the child, then trotted over to her master.

"Good girl." McCoy clicked the leash to the dog's harness and said to Hope, "See you around."

She watched man and dog saunter away.

She glanced back at Walker, allowing herself one, long look into his piercing blue eyes, then felt her own narrow. The man was working a sizeable handful of snow into a tidy little ball.

"You better put that snowball down," Hope warned, hands on hips.

His grin flashed, quick and devastating. "Are you questioning my motives, Ms. Jeffries?"

She looked frantically around for shelter. She found and discarded several options. Then. There. Perfect. Inching toward the bushy pine tree, she picked up speed when

Walker mimicked the windup of a professional baseball pitcher.

The snowball sailed through the air in a wide, looping arc. And...smack!

"Hey!" She brushed the snow off her right shoulder. "You, Dr. Evans, just crossed a line."

He rubbed his hands together. "Now we're talking."

Walker couldn't remember having this much fun in years.

He didn't let his mind go any further than that. Instead, he concentrated on watching Hope's retreat behind a snow-covered pine tree.

"You can run, Hope Jeffries, but you can't hide."

She spewed out a muffled threat that included a bunch of nonsense and a reference to a former softball career in high school.

Laughing, he formed his next frosty weapon with the quick, sure hands of a man who'd won his share of snow-ball fights. Unbeknownst to his opponent, Walker had the patience of a younger brother in a large family bent on teaching him the pecking order. His siblings had under-estimated him. And so, too, had Hope. When Walker Evans set his mind on something, he had the tenacity of a bulldog with a meaty bone.

"You gonna come out anytime this year?"

She made the mistake of peaking around the tree. He fired. And missed.

"You have no idea who you're up against." Since she made the ridiculous threat from behind a tree large enough to hide a small SUV, Walker took his time reloading.

A mistake in judgment. Hope pelted him in the chest with three snowballs. "Impressive aim," he called out.

"I told you I pitched for my high school softball team."

Okay, then.

The twins realized they were missing out on the fun. Walker immediately claimed them for his team. "You make the snowballs," he suggested. "I'll throw them."

Proving to be excellent recruits, the girls got to straight work.

"Hey," Hope called out from behind the tree. "That's three against one."

"Yeah, yeah, a tiny little insignificant detail." Nevertheless, in the spirit of fair play, Walker switched jobs with the girls.

Playing along, Hope came out from behind the tree to give then an easier target. Harper and Kennedy attacked, mostly missing, but Walker praised them for their effort. As did Hope.

She came closer, closer, tossing a snowball from one hand to the other. The twins screeched, running for shelter behind Walker. He opened his mouth to call a truce, but Hope was having none of it. Smiling sweetly, she lifted onto her toes, came eye to eye with him, then smashed the snowball in his face.

He blinked in surprise. Torn between laughing and taking revenge, he settled on roping his arms around her waist and pulling her against him.

"What are you doing?"

Blinking snow out of his eyes, he gave the twins a sidelong glance. "Who wants to learn how to make a snow angel?"

"Me!" they screamed in unison.

"You're in luck. Your aunt has agreed to demonstrate the proper technique." Hooking his foot around the back of her knees, he dumped her gently atop the snow-covered ground.

Flat on her back, she glared. "You are not a nice man."

"Many people in town would disagree."

The twins leaned over her. Harper spoke for the duo. "She's not moving." She swung her gaze up to Walker. "Is she supposed to just lay there like that?"

"She's supposed to move her arms and legs, up and down, in and out, kind of like horizontal jumping jacks."

"I know how to make a snow angel." Hope growled at him. She actually growled. The woman made him smile. It had been a long time since Walker had smiled so much.

"We're waiting."

"Fine." Lips pressed tightly together, she went through the motions, finishing up by pressing her head back into the snow.

"Well done," he praised, earning him another growl.

Laughing, he reached out and waited for Hope to accept his assistance.

Slowly, clearly reluctant, she placed her hands in his. He yanked her up, catching her against him before her feet touched the ground.

The past melted away and his mind went blank but for the woman in his arms. He drew in a sharp breath, his heart beating wildly in his chest.

"My turn," Kennedy declared, the interruption restoring his equilibrium.

A little mournfully, Walker set Hope on the ground, then turned to the bouncing child beside him. "Let's find a clean spot in the snow."

He picked up Kennedy, dumped her gently in the snow and said, "Don't move." Then he repeated the process with her sister. "Okay, go!"

They went a little crazy, but got the job done. In silent agreement, he and Hope pulled the girls to their feet. Kennedy spun around and grinned at him. "That was fun."

Her eyes shone from beneath her dark winged eyebrows, another undeniable Evans trait. Was this what his child would have looked like, Walker wondered? Would she have been this pretty, this sweet and innocent? His knees buckled under the onslaught of emotion that washed over him. Some old and familiar, others fresh and almost optimistic.

It was as if a switch had been flipped in his mind. He hovered in a moment between past and present. His limbs suddenly felt heavy, the kind of weight that came after a long slumber.

"Can we finish the snowman now?"

He had to look away before answering. He swallowed, twice, then managed to say, "Let's do this."

Eyes burning, he took off toward the half-finished snowman. The twins trotted alongside him. Although she moved at a slower pace, Hope followed along, too.

Walker watched her out of the corner of his eye. He couldn't stop thinking about her in his arms. They'd fit nicely together, pretty close to perfectly, her head the exact height for him to rest his chin at the crown. His hands itched to pull her close again, to see if she still smelled of lavender and the great outdoors.

Needing a moment to calm his pulse, he smoothed his hand over the snowman's lower body. For the next ten minutes, Walker focused on the mechanics of stacking three snowballs on top of one another, largest to smallest, while Hope and the twins packed snow between the gaps.

"Nicely done," he said, stepping back to eye the finished product.

Kennedy wasn't even a little impressed. "He doesn't look right."

"That's because he's not finished yet. Hang tight." Walker retrieved the gym bag he'd brought alone. He pulled out a baseball cap, a blue bandana and a few other items he'd gathered from the hospital's break room.

The twins brought the snowman to life.

"Best snowman ever," Hope declared.

"He does have something special," Walker agreed.

The twins launched into an impromptu happy dance that was about as graceful as Bertha's had been earlier, and just as infectious. Walker watched with his heart in his throat. *Brent has lost so much time with them.*

He vowed to redouble his efforts to get in touch with his brother.

Hope met Walker's gaze over the twirling, spinning girls. Something came into her smile. Gratitude. Relief. Fear. And then, determination. A woman preparing for a fight.

"We've monopolized your morning long enough," she said, her voice full of apology and something else, something that put distance between them. He would know. It was a tactic he used often enough.

"I'm good." Granted, he was running on adrenaline at this point, but he wasn't sorry for it. He could sleep next week.

"You're exhausted. Let's go, girls. We need to let Dr. Evans get on with his day."

The arguments began at once.

The twins' reluctance to leave his company gave Walker a kick in the gut. As did Hope's use of his formal title. He wasn't Dr. Evans. He was Uncle Walker.

Now wasn't the time to make that distinction. But soon.

"You'll see Dr. Evans later tonight. Say goodbye."

"Please, call me Dr. Walker," he told the girls, which earned him two identical grins and would make the transition to Uncle Walker much easier.

"But we don't want to say goodbye, Dr. Walker," Harper whined. "We're still having fun."

Me, too, Walker thought, only half shocked at this point by the revelation. He'd flown solo for years and been just fine with that. Or at least resolute. In a matter of hours, the twins had broken through his defenses. He wasn't sorry for it.

No matter what Brent had done to their mother, or what she'd done to him, the twins were family. Harper and Kennedy deserved to know their aunts and uncles and cousins. They also deserved to know their father.

Hope had custody of the girls, for now. Could she make a case against Brent? Without more information, Walker simply didn't know.

He needed to speak with Brent.

If his brother didn't want to be a part of his daughters' lives—and that was a big if—Walker would work with Hope to formulate a plan for the future.

Would she play nice?

Something cold moved through him, wrapping around his heart, redoubling his resolve. If Hope Jeffries had come for a fight, she would get one. "I need your contact information."

She flinched at his abrupt tone. "You think I'm going to run."

He said nothing.

"I came all this way. I'm not going to run now."

Still saying nothing, he held her gaze.

"Fine." She pushed out a sharp breath. "Give me your phone."

He tugged his cell out of his back pocket. She sent herself a quick text from his phone so he would have her information.

Walker studied the screen before tucking the phone

back into his pocket and saying, "I don't recognize your area code."

She lifted a shoulder. "The girls and I live on the East Coast."

Though not unexpected, her vague response put him on guard. She'd come halfway across the country to introduce the girls to their father out of the goodness of her heart? No, there was more to it. Either she would tell him, or Walker would find out on his own. "Where are you staying in town?"

"At the Grand Palace Hotel on Main Street."

"The meeting at Quinn's is set for seven o'clock tonight. I'll pick you all up at six thirty."

"I'll drive us to your sister's house."

Walker started to argue, then thought better of it. He couldn't ask Hope to trust him, if he didn't do the same.

"Suit yourself." He gave her Quinn's address, then placed his hands on his knees. "See you later, girls."

They jumped into his arms. As he held them close, his heart swelled with love—so fast, so unexpected. He pulled in a hard breath. There was a ragged quality to the sound that made him shut his eyes. The moment passed, and he let them wiggle free.

Hope said her own goodbye with a little too much enthusiasm. Which wasn't suspicious at all.

Once she and the twins were out of earshot, Walker retrieved his cell phone again. He called his attorney's private number. Mitchell St. James, a friend since middle school, answered with a smile in his voice. "Hey, Walker, what's up?"

"We need to talk, Mitch."

A pause. Then, "You got a legal problem?"

"Maybe, yeah. I think I do."

"Too bad." A rustle of papers filled the next few seconds. "I have an opening tomorrow at two thirty."

Tomorrow. Walker experienced a slight dropping sensation in his stomach. Although he'd rather meet with Mitch today, he knew the attorney was a busy man. Which meant he probably had to switch a few things around to fit Walker in so quickly.

"That works," he said into the phone. "See you then."

Chapter Six

Back at the hotel, Hope helped the girls out of their coats. Kennedy yawned. Harper copied her. Despite their exhaustion, neither twin could stop talking about their "new friend" Dr. Walker, or the big dog with the super soft fur.

"Yes," Hope agreed with her heart in her throat. "Bertha was very pretty."

"Can we get a dog just like her?" Kennedy asked around another yawn.

Hope murmured a noncommittal answer, then suggested, "What do you say we take a nap?"

Half-hearted arguments followed, accompanied with another round of yawns that proved just how tired they were.

"That settles it." A smile tugged at Hope's lips as she tucked them in the queen-size bed the two had shared the night before.

Covers up to her chin, Kennedy looked up at Hope with an expectant, wide-eyed expression. "When will we see Dr. Walker again?"

Hope answered the question as she had every other time the child had asked. "Later tonight."

"Good." Another yawn. "I like him."

Hope tried not to sigh. Of course the child liked Walker. He'd been spontaneous and easy with the girls, something that had never come naturally to Hope. It wasn't that she didn't try. She simply didn't know how. Even as a child, she'd been more reserved than other kids, which had carried over into adulthood.

From the moment Charity had arrived on her doorstep, Hope had been out of her element with the twins. Dr. Stephens had suggested she let the relationship grow organically. But Hope wasn't one to sit around and wait. She'd read every article and book about child development she could find. She'd attended workshops, asked advice from day care workers and had sought out experts at her university.

She'd also prayed. A lot. She'd searched the Bible for direction, as well. She found the most concrete advice in Proverbs, especially Proverbs 22, which said *Train up a child in the way he should go: and when he is old, he will not depart from it.*

With that in mind, Hope had taken the twins to church every Sunday. Yet here she was, months after assuming sole custody and she was still searching for that relaxed sense of play that had come so easily to Walker.

Oh, Charity, I wish you'd have told me more about the man you'd married. Did you know he came from a large, extended family? Did he really abandon you?

There was so much left unsaid.

Time had run out for her and her sister. She would do better with her nieces. If they wanted a dog, she would find a way to get them a dog. It would mean moving out of her apartment in the city sooner than she'd planned. Finding a larger space near the university wouldn't be easy, as her initial inquiries had proved. Now she would have to broaden her search to include a pet. This was assuming she was able to keep guardianship.

Brent Evans was the unknown factor in the equation. *Solve for X*, she told herself, but she still came up empty.

Hope fired up her laptop and typed *Doctors Without Borders* into the search program. After a quick click through the various pages on their website, she found a personal diary penned by a doctor who'd caught Ebola on one of his tours. It was a pretty harrowing account.

Her heart filled with fear, for Brent, for the possibility that the twins could lose their father before they ever met him.

Her phone vibrated on the desk beside her. Hand shaking, she picked up the device and took a look at the caller ID. The name on the screen did nothing to erase her unease. Stepping out into the hallway, she pressed on the flashing green icon. "Dr. Evans?"

"Walker."

"Walker," she corrected. "Is everything all right? Have you heard from your brother?"

"Not yet."

Hope thought about the account of the Ebola outbreak she'd just read. "Is his silence something we should be worried about?"

"Not necessarily. It's only been a few hours, and the workday isn't over yet."

"That makes sense." Her research had barely skimmed the surface. The Doctors Without Borders website showed pictures from rural locales where regular medical equipment and modern sanitation were limited. But there were also photographs of doctors working with advanced technology. "What kind of physician did you say your brother was?"

"I didn't. He's an anesthesiologist."

That meant he worked in operating rooms with modern equipment. A portion of her concern evaporated. "I assume there's a reason for your call?"

"There is. What kind of pizza do the twins like?"

"You want to know their pizza preferences?" She couldn't explain why this surprised her, but it did. It seemed everyday and normal.

"Quinn put me in charge of providing dinner for tonight's gathering. I don't know how much your background check revealed, but if it came back saying I am a culinary genius, it was dead wrong."

His reference to her preparation for their first meeting—she refused to call it a background check—brought a flush to her cheeks. "They like cheese pizza."

"Seriously? Not pepperoni? Every kid I know likes pepperoni."

"Not Harper and Kennedy." Finally, there was something she knew about the twins no one else did. It was petty of her but, in that moment, she needed the feeling of control.

"What about you? What kind of pizza do you like?"

She sighed. There had been enough evasion and avoidance of direct answers for one day. "Pepperoni."

His soft chuckle did strange, warm things to her insides. She did not like the sensation, not one, tiny, little bit.

"Now that we've settled that," he said, clearly amused. "Let's discuss the rest of the evening."

"Good idea."

They agreed to let Hope do most of the talking. Walker suggested she keep the mistaken identity piece of her story to herself. "I'm not comfortable with that," she said. "Besides, won't your siblings notice the discrepancy on the marriage certificate and put two and two together?"

"Maybe, maybe not. Look, Hope, I'm not asking you

to lie. I'm merely suggesting you gloss over the more unpleasant portion of the story. Your mistake is not important."

She disagreed. Brent had forged his brother's signature. It stood to reason Hope would have come after the wrong man. Clearly, Walker was trying to prevent her from any further embarrassment. Which was really sweet, but totally unnecessary. Hope took a different approach. "Weren't you the one who said a half-truth is a whole lie?"

"Look at you, using my own words against me. I bet you're a tough one in the classroom."

"You…" She wobbled unsteadily and had to brace a hand on the wall to regain her balance. "You know I'm a professor?"

"I did a Google search, *Dr.* Jeffries. You have a PhD in Economics and another in Mathematics, with an emphasis in Statistics. You share your considerable knowledge with both undergraduate and graduate students at Columbia University in New York City. I'm impressed."

There went her insides, turning all soft and warm again. "Don't be. I just like school."

"Apparently." His voice held admiration.

"Was there anything else?"

"Nope. We're done." He disconnected the call before she could respond.

Staring at the blank screen, Hope stepped back into her hotel room and moved closer to the edge of the bed where the twins slept. They looked so peaceful. They'd suffered so much upheaval in their short lives. She wanted to provide them with stability.

She'd dropped them in the middle of more chaos, instead.

Filled with regret, Hope moved to the window and glanced out over Main Street. Christmas had exploded on the streets of Thunder Ridge. What child wouldn't love living here?

Deep-rooted longing filled her. Out of necessity, Hope had learned to rely solely on herself. As a kid, she'd become an island in a sea of rotating homes and faces, good people helping out their beloved, grieving pastor. They'd opened their homes to Hope and Charity, but only temporarily and never for longer than a year, maybe two. Always a new beginning that never lasted.

The twins would not experience that level of uncertainty. They would always have Hope. She would not be pushed out of their lives.

Time to put Plan B in place.

She went back to her computer and composed an email to her department chair. Then she began another Google search, this one to secure her future with the twins.

From his vantage point on the porch, Walker watched Hope's rental car turn into the drive. He waited until she pulled to a stop behind McCoy's Jeep before leaving his perch. He crossed the distance at a deliberately casual pace. He hated the idea of Hope and the twins staying in a sterile hotel room. That was a conversation for another time.

The twins spotted him from the back seat. They waved frantically. He returned the gesture, his heart kicking against his ribs as they scrambled out of the car. Hope had dressed them in their red coats and jaunty caps again. She herself had donned fancier outerwear than what she'd worn this afternoon. This one was made from green wool that matched the color of her eyes.

She'd left her hair free so that it hung in long, unruly waves past her shoulders. As was her habit, she absently hooked a few curling strands behind her ear. The gesture sent his gut rolling into a tight knot.

The masculine interest felt foreign. It made him itchy, like his skin didn't fit quite right. Walker shouldn't be this intrigued by a woman, by any woman, but especially not one he could be facing in a courtroom in the near future.

Harper and Kennedy called out to him, their grins wide and full of joy. Standing next to their aunt, the trio looked like they were ready for a holiday photo shoot and, despite knowing the danger of opening his mind to the possibility, Walker envisioned a different future for himself. Something more than returning to an empty house after a long shift in the ER.

He pushed the image aside. "Here you are, the three prettiest ladies in town."

The girls giggled.

Hope remained silent.

"I like it here," Kennedy said, gaping at the house behind Walker. "It's so pretty."

Walker glanced briefly over his shoulder, considering the house from an outsider's perspective. "My sister dresses up her home for all the holidays, but Christmas is her very special favorite."

"What other holidays?" Hope asked, her eyes nearly as wide as the twins as she gazed at the house.

"All the big ones. Valentine's Day, St. Patrick's Day, Easter, Fourth of July, Founder's Day, Oktoberfest, Thanksgiving and…" He took a breath. "I think I missed a few."

"So many?" Hope's eyes were slightly misty as she spoke. Her emotional reaction seemed to hold a kind of longing that didn't fit with her polished facade.

Walker wished he knew more about her. His internet search had been short due to time constraints. He'd found her curriculum vitae from two years ago, but she wasn't on any social media. He'd located a few images of her at various black-tie events related to the university where she worked, but not much else.

"This house is the bestest of all the others we passed," Harper said, her voice filled with little-girl awe.

Walker attempted to take in the house with fresh eyes. Sitting on five acres of prime Colorado real estate, the rambling two-story house was nestled on the banks of Thunder Ridge Lake and had the quintessential wrap-around porch. Quinn had decorated the exterior tastefully, but with what Walker considered a heavy hand.

Thousands of white twinkling lights—*not* an exaggeration—hung from every roofline and easement. Illuminated wire reindeer fed on a blanket of snow. And that was only the beginning. "The inside is just as amazing as the outside."

"I can't imagine." Walker heard the faint wonder in Hope's voice as she pulled out her cell phone and took a photo, then several more. "You're fortunate to be a part of all this."

She swept her hand in the general vicinity of the house. Once again, he regretted not digging deeper into Hope's past. His need for information hadn't been strong enough for him to invade her privacy any further. Walker hoped he hadn't made a mistake. Two little girls' futures depended on him knowing everything he could about their aunt.

Had she been given the love and security that came from strong family ties? Hope could prove herself a woman who didn't value family. He dismissed the thought. Her devotion to the twins was too strong, too genuine.

The front door swung open and the entirety of his family spilled out onto the porch, including dogs and a cat

Walker had never seen before tonight. "Looks like the gang's all here."

"I...oh, my." Hope fell back a step. "I knew there were a lot of you. I just didn't realize there were *so many* of you."

Walker smiled to himself. Rachel had been equally blown away by the sheer number of Walker's family members. She'd eventually gotten used to it, but it had been touch and go for a while. They'd even discussed moving away, which had been a source of contention between them.

The thought felt like a betrayal to his wife's memory.

He eyed the Evans clan, which included two of his three brothers, Quinn's husband, Grant, both sisters and a collection of mangy dogs running around his twin nieces, Bertha leading the pack. The only animal missing was Quinn's dog, Daisy, a pug-beagle mix that had recently given birth to a litter of puppies. "We're pretty overwhelming at first. But we don't bite."

"If you say so."

He gave Hope's hand a reassuring squeeze, then turned to the twins. They were clutching onto Hope with wide, uncertain eyes. Their inherent shyness had kicked in. Walker decided to ease the next few moments for them, and their aunt. "Wait here."

Leaving the twins with Hope, he hustled toward the porch.

Quinn met him at the bottom of the steps. "What's up?"

"The welcome committee is a bit too much for the twins."

Quinn glanced over her shoulder. "I didn't think. I was just so excited to see them again."

"I understand." Walker had felt the same way. "How about we hold off on the introductions until after the four of us enter the house?"

"Good idea." Quinn started ushering everyone inside. Skylar and Sinclair weren't as agreeable to the change of plans as the rest of the family. "But we want to meet Walker's friends now."

He breathed a sigh of relief, silently thanking Quinn for holding off telling the family too much about the twins.

"You'll get to meet the girls soon," their father said, glancing at Walker, who gave him a short nod.

Quinn picked up the conversation from there. "Let's think of a way to entertain the twins while we wait for the pizza to arrive?"

Two little faces scrunched in concentration.

"We could show them the puppies," Skylar suggested.

"And maybe we can put pretty ribbons on them," Sinclair added. "You know, dress them up a little."

"I have just the thing in my bag." His sister Remy, the family's resident veterinarian, said. "Come on, I'll show you."

Remy and Quinn led the twins inside the house.

Grant followed a step behind the women, Casey one step behind him, his matching pair of English bulldogs hard on his heels. When McCoy attempted to bring up the rear, his hand on Bertha's harness, Walker stopped him. "Hold up. Can I borrow your dog?"

McCoy's brows went up.

"The twins like her."

"Yeah, sure." He patted the animal on her head. "Be a good girl."

Bertha gave him an insulted doggie glare, as if saying she was always a good girl.

To his relief, the dog proved the perfect transition from car to porch. The twins were still petting Bertha when Quinn popped out of the house with her mom-smile in place. "Hello, girls. I see you like dogs."

They nodded.

"Do I have a treat for you." She reached out to them. They took her hands without hesitation.

Quinn paused at the front door and captured Hope's attention. Walker glanced at her, as well. Everything in her seemed a little deflated. As if reading her trepidation, Quinn smiled softly. "Our dog just had puppies."

The girls' squeals of delight drowned out Hope's response. Walker didn't need to hear her words to interpret the signs of defeat in her downcast eyes and slumped shoulders.

Clearly, he and his siblings had won this round. They were one step closer to bringing Harper and Kennedy into the family fold.

This was what Walker wanted.

They why did he feel like a world-class heel?

Because the twins were also a part of Hope's family. Impulsively, he reached for her hand then thought better of it. "Ready to head inside?"

She heaved a sigh. "Ready as I'll ever be."

Chapter Seven

Hope followed Walker inside the most perfect home she'd ever seen. Not magazine cover–worthy, but in a welcoming, come-inside-and-relax sort of way. She wanted to drink it all in at once. Her arms suddenly felt limp and her feet turned into heavy, clumsy blocks. She tried to focus on her surroundings, but she didn't know where to look first.

The house was at least a century old, probably built by some mining baron during the gold rush. The original woodwork gleamed, proving it had been given great care through the years. The scent of lemon wax and freshly baked cookies reminded Hope of her favorite temporary home. Mrs. McClain had been older, sweet and patient, and had taught Hope how to cook.

Quinn had decorated the interior of her home with as much abandon as she'd applied to the exterior. Crimson and gold dominated. Poinsettias lined the entryway and the sweeping stairwell that led to the top floor. Bowls filled with ornaments sat on end tables, garland hung on the doorways. And was that…mistletoe? She would make sure to steer clear of that.

"The others will already be in the kitchen," Walker told

her, his voice distant, as if he was speaking at her through a wall of water. "This way."

He led the way down a hallway lined with an assortment of family pictures. Hope counted three Christmas trees along the way. Two of them carried the red-and-gold theme. But the tree standing in the corner of what looked like a children's playroom was decorated with less attention to order. A kids' tree. Hope nearly stumbled, wishing for something she'd never had.

Walker seemed to notice her mood change. He took her hand, his hold firm and supportive and somehow exactly right. "It's going to be okay."

The soothing words filled her in a rush and what had been a terrible moment was shoved into the past, already forgotten. "You better be right."

"I am." The words were spoken with such confidence, and without an ounce of arrogance, that Hope found herself smiling.

In the next instant, they were entering the kitchen. It was another large, homey space with granite counters, shaker cupboards and a backsplash of white subway tiles. The scent of baking cookies hung in the air.

Hope barely had a chance to take it all in before Walker began the introductions. "You've already met Quinn. And my brother McCoy. This is Casey."

The man nodded. He had the Evans eyes, but his hair was two shades lighter than Walker's.

Walker introduced Quinn's husband next. Grant Holloway looked every bit the high school principal he was, from the tortoiseshell glasses, khaki pants and polished brown shoes to the blue shirt under a dark brown argyle sweater vest.

The final person in the room introduced herself. "I'm

Remy, the youngest in this massive brood. And before you say anything, I know what you're thinking."

Hope doubted that very much.

"You're thinking, isn't Remy usually a boy's name? Well, not necessarily. In my case, Remy is short for Reims, aka my mother's favorite city in France. And…" She shook her head, laughing softly. "That was probably way more information than you wanted to know about me."

Hope attempted a smile at the self-deprecating remark but came up short.

It's over, she thought with bitter grief.

By sheer numbers, the odds were in the Evans family's favor. If they chose to form a united front, Hope was doomed. She'd known coming to Colorado had been a risk, but now that she was confronted with the reality of this big, large, tight-knit family, she felt like a David up against a formidable Goliath.

"Hey now, there's no need to look so deflated." As if to prove they were allies rather than enemies, Quinn slid her arm through Hope's and said, "We're all on the same side here."

Bold words, but Hope could feel the twins slipping away. "And what side is that?"

"Your nieces. Or rather—" she pitched her voice for Hope's ears only "—*our* nieces. We're in this together."

Walker had uttered similar words.

"Anyone gonna tell us why we're here?" McCoy glanced from Hope to Walker to Quinn, then back to Walker. "And why those little girls look so much like you?"

"I'll let Hope explain."

Extricating herself from Quinn's hold, Hope began at what she considered the beginning. "I met Harper and Kennedy ten months ago when my sister, Charity, their mother, showed up on my doorstep out of the blue. I had no idea of their existence before that day."

"Wait." Remy pushed away from the counter she'd been leaning against. "You didn't know your own sister had given birth?"

"I'm sorry to say, no." Hope sighed. "We were estranged."

"That's rough." Remy looked around the room, held a few gazes, before zeroing in on Walker. "Siblings should be able to work through their differences, wouldn't you agree?"

"Let her finish the story. Go on, Hope. Continue," Walker said.

Not quite understanding the undercurrents between brother and sister, she kept to the basics. She glossed over the details of Charity's decline in favor of focusing on what she knew about the Las Vegas wedding and the twins' birth a little over nine months later.

"I found these two items in my sister's belongings just before her death." Hope passed around the marriage certificate and wedding photo. "When I confronted Charity, she admitted that the man in the photograph was the twins' father."

Silence fell over the room as one by one the Evanses took turns studying the marriage certificate then the picture. McCoy was the first to notice the discrepancy. "Hold up. The name on the marriage certificate says Walker Bartholomew Evans, but—" McCoy snatched the photograph out of Casey's hand "—that's Brent in the photo."

Casey snatched the picture back, studied it a moment and then shook his head. "Oh, man. That's definitely Brent. And the woman looks like—" he zeroed on Hope "—you?"

"My identical twin."

Remy took the picture next. She already had hold of the marriage certificate. "What was he thinking signing Walker's name instead of his own?"

"I have a good idea," Walker said with a wry twist of his lips. "As I'm sure the rest of you do, too."

Six heads bobbed up and down.

Hope had no time to wonder what that meant. Walker was speaking again. "Only Brent can explain what was truly going on in his head at the time."

"So, question." Leaning back against the counter, Remy captured Hope's gaze. "If Brent led your sister to believe he was Walker, whose name is on the twins' birth certificates?"

Heat spread through Hope. There it was. The question she'd been dreading. She was about to lose the bargaining chip she had if this went to court. Hope had managed to convince herself she could keep the information to herself.

But now, with six pairs of eyes on her, she knew she couldn't withhold the truth any longer. "Charity didn't provide the father's name on the birth certificate."

"She left it blank?" Remy asked.

Hope nodded, feeling the same draining away of energy she did every time she looked at the documents. She expected an interrogation from Walker, but he only looked at her with a curious sort of silence, as if he was trying to figure out her angle.

"Is there any doubt Brent is the father?" This, from McCoy.

How she wished she could say yes. She rattled off the twins' birthdays, then after they did the math added, "You've seen them. What do you think?"

"I think I have a pair of adorable nieces," Remy said. The others agreed with equal wonder and, to Hope's sorrow, enthusiasm. This was not the reaction of a family that would just hand them over to a woman from New York.

"Has anyone attempted to contact Brent?"

"I've reached out several times," Walker said. "So has Quinn. He's not responding."

McCoy shook his head. "Let's see if he'll answer me."

"Or me," Remy said.

Cell phones appeared in rapid succession. Texts were sent. Calls were made, all of which went straight to voice mail.

While the siblings concentrated on their individual devices, Quinn pulled Hope away from the others. "Something's been bothering me all afternoon."

Hope flinched. "Go on."

"There's no way you could have known that was Brent in the picture. That means you thought Walker was the twins' father."

Heat rushed through Hope. "I did, yes."

Quinn's expression softened. "Let me apologize on my brother's behalf."

"That's not necessary, really. Once we sorted out my mistake, he's actually been pretty great." Walker could have been difficult. He could have blocked her from getting in touch with Brent.

He still could.

But now that all the siblings were involved it would be harder.

Hope took that to heart as the flurry of cell phone activity came to an end.

"Well," Remy said, amusement in her voice. "We certainly gave Brent something to think about. Poor guy won't know what hit him."

Poor guy? The man had abandoned his pregnant wife. He'd chosen to serve in a country of strangers instead of taking responsibility for his family. Hope's father had done the same, leaving her and Charity in the care of others while he flew halfway around the world to minister to lost souls.

Walker brushed her arm with a whisper-light touch. "You okay?"

"Don't be nice to me."

"You'd rather I be cruel?"

"I'd rather... I need a moment."

She tried to turn and go. He caught her arm. "Wait. Let's see if Brent responds to any of us."

And when he did, it would be the beginning of the end. Why had she come here?

This tangle of feeling in the pit of her stomach was grief. "Please, Walker, let me go. I need to be alone right now."

"Go on, then." He lifted his hands in the universal show of surrender.

Free at last, she rushed out of the room.

Walker gave Hope ten minutes to pull herself together. He used the first five to formulate a plan for telling Brent about his daughters. The siblings agreed that, no matter which of them Brent contacted first, the news should come from Hope via Walker. They also agreed to hold off telling the twins about their father. That, too, should come from Hope. Or possibly Brent. How he responded to the news would determine which of them would do the talking.

Satisfied with the plan, Walker found the twins playing in the basement with Sinclair, Skylar and eight squirming puppies. They didn't notice his arrival, which gave him the opportunity to watch them without interruption.

What he saw sent a wash of relief through him.

No longer looking lost and overwhelmed, Harper and

Kennedy were laughing and kissing puppies and generally behaving like normal five-year-old little girls. The similarities between the pair of twins were obvious, mostly in the eyes, all four had Evans eyes. But where Grant had passed on his brown hair, Harper and Kennedy had inherited Brent's blue-black hair.

Kennedy picked up one of the puppies and buried her face in the furry neck. The gesture was so similar to the way Brent had reacted to his first dog that Walker found himself blinking in surprise. The girls really were Brent's daughters.

Satisfied the twins were in good hands, Walker went in search of Hope. He found her standing beneath the vaulted ceiling staring into the flames snapping in the hearth. Her hair took on the fiery colors. Seemingly lost in thought, she looked up at the Christmas tree. Tears had collected in her eyes, but none had spilled over. Bertha sat beside her, gazing up at her with adoration as she accepted Hope's gentle strokes.

Walker felt his own eyes burn at Hope's raw, uncensored look of grief, as if she'd lost her way and didn't know what came next. He knew that feeling, had lived with it for too many years to count on one hand. He approached her slowly, drawing to a stop on the other side of the dog. She looked over at him and their eyes met. The impact nearly threw him back a step.

How he wanted to reach to her, to comfort and soothe. And there, in the wanting, was an utter sense of betrayal for everything he'd ever felt for Rachel. In all these years since her tragic passing, Walker had never wavered in his loyalty to the vows he'd spoken in front of God. Until now.

Until Hope.

A tear wiggled to the edges of her eyelashes. He automatically reached to wipe it away but dropped his hand just as quickly. "You okay?"

"No." She swiped at her eyes with a single, furious brush of her fingertips. "But I will be, eventually."

He wasn't sure he believed her.

They continued staring at one another. "I checked on the twins. They're neck-deep in puppies and about as happy as I've ever seen two little girls."

"I'm glad." She continued stroking Bertha's fur, as if the connection with the dog somehow grounded her.

Walker felt a crack slit through his heart. He suddenly wanted to know everything about this woman. Her past, her present, her plan for the future.

Why her, Lord? Why now?

He wasn't ready to let Rachel go. But in that moment, he needed to comfort Hope more than he needed to hang on to the past. "We aren't going to take the girls away from you."

"You can't make that promise."

Maybe not. If she took this battle to court, Hope had a claim. She'd been the twins' custodian for months.

Not if Brent steps up. Not if we form a united front against her.

The thought of becoming her adversary made him sick.

"You should know, Walker—" Hope pivoted to face him directly, her expression fierce "—if my sister was right about Brent, if your brother abandoned Charity and the twins, I will not hesitate—"

"You don't want to finish that statement."

She pressed her lips tightly shut. Mutiny burned in her eyes.

"We aren't at war, Hope. We both want what's best for *our* nieces." He emphasized the word to remind her they were on equal footing. "You can't know what Brent did or did not do until we speak with him."

"Are you that confident he's innocent? Can you honestly say my sister lied about him?"

"I know my brother. He wouldn't have abandoned his pregnant wife."

Her bottom lip began to tremble. "Are you certain?"

"Yeah, I am."

"It's been a long day," Hope said, her tone defiant. "The girls and I should go back to the hotel and—"

"You need to eat."

"Yes, we do." She conceded. "But once the twins eat, we're leaving."

She didn't trust him, he got that, and she definitely didn't trust Brent. Hope only knew what her sister told her. Perhaps Walker could provide some clarity. "Come, sit for a minute. I want to tell you a story." He sat in a wingback chair, indicated she take its match. "It's about Brent and what he was going through when he married your sister."

Hope sat in the chair, Bertha's chin resting on her lap. "I'm listening."

Walker took his time organizing his thoughts. Retelling Brent's story would mean revisiting his own loss. That both he and his brother had suffered losses so close to one another had been a cruel twist of fate that should have brought them closer. If not to each other, then to God. Instead, Brent and Walker had turned their backs on one another and the Lord. "It happened over six years ago."

"What happened?"

"The accident."

Hope's eyes widened, but she didn't interrupt. Walker appreciated that. It gave him time to push aside the images bombarding his mind. Rachel writhing in pain in the ER. Her insistence the doctors focus on the child in her belly, instead of her. If Walker had refused, if he'd focused on Rachel, then maybe—maybe—he could have saved both his wife and daughter.

He shut away the memories.

"Brent had just finished his residency in anesthesiology." Walker left out that he had been too caught up in his own grief to welcome his brother home. "He'd returned to Thunder Ridge to marry a woman he'd known since childhood. Brent and Nicole and their group of friends from high school were avid rock climbers. The weekend before the wedding, they went on a climbing trip."

A gasp slipped out of Hope.

"I won't get into the details, that's Brent's story to tell. His fiancée and another woman fell from a considerable height. Nicole died in the ambulance on the way to the hospital. The other woman recovered, but she was left with a permanent limp. Brent blamed himself."

Walker had understood his brother's need to take responsibility. He'd done the same after Rachel's death. The guilt still clung to him today, always there, at the edges of his consciousness.

"Was the accident his fault?"

"There was an investigation. Turned out the rope had been made of faulty material. Brent was exonerated of any blame. But Nicole was still gone."

"That's tragic."

"There was a lawsuit. But Brent wanted no part of that. He said it wouldn't bring back Nicole."

Walker stared into the fire, remembering his brother's pain and the helplessness he himself had felt when he couldn't seem to set aside his own grief to help Brent through his. Walker simply hadn't tried hard enough. He knew that now.

He had words of apology to say to his brother, if only

Brent would call him back. "My brother went a little wild after the accident."

"Wild, like taking impromptu trips to Las Vegas?"

"Apparently. Brent would disappear for days at a time, then show up full of remorse and determined to get his life back on track. But then the cycle would begin again. This behavior went on for months."

"I think I understand."

Did she? Walker wasn't convinced. "You've met my family so you can figure out how we reacted. We called in the pastor from our church and, with his help, attempted an intervention. Which only managed to push Brent further away. Then, suddenly, after an exceptionally long binge, he called a family meeting and told us he'd signed up to work for Doctors Without Borders. He left for Africa a week later."

As if trying to form a mental picture, Hope watched Walker closely. "How long ago was this so-called epiphany?"

Walker did a quick mental calculation. "A little over five and a half years ago."

Her hand stilled on Bertha's head. "No mention of a Las Vegas wedding before he left, an annulment, anything?"

"No. Nor was there any mention of your sister or the possibility of a pregnancy."

"He may not have known Charity was pregnant," Hope conceded in a small, strained voice. Her reluctance at the admission was evident in her tight shoulders and pinched expression.

"Look, Hope, we could spend the rest of the evening jumping to conclusions, but I'd rather we didn't."

She looked ready to argue the point.

Walker didn't give her the chance. "Brent will respond soon, and then we'll know more."

"You seem certain he'll call."

"The family blew up his phone. He'll know something's up."

Hope let out a breath, sucked it in again, then slowly nodded. "I hope you're right."

"I usually am."

She smiled.

He smiled back, deciding it was best not to dwell on his own doubts concerning his brother's behavior. Hard not to. Brent hadn't been in his right mind when he'd married Hope's sister. Walker prayed his brother hadn't done something unforgiveable, like knowingly abandon his pregnant wife.

But if he'd done just that? Then Brent would make restitution. Walker would insist.

Chapter Eight

Once again, Hope thought that Walker knew their nieces better than she did. She watched, eyes wide, mouth slightly open, as the girls each consumed a slice of pepperoni pizza, then devoured a second. When they reached for a third, Hope turned to Quinn. "Three slices? Is that normal?"

"They're five," Quinn said on a laugh, seemingly unconcerned the twins were gobbling down their food. Probably because her daughters were doing the same. "And... pizza."

Hope shook her head, opened her mouth, but Quinn was still talking. "Come. Sit with me on the porch swing a moment."

She hesitated.

"The twins will be fine."

"I know, it's just..." She was being overprotective. There were five other adults in the house. Including Walker, who currently sat between the two sets of twins, consuming a slice of pizza with as much gusto as the girls.

Grabbing her coat and gloves, Hope followed Quinn out onto the front porch. They sat together on the swing.

After a moment, Quinn broke the silence. "You're holding up well."

Amazing, how the other woman's understanding tone gave Hope the desire to let down her guard. "I never expected to become a mother, not so soon, anyway. Now? I can't imagine my life without the twins in it."

"What will you do when Brent comes home?"

"Are you sure he will come home?"

"Of course. That's why you brought the twins to Thunder Ridge, isn't it? To meet their father?"

Hope felt suddenly weak, and very aware of the cold moving through her. A cold that had nothing to do with the weather. "Honestly? I wouldn't have been able to live with myself if I hadn't looked for their father, knowing he was out there somewhere."

Quinn was nodding before Hope finished speaking. "That says a lot about your character."

They'd reached a tipping point. Hope sucked in a steadying breath and made her decision. No more evasions, no more half-truths or whole lies or pretense. "I haven't told you everything I know about my sister and your brother."

"I assumed as much."

Hope looked away, feeling a little sick to her stomach again. At some point in the evening, as she'd watched the family take in the news of Brent's marriage to Charity, as she'd seen the concern for their lost brother coupled with their obvious love and affection for him, Hope had begun to believe Brent was not the cad her sister had portrayed. At the very least, he was a man who deserved a chance to tell his side of the story.

"What aren't you telling me, Hope?"

She looked back at Quinn. "According to my sister,

Brent knew about the pregnancy and that was the reason he insisted on ending the relationship."

"You're claiming my brother abandoned his pregnant wife?"

Hope gave a long sigh. "I'm not claiming anything. I'm telling you what my sister told me."

Another long sigh followed, this one from Quinn. "I pray your sister was wrong." She glanced off in the distance. "It seems we won't know until Brent makes contact."

Hope shifted on the swing and stared at the other woman's troubled profile. Had Quinn told her to jump off a cliff, Hope wouldn't have been more surprised. She did her best to park her shock. "You aren't immediately coming to your brother's defense?"

"I wish I could." She sighed again. "Brent wasn't in a great place before he left for Africa. He'd suffered a tragedy that changed him beyond all recognition of the brother I knew."

"You're referring to the accident that killed his fiancée."

"You know about that?"

Hope gave a slight shrug. "Walker—"

"—told you. Of course, he did."

"He thought it would help me understand Brent better."

"And did it?"

"Yes," she admitted. "I can't imagine the pain of watching—"

She was cut off by the sound of the front door swinging open.

Both sets of twins came rushing out of the house, all four speaking at once. Hope could barely keep up, but was pretty sure she heard the words puppies, ice castles and then...sleepover.

Clearly more competent at deciphering little girl chatter, Quinn held up her hand to stave off any further chatter. "Hope and I will discuss it."

"Oh, please, Aunt Hope," Kennedy begged, taking her hand and bouncing on her toes. "Please, please, can we sleep over?"

Hope thought her heart might explode with equal parts love and dread. *Look at them*, she thought. *So happy, so normal. And so totally enamored with their cousins. Their family.*

Family. There was that word again, the one that threatened to rip the girls from her. "We'll see."

"That means no." The child's crestfallen expression made Hope feel even more like the enemy. She had a momentary falling sensation in the pit of her stomach.

"It means, I need to speak with your—" Aunt, she'd almost said aunt. "Miss Quinn and I will discuss it. Now go back in the house, please, so we can talk."

She waited for the girls to rush off, before addressing Quinn. "They don't have their pajamas or toothbrushes."

And Hope wasn't sure she should leave the girls overnight with strangers.

Not strangers. Family.

"We have extras of both."

Hope dragged her bottom lip between her teeth. "What if they get homesick?"

"Then I'll call you and you can come get them."

Dr. Stephens's words filled her thoughts. *If you want them to be normal children, then you have to let them experience normal activities.*

Hope closed her eyes, feeling completely out of her depth. The falling sensation in her stomach turned into a tidal wave of anxiety.

"We'll keep them safe," Quinn said, her tone mother to mother, as if understanding the core of Hope's reluctance.

"I suppose it'll be okay, so long as you make sure they get to sleep at a decent hour and promise to call me if anything happens."

"Done and done."

"I'm staying at the Grand Palace Hotel, room 303. Walker also has my cell phone number."

"I'll get it from him before he leaves tonight."

And just like that, the sleepover was a done deal.

Quinn let Hope give the girls the good news. Their excited shouts brought, if she were being honest with herself, a moment of utter grief. Harper and Kennedy were already bonding with their cousins. And pulling away from Hope.

She felt a little lost as she watched the girls rush up the stairs.

Turning to speak with Quinn, she found Walker standing in his sister's place. "Oh." Her hand flew to her throat. "I didn't hear you come up beside me."

"I don't doubt it." He chuckled. "A bomb could have gone off and you wouldn't have heard the explosion over all that screaming. Those girls have a healthy set of lungs. I know these things, I'm a doctor."

She laughed in spite of the sorrow moving through her. "I should get back to the hotel."

"I'll walk you out."

Hope said her goodbyes after she and Quinn made plans to meet for lunch and the kid exchange at Latte Da, a local diner known for its gourmet burgers and fancy fries.

Was this to be her life, then, she wondered as she joined Walker in the foyer. Kid exchanges at restaurants or airports after small snatches of time with the twins?

She closed her eyes and tried to recall a Bible verse that would bring her a moment of peace. She recited one from Proverbs she had etched on a pillow back in her apartment.

Trust in the Lord with all thine heart; and lean not unto

thine own understanding. In all thy ways acknowledge Him, and He shall direct thy paths.

Hope let the words sink in as Walker ushered her out of the house. She paused and stared up at him. Under the soft glow of the porch light, he looked like a man she could count on, steady and sure, and very masculine. Hope had been around good-looking men before, including less than an hour ago in Quinn's kitchen. But none of them had affected her breathing like Walker did.

Why did he have to mess with her breathing?

His gaze tracked over her face, sending heat through her limbs, making them heavy and full of tension.

Oh, no. No, no. No matter how good-looking he was, or how he made her breath hitch in her throat or made her knees a bit wobbly, he was not the man for her. Too much stood between them. Or rather, two little girls stood between them, figuratively speaking. On the other hand, what if she allowed herself to dream, only for an instant? If things were different, could she see her and Walker becoming something more than adversaries? More than friends?

"Do you and the twins have plans for Saturday?"

For a moment she just stared at him, the what-ifs and possibilities vanishing in the cruel light of reality. She'd hoped to be back in New York by Saturday filing papers that would make her the twins' mother. Best-laid plans... "Not really."

"What do you say I take the three of you to the Ice Castles?"

She stared at a spot just over his left shoulder, trying not to notice how her pulse rushed in her ears. "When the girls mentioned Ice Castles, I thought they were talking about a movie."

"Not even close. It's a city made out of ice. McCoy and

his team harvest tens of thousands of icicles daily. Then they hand place them to create sculptures, tunnels and, as the name implies, ice castles."

"Sounds like a complicated process."

"And completely worth a visit." He went on to explain in greater detail.

While he spoke, Hope pulled out her phone and began a quick search of the Ice Castles. The images were spectacular, especially the night views. "The girls will love this."

Walker leaned in to look at her phone. "I think McCoy took those pictures himself."

"He's very talented." Hope was losing her cool. With Walker's face inches from hers, his warm, woodsy scent was slowly reeling her closer.

Time seemed to stutter to a stop as she looked up at him. She yearned for something. She couldn't quite say what. To soothe, or maybe smooth away that hint of sadness that seemed a part of him. She nearly reached up to push a lock of hair off his forehead, then caught herself. Taking a not-so-subtle step back, she quickly put her phone away and continued down the steps toward her car.

"Hope, wait." Walker caught up with her, his long, ground-eating strides making quick work of the distance. "You never gave me an answer."

She paused. "To what?"

"The Ice Castles, you, me, the twins. Tomorrow night."

This caused her a moment of indecision. She should say no. She didn't want to say no. "Sure. Why not?"

A bark of laughter slipped out of him. "I'm overwhelmed by your enthusiasm."

"Sorry, I…" He moved a step closer and she temporarily forgot what she'd been about to say. "It sounds fun. No, really, don't raise your eyebrows at me. I'm actually looking forward to seeing McCoy's Ice Castles."

"Uh-huh."

Their eyes held one beat, two.

"I'm *super* excited." She gave him a big, toothy grin. "Convinced now?"

"Getting there." His gaze tracked across her face. There was a look in his eyes that made her breath hitch in her throat. A mix of masculine intent and secret sadness.

It was the sadness that called to her. She stepped closer and surprised them both by pressing her hand to his chest. Neither moved. They didn't speak. All that was left was the staring, and the sharp intake of a quick, unsteady breath.

Beneath her fingertips, Hope felt the rapid tripping of his heartbeat. Her own caught the erratic rhythm. She could close the distance between them without much effort. All it would take was a little stretch. A slight lift onto her toes.

"You won't regret it."

Hope blinked. It took her a moment to realize he was talking about the Ice Castles.

Her hand dropped away, but she couldn't seem to force her feet to move.

Eyes still locked with hers, Walker gave her a slow, careful grin. "I'm glad you brought the twins to Thunder Ridge, Hope."

"I'm not sure I am." She hadn't meant to stay that out loud.

"Don't go negative on me." He put a finger beneath her chin and applied light pressure until her head tipped back ever so slightly. "We're going to figure this out."

We. There he went again, acting as if they were a unit, a team. Feeling slightly off balance, she breathed in a slow, careful breath.

What was it with her and the chaotic breathing all of a

sudden? She'd never had respiratory issues. It must be the Colorado air. Too thin for her New York lungs.

Fat, languid snowflakes floated around them, lazy, unhurried, creating a surreal, almost wistful feel to the moment. "Is it wrong of me to want the girls to miss me tonight, just a little?"

"I think there's something very right about wanting them to miss you."

Why did he have to be so understanding?

Her life was about to change dramatically, once again, as it had eight months ago. She wasn't any more ready now than she'd been back then.

Sighing, she glanced at the perfect house behind Walker, and thought of the close-knit family, the loving siblings. But what of the parents? Where were they? Did Harper and Kennedy have grandparents? "What about your mother and father? Are they no longer living?"

"They are very much alive and kicking. Happy and healthy, and enjoying an active retirement in Arizona as we speak."

Of course, she thought a bit bitterly. *Perfect grandparents to go with the perfect family.* She hadn't realized she'd said that out loud, until Walker corrected her. "Not perfect, none of us are."

It was her turn to raise her eyebrows.

He stood there a moment, steady under her gaze, then shook his head. "We've had our share of tragedy and loss."

Brent had. What about Walker? "Even you?"

He hesitated. His expression could only be described as devastated. "Especially me."

The two words came out raw and full of pain. His gaze turned troubled, matching the sound, and Hope had done that to him. She'd been quick to judge this family, this man, and she regretted her behavior. It was clear Walker had suffered a tragic loss. Her private detective had either failed to uncover this bit of information or had chosen not to tell her.

What did it matter now?

"Too much death," he muttered.

In that, they agreed. Hope had lost her sister. Brent had lost his fiancée. Walker had lost someone he'd loved. She wanted to ask who she was, and what she'd been to him, but Hope didn't have the right to dig into this man's private pain.

She was still trying to sort through her confusion when his hand touched the back of her neck.

Her breath stalled in her throat.

Was he going to kiss her?

She had her answer when he guided her head to his shoulder, then wrapped his arms around her. He said nothing, simply held her against him. A moment of solidarity passed between them.

Only a moment before, Hope had been trying to figure out a way to offer comfort to Walker. Instead, he was consoling her. She wanted to weep, and to let his strength wash through her.

What must it be like to rely on someone like this good, decent man, to know she wasn't alone? But Hope was alone, and this was only a moment.

Too soon, Walker set her away from him. But then he pressed his lips to hers in a quick, matter-of-fact kiss.

He stepped back, stuffed his hands in his pockets. "I'll pick you up sometime after three."

"I thought you said the best views were at dusk."

"I'm guessing you and the girls didn't bring your snow pants."

"We don't own snow pants."

"You'll want them for the Ice Castles."

Feeling a stab of uncertainty, Hope looked out into the darkened distance. She didn't like the idea of shopping with Walker and the twins. It made them seem too much like a family. "I can take the girls shopping after I pick them up at the diner. We'll have time."

"I'm sure you will. But I'm friends with the owner of The Slippery Slope. He'll give you a better deal if I'm with you."

Arguing any further would only make her appear petty, or afraid. She was neither. Okay, she was both, but Walker didn't need to know that.

"See you tomorrow, Hope."

She nodded, then climbed into her car and drove away. Two blocks later, she braked at a stop sign and pressed her fingertips to the spot where Walker's mouth had touched hers. It had hardly been a kiss, nothing more than a brief meeting of lips.

Then why couldn't she stop smiling?

Her hand went back to the steering wheel and she continued through the intersection.

Walker wasn't the first man Hope had kissed. She'd had romantic relationships, several of them. Only one had left a few scars in his wake, a fellow professor with a fondness for dating several women at a time. When Hope had discovered his unfaithful ways, she'd cut him loose.

She'd been angry for weeks, but then something odd had happened. She'd listened to a sermon online about forgiveness. The preacher's words had resonated and she'd realized Jeff wasn't worth the anguish. Bitterness would not live in her heart because of him.

If Walker turned out to be the same as Jeff, Hope wasn't sure she'd get over him that easily.

Chapter Nine

Feeling more alone than he had in years, Walker suffered a fitful night, alternating between wakefulness and sleep. It wasn't that his body was out of sync with the change in his work schedule, although that probably played a role. He'd spent too long reviewing that moment when he'd forgotten himself, his past, *everything*—except the feel of Hope in his arms. The kiss had been as natural as breathing, and more of a betrayal because of it.

At one confused point in the night, he dreamed he was back in the ER. Rachel was there, too, her belly swollen with his child, the stomach pains bending her over at the waist. Walker kept reaching for her, always coming up short and gasping awake. At which point he would try to recall her features. Again, he came up short.

He abandoned sleep hours before dawn. As he showered and dressed for the day, he rehearsed the upcoming conversation with Brent, over and over. Time passed by until his phone buzzed, startling him out of his thoughts.

Walker checked the screen, blew out a relieved puff of air. "Finally."

His relief was cut short as he studied the text. His brother had only responded to him, not the rest of their siblings. The message was short and pure Brent. How "important" are we talking here? 1—10.

Walker frowned, recognizing his mistake. In his desire to keep from spooking his brother, he'd failed to instill the proper amount of urgency. Time to rectify that.

Walker typed, Not life or death, but a solid 8.5. Call me. Now.

A series of dancing bubbles showed, proving that Brent was in the process of responding. Then…nothing. He'd stopped typing. Walker drummed his fingertips on his thigh. A second later, Brent's reply came through. Heading into surgery, which IS life or death. Will call when the patient is awake.

Which could be an hour or longer, hard to know with the little information Brent had provided. Same old evasive Brent.

Blowing out a hiss, Walker checked the time. Early, but not too early to text Hope.

She responded immediately. At least we know he's safe.

Walker blinked at the phone, surprised at her response and yet…not.

His mind traveled back to the moment he'd pulled her into his arms last night. There'd been nothing romantic in the move. She'd needed comforting and, truthfully, so had he. Walker hadn't thought past the need to connect with another human being. But as soon as he'd held Hope against him, his motives had turned foggy, his loyalties divided.

Restless, edgy, he prowled through the house, turning on lights, looking around with a critical eye. He'd bought the house a year ago but hadn't done much with the decor. This was supposed to have been his fresh start. But without Rachel, he simply hadn't had the desire to make the house a home.

He paused in the living room. The ceilings were high and vaulted, with thick wood beams and posts. At the center was a wood-burning, stone fireplace. The floor-to-ceiling windows facing the lake revealed an awe-inspiring view, but the room still lacked warmth.

What would Hope think of the place? Would she want to add frills, or large throw blankets and sturdy furniture? Maybe pictures on the wall and—

Walker stopped himself. How could he be thinking of one woman when he'd pledged his heart to another? *Rachel has been gone a long time.*

She died a lifetime ago, and yet it had only been a handful of years on the calendar.

It was long past time he let her go. Walker knew this. He understood how unhealthy it was to hold on to her this long. Rachel had been beautiful and kind, a pediatrician with a big, loving heart. She wouldn't want Walker living like this, half alive, moving through life on autopilot.

He didn't know how to let her go.

The process had already begun, he realized. He shut his eyes, desperate to call up Rachel's image. Again, nothing. Needing to see her, to remember, he went into his study and booted up his computer. He spent the next hour scrolling through pictures from their wedding, their honeymoon, the gender reveal party at Quinn's house.

The back of his eyes burned. He rubbed at them, clicked on the next image. His arm was slung over Rachel's shoulders. They looked so happy, blissfully unaware she would be dead three months later after a perfect storm of complications.

His phone buzzed.

Brent, it had to be. Happy for the distraction, he glanced at the screen. Not Brent, Hope. He couldn't talk to her right now.

Placing his thumbs on the screen, he started to decline the call, then reconsidered. He didn't want to be alone with the past. He wanted to hear Hope's voice. Hand shaking, he moved his thumb and pressed on the screen. "Hey."

"So, I was wondering—"

"Brent hasn't called yet."

A pause. "Okay, good. That's actually why I called. I was wondering if you would consider having me there when you talk to him."

It was Walker's turn to pause.

"I can answer questions he may have about Charity and the girls."

Admittedly, it wasn't a bad idea. "What about the twins?"

"I don't pick them up until noon." She explained about the plans she and Quinn had made to meet at Latte Da, then added, "I can come to you."

Walker thought of Hope in his home and realized he didn't hate the idea. He actually liked it. But then his gaze landed on the computer screen, on Rachel smiling out at him. McCoy had taken the picture just as the wind had picked up, sending her long red curls in a flurry around her face.

As he stared at the photo, Walker felt distant from the man standing next to his wife.

That was another time, another life. He went hot, then cold, and the room started to spin. "No." The word came out slightly tortured. "I'll come to you."

Twenty minutes later, he was standing in the empty hotel lobby, waiting for Hope to join him. She exited the elevator looking young, fresh and alive. So very alive. She smiled, and it was a really great smile. Something inside him came to life, something he thought dead. He forgot all about court battles and DNA tests.

His phone buzzed.

Hope caught up with him at the same moment he looked at the screen. "It's Brent."

Her eyes filled with nerves. "Aren't you going to answer the call?"

Answer the call. Right.

Walker directed Hope to a quiet alcove off the lobby. Satisfied they were alone, he pulled the phone up to his ear, then decided to put the call on speaker. "Brent," he said, his tone neutral.

"Walker."

Apparently, this was how brothers greeted one another after five years of limited communication. Accepting his share of the blame, Walker softened his tone and tried again. "How did the surgery go?"

"The patient lived. Look, Walker." Exasperation sounded in Brent's voice. "I have three more surgeries ahead of me. What's so urgent that you felt the need to involve the entire family?"

Brent sounded irritated. Yeah, well, so was he. Which explained why his words came out as clipped and angry as his brother's had. "How about we discard the chitchat and you tell me about your Vegas wedding to Charity Jeffries?"

A long, tense silence met the statement, then a slow hiss sounded through the speaker. "Ah, that."

Walker shared a look with Hope. "Yes, *that*."

"You're mad because I signed your name on the marriage certificate."

Not mad, confused.

But time was short and the whys behind Brent's behavior was for another conversation. "We'll talk about that later. For now, I need to know about the annulment. Whose idea was it, yours or your bride's?"

"We...hang on a minute." A series of mumbles followed the command, as if Brent had covered the speaker with his hand while he had a brief conversation. When he came back on the line, his voice was filled with impatience. "What did you want to know again?"

Walker forced down his own impatience. He chose his words carefully, ensuring he didn't lead Brent to respond in a way that could be held against either of them in the future. Or in a court of law. "Your marriage to Charity Jeffries," he said. "And the subsequent annulment. Walk me through it."

"Now?"

"It's important."

"You aren't going to let it go, are you?"

"Nope."

"Fine. We got married the same night we met. We pretty much realized our mistake a few days later, but we managed to hold it together for about a month, maybe a bit longer." Brent spoke as if he were under interrogation. "I was pretty shook up by the events of a night I could barely remember. I committed to cleaning up my act, for good this time. But Charity didn't much like the sober, responsible Brent. And, quite frankly, I didn't like how she was always looking for the next party. We agreed to end the marriage. The End."

Not the end, Walker thought. But he said, "So, it was a mutual decision to break up?"

"That's what I said, isn't it?"

Walker glanced at Hope, caught the momentary tightening of her mouth, as if she were deciding whether to challenge Brent's story or let him talk. Walker rushed to fill the silence before she could. "One more question."

"Fire away." Brent sounded resigned, and a little snarky. Walker figured he deserved the latter.

"Did you know your wife was pregnant when you ended your marriage?"

"I…wait, *what*? Did you just say Charity was pregnant?"

"As a matter of record, your wife gave birth to two healthy baby girls forty-one weeks and three days after the date of your wedding."

"Did you say *two* baby girls?"

"That's right," Walker confirmed, then pressed for answers. "You really didn't know about the pregnancy?"

"Of course I didn't know." The irritation was back in his voice.

The conversation went quickly from there, mostly with rapid-fire questions from Brent and equally fast answers from Walker. As would be expected from a man who was just finding out he was the father of five-year-old daughters, Brent wanted to know why he was only hearing about the twins now, were they healthy, happy, what were their names, where were they were now. And on and on.

The conversation turned somber when Walker told his brother about Hope, and her appearance in Thunder Ridge the day before—had it only been yesterday?—which led to the inevitable, "But what about Charity? Where is she?"

Walker saw Hope's mouth working and decided to let her take over the conversation. "My sister died three months ago. Cancer."

"I'm really sorry to hear that. She was a special woman." Brent paused, then made a sound deep in his throat. "We weren't meant to be together, but I was lucky to know her."

There was no doubting Brent's sincerity.

"Hang tight, I'm about to send you a few pictures of your daughters."

They all fell silent as technology worked. A gasp

sounded from the other end of the phone, and then Brent said the words that would change all of their lives. "I'm coming home."

Walker was glad, until he got a look at Hope. She'd turned a pale shade of green.

"I'll be back in touch once I confirm my travel plans," Brent said. "It may take a while."

"Understood." This was what Walker had wanted to hear. Then why wasn't he happy? Where was the relief? "I'll look forward to your call."

He was aware of his heartbeat as he disconnected the call, and the look of defeat on Hope's face. Eyes closed, she sagged against the wall behind her.

Walker reached to her.

As if sensing his attempt to touch her, she shook him off with a wave of her hand.

Silence fell over them, a silence neither tried to break. Her eyes opened at last and Walker could feel the metaphorical wall she'd erected. They were back to being strangers again. It made him feel as wretched as she looked.

He wanted to feel enthusiastic his brother hadn't known about Charity's pregnancy, but instead felt a weight of despair. Not for himself or for Brent, or even the twins, but for Hope. She'd been so certain Brent had abandoned her sister.

Looking at her now, seeing the defeat in her eyes, Walker knew—he *knew*—she'd come to Thunder Ridge with the idea of gaining custody.

Hope had lost. Brent was coming home. He hadn't mentioned anything about next steps once he arrived. He could turn out to be just like her own father. He could choose helping strangers living halfway across the world over raising his own daughters.

Hope allowed herself the luxury of wallowing in a moment of wishful thinking. She hadn't lost yet. But she wasn't any closer to winning, either.

"Hope." She couldn't look at Walker, not yet. "Stay through the holidays."

Surprised, she met his gaze and felt his struggle. He, too, wasn't sure what came next. She told herself not to care that they seemed to be on the same page, but she couldn't do that.

We're in this together. In that moment, she realized he cared about the twins as much as she did. And...

He'd been speaking. "I'm sorry, what did you say?"

"I'd like you to consider staying through the holidays. There's no telling how long it will take Brent to make arrangements to come home. It could take days, or possibly weeks."

"That long?"

"Depends on whether he's planning a temporary trip home, or something more permanent."

A lump lodged in her throat.

"We have a lot of great traditions here in Thunder Ridge. Aside from the Ice Castles, there's the Tree Lighting Festival, the live Nativity Play, the annual parade on Christmas morning. You get the idea."

Every one of the events he mentioned sounded amazing. "I can't think past your brother's return. If he refuses to step up and be a father to the twins, I will need to—"

"That's a conversation for later."

Was it? There were steps Hope needed to consider, decisions to make, whether she went with Plan A or Plan B or Plan C, D or E.

Walker appeared to be thinking through a few plans

himself. His next words confirmed her suspicions. "From everything you've said, I get the impression Harper and Kennedy haven't experienced a Christmas like the one Thunder Ridge puts on."

The twins weren't the only ones.

Hope smiled politely, ignoring the way Walker was looking at her with that infuriating mix of surety and challenge. "If we stayed—"

"I knew you'd see things my way."

"*If* we stayed," she began again. "That would mean at least three weeks in a hotel. I'm not sure that's a good idea for the girls."

As soon as the words left her mouth, she regretted them. There were a lot of other places for the twins to stay besides a hotel. Quinn's house, for example. Hope should have come up with a better excuse. Now she would be alone for the holidays, or mostly alone, on the outside looking in. It was her childhood all over again.

"I have another idea."

She just bet he did. But would it include Hope?

"The three of you can move into my house. No, don't say anything. I'm not through. Let me finish. There's plenty of room. I live on the lake just two houses down from Quinn, close enough to walk, even in the worst of weather."

"No."

"Why not?"

There were so, so many reasons. "The twins and I couldn't possibly stay in your house with you living there as well."

"Not at all what I meant. I'll move in with McCoy. You and the girls can have my house to yourselves."

Hope ignored the little flutter in her stomach, the one that wanted to experience everything Thunder Ridge had to offer, not just for the holidays, but for a lifetime. "You would do that for us? You would move out of your own house?"

"Consider it already done. What do you say? Want to join forces and give the twins a family Christmas like they've never had before?"

It was a dangling carrot.

She looked into his eyes for any signs of ulterior motives. She found several. Of course Walker had ulterior motives. They both did. But he'd offered to join forces, which meant he didn't plan to cut Hope out of the Christmas festivities.

Oh, boy, this was bad. In a really good way, but also a very, very bad way. The twins deserved to experience a Christmas in this town. And Hope wanted to give it to them. But at what cost?

She should say no.

She prayed for guidance, instead, knowing it would be wrong of her to take the twins back to New York now. And so, she caved. "When can we move in?"

"Is now too soon?"

Despite her misgivings, she laughed. The man had a good sense of humor. She wished she didn't like that so much. "How about first thing tomorrow morning?"

His smile turned a little crafty. "You won't regret this."

She worried that she already did.

Chapter Ten

At half past three Saturday morning, Hope hustled the twins out of their hotel room. They'd been grumpy ever since she'd relayed the message that Walker was running late. Apparently, some important meeting had run longer than he'd expected. Now that he was waiting for them in the lobby, Harper and Kennedy had become darling little angels, talking nonstop about their new friends, Skylar and Sinclair.

Hope predicted they would be thrilled when they learned the Holloway twins were their cousins. And that more sleepovers were in their future. Tears blurred her eyes. She wanted to weep, possibly forever.

Still, this was not the future she'd envisioned for herself and the twins.

She ushered the girls into the elevator, while they continued to extol the virtues of the Holloway family. It took tremendous effort to focus on their words. Ever since making contact with Brent, Hope's mind had been running through next steps. At some point, Harper and Kennedy would have to be told he was their father. Hope was still undecided if that conversation should take place before he came home or after.

In the meantime, she'd taken action securing her own future, one that would keep her in the girls' lives a little longer, regardless of what Brent decided to do about his daughters.

The conversation turned to the newborn puppies. "They were so cute."

Hope wouldn't know. She'd been unable to drum up the courage to walk down the basement stairs. She'd been too afraid she'd leave the Holloway's home with a puppy in her possession. She'd always wanted a dog. But her apartment building back in New York didn't allow pets.

Of course, Plan B would solve that problem.

The elevator dinged their arrival to the bottom floor.

As expected, Walker was waiting for them in the lobby.

A small smile played across his handsome face. He appeared rested. His hair was in a bit of disarray, as if he'd run his fingers through the dark, thick mass more than once. Since when had Hope become a sucker for the disheveled look? Since meeting Walker Evans, apparently.

He wore dark-washed jeans that hugged his long legs and a light blue sweater that matched his eyes. The hiking boots on his feet were worn. Overall, there was a masculine, outdoorsy feel to him. Refined yet rugged.

And there went her heart, pinging again.

The girls rushed straight to him, no hesitation.

In a gesture that was becoming as familiar as the man himself, Walker crouched to their level and opened his arms wide. The twins flung themselves at him. Laughing, he pulled them close, kissed each of their heads, then set them back and rose.

He greeted Hope with a slight touch to her hand. That simple brush of fingertips was oddly intimate, and her mind sped back to their kiss the other night. She shoved the memory aside and followed Walker outside. Hope breathed in the fresh mountain air, then looked around for Walker's SUV. It was nowhere in sight.

As if understanding her confusion, he pointed down the street in a northerly direction. "I'm parked in front of The Slippery Slope."

Two blocks later, Hope paused on the threshold just inside the ski shop and glanced over the impressive collection of skis, snowboards, walking sticks, sleds, snowshoes and all the accompanying outerwear.

Apparently, the people of Thunder Ridge took their winter sports seriously.

She was still taking it all in when a man about Walker's age approached. He walked like an athlete. He had a tall, rangy build, spiky blond hair, and was really good-looking, in that skier sort of way. Hope was certain she'd seen him before. On a poster somewhere? A magazine cover?

Walker began the introductions. "Hope, this is Reno Miller. Reno, Hope Jeffries."

Hope recognized the name immediately. She tried not to gawk, but...wow. "You're Reno Miller!"

"One and the same." He punctuated his words with the lazy, flirtatious grin she had, indeed, seen on a poster. And the cover of every sports magazine known to man.

Reno had won five Olympic gold medals and two world championships. Some of the news outlets called him a national treasure. Others called him the bad boy of the slopes. "You're a professional downhill skier."

Reno's smile never wavered, but his eyes went blank, distant. "*Former* professional skier."

"Right. Sorry. I knew that." She only just remembered the news stories about the terrible crash that had ended his career. According to the reports, the man was lucky to be alive. "I didn't mean to—" she paused, worrying that anything she said would bring back bad memories "—gush."

He lifted a shoulder. "It happens."

"Probably more than you would like."

It was the right thing to say. His manner turned less distant and his eyes held that warm, friendly note again. "What brings you to The Slippery Slope?"

"Walker is taking the girls and me to the Ice Castles. Apparently, we are not appropriately dressed."

"Hmmm." Reno's gaze slid over her. His eyes held a teasing light. "I've got just what you need."

If Hope wasn't mistaken, Reno Miller—*the* Reno Miller—was flirting with her. And if Walker's scowl was anything to go by, he was not amused. Was he jealous?

She wasn't sure what to think of that.

Clearing his throat, Walker stepped between her and Reno, practically shoving his friend out of the way. "We're on a time crunch, man."

"Are you, now?" Reno's amused expression bounced between his friend and Hope. "Can't say I blame you." His gaze dropped to the twins. "And who might you be?"

"I'm Harper and this is my sister, Kennedy."

"Please to meet you, Harper and Harper's sister, Kennedy." Reno shook each of their hands, then, proving why he'd once been the darling of social media, spoke to the twins as if they were just as important as any adult. "You're going to want a pair of sleds to go along with your snow gear."

Two pairs of eyes lit with curiosity. "Really? Why?"

"For the tunnels. Way more fun on a sled. Come with me. I have the perfect ones in mind."

"Are they pink?" Harper asked him, taking the hand he offered.

"Please. What other color would they be?"

"Maybe purple?" Kennedy suggested, trotting over to his other side.

"My friends—" he divided a look between the twins "—I am about to hook you up with the best pink and purple sleds in town."

The next half hour was spent shopping for the proper gear to experience the Ice Castles. Much to Hope's amusement, Reno proved to be an outrageous flirt. Walker ran interference whenever the man got too cozy with her. It sent a little thrill through her every time he literally stepped between them.

Instead of being deterred by his friend's heavy-handed antics, Reno upped his game and told Hope embarrassing stories about Walker. It was apparently all in good fun, because the two finished by firming up plans for a day of snowboarding five days later.

By the time they left The Slippery Slope, Hope and the girls had changed into their new snow pants, ski jackets and sturdy boots. Walker carried the sleds to the car, one pink, one purple. After the four of them piled into the SUV, Walker kept up a running commentary about what they could expect at the top of the mountain. He interjected a few really corny jokes, which made the girls giggle and Hope roll her eyes.

They felt like a family, the four of them. An illusion Hope knew better than to let take hold of her heart. Brent would be home soon, and that would be the end of these types of outings.

Hope forced herself to make small talk. "How long have you known Reno?"

"Since before we could crawl. Our parents are best friends and have been for well over three decades. In fact, they retired near each other down in Phoenix."

Hope wondered what it must be like to have lifelong connections. Not to mention friendships that had started during your diaper days. "I liked Reno."

"I noticed."

Hope resisted the urge to laugh. "He's nice, but definitely not my type."

"No?" Walker gave her a sidelong glance. "What is your type?"

Men who are dedicated to helping others. Hope straightened in her seat. Where had that thought come from?

She glanced out the window, not really seeing the scenery as she answered his question. "I suppose I like them to be a tad more cerebral than the average bear."

"I've read *Moby Dick*, *Beowulf* and *A Tale of Two Cities*." He wiggled his eyebrows. "I also know all about Keynesian economic theory."

"Prove it."

He shot her a smug grin before returning his gaze to the road. "Keynes believed that consumer demand was the driving force in any economy. He supported increased government spending during recessionary times and government restraint during a rapidly growing economy."

"Well, okay then." Hope blinked. "That was pretty spot on. I'm impressed."

"Don't be." His lips twisted at a wry angle. "I looked it up on my phone while you were flirting with Reno."

"I was not flirting."

He lifted a brow.

"Okay, I was flirting, but only a little, and he started it. What can I say?" She tilted her head back to look into his eyes. "I'm a sucker for bad boys."

"I thought you liked them smart."

"A bad boy can be smart."

He considered this in silence as he turned onto another steep, winding mountain road that took them up, up, up. Distracted by the awe-inspiring view, Hope gave a short, happy gasp.

"Is that an eagle?" She pointed to a bird with a massive wingspan.

"A hawk. And that—" Walker nodded toward an animal grazing on a small ledge halfway up the rocky cliff "—is a mountain goat."

Hope eyed the creature with the massive twisting horns. "He's beautiful. It's all beautiful. Colorado is amazing."

"You are not wrong. Look, girls, the Ice Castles are just up ahead."

A chorus of delighted squeals rose from the back seat. Hope nearly joined in. Even from this distance, she could tell Walker had not been exaggerating when he'd claimed the sculptures were enormous. Some of the structures appeared to be several stories high.

"McCoy is a genius."

"He would tell you the same. Humble, he is not." Walker's tone was full of good humor as he steered the SUV through a wooden gate.

He'd barely parked before Hope was hopping out of the car.

As if they'd done this a million times, she and Walker helped the twins out of their car seats in the back. While she straightened their coats, he went around back and retrieved the sleds. Tucking them under his arm, he winked at the girls. "Ready to party?"

Hope directed the girls toward a ticket booth, but Walker stopped her. "Already taken care of. You forget, I have connections."

The man was nothing if not prepared. *A kindred spirit*, Hope thought, with a little twinge in her heart. She studied Walker out of the corner of her eye. A strange sensation washed through her, as if she was poised on the edge of something significant. Good or bad, she couldn't yet say.

With Walker guiding them through the entrance, she

felt a part of something bigger than herself. Instead of overthinking it, a bad habit of hers, she resolved to enjoy this adventure with Walker and the girls.

If her brain wanted to do a little wishful arithmetic, making one plus one plus two equal a family of four, then she would go with it.

But only for today.

Once they passed through the entrance, Walker turned to Hope. "Prepare to be amazed."

"I already am."

"Do you have a dog?" Harper asked Walker.

He blinked at the random question, a distant look on his handsome face. "I used to. But not anymore." He seemed caught in a memory that brought more sadness than joy. "We're here."

The four of them stopped at the base of a working fountain made of ice. There was no more talk of dogs or puppies. The girls were too busy spinning in circles, looking everywhere at once.

Hope bounced her gaze past the fountain, to a group of animal sculptures, a miniature princess castle, a perfect replica of Santa riding his sleigh, then back to the fountain. "It's a whole world made from nothing but ice and water."

For the next hour they explored the frozen world. Walker encouraged the girls to touch one of the structures. They sat on kid-size thrones next. Then crawled through tiny ice tunnels, which earned them high praise from Walker.

At one point, he pretended to get stuck in a tight walkway. "We'll save you, Dr. Walker," the twins cried out. Taking their role as his rescuers very seriously, they tugged on his hand until he slid through the tight quarters.

Hope rode down a slide behind the twins, more than a little grateful Walker had insisted on the snow pants. She crawled through a tunnel lit by blue and pink LED lights. He caught her hand from the other side and pulled her through the final few feet. Her breath caught and a belly-clenching thrill rolled in her stomach.

"Look up."

Hope gasped. Thousands of icicles hung over her head.

They finished their journey where they'd begun. McCoy stood at the fountain illuminated with red and green LED lights, Bertha by his side. He was talking to a woman dressed in faded jeans, battered boots and a forest green puffy jacket. Her hair was a light, golden brown with plenty of blond streaks, shiny and thick, and just barely brushing her shoulders. She was also leaning heavily on a cane. "Who's that with McCoy?"

"That's Bertha."

"Not the dog, the woman."

"Emma Summerland."

"I didn't know McCoy had a girlfriend."

"She's not his girlfriend." Walker glanced at the twins, back to Hope, indecision in his eyes. Then he spoke. "Emma was on the rock-climbing trip with Brent."

Hope felt her heart sink. Emma Summerland was the other accident victim that had sustained a life-altering injury.

As they drew closer to the fountain, Hope studied the other woman. Emma was very pretty, gorgeous really, and appeared near her same age. Her manner was light-hearted despite the cane, as if she was happy with her life. Her sparkling eyes held no bitterness. They were a pretty shade of light green and, at the moment, full of curiosity.

Dividing her gaze between Hope, Walker and the twins, her eyebrows drew together. She appeared to be puzzling over the family resemblance.

Would everyone in town assume Walker was the twins'

father, and that Hope was their mother? The thought brought a wistful tug somewhere in the vicinity of her heart. She liked the idea of her and Walker raising the twins together. Maybe a little too much.

Surely, she wasn't falling for a man she'd only just met.

"Bertha!" Kennedy's shriek rent the air.

Both twins ran to the dog without a second thought to their safety. Hope called after them to slow down, which was promptly ignored.

Walker chuckled beside her. "I think it's love."

"The twins or the big, furry dog?"

"All three."

Their eyes locked, held. A moment of silent understanding passed between them, something that was altogether theirs alone.

Hope looked away, and right into Emma's all-too-knowing smile. The other woman thought Hope and Walker were a couple. Hope should correct her assumption. Except...

How did she go about correcting a misconception that hadn't actually been voiced? She didn't.

As Walker made the introductions, Hope attempted a bland smile. A wasted effort. Emma's full attention was now on the twins. "Who's who?"

"I'm Harper." This was said absently. The child's focus was solely on the dog.

"That must make you Kennedy."

The little girl glanced up. "That's me."

Emma's delighted expression stayed hooked on the twins. "I really like your sleds."

Kennedy continued looking at her. "They're new."

"Even better." So began an extensive dissertation on their shopping expedition at The Slippery Slope. Kennedy did love her shopping trips.

Apparently, Emma did, as well.

Walker pulled Hope aside. "Emma is a kindergarten teacher at the Thunder Ridge elementary school."

Which explained her ease with the twins, and her ability to understand the storytelling of five-year-olds. As she watched the interaction, Hope stood rooted to the spot by a deep, undefined ache in her chest. If Brent won custody, the twins would attend school in Thunder Ridge. Emma would probably be their teacher.

Proving he just might have mind reading skills after all, Walker took her hand. "It's going to be okay."

No, it wasn't. Hope's life was unraveling right before her eyes. She tried to pull her hand free, but she couldn't seem to do so. She didn't want Walker's comfort. And still, she held on to his hand, barely resisting the urge to cling.

She wanted to watch the twins grow into adults. She wanted to be a part of their lives every step of the way. She wanted to celebrate every triumph. Bandage every skinned knee, kiss away every hurt.

How, Lord? How do I let them go?

Chapter Eleven

Night had fallen by the time Walker drove down the mountain. The Ice Castles were nothing more than a collection of LED lights and sporadic shadows in the rearview mirror.

Walker could feel the turmoil rising in him. His connection to Hope was growing stronger, and more impossible to ignore. Even worse, he hadn't thought of Rachel at all throughout today's adventures. Guilt sent his heart thumping hard against his ribs and his palms sweating inside his gloves. *Set it aside,* he told himself.

Stay in the moment.

He glanced over his shoulder. The twins were talking to one another in low, excited tones. They were happy, exhausted and, according to Harper, really hungry. Walker made suggestions for dinner, mostly nicer restaurants.

The twins had their own idea. "We want to go to the Latte Da."

Walker turned to Hope. "Isn't that where you went for lunch today?"

Even in the dim light from the dashboard, he could see a dozen thoughts racing in her eyes, none of the happy variety. "It was a big hit with the girls."

"You don't mind going there twice in one day?"

"If the twins are happy, I'm happy." Her voice matched her somber mood.

Something was up with her, that much was clear. Walker wondered if she would confide in him, or if he would have to go on a fishing expedition. He would prefer she opened up on her own, so he waited for her to break the silence. And waited. And waited.

After a series of sideways glances in his direction, she turned her head to look out the passenger-side window. At last, she spoke. "I liked Emma."

An odd segue. Walker kept his answer neutral. "Most people do. Emma is a likable person."

"But—" Hope swallowed audibly "—is she a good kindergarten teacher?"

Yep, Hope had gone right where Walker guessed. Whether she admitted it out loud or not, she was already thinking about a future for the twins in Thunder Ridge.

Walker should be elated.

Hard to be when the sigh that leaked out of Hope carried an edge of defeat. He didn't want to win this way, not if it meant Hope had to lose. "I can't say what kind of teacher Emma is. Quinn would know. Her daughters were in Emma's class two years ago."

Nodding, Hope said in a slightly unsteady voice, "I'll definitely speak to your sister. It would help to know what she thought about…"

She turned to look out the window without finishing her thought. She didn't need to finish. Walker knew what she meant.

In that moment, he felt profoundly that he'd failed Hope. The sensation grew stronger when he considered the meeting with his attorney two days ago. Mitch had assured Walker that Brent had a strong case for custody. Especially if, as Brent claimed, Charity had kept her pregnancy a secret from him. And Walker believed his brother.

Hope seemed to be withholding final judgment until Brent came home. Once he did, would she dig in her heels on her sister's behalf, a woman who couldn't defend herself? Would it even matter?

This was a classic case of he said/she said, which gave Brent the advantage since he could make his case in front of a judge. Walker didn't want to be on the opposite side of Hope. He wanted to work with her, as he'd promised.

Set it aside.

He reached out in the darkened interior of the SUV and took her hand. He considered it a win that she didn't pull away for several life-affirming heartbeats.

Dinner was a combination of hot dogs, french fries and an enthusiastic revisiting of their recent adventure at the Ice Castles.

Heart full, Walker joined the conversation.

During a brief lull, he greeted the duo seated at the table next to theirs. "Wyatt." He nodded to the little boy with him, a child a few years older than the twins. "Samson. Wyatt is the newly elected sheriff in town," he added for Hope's benefit.

Hope seemed a little shocked.

"What?"

"Do you know everyone in Thunder Ridge?"

"Only the important people." He winked at Samson, who beamed back at him.

Walker was pleased to see the boy smile, a rarity since his mother, Wyatt's sister, had been found guilty of a felony drug charge. The whole ugly mess had been a big scandal in town, made worse because Wyatt was the arresting officer.

CiCi wasn't a bad person, just really lost after the death of her husband in the car accident she'd caused. A series of bad decisions had sent her down a path of self-destruction that had endangered her son. Samson was doing better now that he was living full-time with his uncle.

"We went to the Ice Castles," Harper told Samson with no small amount of pride.

"Did you crawl around in the tunnels?"

"Well, yeah." Kennedy rolled her eyes in a gesture filled with little girl impertinence. "Duh."

Hope gasped. "Kennedy, don't be rude."

The child looked completely unrepentant. "It was a dumb question, Aunt Hope."

Hope and Samson responded at the same moment. "No, it wasn't."

"Say you're sorry," Hope urged the little girl.

"I'm sorry," Kennedy spat out the words, while Hope, looking both distraught and embarrassed on her niece's behalf, gave an apologetic grimace to Wyatt.

Samson swung around, putting his back to their table, but not before saying in a voice loud enough to be heard three blocks over, "Stupid girl."

Now Wyatt looked distraught and embarrassed. "Samson! We don't use that word, ever. Apologize. Now."

Samson swung a scowl in Kennedy's general direction. "I'm sorry I called you a girl."

Wyatt sighed. "You know that's not what I meant. Try again."

"Fine. I'm sorry I called you stupid." The little boy growled out each word through clenched teeth.

Hope nudged Kennedy's shoulder. "Your turn. Say you're sorry, and mean it this time."

Arms crossed over her chest, the little girl gave her aunt

the stink eye, then turned the same look onto Samson. "I'm. Sarr. I'm…sar." She huffed out a whooshing sigh. "I'm sorry."

The two children scowled at one another, accepting the other's apology with grudging nods. Hope and Wyatt apologized to each other on the children's behalf.

Walker did his best not to laugh, and managed to succeed, mostly. Except for a low snicker in the back of his throat, which earned him an adult version of the stink eye from Hope. He maintained his composure until the girls were secured in the back seat, with the SUV's doors closed behind them.

"What's so funny?"

"Kennedy and Samson." He gave his laugh free rein. "Priceless."

Looking ready to rumble, Hope's eyes narrowed. "I don't see the humor."

"Come on, Hope. Those apologies were funny, and you know it."

Her lips twitched. But she didn't give in to a laugh. "I don't know what got into Kennedy. She's never been rude like that."

"She was behaving like a normal kid." He moved in closer, feeling the tug of this woman as if they were tethered by an invisible cord. "Call your therapist and see what she has to say about it."

Hope's chin lifted at a haughty angle. "Maybe I will."

Walker was only half surprised she didn't pull out her cell phone and make the call right there on the street corner. Still smiling—he couldn't remember when he'd smiled this much—he dropped off the trio at their hotel. They made final plans for the big move the next day, agreeing mid-morning would work best.

That night, for the first time in months, maybe years, Walker entered his home with a woman other than Rachel on his mind.

The next morning, while the girls packed their suitcases, Hope stepped into the hallway and made a call to New York. She disconnected a few minutes later. Dr. Stephens had agreed with Walker's assessment about Kennedy's rudeness at the diner, calling it normal five-year-old behavior. Hope was relieved.

The twins had been entirely too timid and distant prior to coming to Thunder Ridge. The change to normal five-year-old behavior was a blessing she'd been praying for since they'd come into her life.

What worried Hope was that the girls' transformation could be directly attributed to their interactions with Walker and the rest of the Evans family. *Family.* There was that word again. She swallowed back a sob. And went back into the hotel room to finish her own packing.

"I can't wait to see Dr. Walker's house," Harper said.

Hope was equally curious.

"I wish he was going to live there, too."

Hope had already explained why that wasn't possible. Or rather, she'd given the girls an explanation that a kindergartener would understand. "We can't stay in the same house with a man we only met a few days ago. It wouldn't be appropriate."

"You could always marry Dr. Walker," Kennedy suggested. "And then he could be our daddy and you could be our mommy."

Hope's heart lodged in her throat. It was pointless to argue with five-year-old logic, especially when she didn't hate the idea as much as she should. She could picture the four of them as a family. She could picture being married to a man like Walker.

"Dr. Walker and I are not getting married." She said this as much for the twins' benefit as her own.

"Why not? You like him, don't you?"

"We haven't known each other long enough."

Harper and Kennedy shared a look full of silent twin messages. "Okay."

Okay? Hope blinked at the pair. When had either child ever given in that easily on, well, anything?

"If you won't get us a daddy," Harper said for the pair. "Can we have a puppy instead?"

More five-year-old logic that sent a ripple of frustration through Hope. "We'll see."

"Is that a yes," Kennedy asked. "Or a no?"

"It's a 'we'll see.' Now, if you're finished packing, it's time to go."

"We're finished." All conversation of fathers and puppies were dropped in favor of hurrying out of the room.

Twenty minutes later, Hope drew to a stop outside the address Walker had given her. She cut the engine and stared out at the massive two-story house overlooking Thunder Ridge Lake.

That is a lot of wood and glass, she decided, really enjoying the way the house seemed to merge with its rustic surroundings while still having a modern appeal. She could see herself coming home to a place like this after a long day of teaching.

As if she'd somehow called him with her thoughts, Walker exited the house and stood, hands stuffed in his back pockets, waiting for her and the twins. This is what he would look like if they were married and, and...

She stopped herself before she went any further in her

mind. Pocketing her car keys, she swiveled around to face the back seat. "We're here."

The twins fist-bumped, then waggled their fingers as they said in unison, "Firecracker!"

Hope's heart twisted. Walker had taught them the gesture last night. He'd become such a part of their lives. She tried not to resent that, and almost succeeded, but her mind kept circling around an irrefutable fact. Her life with the girls as she'd known it was coming to an end.

So little time left. Hope climbed out of the car, the twins right behind her. Walker went on the move, heading straight for her.

Her stomach performed a quick, hard roll at the sight of all that masculinity coming her way. He wore all black, save for the pristine white collar peeking out from beneath the neck of his sweater. His eyes were a pale blue under the bright sun. His smile a mere tilt of one corner of his mouth. Hope thought she detected a hint of humor in his expression, and something that looked like affection. For her, the girls, all three of them?

The responding tug at her heart felt too real. How was she supposed to remain immune to the man when he looked at her like…like…*that*?

"Good morning." His deep voice fell over her like a warm caress.

She had no time to respond before Harper was tugging on his arm. "Aunt Hope says you can't be our daddy."

His gaze swung back to Hope. "Did she, now?"

"Yeah." Harper took a quick, audible breath. "But she said we can get a puppy, instead."

"I said we'll see."

"Okay, yeah," Harper admitted, engaging Hope in a stare-down that claimed she would not be denied this request. "But that's almost the same thing as yes."

Hope held the child's glare with an unflinching one of her own. "I made no promises, Harper."

Walker's chuckle interrupted the staring match. "Wise woman."

And now she was locked in a silent contest of wills with him. Their gazes held a long, silent beat. An unspoken message passed between them, but Hope couldn't quite decipher the meaning.

Walker broke eye contact first.

"Ready to move into your new home?" The words were directed at the twins, but Hope felt them all the way to the depths of her soul.

The words, spoken in that rich, masculine baritone, and the carefully constructed life she'd envisioned for herself with the twins morphed into something new. Something different.

And, for the first time in her life, unrealized dreams seemed possible.

Chapter Twelve

Walker tried not to look at Hope. He tried not to look at the twins, either. The moment he'd caught sight of all three exiting the rental car, his mind had focused on one word. *Mine.*

Except, they weren't his.

Harper and Kennedy belonged to his brother. And Hope, well, she had a life in New York. It would be unwise to think of her as anything beyond the twins' aunt. She'd agreed to stay through the holidays, nothing more, and only for the girls. Still, his mind wrapped around one, unrelenting truth.

It isn't long enough.

"Are we going inside now?"

Walker smiled down at Harper. "Let's go."

"What about our suitcases?"

"I'll get them later."

He led the way, first onto the front stoop and then inside the house itself. Where was the trepidation of welcoming them into his home? Nowhere to be found, he realized with his second jolt of the day. He'd bought the house barely a year ago, with the idea of finally putting the past behind him. He'd planned to start the next chapter in his life.

He'd clung to a series of blurred images and hazy memories, instead.

His gaze hooked on Hope. Something inside him shifted. Walker wanted this woman in his home, in his life. The thought pulled him up short. Ever since Hope had barged into his ER, Walker had begun looking to the future instead of dwelling on the past.

He glanced down at the twins. They'd played a role, as well. "Let's get you out of your coats."

A lot of shuffling and giggling filled the next few minutes as he and Hope removed the children's outerwear. The happy sound bounced off the walls and landed straight inside Walker's battered heart. He heaved a weighty sigh and, determined to live in the moment, concentrated on hanging the girls' coats on hooks near the front door.

Hope rested a palm on the banister leading to the upper level and looked around with an assessing eye.

"Well?" he asked. "What do you think of my house?"

She checked herself slightly at the question, so slightly Walker almost missed it. "You really want to know?"

"I do." Her opinion mattered.

"It's nothing like my apartment. There's a lot of wood and glass, everywhere."

He glanced around, trying to take in the house from a woman's perspective. "Is that a problem?"

"Not even a little bit. My view in New York is of the building across the street. The girls and I have to walk five blocks to get to a park. But here? It's as if the architect managed to bring the outdoors right inside with us, while also maintaining a comfortable, welcoming feel."

Nice compliments, and yet he sensed she was holding something back. "But...?"

"The decor is a bit sparse. And I noticed yours is the

only house on this side of the lake that isn't decorated for the season."

"I've been busy." It was a lame excuse even to his own ears, but she gave him a pass.

"No doubt. Anyway." She craned her neck to look past the foyer into the main portion of the house. From her vantage point, she could easily see into the living room, to the far wall made entirely of picture windows that looked out over the lake. "Whew. That's some view."

"One of the reasons I bought the house last year."

"You've lived here an entire year? Interesting."

He knew she had more to say, he could see it in her eyes. But she held silent for a moment. His impatience got the better of him. "Do you like the house, or not?"

"I think it's amazing. But, like I said, a bit sparse." She shot a significant look into the living room. "Christmas decorations would help."

He followed the direction of her gaze, pausing over a large empty space near the bay of windows. A Christmas tree would fit perfectly there. Some garland would be nice, too. Some of those twinkling little lights would add color.

"Do you have any available?" Hope wondered aloud.

"Sure, I do." He swung back around to face her. "They are currently sitting in one of those big-box stores waiting for me to purchase them."

As intended, she laughed. "Cutting it close, aren't you?"

"I have well over two weeks until the big day."

Hope tapped her wrist. "Ticktock, doctor."

He opened his mouth to defend himself, but the twins cut him off. "We'll help you decorate," Kennedy said, with Harper adding, "Yeah! It'll be fun."

"Consider yourselves drafted into service."

"Yippee!"

Walker smiled down at his two new recruits. Their joy

was infectious. "Why don't you go explore your new home while your aunt and I retrieve your luggage from the car?"

"Can we, Aunt Hope?"

She gave her permission with a short nod.

The girls didn't need to be told twice. Off they sprinted, their shouts filling the empty house and, just like that, the crack in Walker's heart opened a little more.

"You just wait, Walker Evans. The girls and I are going to turn your house into a home this holiday season."

Home. The word rolled off Hope's tongue naturally, leaving Walker wanting something more, something he'd thought lost forever.

He wanted tomorrow.

He was actually reveling in the sensation, until Hope touched his arm and asked a question that killed his mood. "Any news from Brent concerning his travel plans?"

"Nothing yet."

Her eyebrows drew together. "I hate waiting."

Walker did, too, usually. Right now, he was a big fan of a nice long delay. Every hour Brent was held up in Africa was another hour Walker got to spend with Hope and the twins.

As if to mock him, the antique clock above the fireplace chimed the hour. The sound reminded him that time was running out. Or, as Hope so eloquently said...

Tick, tock...

Due to a change in his work hours and other scheduling difficulties, Walker didn't see the Jeffrieses for the next several days. He'd texted Hope, mostly to make plans to purchase a Christmas tree and other decorations for his house. Hope had also agreed to meet him outside the church building this morning, which happened to be Sunday. He'd used the excuse that he'd show her and the twins around, but he really just wanted to make sure they sat with him during service. He was starting to feel territorial.

That could be a problem.

And yet, here he stood, on the steps of Thunder Ridge Community Church, watching their approach with his heart lodged in his throat. He was reminded of the first time he'd seen the trio moving toward him. He'd been struck speechless by the sight they made, the very picture of the kind of family he'd once craved.

The sensation was even stronger this morning, because now Walker knew what he wanted. A second chance at happiness. More than that, he wanted the dream he'd nearly had once before. A wife, a houseful of children, a few rambunctious dogs, all of it.

The twins caught sight of him first. They broke into a run and all but leaped into his outstretched arms. His greedy heart soaked in their joy. All too soon they wiggled out of his embrace.

"Will you sit with us?" Kennedy asked.

Walker smiled down at the little girl. "That's the plan."

He switched his attention to Hope. The harsh morning sun cast her in its stark glow, highlighting the purple shadows beneath her eyes. "Bad night?"

She looked ready to deny the gentle accusation. But then she shook her head and sighed heavily. "I tossed and turned," she admitted. "Any news from your brother?"

As if on cue, Walker's cell phone dinged. He thumbed open the message. "It's from Brent."

"What does it say?"

He allowed a brief silence to elapse, then looked up. He saw tiredness in Hope's eyes, and a shred of fear. "Read it yourself." Boarding a flight to Germany. Will contact you again when I land.

"So, he's officially on his way home," Hope said.

"It would appear so."

Her face did a funny little twist as she handed him back the phone. She looked dazed, lost, but also determined.

"We'll talk more after church. For now—" Walker reached out "—let's get inside and find our seats."

Hope accepted his silent invitation, taking his hand without hesitation. But she couldn't prevent a small sob.

"We'll figure it out, Hope."

"I know." Then, just as smoothly as he'd taken her hand, she reached out and grasped one of Kennedy's. Walker took Harper's, and the four of them entered the church linked together hand in hand.

The dream just became a lot more real.

Walker directed their tiny group to one of the back pews. Almost as soon as they were settled, the worship team began playing the first cords of a familiar Christmas hymn.

Proving Hope hadn't neglected their Christian education, Harper and Kennedy launched into the song with enthusiasm. The girls knew most of the words. They mumbled over several of the more difficult phrases, then all but shouted out the chorus, putting solid emphasis on *away* and *manger*.

Walker and Hope shared a smile over the children's heads, the silent message that passed between them seemed to say, "How could anyone not love these two girls?"

The lead pastor took the pulpit. His sermon focused on God's love given to humankind in the gift of His Son. An appropriate message for the season and one Walker considered while the girls silently drew on paper Hope had brought with her.

"We are an active participant in this transaction between God and His people," the preacher continued. "We are to accept this gift that is freely given."

The man's word choice had Walker sitting a little straighter. *We are an active participant.* For years, Walker had remained passive. He'd ignored his blessings in favor of focusing solely on what he'd lost. He'd allowed what might have been to overwhelm what could be.

"Accepting a gift, any gift, starts with a choice."

A choice. Yes, Walker had a choice to make. He could remain stuck in the past where everything was sad yet familiar, or he could reach for an uncertain future full of unknowns. Letting go would not be easy. Rachel's death had shattered his heart. Walker had truly thought he'd buried his one chance at happiness with his wife and daughter.

However, for the first time in years he wanted to try for happily-ever-after again. And it was all due to the woman sitting on his right. The girls had played their role, as well. Walker wanted to be a husband *and* father. He'd quit wanting either. Unable to stop himself, he glanced at Hope over the twins' heads. She was leaning forward, listening intently to the sermon. In a flash, Walker saw what his future held. And whom he wanted to share it with.

Dare he take a leap of faith?

The sermon concluded and the worship band took their place. They played the final song, another Christmas staple. The pastor dismissed the congregation with a prayer and a blessing for the coming week.

Walker and Hope went through the process of swathing the twins in their winter-weather gear. With Hope riding shotgun, and the twins buckled up in the back seat, Walker pointed his SUV toward Quinn's house. When Hope asked why, he simply said, "Tradition."

Her eyes filled with that same look he'd come to recognize as longing. "I thought we were going to buy a Christmas tree."

"After lunch."

Five minutes later, he was pulling his SUV in behind McCoy's beat-up Jeep. He and Hope were helping the girls out of the back seat when Reno's pickup pulled to a stop behind them. "I thought you said this was a *family* tradition."

"Extended family," he corrected. "Which includes lifelong friends, distant cousins and random people any of us want to invite."

"Random people like me." She clearly meant it jokingly, but there was hurt in her tone.

"There is nothing random about you."

Hope gave him a wry smile. Again, Walker wondered about her past, namely her childhood. He wasn't able to ask the question, because Reno hopped out of the truck and stretched his long legs as if working out invisible kinks. His face held signs of pain.

The doctor in Walker frowned at his friend. "You went skiing?"

Reno made a face. "Knock it off, *Mom*. I hit the slopes this morning. Snowboarding, not skiing. And look who it is. Hey, girls. Hope."

"Hi, Reno."

From Walker's point of view, Reno's smile was a little too friendly. As was the one Hope gave him in return. Walker shifted between the two. The move lacked finesse and Reno, hardwired to cut Walker zero slack, made a snarky remark. "Real smooth, man."

Bertha barked a greeting from the porch.

Squealing in delight, the twins took off. Hope shot after them, all but begging them to slow down. A minor commotion ensued at the top of the steps. Then, after a cursory knock on the front door, everyone entered the house.

Walker and Reno pulled up the rear. Reno, incapable of keeping his nose out of anyone's business, wasted no time fishing for information. "What's going on, Walker?"

He pretended to misunderstand. "You and I are about to embark on some serious carbo-loading thanks to my sister's world-famous mashed potatoes."

Reno paused at the foot of the steps, forcing Walker to do the same. "Nice redirect, but something's definitely up. I'm not blind. I see the family connection. Either come clean about those little girls, or I'm going to start drawing conclusions."

"Let it drop, Reno."

"No can do. You're happy again." The other man arrowed a finger in Walker's direction. "And we both know why."

Walker attempted to sidestep his friend and ascend the steps.

Reno moved directly in his path.

"Move out of my way."

"Are Harper and Kennedy your daughters?"

Walker suppressed a ragged sigh. It swelled inside him, hurting like a sip of scalding coffee heading down his windpipe. "No."

Expecting more probing, Reno surprised him with shake of his head. "Too bad. You've been walking around half-dead for way too long. It's been nice seeing you come back to life."

There were a lot of ways Walker could respond to his friend's assessment. He could attempt denial, but why? Reno was right. He'd been moving through life on autopilot for years.

"Yeah, yeah, I get it. Mind my own business." Reno

slapped Walker on the back. "Now that I'm through making startling insights, and watching you squirm, I could get down with some serious carbo-loading."

Although he knew this was only a pause in the conversation—Reno was nothing if not persistent—Walker was relieved his friend had let the matter drop for now. "After you."

They entered the house, Reno seeking food, Walker breathless with a different sort of hunger. The kind that couldn't be sated with mashed potatoes. He wanted what Reno accused to be true. He craved a family of his own. Not just any family, either, but the one that could never be his.

He was suddenly aware of the wild beating of his heart.

In silent agreement, he and Reno moved past the entryway, into the living room. An eclectic mix of people had gathered, some sat, others milled about with plates overflowing with food. The majority was family, but a few friends and locals were also in attendance, most of whom Walker had known since grade school. Some, like Reno, he'd known even longer.

A grin slid across Reno's face. "Lunch is served."

Without another word, his friend took off for the dining room, leaving Walker alone with his thoughts. The exact place he did not want to be. Thankfully, a loud *woof* heralded Bertha's arrival. The massive dog wheeled around the corner, then let out another serious of barks when she eyeballed Walker.

"Hey, big girl." He reached down to pet the dog's head.

"Look what the dog dragged in." Dressed in jeans and a wheat-colored cable-knit sweater, Grant greeted Walker with a grin. "Hope is in the kitchen with my lovely wife."

"Who said I was looking for Hope?"

"Weren't you? My mistake." The man sauntered off chuckling under his breath.

Walker hung back, torn between seeking out Hope or the food. The matter was settled when Reno returned, plate in hand, a snarky look on his face. "You going to stand there petting the dog all day or eat?"

"I'll eat. Thanks, man." He yanked the plate out of Reno's hand and disappeared in the living room to the sound of his friend's outraged sputtering.

Barely ten minutes after entering the Holloway's home, Hope found herself elbow-deep in flour and cookie dough. This home, these people, they took family to a whole new level. Traditions were as ingrained in their DNA as their hair color. Hope had seen glimpses of the same in her temporary homes, but never before had her mind been able to reach beyond a hazy, unrealized dream and formulate a clear picture of the kind of family she wanted for herself.

Quinn rattled off the recipe's ingredients. Hope was familiar with most, but the last one had her looking up, mystified. "Cardamom?"

"There's something cozy about the spice, don't you think?"

"I have no idea." Hope wasn't even sure what cardamom was.

When she voiced her ignorance, Quinn smiled. "It's a spice from India."

"Did I hear you say cardamom?" Walker appeared in the doorway. "Please tell me you're making my favorite cookies."

Hope angled her head. "Really? They're your favorite?"

"Fastest way to my heart."

His words seemed to have a hidden meaning. Or maybe not so hidden. The moment Walker's gaze locked with hers, Hope thought of family again, of cozy wood and glass houses nestled on a Colorado lake.

For several, painful seconds, her lungs refused to work properly.

Why him, Lord?

Hope knew so little about the man, and certainly nothing about the loss he'd endured that had born that hint of sorrow he wore like a second skin.

The room suddenly felt too small, too hot and crowded. Hope shoved a strand of hair off her face with the top of her wrist. It fell back over her forehead almost immediately. Couldn't her hair at least cooperate, if not her heart?

Walker shifted, splintering the tense moment.

"Stop distracting my helper." Quinn gave him a little shove. "Hope and I have serious work to do."

Walker dug in his heels, making a snide comment about bossy big sisters. Quinn countered with a remark about bratty little brothers. The affection between them was obvious. Hope felt a tug in her heart. She'd seen siblings interact like this. But she'd never really been a part of the good-natured teasing.

Always on the outside looking in. Story of her life. The tug in her heart turned into an ache.

"Go find someone else to bother." Quinn gave Walker another shove.

"All right, all right, but only because the sooner I leave, the sooner you can get those cookies baked." He gave Hope one long look, then left the kitchen muttering something under his breath she didn't quite catch.

"What was that?" Quinn yelled after him. "Did you just call me a nag?"

His only response was a brief wave over his head.

Hope kept her expression bland as she watched Walker's retreat. She tried to appear nonchalant, easy breezy. But when she realized Quinn was watching her, she was hit with a wall of nerves. Had she just given away her attraction for Walker away? *To his sister?*

Proving she took her role as big sister seriously, Quinn addressed the matter head-on. "What's going on between you and my brother?"

Hope busied herself with picking up the recipe card and pretending avid fascination. "It's not what you think. Walker and I agreed to work together to provide the twins a happy Christmas."

"Admirable, to be sure." Quinn took the recipe card out of Hope's hand. "I'm glad you and Walker have become friends. He needs a friend. He's been alone too long, ever since..."

She let the rest hang in the air. Hope had so many questions. Walker had been alone ever since...what? Would Quinn tell her if she asked? The woman's continued silence was answer enough. "How many cookies are we making?"

Quinn appeared relieved by the change of subject. "Three batches of thirty-six, one for today, the rest for Grant's office."

"One hundred and eight cookies it is." Hope grabbed the jar of flour, giving Quinn a bland stare before rolling her gaze over the recipe card she still held. "Ready to get back to work?"

The next hour was spent mixing ingredients, rolling out dough, applying cookie cutters and then baking batches of two dozen at a time.

The spicy aroma of cardamom was mouthwatering. "I can't wait to taste these."

"You shall be the first."

Only after the last batch was out of the oven did Hope take Quinn up on her offer. The mix of sugar, butter and cardamom slid over her tongue. "I'm stealing this recipe."

"No need. It's yours."

She'd barely taken a second bite when they were interrupted by two sets of very excited twins. Apparently, sledding was on the afternoon's agenda. "Dad and Uncle Walker are meeting us at the top of the hill," Skylar said.

"Let's sit out on the back porch and watch the shenanigans," Quinn suggested. "Unless you want to join the fun."

"I'm perfectly happy observing."

"I was counting on you saying that."

Outside, Quinn pointed to their left where the sledding party had gathered near a clump of pine trees. The grade of the slope seemed a bit steep for Hope's liking, but it faced away from the lake and leveled out into a flat, snow-covered plain.

Harper and Kennedy bounced around Walker, talking all at once. From this distance, Hope couldn't hear their specific words. She didn't need to know what they said. Their obvious excitement was enough to warm her heart. For his part, Walker looked like—Hope swallowed—he looked like a father as he loaded the twins onto a two-person sled.

He guided them in position, and then...

Whoosh! Down the hill they went. Harper screamed. Kennedy screamed.

Hope jumped to her feet.

She was halfway down the back steps when the shrieks turned to giggles, then to bellyaching laughter. At the bottom of the hill, both girls rolled off the sled, then, hopping to their feet, began jumping up and down and begging to do it again.

Walker ran down the hill, grabbed the sled and trudged back up the slope, the girls scrambling along behind him.

Still shaking a little, Hope returned to her seat next to Quinn and continued watching the fun. This carefree afternoon with family was the life the twins deserved, and so much more than Hope could provide them.

Had she once thought she could take them back to New York and none of this would matter anymore?

"It's a relief to see Walker happy again. He's shut himself off from the world for so long I'd forgotten how good he is with kids, not just my daughters, but other kids, too."

Hope had a million questions. She settled on, "Has he always worked the night shift?"

"No." Quinn waved at one of her daughters. "He says the hours suit him. But I know it's not true. It's just an excuse to avoid personal connections outside of family."

Too intrigued to let that go, Hope said, "That's the second time you've referenced Walker's past. What aren't you saying?"

"He hasn't told you about Rachel?"

Rachel. Hope now had a name to put to Walker's private pain. There'd been a woman, one that still lived in his heart, if not his life. Hope wanted to retreat inward and isolate herself from the moment. Her curiosity was too strong. "He's never mentioned a Rachel, or any woman for that matter."

"I'm not surprised." Quinn's gaze followed Walker as he loaded the twins onto the sled again. "Brent isn't the only Evans brother who suffered a terrible loss."

"No?"

"I'm sorry. I've said too much. Walker should be the one to tell you about his wife."

"Walker is married?"

How had her private detective missed that vital piece of information? How had she?

"*Was* married. It was a long time ago."

"What happened?"

Quinn shook her head. "I shouldn't say. If my brother wants you to know what happened, he'll tell you himself."

Hope looked over where Walker stood, laughing with Grant over something one of the little girls said. He seemed genuinely happy. But with Quinn's words rolling around in her head, Hope studied him closer. She noticed how he held himself a little separate. In the moment, and yet not fully there. His loneliness called to her. Hope wanted to go to him and offer what comfort she could. She wanted to listen to his story, maybe soothe away his pain. She wanted to provide him with new memories to chase away the bad ones.

Did she have that right?

"You like him."

Hope gave a weighty sigh. "Of course I like him. He's a friend. I like *all* my friends."

Quinn's lips curved upward. "No man looks at a friend the way my brother looks at you."

Hope shut her eyes. There was no excuse for feeling moved by Quinn's observation. "If Walker considered me more than a friend, he would have told me about his past."

That, Hope realized, was the critical detail she must not forget. She'd put Plan B in motion to secure her future with the twins, not Walker.

"Hope, is it really out of the realm of possibility that you and Walker could be more than friends? Have you considered—"

The man himself interrupted. "We have hungry kids out here. Cookies ready yet?"

Quinn gave him a thumbs-up.

A commotion ensued as adults and children took a break from the sledding. The twins were digging into their first cookie when Kennedy swung a perfectly innocent gaze up to Hope. "Have you thought any more about getting us a puppy?"

Nothing like putting her on the spot.

"You really should take a look," Walker said.

Hope was shaking her head before he finished. "I don't want to see puppies."

"And yet your face says you absolutely do."

"I absolutely do not." She sighed. "I'll just fall in love."

Walker held out a hand. "Come on. You can take a quick look. Five minutes, and that'll be that."

Hope grappled with indecision. "Five minutes, not a second more."

"I'll start a timer." He pointed to his sports watch, then stopped the twins with another point when they scrambled out of their seats. "You cannot come with us."

Identical scowls formed between their brows. "Why not?"

"Because you'll start begging your aunt for a puppy—" he lowered his voice to a stage whisper "—and then she'll say no for sure."

With their faces full of little-girl mutiny, they relented.

At the top of the basement stairs, Hope hesitated. "Before we head down, I need to know whose side you're on, mine or the twins?"

He gave her a wounded expression. "Must you ask?"

"Actually, yes. Am I about to be manipulated into adopting a puppy?"

"Honestly?" His grin flashed. "Only if you really, really, really want one."

Bracing herself, Hope descended into the basement. Daisy lay peacefully in the basket with her puppies. Four were feeding, but the other three were engaged in a raucous play session.

"They're so cute." Hope lowered to her knees, her eyes

filling with tears as she took in the miniature round, tawny bodies, squat legs, black ears and smashed-in snouts. "I can hardly stand it."

A daring puppy belly-crawled to the edge of the basket. He wiggled over the top and tumbled onto the floor. After a seriously cute dance to gain his feet, he found his balance and shot across the basement at lightning speed. He came to a dead stop, then spun in a circle and sped back in the direction of his siblings. This time his bubblegum-pink tongue flapped out the side of his mouth.

Before Hope could reach for him, the puppy took a flying leap in the air. With momentum on his side, he cleared the edge of the basket and landed on top of the other puppies with a belly splat. He wiggled around, chomping and nipping at random paws, floppy ears and nub tails. Hope stared in momentary shock then, shaking her head, burst out laughing.

With Walker's accompanying chuckle filling the room, she scooped up the troublemaker. He came up wriggling and twisting, little legs running in the air. "Rambunctious little guy, aren't you?"

He continued his antics, sufficiently getting in several licks across her chin. Laughing despite the impromptu bath, she held on tight and studied the animal through narrowed eyes. "You are breaking my heart."

When he stopped thrashing, Hope put him on the floor. He spun around, caught sight of his mother and immediately instigated a wrestling match with her. The good-natured Daisy obliged her rabble-rousing offspring.

"Time's up." Walker stretched out his hand. "It's been five minutes. Ready to go?"

Hope wasn't ready to leave. "One more minute."

"I'll give you two."

She took ten.

Then, heart heavy, she ascended the basement steps

in silence. Walker brought up the rear. Upstairs, he took her hand, pulled her close enough she could feel the heat coming off him in waves. "Why so sad?"

She shrugged.

"Talk to me, Hope." He drew her a step closer, so close she could smell the remaining hints of his shampoo—a masculine, spicy scent that brought to mind a forest of fresh pine trees covered under a blanket of snow. They were nearly touching now.

She drew in a shaky breath.

"You were smiling and laughing down there, kissing puppies and letting them kiss you back." He angled his head. "Now you look like you want to cry. Tell me what's wrong."

Hope said nothing as he guided her to the kitchen table, now empty but for abandoned plates full of cookie crumbs.

Without really thinking about what she was doing, she sat.

Walker took the chair beside her.

"Did you have a dog as a child?" he asked. "I'm shooting in the dark here, but…did he get hit by a car or something?"

"I never had a dog. I always wanted one. But it was out of the question." She looked down at the distressed farm table, dragging her thumbnail along a jagged scar. "Charity and I were shuttled from home to home, some large and full of other kids, some smaller. A few older couples took us in, all of them doing their Christian duty, taking care of the widowed pastor's daughters, 'the poor little dears.'"

Hope hated the bitterness she heard in her tone. She rarely talked about her childhood for this very reason.

"Where was your mother?"

"She died when Charity and I were a few years older than the girls."

"And your father? He was a pastor?"

She nodded. "After my mother died, he became a missionary, working in various undisclosed regions of the world, probably the Middle East, maybe China, but always somewhere dangerous. He came home occasionally, then off he would go again. The church rallied behind him, financially supporting his work and taking turns caring for Charity and me."

"So, your father basically abandoned you and your sister."

She shrugged.

"At least you had each other."

If only it were that simple. "Charity and I weren't close like Harper and Kennedy. We never had that twin connection. We were wired differently. Charity considered every move to a new home as a wild adventure. I dreaded having to start all over again. Holidays were the worst."

"Because of your father's absence?"

Hope didn't want Walker rooting around in her head and making himself at home. *Too late.* She'd already let him in. "He served people living in the worst of conditions. It changed his perspective. He considered America far too indulgent. He disliked Christmas most of all. We were not to celebrate or accept presents. We were to contemplate the plight of others less fortunate."

"That's a lot to ask of children."

"It was especially difficult when we were living with families that had other kids our age."

"Because those kids accepted the full Christmas experience as just a part of their normal existence?"

"Exactly."

"What about other holidays, birthdays? Were those off-limits, as well?"

"They were treated the same as Christmas." She closed

her eyes, trying not to remember the shame of wanting something special from her father, nothing big, just something tangible she could hold on to when he left her in the care of strangers. "I don't want that for Harper and Kennedy. I want them to love Christmas. Not because of the presents, my father had a point about that, but about the celebration of family. I want them to know the joy of the season. The food, the baking, the decorations."

"Your sister didn't give them those kinds of Christmases?"

"I'm not sure. I don't think she had the money, or even the inclination." Hope sighed. "It's hard to know. I've asked the twins about their life with their mother. But they only know what they know. What seems normal to them isn't normal for other children."

In a stilted tone, she told him about their request to stay in the car while she went into the hospital to confront him. As he listened, Walker's expression mirrored the concern swirling inside Hope. "I fear my sister may not have been the most conventional of mothers."

A long pause met her confession. Then, with the insight she was coming to understand as part of who he was as a doctor and as a man, he said, "You're afraid she was abusive?"

"No! Charity made mistakes, but she loved her daughters. It's just... I worry she neglected them."

"Let me ease your mind. I've treated hundreds of children in my ER. Part of what I have to do is to look for signs of abuse. Harper and Kennedy show no signs of it. Yes, they're more reserved than most five-year-old children, and they can be clingy when they're tired or thrown into new situations, but they know they're safe and loved. They're going to be fine."

"That's pretty much what Dr. Stephens said."

Walker considered her with a thoughtful expression. "You've taken excellent care of them, Hope. Never doubt that."

But she did, all the time. "I can't give them everything they need. Although I've tried, I can't be both mother and father to them. And I can't give them a family Christmas, not without your help."

He smiled then. And the look in his eyes—*that look*— was full of unspoken promises. "We're going to give Harper and Kennedy the best Christmas of their lives. Actually, we've already begun."

She supposed they had.

"And you, Hope." He touched her sleeve, nothing but a slide of his fingertips, but she felt the contact all the way to her toes. "You deserve to experience the joy of a family Christmas as much as the twins. Let me give that to you."

She wanted to believe this time would be different. "I'm not family."

"Now see, that's where you're wrong." He pulled her close and kissed the top of her head. "You are family."

Oh, Walker.

"Now, let's round up the twins and go buy us a Christmas tree." He stood and reached for her. "You with me, Jeffries?"

With fingers shaking slightly, she placed her hand in his. "I'm with you, Evans."

Chapter Thirteen

Walker and Hope found the twins in the living room. They were listening, eyes wide, as McCoy gave his opinion on what kind of tree they should choose. According to his brother, the tree should be at least seven feet tall, a Colorado blue spruce and the only place to find it was Coach's Christmas Tree Lot.

Aware his brother could go on for another thirty minutes, Walker interrupted the one-sided discussion. "Who's ready to pick out our Christmas tree?"

Harper and Kennedy answered immediately. "Me!"

Goodbyes were said. Then, after loading Hope and the twins in his SUV, Walker set out in the direction of Coach's Christmas Tree Lot. He pulled into an empty parking space next to the hand-painted sign announcing he'd found the right place.

As they climbed out of the vehicle, Harper informed their group, "We have to get a Colorado blue spruce. Or nothing at all."

Walker met Hope's amused gaze over the little girl's head. "I'm told this particular lot has a wide variety of blue spruces."

"They have to be *Colorado* blue spruces."

Walker gave the child a fist bump. "Got it."

With the help of one of the coaches, they found the perfect tree. A Colorado blue spruce that was just over seven feet tall with full branches, a straight trunk and no bald spots.

"For an additional ten dollars," the man informed them, "we'll deliver the tree to your house within the next twenty-four hours."

"Thanks, but I think we can manage it ourselves."

It was past dusk, the sky more purple than gray, when Walker drove into his driveway.

By mutual agreement, Hope occupied the twins so he could wrestle the tree off the roof of his SUV and secure a stand to the trunk. When he brought the tree inside the house, he was pleased to discover Hope and the twins had prepared the perfect spot in the living room.

After setting the tree in the now empty space overlooking the lake, he moved it around until Hope was satisfied with its position. "There," she declared. "Right there. Perfect."

Walker removed his gloves and studied the overall effect. "We made a good choice."

He caught Hope's smile, found his own widening in response. This moment with her and the twins felt good. It felt right. No guilt, no looking back, just a full heart and a lot of joy.

Something was churning inside him, something directly related to the smiling woman standing beside him. Each moment in her company was becoming more and more precious. The twins added the exclamation point to every encounter.

Walker's house felt like a home now. The tree wasn't the only reason.

Anticipation sang in his veins, and then…

Ah, yes, there was the pang of familiar guilt he'd been expecting. Tonight, however, the pain that always accompanied the sensation was decidedly less. Time and distance had softened the rough edges of his grief. And now, Walker was ready to admit he had feelings for Hope. She made him want to start living again.

Why not start now?

"Okay, girls, now for the important question. Do we go with white lights or multicolored? No, wait." He held up a hand to stop the twins from shouting out their preferences. "Think very hard before you respond. There is only one right answer."

Both girls turned to Hope. Kennedy spoke for the pair. "Can we show him what we got?"

"Now is as good a time as any." Hope smiled. "Be right back."

With her expression giving nothing away, she disappeared into the kitchen. When she returned, she carried an armful of plastic bags from the big-box store on the edge of town. With a flourish, she dug inside one of the larger bags, then pulled out a box of lights.

Walker's gaze landed on the picture of a Christmas tree aglow with every color in the rainbow. "Now that's what I'm talking about."

Harper rummaged through the other bags. Kennedy, sweet girl that she was, only had eyes for him. "Are you going to stay and help us decorate the tree?"

The question should have thrown him off balance. Walker hadn't decorated a tree since Rachel's death. He waited for images from the past to encroach on the moment. They didn't come. Instead, a very clear picture of Christmas morning swam in his mind. The twins were in flannel nightgowns, sitting among discarded wrapping paper and way too many presents. Walker and Hope drank coffee and watched them tearing into yet another gift.

He was so caught up in the image, he hadn't realized Kennedy was still talking to him.

"Here." She shoved a box of shiny red ornaments into his hands, her eyes full of little-girl excitement. "You can put these on the tree."

Walker automatically closed his fingers over the box. "Ho-kay."

The next two hours went by in a whirlwind of decorating and giggling—on the twins' part—and organized chaos. When the last ornament was hung, Walker stepped back and studied their collective handiwork.

"It doesn't look right," Harper complained.

"That's because the little lights aren't twinkling." He turned to Hope. "Want to do the honors?"

"You better believe I do." Looking happier than he'd seen her all day, she trotted to the wall socket and plugged in two sets of cords.

An explosion of color erupted from every available branch.

"Best tree ever," Walker declared, earning him a pair of matching fist bumps from the twins.

Hope returned to his side then, stunning him speechless, she linked her arm through his and laid her head on his shoulder. "We make a great team."

"We do."

She lifted her head.

Their gazes locked, held. Walker couldn't look away. Hope seemed caught with the same affliction. The twins settled in on either side of them, gazing up at the tree with wonder.

Walker's heart filled with a flourish of warmth and

long-missed happiness. In that moment, the future seemed as bright as the multicolored Christmas tree.

Both girls were practically asleep in their chairs by the time Hope served dinner, a simple meal of pasta and a green salad. They'd been able to convince Walker to stay for the meal. Hope watched him out of the corner of her eye, an uneasy sensation making her shoulders bunch.

Something had changed in the last few minutes. Over dinner, they'd fallen into an easy conversation about random topics from the weather to Walker's plan for decorating the outside of his house. "I'll get it done this week."

"Tell me what I can do to help."

"I'll send a long, extensive list."

They shared a laugh. And everything seemed right in the world. However, now, beneath the girls' sleepy chatter boiled unspoken tension. Hope thought they'd gotten on well today and were beginning to trust each other. But she'd caught Walker watching her from across the table, his brows knit together, as if he had yet to determine if she was his enemy or his ally.

She wasn't sure herself. Which probably explained the strain.

Needing to alleviate a portion of the awkwardness, she smiled at him. He smiled back.

"It was a great day," she said.

"The very best."

Yawning loudly, Harper rubbed her eyes. "Will you read to us tonight, Aunt Hope?"

The question sent warmth washing through her. She and the girls may be staying in an unfamiliar town, in an unfamiliar house, but Hope could—and would—continue reading to the girls at night. Dr. Stephens had emphasized the importance of routine. All Hope knew was that the bedtime ritual was as important to her as it seemed to be for the girls.

She realized she hadn't answered the question when Kennedy chimed in. "Will you join us, Dr. Walker?"

Hope didn't want Walker invading her special time with the twins. But the silent plea in the little girls' eyes nearly wrecked her. How was she supposed to say no to that look? She locked eyes with Walker. The longing in them made her decision for her. "Do you want to come upstairs and read to the girls with me?"

He lifted a shoulder, trying to look nonchalant. Hope wasn't fooled. He wanted to join them. "What are you reading?"

"The Night Before Christmas."

"My favorite."

The four of them trooped out of the kitchen, the girls dragging at an impossibly slow pace that spoke of their exhaustion. Hope figured they wouldn't make it past the first page.

At the last minute, Walker turned back in the direction of the kitchen. "It's trash day tomorrow. I better take the can to the edge of the drive before I forget."

She nodded, then he did, and they went their separate ways.

By the time the twins were tucked into the queen-size bed in one of the upstairs bedrooms, their faces washed, teeth brushed and prayers said, Hope's heart had taken a series of hits. The twins had prayed for her, for their mother in heaven, then had added several more for Walker, Quinn, the Holloway twins, McCoy. They'd finished with Bertha and Daisy.

Then Harper had added, "Please, Lord. Make Aunt

Hope change her mind so we can get one of Daisy's puppies."

Kennedy had her own final request. "Can you make it so we can stay in Colorado forever and ever? And can you make Skylar and Sinclair our best friends? Dr. Walker, too? We like him a lot."

"A lot, a lot," Harper added.

The girls had opened their eyes, grinned at each other, then said, in unison, with one solid nod in agreement, "Amen."

Eyes stinging, heart shattered into a million pieces, Hope accepted the truth. Harper and Kennedy were already thinking of themselves as a part of the Evans family. Or certainly wanting it to be true. They would be thrilled when they discovered the truth.

She sat in a chair next to the big bed they shared, opened the book in her lap and looked over at the twins.

Two pair of big blue eyes stared back at her. They had something on their minds.

"Girls? What's up?"

They looked at one another, exchanged one of their silent twin messages, then turned back to study Hope with identical expressions of wistfulness.

"Do you like Dr. Walker?" Harper asked.

Hope knew where this was going. She'd assumed the twins had let this particular topic go. "Of course I like him. I think he's nice."

"Do you think you could marry him?" the child asked. "And then you could be our mommy and he could be our daddy and we can live in this house forever and ever."

Hope sighed over the vulnerable expression in the young girl's eyes. "Dr. Walker can't be your daddy."

"But you said you liked him," Harper whined. "And

when Momma said she liked a man, he would move in with us."

Oh, Charity. A keen ache pierced the center of Hope's soul.

She was going to have to tell the twins about Brent if he didn't arrive in the next few days. In the meantime, she sidestepped the issue of fathers altogether by saying, "It's best Dr. Walker and I stay friends for now."

For now? Why had Hope added that qualifier?

You know why.

And so, apparently, did the twins. They exchanged another look. Hope feared two little matchmakers had been born tonight. Praying she was wrong, she lowered her head and started reading. "'Twas the night before Christmas and all through the house…"

Walker stood outside the twins' bedroom, listening as Hope's soft, lilting voice read the popular Christmas story. Her voice was filled with an underlying tenderness, as if she was feeling especially emotional tonight.

Unwilling to interrupt the tender moment, he peered into the room. His gaze sought and found Hope. Head bent, there was a softness about her that sent his head reeling. He had to look away to catch his breath.

Walker tried not to read too much into his reaction. Hope was reading to his nieces. His nieces! The knowledge was still new, making him as emotional as she sounded. The three were living in his home, as if they were family.

They were family.

Just not *his* family.

Hope paused, looked up and caught him staring. She kept reading from memory, her green eyes searching his as she spoke. Her gaze was full of profound gentleness, as if she shared the conflict waging inside him. He wanted to go to her, let her soothe away whatever this was moving through him.

She mercifully looked back to the book.

On surprisingly unsteady legs, Walker quietly slipped down the hallway. He left the house through the back door and sat heavily on the stoop. He drew in a deep breath, let it out slowly and then stared up at the clouds skidding across the full moon.

He attempted to picture Rachel in his mind. She came to him, the image clearer than in recent years. He breathed in. Out. And then…he let his wife go.

Peace enveloped him.

The process had been so simple. Why hadn't he done this sooner?

Because Hope hadn't come into his life, making him wish for something more than a bland existence and terrible work hours. She'd awakened a desire to start living again, without grief weighing him down.

What if she left Colorado?

What if she didn't?

Working the question around in his mind, he stared out over the lake and watched the moonlight shimmer across the water.

Behind him, the door creaked on its hinges. "Walker?"

"Out here," he called over his shoulder. "On the back stoop."

Hope poked her head out the doorway. "I thought you'd left."

"Not yet." Without thinking too hard about what he was doing, he patted the spot beside him. "Come. Sit with me a moment before I head out."

"Let me get my coat."

She returned in less than a minute and sat.

Walker could feel her eyes on him. She had to be wondering why he hadn't come into the room to read with the twins as he'd promised.

He wasn't sure how to explain it.

Gathering his thoughts, he looked up at the sky.

As if sensing he had something important to say, she reached out and covered his hand with hers. The tension drained out of him and he knew where to start. "I like having you and the twins in my house."

"Thank you for inviting us."

"It made sense." He swiveled his head in her direction and decided to be candid. "I heard your conversation with the twins tonight."

"Which part?"

Rather than rehashing the conversation, he said, "It's not a bad idea, you and me."

"It's a terrible idea." He would have been insulted if not for the tender expression in her eyes, and the yearning. "They think if we got married, you would become their father. You can't be their father."

She was right, of course. Brent had that honor. The reminder felt like another loss.

"Even if your brother denies paternity, or fails to—"

"He won't."

"Then there's nothing more to say."

Oh, but there was. "There's something between us, Hope." He took her hand in his. "I know you feel it, too."

"We barely know each other."

"We know enough."

"You may know enough about me. But I know very little about you."

"That's not completely true."

"No?" She turned her face away from his. "What about your wife? Were you ever going to tell me about Rachel?"

Not expecting that, Walker stared out at the lake. He

traced the moon's path across the water, gathered his words. "How much did your investigator tell you about Rachel?"

"Nothing, actually. It was Quinn."

Quinn, of course.

Dragging in a ragged breath, he turned to face Hope. "Did my sister tell you Rachel was five months pregnant when she died?"

His voice sounded as empty as he felt.

"Oh, Walker. No." Tears filled her eyes. "I... I didn't know. I'm so sorry."

He rose, unable to sit still, and paced a few steps toward the lake. He stopped and shoved his hands in his pockets. "Rachel had just reached the halfway mark in her pregnancy, about nineteen and a half weeks along, when the pain began."

"She was losing the baby?"

"That's what we both thought. What we didn't know was that her appendix had ruptured. By the time the doctors realized the problem, it was too late. The toxins had already moved into her blood. The baby survived in the NICU for a few days after Rachel died, but..."

The rest of his words floated over the lake.

"Oh, Walker." Hope moved to stand beside him. "I'm sorry."

They shared a sad smile. He looked down at his open palm and dusted it with the other. He'd never confided so much to anyone outside the family, and certainly not to a woman. But now that he'd begun, he needed to tell Hope the rest, the part that came after Rachel's death. "I didn't allow myself to grieve. It felt too... I don't know, indulgent. I turned to work to numb my pain and have been living that way ever since."

He shut his eyes a moment, tried to bring up one last

image of Rachel. But the reality of Hope was too strong. Her lovely, oval face, the gentle, bowed lips and green eyes, their color so unique they seemed to contain hints of some undiscovered shade. His mind filled with her. How could a woman so deserving of love have received so little? Walker wanted to give her the love she deserved.

The Lord had blessed him with a second chance at happiness. He forced opened his eyes and focused solely on Hope. He swallowed.

She did the same.

"I was happy enough going through the motions, moving from one day to the next, but not really living. Then you and the twins strolled into my ER and everything changed."

She blinked, but didn't say anything.

"Tonight, in my living room," he said. "You, me, the twins, we were a family."

"But, Walker." A sob sounded in her throat. "We can't be a family. Brent is the twins' father. We have to tell them."

Something hot and miserable moved through Walker. "I'm not convinced we should. Brent will be home in a few days. The news should come from him."

She looked so panicked, so defeated, Walker forgot all about his own pain and dragged her into his arms. For a moment, they simply stood wrapped in each other's embrace.

"Hope." He spoke her name with as much gentleness as he could. "Even if we don't tell them about their father, they should at least know they belong to the Evans family."

She stepped out of his arms. "What if they react badly?"

"Do you honestly believe they'll find the news upsetting?"

"No." She sighed. "They'll be thrilled."

Knowing how hard that was for her to admit, Walker pulled her back into his arms and received the shock of his life. It was him that was immediately soothed. Him that felt the rightness of them being together.

"Walker?" Hope whispered his name, encouraging him to tap into the part of his nature he'd buried with Rachel. "I don't know how I'll bear losing them. I… I don't want to be alone anymore."

"You're not alone," he whispered into her hair. "You have me."

She shifted in his arms and looked into his eyes. He saw the truth gazing back at him. She wanted what he wanted, but she was afraid to believe it was real.

He had those same fears.

A severe sensation took over his body and he felt the blood rush through his veins. Her silent call was too strong to ignore. He lowered his head, stopped when his mouth was mere inches from hers. "Tell me to step back. Tell me to let you go. Tell me you don't want me to kiss you."

Her answer was to slip her hands around his neck. It was all the encouragement he needed. His mouth moved over hers.

She sighed into him.

The sound brought him to his senses. Things were moving too fast, for both of them. He abruptly let her go.

A shaken breath escaped her.

"Hope…" He was talking to her back.

Walker didn't follow her inside the house. They both needed time to sort through their feelings. And then? *Then* they would discuss the future.

Chapter Fourteen

Hope woke the next morning to clear skies and an unmistakable reality. She'd lost her heart to Walker Evans. This wasn't supposed to have happened. She'd come to Thunder Ridge to confront the twins' father, obtain his signature on the custody papers, then return to New York with her future set.

Nothing had gone according to plan.

Hope had been naive when she and the twins had boarded the plane in New York. Now, she felt lost, unmoored. She didn't know what came next, or where to turn. Her gaze fell on the Bible she kept by the bedside. Couldn't hurt. She opened to 2 Corinthians and contemplated the highlighted section in the twelfth chapter.

My grace is sufficient for thee: for My strength is made perfect in weakness.

She wasn't alone. She had the Lord. And, according to the man himself, she had Walker. Her feelings for him were growing every day. What they shared seemed real, but Hope wasn't sure if the twins formed the glue that bound them together, or if it was something more.

They needed time, which they would get now that she'd put Plan B into motion. Of course, nothing could be decided until Brent came home. Everything hinged on his arrival.

Putting the future out of her mind, Hope helped the twins dress for the day. In the kitchen, she pulled out the ingredients for their breakfast. As her hands scrambled eggs, her mind went back to Walker. Hard not to think of him when she was living in his home. If Brent didn't step up as the twins' father, could she and Walker make a home for them here? The thought brought such anticipation, she had to take in a few slow breaths.

Kennedy chose that moment to come running into the kitchen, her little face scrunched up in a picture of concern. "Christmas is next week."

"You are correct."

"But we haven't bought any presents for Dr. Walker or Miss Quinn or the twins or the puppies or for, well, anybody."

This, Hope decided, was an easy enough problem to fix. "We'll go shopping after breakfast."

Thirty minutes later, she was parking her rental car outside The Slippery Slope. "We'll buy something for Dr. Walker first."

The idea was met with excited approval.

She escorted the twins inside the shop and looked around for Reno. Surely, he would know what they should buy his friend. A salesclerk with a mouthful of braces told them the owner wasn't in yet, but she'd be happy to help them. "We're looking for a Christmas gift for a man who likes to ski."

"Does he prefer skiing, or snowboarding?"

Hope felt a moment of sheer panic. How could she have fallen for the man when she didn't even know whether he preferred skiing over snowboarding? "Maybe we should go with something simple, like gloves."

"I can work with that." The clerk led them to a table filled with a wide variety, including mittens, which according to the teenager kept your fingers warmer than gloves during a long day on the slopes. Hope figured someone living in Colorado would know this.

"There are so many choices," Kennedy breathed.

That was an understatement.

It took less than two minutes for Hope to realize she'd made a bad decision. The twins couldn't decide on color or style or whether they should go with gloves or mittens.

"Let's see if I can help." The salesgirl asked a few questions, then began pulling out several options.

The girls agonized over their selection. "It has to be just the right pair," Harper declared.

Eventually, they narrowed the decision down to two possibilities. When they couldn't come to a consensus, Hope stepped in. "Why don't we get both?"

The clerk offered to get two boxes, which were in the back. While she was gone, they wandered around the store. In the kids' section, her eyes landed on tiny snowboards and miniature skis. Would Walker teach them? Or would their father?

One thing was for certain, it wouldn't be Hope. Needing to distract herself, she asked the girls, "Have you thought about what you want for Christmas?"

"We think about it all the time." Harper's eyes settled on her with a clarity that gave her a bad feeling in the pit of his stomach. "We want a daddy of our very own."

"And we want it to be Dr. Walker," Kennedy added.

"We talked about this already," she croaked out. "Dr. Walker is—"

Kennedy cut her off. "—the daddy we want."

Harper agreed with a vigorous nod.

The wistful look both girls sent Hope shot past every

argument she could come up with, except one. The twins already had a father who was currently traveling across the globe to meet them. She wished Walker was with them. He always seemed to know what to say.

"Let's think of other items to add to your Christmas list," she said carefully, attempting to diffuse the situation with a bit of old-fashioned distraction. "In case other people in town want to know what to get you."

"If we can't have a daddy," Harper said, eyes flashing, "then we want a puppy."

Hope nearly agreed to the request. For all the wrong reasons. "I'm still thinking about that, but it's a definite maybe."

The two turned their backs on Hope, then huddled together over a bin of beanie toys. They were subdued the rest of the day. Later that night, once the girls were asleep, Hope lay in own bed, staring up at the ceiling. The twins had asked her about Dr. Walker during bath time, then again after prayers. Hope had told them he was working at the hospital, which seemed to appease them. For now.

It wouldn't last long. The twins were already too attached to Walker. They needed to understand why he couldn't be their father. Knowing it was time to tell them the truth, she picked up her cell phone and composed a text. Any news from Brent?

Walker's response came a few minutes later. Just another update to tell me he's still en route.

Hope blew out a frustrated breath. The girls are asking questions. It's time we tell them about Brent.

Heart pounding, she watched the floating bubbles on the phone's screen. Walker's answer was heroically neutral. I'll come by first thing in the morning after my shift. We'll tell them together.

Hope sent a thumbs-up emoji, then set aside her phone.

There was nothing left to do but mourn what might have been had Walker been the twins' father instead of Brent.

Walker was still thinking about Hope's text as his shift wound down. The last time they spoke, she'd seemed okay letting Brent tell the twins he was their father. Something had changed her mind, and Walker had a good idea what as he reread her text. The girls are asking questions. It's time we tell them about Brent.

Translation: the twins were asking for a father. Had Walker's name come up again? The yearning that came with the thought was a physical ache in his chest. He was ready to join the living again. No more pretending the overnight hours suited his biological clock. No more burying himself in work so he could avoid personal connections.

His awakening didn't mean he would forget Rachel. She would always hold a special place in his heart. But she was his past.

Hope was his future.

The tricky part would be convincing her of that.

Not bothering to change out of his scrubs, he grabbed his gear. Before he could head out, one of the ER nurses peeked her head over the top of his cubicle. "Dr. Evans, you have a visitor. He's waiting for you in the employee break room."

Brent. Who else could it be?

Walker could hear nothing but the sound of his pulse rushing through his veins. Time seemed to crawl. Brent's arrival meant Walker's time with Hope and the twins was over. He'd still see them, but it wouldn't be the same. He tried to shove aside the bitterness that took hold. Tried and failed.

Hope needed to know Brent was home. Walker pulled

out his phone. As he typed, he said, "Tell my brother I'll be there in five minutes."

The nurse didn't move. "How did you know it was your brother waiting for you?"

Walker lifted a shoulder. "Lucky guess?"

She left shaking her head.

Alone, Walker texted Hope the news of Brent's unexpected arrival. Almost immediately floating bubbles appeared on the screen. They disappeared for an extended period of time, then came back up. They disappeared again and then—finally—her response came through. Nothing more than a brief Thanks for the heads up and a promise she would have the girls dressed and ready to meet their father.

With leaden steps, Walker made his way to the employee break room. His brother's voice wafted through the open doorway. "You said he'd be here in five minutes." Brent's low-pitched baritone teemed with frustration. "It's been ten. Are you sure he's coming?"

"It's been seven and, yes, he's coming."

Same impatient Brent. Walker shook his head.

Eyes gritty, throat raw with emotion, he stepped into the doorway and confronted his brother's scowl. No doubt his own expression was equally fierce. His suspicion was confirmed when the nurse glanced from one brother to the other, then beat a hasty retreat.

Arms crossed over his chest, eyes narrowed, Brent waited for Walker to enter the room. The calm demeanor was a facade. The man practically hummed with barely controlled energy.

Walker felt a snap of impatience himself.

Clearly, the years of separation hadn't eased the tension between them. And the blame fell firmly on Walker. A sense of inevitability slammed through him. It was time he humbled himself and healed the rift he'd created.

He quickly scanned Brent's face, noticing the dark circles under his eyes and the lines of strain around his mouth. "You look awful."

"Good to see you, too, bro." Brent's lips twisted at a wry angle. "What can I say? Flights out of Africa aren't exactly easy to come by on short notice."

"You were supposed to contact me when you arrived in Germany."

Brent broke eye contact. "Yeah, well, I didn't."

The hostility was nothing new. Again, Walker's fault. He was handling their reunion poorly. Putting his brother on the defense was the exact opposite approach he should be taking. "I'm glad you're home."

Brent's eyebrows slammed together.

Walker recognized that look. *Here it comes.* The push-back, the detailed list of past transgressions, the reminder he'd made a complete mess of their relationship with his lectures and holier-than-thou comparisons.

The fault was his, Walker knew, and he should take the first step toward reconciliation. "I'm sorry, Brent."

"What, exactly, are you sorry for? That I had to beg, borrow and sell half my possessions to get on a flight home? That I had a three-day layover because of bad weather? Or maybe you're sorry because you just can't stop judging me?"

"I'm sorry for all of it. I'm sorry for my lack of understanding after Nicole died. I'm sorry for expecting your experience to be the same as mine, and for spouting off the same tired sermons about it not being too late to change your ways."

"That was certainly a mouthful."

And Walker wasn't finished. "You had every right to

grieve Nicole in your own way, as I had the right to grieve
Rachel in mine. Who better than me to understand what
you were going through? But instead of offering understanding, I lectured and judged you. I was wrong."

Brent gave him an odd look. "You finished?"

"Not quite." He yanked Brent into a ferocious hug.
"Welcome home."

Brent returned the hug, added a few slaps on the back,
then stepped away and eyed Walker thoughtfully. "You've
changed."

"I had help."

Questions lit in the other man's gaze, but he didn't voice
them. The restraint was new. As was the apology in his
eyes. "You were right to lecture me," Brent admitted. "I
was on a bad path. I hurt a lot of people, and all I can do
is start making amends, beginning right now. I'm sorry,
Walker."

"Don't be too hard on yourself. We both made mistakes,
but I know what kind of man you are. And I know once
you meet the twins you'll do the right thing."

"The twins." Brent moved to the window and looked
out, his shoulders tense. "You're sure they're my daughters?"

"You'll take a DNA test but, yes, I'm sure. I sent you
pictures."

"I've looked at them a million times. They…yeah, I
believe they're mine." He took a long, slow inhale of air.
Blew it out. "I don't know anything about being a father."

"You aren't in this alone, Brent. We'll help you every
step of the way."

Still looking out the window, Brent rocked back on his
heels. When he turned back around, his expression was
full of suspicion. "We?"

"Me, the family, their aunt."

"The one I spoke with on the phone? Charity's sister."

"That's the one."

Brent didn't look convinced. "The last time we saw each other, you told me I was immature, reckless and irresponsible. That's not a man who should father two little girls."

"I was wrong."

"But that's the thing. You weren't wrong. I was everything you said." Brent ran a hand over his face, drew in another long pull of air. "There are some mistakes a man can never outrun, mistakes that can't be forgiven."

"That's not true. The Lord forgives our transgressions. If you would just turn to Him and—" Walker cut off the rest of his words before he fell into the same old trap of lecturing his brother.

Brent didn't seem to notice his restraint. "The Lord forgives, that's true. But He doesn't always take away the consequences of our sin. You said that to me once, Walker, and you were right. I may never make restitution for my actions, but I'm here to try."

"I didn't say you had to *earn* forgiveness by hopping on a plane to Africa."

"I had one motive when I left the country, and that was to forget what I did."

"You didn't kill Nicole."

Brent's eyes glazed over, as if he was trapped in a horrible memory and couldn't find his way out. "Didn't I?"

"There was an inquiry," Walker reminded him. "The rope's manufacturer was at fault. You were exonerated of any blame."

Walker understood Brent's deep-rooted anger at himself. Until recently, he'd struggled with the same emotion. Brent had been selfish, prideful and determined to live life on his own terms, all because he'd been grieving. Walker, on the other hand, had buried his grief in work.

Neither had found freedom, only a self-made prison of their own making.

"Now that we've covered the past," Brent said, moving away from Walker to pace the room. "Tell me about my—" his steps slowed "—daughters."

Walker did as his brother requested, in great detail. Concluding with, "They're incredibly sweet and beautiful, and you are the most blessed man I know."

"Blessed? I've lost five years of their lives." Brent sounded outraged, a man who'd been wronged by a woman he'd hardly known. He also sounded like a father.

"You really didn't know Charity was pregnant?"

"After we decided to go our separate ways, she cut ties completely." Brent made another pass through the room. "I tried to contact her before I left for Africa. My calls and texts went unanswered. I never knew about the baby. I mean, babies. There are two of them." Wonder filled his voice. "I have *two* daughters."

They grinned at each other, and another layer of hostility fell away.

"When can I meet them?"

Walker moved to the doorway, "How about now?"

Brent joined him on the threshold, paused. "You shouldn't be this easy on me."

"You'd rather I was difficult?"

Sighing, Brent shook his head. "No."

"I need to tell you about Charity's sister," Walker said in a voice as normal as he could. "Hope did the right thing, searching for the twins' father. She didn't have to bring Harper and Kennedy to Thunder Ridge, but she did."

"Your point?"

"The twins love her. She loves them. I won't let you tear them apart."

"You care for her? For Hope?"

"Yes, very much." The truth hit him at last, staggering in its impact.

Walker didn't just care for Hope. He loved her. His feelings were different than the ones he'd had for Rachel, because Hope was different. Walker was, too. And now, he had to trust that God was in control. He had to accept the blessing that had come into his life. "I'm going to ask Hope to stay in Thunder Ridge."

"I see." From the knowing look in his brother's eyes, Walker figured Brent saw the situation pretty accurately.

Walker stepped into the hallway. "Ready to meet your daughters?"

"I've been ready since I learned of their existence."

Chapter Fifteen

Hope waited in the living room for Walker to arrive with his brother. She stared out at the lake without really seeing it. She wasn't sure how long she'd been standing there. A few minutes? Ten? Twenty? She'd lost all concept of time.

Snow fell from the sky in a soft, gentle rhythm, blanketing the lawn in pristine white. The peaceful scene was at odds with the anxiety beating against her ribs. Behind her, the girls strung popcorn and discussed their trip to meet Santa the next day. They agreed they would speak to him together. Harper would sit on Santa's right knee while Kennedy sat on his left.

They plotted what they would ask for from the big guy. A puppy was on the top of their wish list. Apparently, they'd let go of wanting a father. Or so Hope assumed. But when their voices dropped to a whisper, she heard Walker's name, followed by her own.

She glanced over her shoulder. Two identical heads were bent together, conspiring about very important matters. Whatever they were saying to each other, it wasn't meant for her ears.

Probably for the best.

Their father was en route from the hospital, riding shotgun in Walker's SUV. Nothing would ever be the same after he stepped into this room.

Lord, please...

The front door opened and then shut with a soft click. The twins were so involved in their plotting they didn't notice. The sound of masculine voices wafted on the air, and still the girls whispered among themselves.

Walker said something low that made the other man laugh softly. Walker spoke again, his words muffled, but Hope knew it was his voice. Odd that she recognized his rich baritone immediately. They'd only known each other for a few weeks.

The voices grew louder.

Hope turned to face the hallway. No decisions had to be made today.

The voices grew louder, closer, mingling with the heavy, masculine footsteps.

Hope's breath clogged in her throat. The twins looked up.

Now came the moment of truth. No regrets, she told herself.

This is what you want for them.

She forced herself to step back, away from the twins. She'd promised herself she would remain a witness to this first meeting, a bystander.

Always on the outside looking in.

"Dr. Walker's here." The girls hopped to their feet.

Another second passed.

And then...

Walker entered the room, still dressed in scrubs, his jawline tight and peppered with dark stubble.

"Dr. Walker." Harper and Kennedy squealed in delight and rushed to him.

He greeted them with the customary hug and fist

bumps. Over their heads, he sought Hope's gaze. Something passed between them, a silent message that her heart understood but her mind refused to comprehend. She was reminded of that first time their eyes met in the ER. Her heart had taken a hit that day. She had never fully recovered.

Another man entered the room, a near carbon copy of his older brother. His movements were full of unmistakable nerves and... Hope's heart dropped to her toes. Brent's gaze was filled with anticipation. He looked at Hope, gave her a short nod, which she returned. And then he smiled directly at the twins.

They started toward him without an ounce of hesitation, as if something in their DNA gravitated to its source.

Hope fell back a step. She hadn't expected that immediate connection.

Walker came to stand beside her. The sorrow in his expression matched her own. *We're in this together.* She felt a little bit less alone.

He took her hand and her restraint nearly shattered. Every bit of moisture dried up in her throat. She'd found a purpose with the twins and could only watch it melt away as Brent Evans lowered to his knees in front of them. "Hi, there. You must be Harper and Kennedy."

Hand in hand, they nodded, drawing closer to him. Closer. Closer.

He began speaking to them in soft tones, commenting on their clothing, their pretty eyes, asking questions about their likes and dislikes, becoming their father with every careful word he spoke.

Hope heard the wonder in his voice. She saw the gleam of fatherly pride swimming in his eyes, and the tears. It was the tears that shattered the last of Hope's doubts.

Brent hadn't known about his daughters until Walker's phone call.

That meant Charity had wronged him in one of the worst possible ways a wife could wrong her husband. Hope felt her knees buckle under the realization that her sister had lied to her. Walker kept hold of her hand, an anchor in the storm of her swirling emotions.

What was she supposed to do now?

Nothing. Hope was supposed to do nothing. Five years ago, Brent Evans and Hope's sister had created two perfect little girls. For years, Charity had kept Brent from knowing his daughters. He deserved to know them.

The twins were equally in awe of the man kneeling in front of them, as if somehow sensing he was theirs.

Feeling mildly desperate, torn between grief and joy, Hope glanced at Walker. He was watching the interaction with watery eyes.

No help there.

At some point, someone would have to tell the girls Brent was their father. But not now.

Kennedy beamed up at him. There was no nervousness in the child, no fear. Just innocent curiosity. "You look like Dr. Walker."

Brent gave the child a warm smile. "That's because I'm his brother."

"Like Aunt Hope was our mom's sister."

He glanced at Hope, giving her a quick once-over. "Sort of like that, yes." His voice was hoarse with emotion. "I'm your..." He swallowed again. "I'm Brent, and I'm your fath—"

He cut off the rest of his words, something preventing him from declaring himself just yet. Perhaps he simply wanted the children's easy manner to continue, or maybe he didn't want to watch their smiles disappear when he declared who he was and why he hadn't come to them sooner.

"Do you have a dog?" Kennedy asked him.

"No, but I want one."

"Daisy had puppies. You want to see them?"

He ran his gaze around the room, landing on Walker. "You got a dog?"

Kennedy giggled. "No, silly. Daisy is Miss Quinn's dog. You should take us over to look at the puppies."

"Can we go over there now, Aunt Hope?" Harper asked. "Can we?"

Brent glanced over to Hope, rose to his full height and studied her a few seconds longer. "You look just like her."

"We were identical twins."

"I see it now. I know it's been a rough few months, and you didn't have to search for me, so…" He paused, his eyes held hers for a few beats. "Thank you."

Two words, that's all it took, and Hope knew she would relinquish the girls without a battle. Eventually. Not yet, though. There were too many details to work out. Legalities to sort through. All of this, assuming Brent wanted to be a full-time father.

He could decide to return to Africa.

Hope didn't want him to do that. She didn't want the twins to have to suffer the same childhood she had.

As if reading her mind, he said, "I'm home for good."

She didn't know whether to laugh or cry.

"You have questions?"

"Several."

His gaze dropped to where her hand was joined with Walker's. Looking as if he had a few questions of his own, he said, "We'll talk later. Right now, I have a litter of puppies to admire. Do you want to come with us?"

She glanced at the twins, both of whom seemed to have

forgotten she was in the room. They were too busy gazing up at their father with adoration.

"I'll follow along in a few minutes."

"Good enough."

Hand still clutching Walker's, Hope watched the three leave the house. The door closed with a sharp snap. And that, she realized, was the end. She'd lost the twins to their father.

Tears welled in her eyes. In that moment, Hope didn't think she could feel any more destitute. She was wrong. Walker released her hand, and it was as if the entire world had turned against her. What was she supposed to do next?

Protect the twins.

Protect them against what? A happy childhood with a loving father who came with aunts, uncles and cousins. And, oh yeah, puppies.

The tears fell then.

Walker drew her into his arms. "This is a good thing, Hope."

His voice held as much raw emotion as she felt. "I know."

"You could still fight him for custody."

She could. "That would only end up hurting the twins."

He continued holding her, rubbing her back, whispering words of comfort she desperately needed. Tossing aside her pride, she clung to him. "You will always be their aunt."

It had to be enough.

Conversations would have to occur in the next few days, dozens of them, but the most important question had been answered. Brent was going to step up.

"He won't cut you out of their lives." Walker set her away from him and stared into her eyes. "I won't let him."

The situation was unbearable, and this man's kindness

was only making the pain harder to bear. She lowered her head.

"Hey, look at me." He applied gentle pressure under her chin until she did as he requested. "No decisions have to be made today."

She'd had the same thought, but the sooner the future was settled, the better for the twins. "I thought we were going to be a family."

"Me, too."

They'd never said the words aloud until this moment. They hadn't needed to say them. It had been understood.

"It hurts to discover we were wrong."

She nodded.

"I'm sorry, Hope. So very sorry for us both." He gave her lips a gentle kiss, the kind that was meant to soothe. Hope thought her heart might shatter in her chest.

"Christmas Eve is only a few days away." He kissed her temple, lingered there a moment. "Let's focus on enjoying the rest of the holidays."

What was the point? They would basically be putting off the inevitable. But Hope wanted this time with Walker and his family. She wanted it for the twins.

She wanted it for herself.

Chin up, eyes moist, she produced a smile that came at great cost. "I guess all that's left is to go admire Daisy's puppies."

He pressed his forehead to hers. "That's the spirit."

Later that night, Hope sat at the kitchen table in Walker's house. He'd positioned himself on her right. Brent had chosen the chair directly across from her. The girls were sleeping in their beds. Puppies, new friends and the excitement about meeting Santa the next day had worn them out.

Brent looked equally beat, but there was an underlying

joy in him that showed past the exhaustion. He was already in love with his daughters.

Snow fell outside the bay window, obscuring the view of the lake. The lazy, floating flakes seemed in no hurry to find a resting place. Hope felt a little like that, as if she was drifting along without a purpose.

All that was left was a series of conversations. She opened the discussion with a brief history of the twins' lives since they'd shown up on her doorstep. Walker stayed silent throughout the story, letting her explain the situation in her own way. "The girls have had a lot of upheaval in the past eight months."

This seemed to be the opening Brent had been waiting for since sitting down. "Let me take this moment to thank you for taking such good care of them."

"They're family," she said simply. "Family is everything."

"True." The look he shot Walker was full of apology. Hope was happy to see the brothers making inroads toward healing their relationship, something she was never fully able to do with Charity. And now she was sad.

"I was sorry to hear about Charity's death. She was a vibrant, passionate woman. Truly special."

Hope swallowed back a sob. How could he be this kind about a woman who'd lied and cheated him out of five years with his daughters?

"I also want to thank you for seeking me out," Brent continued. "The girls, my daughters…" He paused, choked on a breath, then began again. "My daughters are amazing little girls, beautiful on the inside and out, and I can't believe I've missed five years of their lives. I won't miss another day, that much I promise you."

He was saying all the right things. No, not just saying them. Meaning them. Hope heard the sincerity in his voice. "I believe you."

"I can't begin to repay you for the gift you've given me."

"I didn't bring the girls to Thunder Ridge for you, Brent. I did it for them."

"Understood. But it must have been difficult coming here."

Like ripping her heart out of her chest. "It was the right thing to do."

Silence fell over the table, all three lost in their own thoughts.

Hope started to speak, but Brent had more to say. "I want to tell them who I am."

"I agree." She'd thought about nothing else since he'd walked into the house this morning. "They should hear the news from you."

"Really?" Both Walker and Brent seemed surprised by her immediate capitulation.

Hope lifted a shoulder. "I spoke with Dr. Stephens earlier this afternoon. Her advice was to tell the girls sooner rather than later, before they start asking questions."

"They haven't started asking questions?"

"Actually, they have. They want a father for Christmas." They'd meant Walker, but Hope didn't think that mattered as much as the truth. "You are the answer to their greatest wish."

Brent processed this in silence. "Did this Dr. Stephens give any advice on how I should tell them?"

"You need to keep it simple and direct."

"Simple and direct." He considered the advice. "Yeah, I can do that."

"I think I should be there when you tell them. Walker should be there, too." She looked at him for the first time since sitting down. "In case they don't respond well to the news."

Something passed between her and Walker, a silent agreement to be a united front. In that moment, Hope had a glimpse of what it would be like to have him in her life. The two of them acting as a single unit, the very essence of becoming a couple.

Did he feel it, too? She leaned toward him, wondering. Their connection had started with their mutual love of the twins. Somewhere along the way it had morphed into something more, something between just the two of them.

Brent's voice had her straightening in her chair. "You think the twins won't respond well to the news that I'm their father?"

"Honestly, I don't know."

For a moment, Brent looked devastated. But then he squared his shoulders and put on the face of a man determined to confront his past, and all that that implied. "Okay. If you think it's best that you and Walker be in the room when I tell them, then that's how we do it."

Chapter Sixteen

The following morning dawned as so many did in Colorado, without a cloud in the sky. The snow had stopped sometime in the middle of the night, leaving behind a blanket of fluffy white flakes. Hope lit the Christmas tree and, in the quiet stillness, stared at the twinkling lights. She hadn't slept well, too worked up over what the day held for the twins. Before the Evans brothers had called it a night, they'd agreed that Brent would tell the girls he was their father after their trip to see Santa.

Wishing it was over, Hope tidied up the room, moved a few decorations around, did some more tidying and...

She was procrastinating.

Determined to enjoy her time with the twins, she woke them and helped them into their prettiest dresses. Santa deserved their very best. Due to their excitement, the process took twice as long as it should have. Nevertheless, Hope prevailed before ushering them into the kitchen.

They were just finishing up breakfast when Walker and Brent arrived.

"They're here!" Harper squealed in delight.

Hope met the men at the door, the twins hard on her

heels. Walker smiled at her and ping went her heart. They'd come so close to having a family together.

Walker bent low to greet the twins. They gave him a hug, then, seeing Brent, rushed over to him. He crouched in front of them. "Got a hug for me?"

Without a moment of hesitation, they dove for him.

Hope's breath caught at the sight of Brent's eyes filling with tears. Walker draped his arm over her shoulders and whispered, "It could be worse. They could dislike him."

"You're right."

Brent released the girls so they could show off their fancy dresses.

Once the fashion show came to a conclusion, Walker asked the twins. "Ready to meet Santa?"

They nodded vigorously.

Harper ran to Hope. She bent low as the little girl asked in a stage whisper, "Can Dr. Brent come with us to see Santa?"

"That's the plan."

"Yay!"

After a covert discussion, Walker and Hope agreed to let Brent stand in line with the twins. The excuse they gave the girls was that they wanted to take pictures. In reality, they were letting Brent build the trust he would need to tell them he was their father.

Putting his arm around her waist, Walker pulled Hope close.

Needing his strength, she leaned into him. "It hurts, letting them go."

"They're not gone yet."

They both knew that wasn't true. The girls adored their father already.

Stomach bottoming out, Hope glanced at Walker. He was looking rather worse for the wear, as if he'd had as rough a night as she had. The smile he gave her was full of warmth, and something new. There was a calmness about him that soothed her raw nerves. "We have some decisions to make, you and me."

"What about?"

Still smiling, he bent down to whisper in her ear, speaking what could either be a promise or a threat. "The future."

Two hours later, when they were back in his living room, Walker watched Hope set herself apart from the activity. She stood by the Christmas tree, gazing out the window, her eyes hooked on some unknown spot in the distance. Walker was the only one who noticed she'd retreated.

Brent sat on the overstuffed couch, bookended by his daughters. The twins kept up a running commentary about their time in Thunder Ridge. He did a respectable job keeping up with the conversation.

He was going to be a good father.

Walker wanted to be happy for his brother. But Brent's gain had come at too high a cost. Walker had taken a hit. Hope had taken a bigger one. In response, she'd put up a metaphorical wall. Walker didn't blame her, but he hated that she'd put him firmly on the outside with everyone else.

Brent took advantage of a lull in the conversation. "I have something to tell you girls."

This is it, Walker thought, glancing at Hope. The moment when he and Hope let go of a dream that had almost been theirs.

But this wasn't about them. It never had been.

They were here to support the twins. Together. Walker moved in next to Hope.

For an instant, she let down her guard and he saw his own sense of loss staring back at him. They'd come so close, only to lose the dream. Their shared sorrow was a living, breathing thing pulsing between them. He reached out and touched her arm. Her pain bled into his fingertips. The impact was like a physical blow.

He dropped his hand.

Walker shifted his attention to Brent and the twins.

They'd moved off the sofa. Brent had lowered to his knees, while the twins stood shoulder to shoulder facing him. Hands shaking, he touched each of their cheeks. "I have something very important to tell you."

Eyes solemn, Kennedy moved a step closer. Harper did the same. Father and daughters were united at last, but only one of them understood the gravity of the situation.

Walker was suddenly afraid for his brother. What if the twins didn't want him to be their father? What if this all went terribly wrong?

"Aunt Hope?" Kennedy's face took on a look of deep concern. "Why are you crying?"

Hope swiped her cheek. "I'm not crying. I just have something in my eye."

She laughed softly to make her point. There was something broken in the sound. Walker lifted a hand to comfort her. She moved out of his reach.

Brent gained the girls' attention again. "You know, I came to Thunder Ridge to meet you."

"You did?"

"Nothing could keep me away once I knew the truth." He paused, drew in a deep breath and said in a quiet, calm voice, "I'm your father."

Two pair of eyes widened in shock. Harper recovered first. "You're our daddy?"

"I'm your daddy," Brent repeated, making his point so earnestly it was hard to disagree. "And you are my gorgeous daughters."

Through eyes that didn't seem to want to focus, Walker

saw a watery version of father and daughters. The girls stared at Brent with identical expressions of wonder. Both looked so serious, poised to leap into his arms but not quite ready to do so yet.

They continued starting at him.

Brent stood still under his daughter's inspection, shaking slightly, so big and unsure of himself, shoulders hunched. Walker hurt for his brother. The expression on Brent's face was a combination of desperation and anxiety, as if he was in deep, unchartered waters and the girls were his personal life preservers.

Kennedy came out of her trance first. "Can we hug you?"

A muscle tightened in his jaw and then Brent's arms were open. "Get over here."

They launched themselves into the air. He caught them in a single swoop, clutching them against his chest and holding on for dear life. He didn't attempt to stop the tears from falling down his cheeks. And Walker felt like an intruder.

"We should leave them alone," he said in a hoarse whisper.

He was talking to empty air. Hope had already slipped out of the room. It took him five full minutes to find her. She was in his study, sitting at the desk he'd bought a few weeks after moving in. Her head was bent over the keyboard of her laptop, which was in the process of coming to life.

Something in her stiff posture warned him to tread carefully. "You left without a word."

Swiveling around, she looked at him for a long beat. "I didn't belong in the middle of that."

Turning away, she focused on her computer.

Walker wasn't afraid of much, but everything had been

reduced to a dizzying moment of sheer panic when she opened the web browser and typed in the name of a popular airline. "What are you doing?"

"Checking for available flights back to New York."

No. She couldn't leave him. Forcing the panic out of his voice, he moved to stand beside her. "I thought we agreed no decisions until after the holidays."

"I'm looking for flights for December 26."

Two days. He only had two days to convince her to give him a chance, to give *them* a chance. "Stay." He spun her chair around so he could speak to her face. "Hope. Please. Stay."

"I don't fit in here," she said in a halting voice. "I'm not one of you. I'm not one of anyone."

She was wrong. She was also not in the right frame of mind to hear his objections. "You can't abandon the twins." He knew it was a low blow. Desperation did that to a man. "They'll need you more than ever in the coming weeks."

Hope's shoulders slumped. "Maybe I'm more like my father than I want to admit."

"You know that's not true."

She whipped her head up to glare at him. "My first instinct is to run. All I want is to put distance between the girls and me, because staying is too painful."

Walker placed his hands on the sides of her chair. "Hope." He lowered in front of her. "Stay. At least through the New Year."

He could do a lot with an extra week. He could change the future. One week. That's all he needed. And a lot of prayer.

"The longer I remain in Thunder Ridge, the harder it will be for Brent to build a relationship with his daughters."

"That's absolutely untrue. Your presence will make the

transition easier. No, don't shake your head at me. Listen. Just listen. You're the only stability the girls have known in a long time. They need you."

I need you.

She seemed to consider his words, but then she lowered her head and Walker could no longer see what was going on in her mind.

"Stay, Hope. If not for the twins, then for..." He hesitated only a moment before taking the biggest risk of his life since losing Rachel. "Us. Stay for us."

Her eyes moved to his face, and then away again. "We've only known each other a few weeks."

"Lifelong romances have started on less."

She gave an exasperated sigh.

"I know this thing between us seems to have happened fast because, well, it did happen fast. That doesn't make it any less real."

"Oh, Walker. I—"

"No, don't interrupt. Let me finish." Desperation made his voice gravelly. "All I'm asking is that you give me a chance to—"

His cell phone went off, the ringtone alerting him the call was from the hospital. Of all the rotten timing. "I have to take this. It's the hospital."

He listened for several seconds, then said in clipped tones. "On my way." He ended the call then shoved the phone in his pocket. "There's been a five-car pileup on the highway just outside of town. The ER is short-staffed due to the holidays. I have to go."

Her eyes went blank. "Of course you have to go."

Walker could see her pulling away from him, first emotionally, then physically as she swung back around to face her computer screen.

"I don't know how long I'll be gone," he said.

"I understand."

Unfortunately, Walker sensed her definition of *understanding* was not the same as his. He wanted to promise he'd be back soon, at least in time for the Christmas Eve service at church, but he couldn't know for sure. So he didn't make any promises. And realized his mistake as he watched Hope click on the airline's website for a one-way ticket to New York City.

"I'll be back. I promise."

She kept typing.

"Hope." He gripped the arm of the chair and swiveled her around to face him again. Before she could protest, he pulled her to her feet and straight into his arms. "Don't book that flight until I return."

She said nothing.

"Please." He kissed her then. And, wonder of wonders, she kissed him back. He continued kissing her like she was his.

She is mine, Walker realized. *She's my Hope.*

Several hours after Walker had left for the hospital, Hope stood by the cheerful Christmas tree, feeling anything but cheerful. Now that night had fallen, the lake was cast in an eerie blackness that matched her mood. She didn't think her heart could hurt any more than it already did, but as she thought back to the moment Walker had kissed her goodbye and then driven away in his SUV, she felt another fissure.

She'd never felt more alone in her life.

At the twins' insistence, Brent had walked with them over to Quinn's house. They wanted to tell the rest of the family their exciting news. Hope had been invited to tag along, but she'd opted to stay behind.

She wanted to curl up in a ball and hide from the world.

She wanted to hop on a plane and never look back. For the first time in her life, Hope understood her father's choices. And with understanding came forgiveness. Reverend Jeffries had run from his pain.

Hope had nearly done the same thing.

But there was another way. She could stand and fight for what she wanted. Her life wouldn't look like what she'd thought three weeks ago, or even three days ago when she'd finalized the paperwork for her sabbatical from the university. But if she was very brave, she could reach for a new dream. And a new life. She could have the family she wanted. With Walker.

The sound of masculine footsteps quickened her pulse. He was home. Smiling, she spun around to face her future, only to feel her stomach bottom out. Brent had returned. And he was alone. "Where are the twins?"

"Playing with their cousins." He stopped, stuffed his hands in his pockets. "You and I need to talk."

Hope didn't want to have this discussion. "What do you want to talk about?"

"First, I want to tell you, again, how grateful I am you came looking for me."

Hope didn't want this man's gratitude. She didn't want to see the wonder in his eyes, or the joy of discovering a blessing he knew he hadn't earned. *He's not your enemy.*

Charity had wronged this man.

It helped to remember that Brent was as much a victim as the rest of them. That knowledge softened Hope's heart toward him. A little. Unfortunately, a shred of resentment remained. His gain was her loss. "Everything I've done in the past, and will do in the future, is for Harper and Kennedy."

"I know." He took her hand and gave her a grin reminiscent of his brother's. "Thank you for giving me the greatest gift of my life."

How could she hold a grudge against a man who understood the blessing he'd been given? "You're welcome."

"I'm going to do everything I can to be a good father to Harper and Kennedy. I promise."

She believed him. There would be several bumps along the way, and she would be here to help smooth them over. "I'm willing to work with you every step of the way."

"You're staying in Thunder Ridge?"

"I am." She told him about the year-long sabbatical she planned to take.

"A year isn't enough."

It wasn't. But that conversation was for her to have with Walker. In the meantime, she surprised them both by pulling him into a sisterly hug. "Welcome home, Brent."

"Thanks. So, listen." He stepped back a bit awkwardly. "If Walker doesn't make it home in time, I'd like you to join the family for the Evans traditional family Christmas Eve celebration."

"You want me to attend the church service with you?"

"Church is only one of the activities. Quinn throws a pretty amazing party, family only, which definitely includes you. So? What do you say? Will you join us?"

Under the circumstances, Hope could think of only one answer. "What time do we leave?"

Chapter Seventeen

The five-car pileup resulted in numerous injuries, some of them minor, others more serious and a few life-threatening. It had been a long night that had turned into a long morning. That had left Walker dead on his feet and more than a little worried he'd let Hope down.

He'd missed church. He also missed Quinn's Christmas morning breakfast, and several other family traditions. It was well after noon on Christmas Day before he pulled into his driveway. Exhausted and miserable, he was only partially relieved to see Hope's rental car parked in its usual spot. She hadn't left him. Yet.

She still could. She'd been pretty determined to run yesterday.

No way was he going to let her get away. And he planned to play dirty, pulling out all the stops as he breached the walls she'd built around her heart. The woman wouldn't know what hit her. If words failed him, or if Hope refused to give their relationship a shot, maybe the Christmas gift he'd picked up on his way home would change her mind.

Said gift released a loud yawn from the passenger seat. Walker patted the miniature version of Bertha on the head. He'd planned on giving Hope one of Daisy's puppies, but when he'd called Quinn during a short break last night, she'd informed him he was too late. The puppies were all spoken for, one of them by Brent. Walker smiled. The twins were getting both a father *and* a puppy for Christmas.

Thanks to another call, this one to Remy, the family's connection to all things furry, Walker had been able to find a decent solution to the problem. The Saint Bernard puppy was a better fit for Hope, anyway.

Feeling pretty good about himself, Walker picked up the sleepy animal and studied her face. "Hope is going to love you."

The puppy licked his chin.

Tucking the animal under his arm, Walker exited the car. He was barely halfway up the walkway when the front door swung open. Hope stood on the threshold, looking perfectly at home.

His feet ground to a halt. "You stayed."

Okay. Admittedly, it wasn't a great opening line.

She didn't seem to mind. Not if her smile was any indication. "I've been waiting for you for a very long time, Dr. Evans."

There was something underneath her words he couldn't quite identify. He was too overcome with relief to try. "The accident was a bad one, lots of injuries."

"No, you misunderstand." She crossed the distance between them. "I've been waiting for you all my life. And, now that I've found you, I'm not letting you go."

Walker nearly dropped the puppy. He held Hope's gaze, feeling the anxiety in his chest give way to anticipation. Could winning this amazing woman's heart be this easy? "Yeah?"

"Oh, yeah." Her gaze lowered to the squirming bundle under his arm. "Who's this handsome guy?"

"*She* is your Christmas present."

"Okay, wow." Hope touched one of the enormous paws, then the other. "I mean, wow. Our girl is going to be a monster."

"At least as big as Bertha." Walker swung the puppy forward and held her in the Simba pose so Hope could take a good look.

"Oh, Walker. You're killing me."

"There's more." He jiggled the puppy. "I have it on good authority, our girl is an old-fashioned dog at heart. She expects to grow up with both a mommy and daddy."

Hope took the puppy and pressed her face in the furry neck. When she looked back at him, her eyes were filled with tears. "What are we going to name her?"

We. Walker's heart swelled. "I was thinking we could let the twins do the honors."

"No way. They have their own puppy to name. This one's mine. Or rather—" she kissed the dog on the nose then hugged her close "—ours."

Caught in Hope's gaze, Walker's world tilted, wobbled a bit, then steadied. "I like the way you think, Dr. Jeffries."

"Come inside so I can give you your Christmas present."

The puppy fell asleep as soon as Hope set her on the rug near the Christmas tree. After giving the dog a few strokes, she retrieved a brightly wrapped Christmas present with a shiny red bow on top. "Open it."

Settled on the floor with Hope nestled in beside him, he tore away the paper, dug inside the box and discovered a framed photograph. He studied the image of him and Hope and the twins at the Ice Castles. They'd just arrived and were standing clustered together at the fountain, looking very much like a family.

"McCoy took the picture."

"I remember the day well." It had been one of the happiest of his life.

He felt a thread of pain over what might-have-been, but then came a spurt of joy. God hadn't provided Walker and Hope with the family they'd wanted. But they still had Harper and Kennedy in their lives.

And, now, they had each other.

"That, Walker Evans—" Hope tapped the photograph "—is the day I fell in love with you."

He kissed her, lingering a little longer than planned.

Hope pulled away, laughing softly. "I have one more gift to give you."

This time, when he unwrapped the box and lifted the lid, he discovered a bunch of torn-up scraps of paper. "I don't understand."

"You are holding the remains of the custody papers I had drawn up before I arrived in Thunder Ridge."

So Walker had been right to suspect her original motives. Hope had come to Thunder Ridge with the express idea of gaining full custody of the twins. "So this is your way of telling me you aren't going to sue for custody?"

She slid her fingers in his hair, smiled. "You're asking the wrong question."

"What question should I be asking?"

"It's not that I no longer plan to sue for custody, but rather *when* I made the decision to tear up the papers." She waved her hand in the general direction of the box.

"All right." He studied the box with a long considering look. "When did you tear them up?"

"The morning after the twins met your family." She sighed. "That's also when I put Plan B in place."

"Plan B?"

"I requested a one-year sabbatical from my job at the university."

Walker narrowed his eyes. "You were planning to stay in Thunder Ridge all along?"

"Not all along. Once I realized what you and your family could offer the girls, what I couldn't, I knew I wouldn't be taking them back to New York. But I also knew I couldn't live without them in my life, so I made plans to take the time to search for a teaching position closer to Thunder Ridge."

This woman's willingness to sacrifice for the people she loved would have brought Walker to his knees if he hadn't been sitting already. "That was a very brave thing to do."

She shrugged again. "I don't know about that. I never planned to fall in love with Thunder Ridge, or you, or your family, or—"

"Wait. Just wait a minute. That's the second time you've said you love me."

Hope blushed. "You caught that, huh?"

"I love you, too."

Her face broke out into a lovely smile, the one that never failed to reach inside his chest, grab his heart and squeeze. "Oh, Walker." Her smile slipped. "What about Rachel? Will you be able to let her—"

Walker cut her off with a kiss.

"Okay."

He took her face in his hands and kissed her again. "I won't pretend it wasn't hard letting Rachel go. Losing her nearly destroyed me. She'll always be in my heart. But she's my past. You are my future."

"I don't know if I can be second best in your heart."

His own heart melted at the pain he heard in her voice. How did he make her understand? By telling her the truth. "I hung on to Rachel entirely too long. I convinced myself I already had my one shot at happiness. God would never bless me with a second chance. Then you showed up and everything changed."

"Oh, Walker." She closed her eyes.

"Hope, look at me." When she did, he saw the tears. Felt answering ones well in his own eyes. "God has blessed me beyond what I deserve. He brought you into my life. I will not squander what we have. I will strive every day to be a man worthy of your love."

"You already are that man."

He pulled her close, kissed her, then whispered in her ear, "I could make this next part unnecessarily complicated for us both or I can make it simple."

"I like simple."

He slid to the floor, dropping to one knee.

"What…what are you doing?"

"I'm asking you to marry me." Taking her hand, he said, "But I should warn you, I don't have a ring yet."

"I don't need a ring."

"I should also tell you, I'm not a fan of long engagements."

"How long were you thinking?"

"A week."

She laughed. "Maybe we should consider a bit longer than that. After all, I'm not going anywhere."

And that was the biggest blessing of all.

"Hope Jeffries." He pressed a kiss to her palm. "Will you marry me?"

"Since we're keeping things simple…" Her smile lit the room. "Yes."

Epilogue

"Ten, nine, eight…"

Hope leaned into Walker and looked around Quinn's living room at the assembled group of family and friends. Her family now. Her friends. She gave herself permission to look her fill. Everyone had come dressed in casual clothing, another of the many Evans family traditions she already loved.

Hope's heart swelled to overflowing. God had blessed her with a life and a future far greater than she'd ever imagined.

"Seven, six…"

The Lord had brought her on a journey that had begun with fear and ended with certainty. For the first time in her life, Hope knew where she belonged. Here, in Thunder Ridge, Colorado. With the man of her dreams by her side.

"Five, four…"

She smiled into Walker's eyes. In silent agreement, they joined in the countdown. "Three." Walker grinned. "Two." Hope grinned right back. "One!"

"Happy New Year, Walker."

"Happy New Year, Hope."

Their lips met in an all-too-brief kiss before the twins

separated them with giggles and enthusiastic words. "Happy New Year, Aunt Hope and Uncle Walker."

Lowering to their knees, they took turns embracing the girls.

A few more words, then off they went to find their father.

Hope sighed. She would miss Harper and Kennedy once they moved in with Brent. At least she had them a little while longer. They would stay with her in Walker's home until Brent found a suitable house for the three of them.

More change ahead. More upheaval. But one thing would remain steady. Her love for the twins. Family was, after all, family.

Walker pulled her close. "I have something for you."

Hope wasn't sure she could stand any more blessings. Her heart was already about to explode.

Walker's gaze roamed her features. "You know how much I love you, right?"

"I'm catching on to that, yes."

His hand dug into an interior pocket of his jacket. As if sensing something important was about to happen, everyone began gathering around them.

"I wanted to do this sooner," he said. "And would have. But tonight's gathering seemed the right time because everyone who matters is here with us."

Eyes locked with hers, he stepped around to face her directly. He held a square box covered in navy blue velvet in the tiny space between them.

Hope's hand flew to her mouth. "Is that what I think it is?"

"You tell me." With a flourish, he flipped open the lid.

Hope gasped at the sight of the three-stone diamond engagement ring with a white-gold setting that showed off the sparkling gems. "It's gorgeous."

He took her hand and slid the ring in place.

"It's a perfect fit, Walker."

"We're a perfect fit, Hope. You and me. Forever."

"Forever," she repeated.

He pulled her into his arms and kissed her.

A wild cheer went up from the crowd surrounding them.

Frowning, Walker glanced around, then turned back to Hope. "You don't mind I did this here?"

She smiled at him. "It was the exact right time and place."

Grinning, he pulled her back into his arms. "Welcome to the family, Hope. You're one of us now. For better or worse."

For better or worse.

She could live with that.

* * * * *

If you loved this story,
check out these other books

A Haven for Christmas *by Patricia Davids*
An Amish Holiday Family *by Jo Ann Brown*
The Rancher's Holiday Arrangement *by Brenda Minton*
His Christmas Wish *by Allie Pleiter*
The Christmas Bargain *by Lisa Carter*

Available now from Love Inspired!

Find more great reads at www.LoveInspired.com

Dear Reader,

Although this is my twentieth book with Love Inspired, I had as much fun guiding Hope and Walker to their happy ending as I did my first hero and heroine. I never tire of writing stories where two deserving people find love despite a few bumps along the way.

Every story I've written holds a place in my heart. But I confess there are some characters that stick with me long after I write The End. Hope and Walker fall into that category. There's something special about two wounded souls discovering a second chance at happiness. Walker and Hope didn't get the family they planned. But they found each other and a love that surpassed their previous heartaches. My kind of happy ending.

I have another confession to make. I'm a sucker for Christmas-themed romances. Add in a pair of five-year-old twins, puppies, a case of mistaken identity and—cue the happy dance.

I hope you enjoyed hanging out in Thunder Ridge. This was my first stop in town, but it won't be my last. In the meantime, I love hearing from readers. Let me know what kind of stories you prefer. You can contact me via email at ReneeRyanBooks@gmail.com, or on my Renee Ryan Facebook page. My Twitter handle is @reneeryanbooks.

Happy reading!
Renee

**WE HOPE YOU ENJOYED
THIS BOOK FROM**

LOVE INSPIRED

INSPIRATIONAL ROMANCE

Uplifting stories of faith, forgiveness and hope.

Fall in love with stories where faith helps
guide you through life's challenges, and discover
the promise of a new beginning.

6 NEW BOOKS AVAILABLE EVERY MONTH!

LIHALO2020

COMING NEXT MONTH FROM
Love Inspired

Available December 1, 2020

AN AMISH HOLIDAY COURTSHIP
by Emma Miller
Ready to find a husband at Christmastime, Ginger Stutzman has her sights set on the handsome new Amish bachelor in town. But she can't help but feel drawn to her boss, Eli Kutz, and his four children. Could the widower be her true perfect match?

A PRECIOUS CHRISTMAS GIFT
Redemption's Amish Legacies • by Patricia Johns
Determined to find a loving Amish family for her unborn child, Eve Shrock's convinced Noah Wiebe's brother and sister-in-law are a great fit. But when she starts falling for Noah, the best place for her baby might just be in her arms...with Noah at her side.

HIS HOLIDAY PRAYER
Hearts of Oklahoma • by Tina Radcliffe
Beginning a new job after the holidays is the change widower Tucker Rainbolt's been praying for. Before he and his twin girls can move, he must ensure his vet clinic partner, Jena Harper, can take over—and stay afloat. But could giving his heart to Jena be the fresh start he *really* needs?

CHRISTMAS IN A SNOWSTORM
The Calhoun Cowboys • by Lois Richer
Returning home to his Montana family ranch, journalist Sam Calhoun volunteers to run the local Christmas festival. But as he works with single mom Joy Grainger on the project, the last thing he expects is for her children to set their sights on making him their new dad...

THE TEXAN'S UNEXPECTED HOLIDAY
Cowboys of Diamondback Ranch • by Jolene Navarro
Driven to get her sister and baby niece out of a dangerous situation, Lexy Zapata takes a job near Damian De La Rosa's family's ranch and brings them with her. Now they can stay hidden through Christmas, and Lexy will start planning their next move...if she can ignore the way Damian pulls at her heart.

A DAUGHTER FOR CHRISTMAS
Triple Creek Cowboys • by Stephanie Dees
Moving into a cottage on Triple Creek Ranch to help her little girl, Alice, overcome a traumatic experience, single mom Eve Fallon doesn't count on rescuing grumpy rancher Tanner Cole as he struggles to plan a party for foster kids. Can she revive both Tanner's and Alice's Christmas spirit?

LOOK FOR THESE AND OTHER LOVE INSPIRED BOOKS WHEREVER BOOKS ARE SOLD, INCLUDING MOST BOOKSTORES, SUPERMARKETS, DISCOUNT STORES AND DRUGSTORES.

LICNM1120